THE TEMPLAR

One Knight's Life

Tom and Lori,

         I hope you

like this story.

       Best, Bin

Henry Beyer

Printed in the United States of America.

ISBN-13: 978-0-9989798-8-5

Cover designed by Rebecca Blaesing Design, LLC

DEDICATION

This book is dedicated to my mother, Audrey, who taught me how to write, and to my father, Walter, who showed me how to persevere. Special thanks to Mary Anne Hildreth, my editor; Rebecca Blaesing, my illustrator and Linda, my wife, who gave me both support and good suggestions.

TABLE OF CONTENTS

SECTION I: WE

Table of Contents

SECTION I

WE

THE SKILLS OF FRIGG

December 1080

Mariteth again sat down on the short, three-legged stool, the same stool she'd sat on most of the night while ministring to Audrey. The birthing had been long and difficult but without major complications: no backward or sideways efforts on the child's part, no problems with the umbilical cord and no obvious deformities. The baby was big and strong. His size was most of the problem, too big to get out easily yet too strong and willful to be denied. The mother of course was completely spent. After Mariteth had cut and tied the cord, she'd swabbed down both the baby and the mother. With that done, she directed the two attendants to take Audrey to her own bed where she could rest. Mariteth then completed her examination of Henry—that was to be the boy's name—counting his fingers and otherwise turning him about near enough to the torch light so she could see him well. There were no disfigurements or abnormalities. He seemed, she thought, a very fine child. So with her review completed, Mariteth turned toward the doorway to take the child to his mother.

Audrey was barely awake but, seeing Mariteth enter with Henry, she smiled weakly and reached for the child. For several moments as she held him, Audrey stared lovingly at her baby. Then with a start, she turned her eyes back to the midwife and whispered, "Thank you Mariteth. Thank you so much."

"You're welcome, Lady Audrey," replied the midwife who then looked around the small stone room. There was only one candle burning but she could see a young woman sitting quietly in a shadowed corner. Good she thought, the child will need to be fed by someone who can stay awake long enough to do it.

With mother and child well taken care of, Mariteth returned to the small room where the birth had taken place. There she looked at the bloody straw and soiled blanket lying on the floor and sighed deeply. Her moment of importance was over. Her job now was simply to clean up the mess. At this point in the process, she always felt deflated. Her mother had told her she would. Odin's wife, Frigg, had certainly favored her mother.

Of course Mariteth couldn't voice that comment aloud anymore. The new religion didn't recognize any of the old gods. She didn't really mind this Christianity but she'd never understand why it recognized only one god. The gods of her Norse forefathers had certainly treated their followers well. Odin was a crafty war god and had led them on many successful raids. And they'd conquered this northern land of the Franks. What she didn't understand was why they'd taken on the Franks' language and religion. It was almost as if they'd succumbed rather than conquered. But even if Mariteth couldn't cry out the source of her skills nor publicly proclaim that Frigg had been her mother's teacher, she could still employ the abilities and insights her mother had taught. It might be heresy under this new religion but she still knew from where her skills came. And she could still read the signs, another of Frigg's teachings.

And there were signs, very significant signs! Last evening as she followed the stable boy to the castle, a great gust of wind had twisted a large spruce limb from its trunk and dropped it just in front of them. Surely that was a portent. The spruce was Odin's most revered of trees. This boy would become a warrior. And the screeching wind and swirling snow together with the challenge he had in getting out of Audrey's womb, all these spoke to his toughness. And the new religion's priest coming to the castle just before the baby's birth and the Christ's birthday being just seven days hence. This placement of the boy between the priest and Christ held great meaning too. But exactly what it meant, Mariteth didn't know.

When the graying midwife finally finished cleaning up the birthing room, she looked around to see if anyone else was nearby. Seeing no one, she completed the parturition process as her mother had taught her. "Thank you Frigg for your help in birthing this boy. And thank you Odin, for watching over him."

With her work thus completed, Mariteth lifted her right hand to her forehead and made the sign of the cross.

CONFESSIONS

December 1080

It was the eighteenth day of December in the year of the Lord one thousand and eighty. Of that Andrew was certain because it was exactly one week before Christmas. Lady Audrey had called him to hear her confession. And judging by the size of her belly, her time was close. Childbirth was always risky, so getting a confession in before the event was wise. If she died, it could make a big difference for her soul's journey. In her case, with her confession so recently made, she'd get right into heaven. She was such a goodly person, always praying, friendly to everyone and very charitable to the poor. And of course she always remembered to write a few Latin words for his Christmas sermon. And she had remembered, had it all written out for him on a fine piece of parchment. Andrew patted the breast of his leather jerkin which his wife had made for him. It had a pocket on the inside which held Audrey's note. Of course he couldn't actually read Latin nor any other language for that matter. But she'd showed him how to sound out what she'd written and told him he could practice it daily to get ready. He really appreciated her help since she was the only 'Latiner' he knew west of Caen. And he didn't have to get the sounds just right anyhow because none of his parishioners knew Latin either.

Right after she'd confessed, not that there was much that needed confessing, she told him that she'd felt something and asked him to stay. Then she'd called for Lucas the chamberlain and he sent the stableboy for the midwife. Audrey had then thanked him and excused herself. Realizing that the birthing process could take a while, Andrew had taken himself to the castle's great room where he thought there might be a fire. What he found wasn't much of a fire but it did hold back some of the cold. At dusk a cook brought him some mead, bread and cheese together with two blankets, one to cover him and the other to put under his head. By daylight he was hungry again but, knowing that everyone in the castle was probably praying for Audrey and her child rather than looking for food, he decided to pray for her too.

After he'd done that, he also prayed for Audrey's husband Walter. Andrew had just made novice when he joined the Duke of Normandy's vanguard going to England. By then Walter had four children two of whom were already knights. The oldest, Henry, was nineteen and the second, Walter, was a year younger.

Andrew remembered seeing the red and white banner of Dol tip forward and felt the human mass surrounding him break into a trot. Contact was immediate. Henry the Healer leading the Brettons crashed headlong into the Saxon advance. His sons, Henry and Walter, were right behind him. Being relatively short and well behind the leaders, Andrew's view was often blocked by taller men ahead of him. By chance though, he did see Walter and a Saxon warrior rush upon one another. As the Saxon closed, he was swinging both his axes simultaneously. Walter, also closing, intercepted the first axe with his shield. At almost the same moment, with his sword, Walter managed to deflect his opponent's other axe so its blade passed harmlessly over his right shoulder. As the two men's bodies crashed together, each adjusted to pay out a fresh blow. The Saxon, whose left hand gripped his remaining usable weapon, pulled the axe blade down along the back of Walter's hauberk. The chainmail did its job but it only extended to just below his hip. There the Saxon pulled his axe blade fiercely into the Bretton knight's right leg. In the same moment, Walter lowered his sword and savagely sliced it across his adversary's face, cutting into the man's skull. A great gush of blood spewed forth upon both men. Then, just as Walter began to fall backward, Andrew's view was blocked by another soldier in front of him.

Mortified by what he'd just seen, Andrew halted in mid-step. In his mind he kept seeing that great gush of blood...blood in the air, blood on the Saxon, blood on Walter. Blood everywhere!

Meanwhile the rest of the Bretton contingent continued to move toward the slaughter. But one man, a burly fellow whose chainmail shirt fell almost to his knees, stopped right beside Andrew. The man carefully looked past the youth's noseguard into his eyes. Then quite viciously he banged his shield against Andrew's shoulder.

"Come on lad," he barked, "or you'll hate yourself for the rest of your life."

The blow to his shoulder was enough to shake Andrew out of his torpor. He knew he must help Walter. He cursed his hesitation and lunged toward the place where he'd seen his friend fall. The battle had moved forward but there were bodies everywhere. Fortunately he spied the brown leather tunic of the Saxon who had fought Walter. His body lay on top of the young Bretton knight. Several other bodies lay so close to Walter that their arms and legs also draped across him. The priest dropped his mace, unfastened his shield and began to pull his friend out of the carnage.

"I'll help you," Andrew mumbled while he pulled the covering corpses aside. Then as he pulled the last dead Saxon off his friend, he heard a moan. Walter was still alive!

Quickly the neophyte unsheathed his dagger and looked for some sort of fabric with which to fashion a bandage. His eyes fell upon a homespun shirt worn by one of the dead. Andrew cut it lengthwise and yanked it off the dead man's torso. He then set to work tying it tightly around Walter's wounded leg. As his fingers worked, he whispered almost inaudibly. "Thank You Lord for that thump on my shoulder. I should not have hesitated. Please, Jesus, help me save Walter's life."

And God did help Andrew save Walter's life, and win the battle too. But Walter remained forever-after severly crippled. He had to use crutches to walk and his feet had to be tied together with a cord beneath his horse's belly when he rode. But Andrew marveled at his friend's perseverance. Walter never complained, nor ever slacken in his duties.

THE TUTOR
January 1087

Benito Tusculani's room in the castle was on the third level and faced south. The combination of the drafty arrow-loop, the cold stone walls and Benito's thin Italian blood kept the castle's woodsman busy cutting, splitting and carrying loads of firewood up the three flights of circling narrow steps. On this particular January day, the tutor was in his room staring into a mirror. The glass hung precariously from a nail which had been crudly hammered into the wall between two stones. The mirror was about two feet square. He'd brought it with him when he departed the Abbey of Cluny. Three pack animals were all that Abbot Hugh had allowed him to carry his things—not nearly enough, but the Abbot knew that.

Perhaps, thought Benito, the Abbot was jealous of his family's high stature in Rome and their great influence over Papal elections, or perhaps it was their wealth, or possibly it was just that Hugh didn't like anyone who wasn't a Church reformist. Whatever it was, he and the Abbot had never gotten along. This 'penance' of sending him to Dol was proof of that. But Benito reasoned, God willing, it might also lead to his absolution, a bishopric in Rome, or at least some high papal office there. Abbot Hugh had told him he must learn humility and, with that in mind, he was sending him to Dol to teach a child for some indeterminate period of time—Dol! He'd never even heard of Dol, much less did he know where it was. He understood immediately that it would be a purgatory, like Moses leading the Israelites out of Egypt, a long and arduous travail in a place totally lacking civility, social intercourse and educated people. So he'd negotiated with Hugh and asked the Abbot if, after he'd taught this child, he could be sent back to Rome into some position worthy of his intelligence, education and stature. Hugh told him that if Walter, the Lord of Dol, and his wife, Audrey, both signed and sent a letter to Cluny that indicated that he'd done a good job teaching their child and done so without displaying arrogance or insolence, he would recommend Benito to the Pope for a higher office. Benito didn't like it but at least he could see a positive outcome after what would probably be six years in a place of isolation, ignorance and cultural oblivion. Unfortunately he had no choice.

So now, after he'd been teaching Walter's oldest son, William, for over two years, the Lord of Dol had asked him to take on his second son as well. 'Damn,' thought Benito, 'that would extend my penance here by at least another two years. Damn! And my position in Rome depends on a good reference letter from them. Audrey will write well of me. We get along well enough, read each other's poetry. But of Walter's reference, I'm not sure. He's been square with me so far...at least he's seemed to be. But I can't read him well enough to be certain.'

For several long moments Benito stared appraisingly at his reflection. Then suddenly he raised his hand mirror and aligned it with the wall mirror so he could inspect the top of his head. Yes, his tonsure was neatly shaven, a perfectly round circle of white skin surrounded by a hedge of black hair hanging neatly down like a halo above his ears. He shaved the top of his head every day at the same time he did his whiskers, a scissor clip here, a clip there. Ah, what's that? No...just the fire light. No! It's a gray hair and...and more than one. Damn! It makes me look... Hmm... more sophisticated. Yes...even more sophisticated! The Roman monk smiled. 'I won't cut them out. I'll leave them in. Distinguished... they make me look distinguished.'

He lowered his hand-held mirror slightly and studied his physiognomy carefully. Then he twisted the hand glass slightly to bring his nose into view from the side. It was long and hooked downward. It was, he reminded himself, a distinguishing feature of the Roman nobility. All the emperors' statues had noses like that.

"I have it," Benito yelped out loud. "I'll agree to teach Walter's second son but only till he's twelve and only if Walter agrees to let me write his reference letter to Abbot Hugh! That will surely get me to Rome. It means more years here but it takes away any doubt. I'll make that letter sound so good that Hugh will have to recommend me. How sweet it will be to go back to Rome. Of course it could be sooner if Gregory dies and the cardinals don't elect someone as bent on reform as His Eminence. A traditionalist is what they need; not someone who constantly fights with the Emperor and...and thinks every priest should be celibate and doesn't understand the real world when it comes to making political appointments. Of course Gregory could have died months ago, and being here in this God-forsaken place, we wouldn't have heard about it yet. That time in eighty-three when the Roman citizens nearly overthrew the pontiff, it took six weeks for that information to even get to Cluny and...and another two before we heard the Apulian freebooter Guiscard bought them off with thirty thousand solidi. It could be three months before we'd hear anything here in this metropolis.

"But to the point, I'll plan for the long term and rejoice if it's shorter. I'll see Walter today and tell him I'll do it but with one condition, that I'll write his letter to Abbot Hugh for him. I'll tell him right out why I must have an excellent letter. Of course he can read it before signing it. I'll be open to suggestions. But I must get to Rome!"

HUNTING

March 1087

It was the middle of the night and very dark but Henry wasn't frightened. His mother had taught him that God was always nearby and watching over him. He was wide-awake for a different reason. His father would be taking his older brother William and him hunting. Several times he'd heard sounds in the family's room but his father hadn't gotten up. He looked across the room to see if there was yet a glow on the horizon but the two eastward-facing arrow-loops were stuffed with old clothes to keep out the cold. Finally he slipped his hand beneath the blankets and pressed his fingers toward his brother but when he felt warmth, he stayed his hand before making actual contact. His father and mother slept slightly beyond William, but he couldn't see them at all. At least he knew that his father and William hadn't left without him.

Henry woke with a start. William was poking him.

"Wake up," his brother whispered. "We're going to the stable."

In order not to wake his mother, Henry didn't answer. Instead he twisted his feet out from under the covers and bending forward, reached for his leggings, coat and boots all of which he'd carefully set out the night before. He dressed quickly since he had to follow his father down the stone stairs while William went ahead. Their mother had said to do that 'in case your father starts to fall, you can catch him.'

When they got to the stable, Bart was preparing the horses. Alfred and Glendon were already there. William would ride the new, white stallion and Henry and Glendon would each get one of the old mares. Alfred would ride his father's horse which he and Glendon had just ridden over.

The previous week, for the first time, Henry had ridden all by himself. Before that, he'd always ridden with his father, either just in front of the saddle or behind it. Riding alone had been exhilarating. He'd only fallen off once. This morning he was determined not to fall off at all.

Walter made them stay together and gave them direction as well as an explanation for why they must do things in certain ways. Only William and Alfred were allowed to carry bows and they had to ride very close to Walter and receive explicit permission before they could loose an arrow.

Walter told them, "that the most dangerous thing in the whole world was a man with a weapon. So you must be very careful."

By late morning, Henry's butt ached and he was cold. So he began to think about lunch and the great-room's fire. But he did see and respond when his father raised his right arm to signal their group to halt. Henry immediately reined in his mount and looked around to see why they were stopping. Suddenly he saw a deer just ahead of them no more than sixty feet away. The youth looked to his father. Walter was pointing at William and nodding his head. Henry watched his brother silently lift his bow and draw back its string. Then quite suddenly there was a twanging sound and the arrow leapt forth. The arrow struck the animal squarely in the flank just ahead of its hind leg. The deer leapt forward.

"William, you and Bart pursue," commanded Walter. "We'll follow."

It was less than a quarter-mile when they came upon William, Bart and the deer. The creature lay atop a patch of snow where its blood shone bright red. Bart was busy gutting the deer, a male as Henry could now see. Leaning forward the boy watched with fascination as the entrails were removed and his father identified their functions. Then quite suddenly Henry straitened up and twisted around in his saddle so that he was looking back over his horse's rump. About three hundred feet away a man was dragging some tree limbs in their direction.

"Probably one of our serfs collecting fire wood," speculated Walter.

"There are two," uttered Henry.

Instantly Henry thought he'd misspoken. There was only the one serf...and Henry was about to correct himself when a child appeared from behind the wood-carrier. Henry was completely flummoxed... At first he'd seen only the man yet he'd clearly said two! How could that be?

"Bart," called out Walter, "I can see who that is now. Cut off one of the deer's hind legs and we'll take it to his hut. It's just over there a ways."

Later in the stable, Walter supervised the grooming of the horses. "You must always care for your horse first. In war, your horse is your most important weapon. Not only does it carry you, it provides you the ability to overcome foot-soldiers. Always treat your horse like a member of the family."

So they all dutifully watered, fed and curried their mounts. Walter then waited while everyone finished their work and left. Knowing there was a stone stairway ahead with a hand rope for his father, Henry waited too.

"I have important news for you Henry," said the Lord of Dol. "Beginning Monday morning, you will be joining William in Benito's seminary. Benito will teach you to read and write Latin and to do sums. Who knows, you may become a bishop someday."

Henry gulped. It hadn't occurred to him that Benito might become his tutor too... He wasn't sure he liked the idea.

ATTENDING
March 1087

Henry often recalled his first day in Benito's 'erudition' room. It was really just a small store room on the castle's second level. A wooden bench squatted there awaiting his and William's arrival. Beyond the bench, a small table held the one lit candle in the room. Its glow was meager and the room had no loop-holes to let in more light. The candle's light barely reached the edges of the table.

Henry had been very startled when, on his right, Benito's face and hands suddenly appeared out of the darkness. The tutor's countenance was round and oddly white. It seemed to float amidst the blackness of the dark wall behind him. But this almost supernatural appearance began to fade as Henry started to distinguish the outline of the man's black robe around his shoulders.

"So," began Benito Tusculani, "two neophytes now instead of one." The boys' tutor rubbed his hands together and smiled crookedly before continuing. "Well William, you're not really a neophyte any more are you? So here is my plan: Henry, each Monday through Friday you shall come here at exactly Terce and stay till Nones. William, you shall come at Sext and stay till Vespers and bring my lunch as well as yours. As you can see, in the middle of the day you will overlap. Then I'll teach you together, most probably oratory, history, Latin and logic. Henry in his individual time with me will learn the Trivium for the next two years and you William, having already studied that, will begin the Quadrivium with an expected graduation in three years. That is my plan. Do you both understand it?"

Benito paused for less than a moment and then concluded his introduction. "Good."

"Now today being an unusual day, we'll spend our time until lunch learning Latin. You are very blessed that I am accomplished in both Latin and Greek. Additionally, I carry with me at all times my own copy of Virgil's *Aeneid*. It is a priceless copy dating back to the second century Anno Domini. You must always treat it with the utmost care! Now let us sit together so you can see what I shall be reading."

The monk stepped to the small table that held the flickering candle and pulled the four-legged piece of furniture across the wooden floor until it rested in front of the bench.

"Now," said the Master, "let me sit between you."

Gathering his robe up around his midriff, Benito positioned himself to sit down. Before he did so though, he reached his free hand inside the black robe and pulled forth a leather-bound book. Henry saw the candlelight glint off the smooth, reddish-brown leather. It was only the second book the boy had ever seen. He remembered his mother telling him that a high gloss on a book's cover meant that its owner read it regularly.

"Now, Henry," Benito said as he sat down, "draw the candle nearer so we can all see the calligraphy."

After Henry had moved the candle closer to his tutor's elbow, the monk placed his book on the table and carefully opened it.

"William," said Benito, "you have read this part before. Please read the first three words aloud...first in Latin and then translated into French." The black-robed teacher then moved the book slightly toward William.

Henry's brother cleared his throat before speaking. "Arma virumque cano... Of arms and the man I sing." William's voice quivered slightly as he finished.

"Very good," said the Benedictine proudly. "Now please explain to Henry how you determined that translation...the verb, where it usually lies, where the 'I' came from, which words are the objects and the location of the word 'and'."

"Oh." William responded in a surprised tone. "Well, the verb is usually at the end. In this case it is 'cano' which means 'I sing'...and 'Arma' is the plural of 'armum' which means 'arms' and...'virum' is 'man' and the 'que' on its end means 'and' and joins the words 'arms' and 'man' together."

"Very good William, you have been attending." Benito turned his head toward Henry. "What have you learned from this young man?"

Henry gulped quietly, he hoped, as his mind raced to find answers. "Well," he whispered, "I've learned that the word 'cano' means 'I sing'... and 'que' combines words together like our word 'and'...'arma' means 'arms' and 'virum' must be 'man.'

"Very good," said the monk. "And what did I call the word 'cano?'"

Henry pondered again..."I sing," he finally put forth hesitantly.

"No," replied Benito. "William said 'I sing.' I used a different term. Do you remember it?"

Henry forced himself to recall the conversation. He thought the answer to Benito's question had something to do with what went last, but he couldn't remember an exact word. "No," he finally whispered. "I don't remember."

"Well then," muttered the monk somewhat grimly, "put your left hand onto the table palm down."

Henry looked up into Benito's eyes. They showed no hint of mercy. The youth glanced at his older brother but William's eyes were averted. Finally Henry placed his left hand on the table as he'd been instructed.

The black-robed monk's right hand suddenly rose and fell. Henry saw a yellowish blur as the switch passed through the candle's light and fell upon his hand.

THWACK

Henry felt great pain in his fingers. The throbbing quickly flowed up through his hand and entered his arm.

"You must learn to attend," pronounced a distant voice. "You must learn to attend."

The boy felt tears welling up in his eyes but he didn't intend to let his persecutor see them. For several long moments, he stared at the back of his hand watching the welt on it swell and then begin to turn purple. Finally when he was certain his tears were quelled, the six-year-old turned to look directly at Benito. The monk had turned away.

"William," asked the tutor, "what is the word we are searching for?"

"Verb," Henry's older brother replied softly.

"Yes," said Benito, "and will you please explain the function of a verb to your brother."

THE EULOGY
February 1089

Henry was sitting in the chapel's second row. He usually sat in the front row with his father, mother and William but today was special like Christmas or Easter but with less joy. His uncles, aunts and cousins had all arrived the day before. They seemed more subdued than usual. The only child in the chapel making any noise was Henry's new brother Edmond. He made noises almost constantly even though Audrey was holding him and doing her best to keep him hushed.

"We come here today," began Father Andrew, "to honor Benito Tusculani, a Benedictine monk from the Abbey of Cluny and a tutor to the two oldest sons of Lord Walter and Audrey. Benito was an Italian, born in Rome of a noble family and educated there by the finest scholars. Before he died, Benito asked that this service might include a eulogy presented by his youngest student. So Henry will you please come forward and speak to us of Benito."

Henry rose and made his way forward until he stood directly beneath the chapel's rood beam and its large wooden cross. There he turned around so he faced the gathered assemblage but he did not speak. Instead he silently drew his audience's attention. When at last he judged all the attendees were with him, he began.

"Today I shall assert that we should appraise a man more for his strengths than for his weaknesses, more by what he does to get himself into heaven than to keep himself out. It is a man's positive traits that make him worthy."

"Benito Tusculani, as Father Andrew has said, was a Benedictine monk from the Abbey of Cluny and an Italian scholar from a noble family. Beyond this, few of us knew him well. What we usually saw were his less noble traits. He was haughty, strict, curt, self-impressed, arrogant, overbearing and even fashionable. He wore his ermine coat to show himself to be above everyone else. These were his weaknesses. But if we think about them, we realize that none of them were truly sinful but rather only irritating, humiliating, annoying and even sometimes... funny.

"Benito's strengths were harder to discern. They were his standards and his knowledge. Had you attended his classes as William and I have, you would immediately have become aware of his switch. It was a mean branch taken from some supple tree and used to gain our full attention. On my first day with him when I failed to remember something he'd said, he laid that sprig upon the back of my hand so hard I cried. I feared that switch for a long time until I realized that its real purpose was not to hurt me but to set a standard of expectation. You knights among us remember your trainers of swordsmanship and combat pressing you very hard in order to help you survive when you were in real combat.

"Benito's other strength was his knowledge. He used it to convey moral and ethical values. Perhaps you remember William's presentation when he recounted from Homer's *Iliad* the story of Paris stealing Menelaus' wife, Helen, and the war and deaths which followed that vile deed. Therein, Benito shared his knowledge to make a point. And so, like a priest on Sunday who shares a tale from the bible to warn well-meaning Christians what not to do, Benito shared similar stories as he taught his students in order to show them the path to heaven.

"So, what can we conclude about Benito's strengths, his standards and his knowledge? That he used them to benefit other people, to help others live better lives, to help his students make their way to heaven. These strengths are mighty and most compelling upon those of us who have benefitted from them. So let us remember Benito Tusculani for his strengths and wish him well."

Then still standing beneath the burnished cross above him, Henry pivoted away from his audience. He bowed his head for a moment then whispered to God. "If Your plan should ever take me to Rome, I shall try to contact Benito's family so I may thank them and tell them how well their son conveyed Your purpose. Amen."

A NEW DIRECTION
August 1089

Henry sat watching two bright, orange splashes of sunlight metrically climb the great room's eastern wall. There they reflected boldly amidst the growing gloom. His father had commented on them earlier. "Perhaps," he'd said, "we should add a third arrow-loop on the west wall to denote that we now have three sons."

Walter had since departed the room, so only Henry and his mother remained sitting beside one another on one of the long wooden benches.

"Henry, you know we love you. So please don't misunderstand why we have chosen to send you away. I myself was a novice near Bec, a women's abbey of course, not the monastery. And I will tell you that at first I felt quite betrayed by my father who seemed to have given me away. It took quite a while to realize that he made the choice in my best interest. We all have our own lives to lead and, God willing, they may be long ones. So, preparing for an unclear future requires preparation, years of work in order to be able to do those things most desired by our Lord Jesus Christ. Your father and I both believe that you have been gifted by our Savior with both aptitude and zeal. It is therefore your duty during your life to use those gifts as effectively as possible. Anything less would be ungracious and disrespectful to God.

"Accordingly, as your father has just told you, we have decided to send you to the Abbey at Bec. It is all arranged. They will continue your education where Benito left off and prepare you to become a monk like them or perhaps a priest. Your path here is quite limited as William will become your father's successor as Lord of Dol. Accordingly we wish to put you in a direction that will give you real opportunity. The reform movement within the church is growing and actively seeks those who are bright and zealous.

"But Henry, you must remember this: you may become an oblate and then a novice but you are not irrevocably committed until you are ordained. That final choice will be yours alone. So, if you find that a path toward the priesthood is not what you want, you can simply decline your ordination. Meanwhile the education you receive will stand you in good stead no matter where God's plan takes you."

Appearing to want to hear her son's thoughts on the subject Audrey paused.

Henry glanced away for a moment before turning back to face her.

"Mother," Henry whispered, "what if I want to come back to Dol?"

"Oh Henry," Audrey's voice quivered as she put her arms around the boy and hugged him, "if you really don't like it, let me know and I'll talk to your father." Then pulling back with tears running down her cheeks, she looked him squarely in the eye and spoke in a very controlled tone. "Henry, I really do believe you'll like it there. Bec is the best monastery in Christendom only behind perhaps Cluny and Monte Cassino. Your teachers will be among the best in the world. When I was a novice, Lanfranc was there. He is now Bishop of Canterbury in England and one of the great lords of the realm. The current abbot is named Anslem. He has studied at both the high school in Bologna and in Paris. You are a serious young man, 'precocious' I believe is the right word. People come to the Abbey at Bec from everywhere in Christendom to get this level of education. It is a great honor to have been accepted. And Henry, you do have a duty to God to use the gifts He has given you."

~**~

"Son," Henry's concerns were interrupted by his father's voice, "I want to talk with you up on the battlements. It is dark enough now for me to make an important point."

The huge great-room was shrouded in shadows. But the youth could see his father twist on their bench to free his legs from beneath the table. Simultaneously the older man leaned to one side and clasped his crutches from the floor.

"Father, should I bring a torch?"

"No," replied Walter. "I think we'll be able to see once we reach the top of the stairs. Meanwhile we'll use the hand rope to guide us. Do you want to go first?"

"No," said Henry. "I'll go behind you."

So the two shuffled along the ink-black corridor, both clasping the surety rope until Walter reached the circular stairway, whence he turned and reached across the darkness for the second rope which wound up the tightly turning stairs. Finally the older man stopped his climb and fumbled for a moment with what Henry knew was the latch to the door exiting onto the battlements.

"Ah," breathed Walter as he swung open the heavy wooden door with its iron cross-ties. "We can see again."

Henry saw the glimmer of starlight above him. It had been so dark in the stairway that when he stepped onto the roof, he found the starlight quite sufficient. Before he took his own place, he watched his father laboriously sit down on the wooden beam. Then they sat together silently for a long time viewing perhaps a million twinkling sparks of light arrayed against the midnight blackness that arched above them.

At last Walter broke the silence. "Do you know which is the North Star?"

"I think so," responded the boy as he lifted his right arm and pointed skyward. "It's that one isn't it?"

"Yes it is," said Walter. "And do you know what its significance is?"

"It is the one by which we know our direction. It always points toward the north. So when we see it, we can also tell where east, west and south are."

"Yes," whispered Walter, "and so we trust it. It never moves, never waivers, never falters. It is like God in whom we also trust. Sometimes on a cloudy night we may lose our way but that star will eventually shine forth and lead us back to a righteous path. And so it is with God Henry. When you may be filled with doubt, you must trust in Him and know that He has a purpose for you even if it is not yet clear exactly what that purpose is."

"I tell you this not because your mother and I are certain that God wishes you to study at Bec but because we feel it is the best place to put someone with your aptitude. When you are older and have begun to see God's intentions for you, you must of course adjust your own direction accordingly. Meanwhile please trust that we are doing our best for you."

A long pause ensued during which Henry thought about what his father had just said. Eventually Walter spoke again. "Do you understand what I mean?"

"Yes father," replied the boy. "You mean that God has chosen a path for me and that neither of us yet knows exactly what it is. But if I keep looking to God for direction as I would to the North Star, I shall eventually find it."

"Yes," said Walter. "That's exactly what I mean. Thank you for listening."

Thinking that it was really his father who deserved the thanks, Henry was about to say so but his father spoke first.

"You know Henry after I received my wound at Hastings field, I thought I'd never marry. What woman would want a cripple? And so I did not look for a marriage. But God had a different plan and so through my father's best friend Duke William, your mother was presented to me. She has been a wonderful wife and has given me three wonderful sons."

With emotion then overtaking his speech, Walter looked up into the sea of stars above him and unerringly pointed to the never faltering North Star. "God," he said with his voice regained, "will always give you the right direction Henry...always!"

MAGWOLF AND ABRAHAM
August 1089

About mid-morning Magwolf and Henry were picking their way through a moderately thick forest when Magwolf raised his right hand to signal a stop. Henry was about ten paces behind the older man and still leading the two pack-mules. Accordingly he couldn't see as far ahead as his friend. The boy knew from his hunting forays that quiet was called for. So without speaking he leaned in his saddle to get a better look at what was ahead. As he did, Magwolf began to back his mount. When he reached the boy he turned his head toward Henry and whispered.

"Ahead there are several men on horses...perhaps robbers."

Henry couldn't see anyone but he did reach his free hand across his saddle and touch his belt to make certain his knife was still there... It was.

Magwolf's next whisper was much gruffer. "Just sit as you are. I promise they'll not touch you. We'll wait here to let them pass. If they do try to take us, drop the cord to the mules and ride back as fast as possible. I'll delay them as long as I can."

"God, please help us get safely to Bec," the boy murmured, "and please watch over Magwolf should he have to protect us." As Henry ceased his prayer, his mind immediately went to his two most prized possessions: Benito's book and his father's chess set. Both were aboard the second mule behind him. Henry immediately promised himself, that if he and Magwolf got through this encounter, he would ever after carry those two items on his person or at least in his horse's saddlebags.

"That's close enough," called out Magwolf.

Henry peered past his friend to see who he was addressing. As he did, he noticed that his father's liegeman had put his helmet on his head and rotated his shield from behind his shoulder to his left arm. In the woods ahead of them was a similarly dressed man astride a grey mare. Neither warrior had yet drawn his sword.

"Hail and well met," replied the stranger. "We are not brigands and mean you no harm. But of course," he continued, "I must be sure that you aren't the vanguard of some band of thieves. Can you vouchsafe yourselves?"

"We can," responded Magwolf, "but since your company is more numerous than ours, perhaps you might provide your credentials first."

The soldier on the grey thought for a moment. "All right," he finally said, "you can leave your mules and the boy here. But you'll have to come half-way to our train and I'll bring our headman to you. Is that satisfactory?"

"Yes," said Magwolf.

"Good," said the other man as he wheeled his grey around.

Magwolf then twisted in his saddle and yelled to his charge. "Henry, remember my instructions and follow them exactly should anything foul occur." With that, Magwolf twisted away and kneed his horse.

Henry immediately became nervous; his mind was racing with frightening and conflicting thoughts. Would he have to gallop off? Shouldn't he stay and try to help Magwolf? Or would that simply make the sergeant's task more difficult? What about his book and game? Should he go straight for Dol or try to find some local noble to help them? Were these people ahead of them robbers? Or perhaps just travelers like themselves? Why was he having so much difficulty deciding what to do? Suddenly he raised his right hand and slapped his cheek with a puissant blow. For a moment tiny splotches of orange light spun before him. Then he felt his sprinting mind slow down. He would follow Magwolf's orders exactly as they had been given. And in the future he would identify all possible risks that might lie ahead and, through forward planning, be prepared. And so, trusting in God and his father's knight, the youth set his concerns aside.

Meanwhile, until Magwolf signaled him to run, Henry was determined to be as useful as possible. He slowly rotated his head first to his left and then to his right studying every tree, bush and shadow. Finally he looked directly behind him where they'd just come from. The only living creatures he saw were the two pack-mules which stood contentedly, perhaps even happily, staring at the ground in front of them. At last Henry returned his questioning stare to the forest ahead. Magwolf had halted his advance perhaps thirty paces away. What seemed like quite a bit of time passed before the boy finally saw the soldier on the gray riding back toward Magwolf. There were two other men riding with him. One was fitted out exactly as the first with helm, hauberk, shield and horse. The second rode a fine black stallion that even from afar, anyone could tell was a magnificent horse. His appearance though was nothing like Henry had seen before. The fellow was short, wore a black robe with drooping, almost billowing, long sleeves and atop his head, he wore a bell-shaped hat that appeared to be a deep, dark blue.

Magwolf turned in his saddle. "A Jew!" he yelled to Henry. "A blood-sucking Jew!"

Henry had never met a Jew before. He'd heard of them of course, that they were the ones who'd killed Christ, usurers, sly in their dealings, not to be trusted. Then again, Christ had been a Jew.

Magwolf waved his arm for Henry to come forward.

The boy clapped his knees to his mount's flanks. The two mules followed. Relief washed over the boy as he realized that he'd probably not have to ride for his life, lose his book and chess set or see Magwolf slain in combat. "Thank you Lord for watching over us...and I promise to be better prepared next time." He halted his horse beside his bodyguard and faced the three strangers. Beyond them he could see a long train of pack-mules as well as several attendants who were now awaiting the outcome of their meeting.

The fellow on the grey spoke first. "As you can see, we are a merchant's train on our way to a fair. Are you two alone or are there others nearby?"

"There are only two of us," responded Magwolf. "We are traveling east to place this young man at the Abbey of Bec. We can be out of your way in moments."

Suddenly Henry heard a buzzing sound near his right ear and then felt some flying insect land on his neck. Instinctively he slapped it. As he did, the Jew's black stallion whinnied and abruptly reared high into the air. The second soldier clasped the black's reins so quickly that Henry wasn't sure he'd even seen the man move to do so. But as fast as the fellow was, he wasn't fast enough to keep the Jew from falling onto the forest floor in a heap.

"Run," the soldier yelled to the black robed man on the ground. "We're in a nest of hornets. Run for the train." Both soldiers then slapped their mounts and galloped toward the baggage train.

Henry felt a hornet land on his cheek and immediately slapped it. As he did, he saw the black robed Jew get to his feet. The boy thrust forth his hand intending to help the man get up behind him so they could both escape the hornets. The Jew's attention however was on the swarm of insects buzzing around his head. So, without seeing the youth's offer, he began to run back toward his baggage train.

Seeing this, Henry was about to kick his horse forward when he saw on the ground below him what looked like a small book bound in leather. Thinking it was his *Aeneid*, the youth leapt down from his saddle, grabbed up the book, remounted and clapped his legs to move his mount. Only a few moments later he, his horse and the two pack-mules all arrived at the merchant's caravan without a single one of them having been stung. Henry was contemplating how lucky he'd been when it occurred to him that he couldn't understand how his book could have gotten out of its wrappings onto the ground. He lifted the tome and looked at it. It was not his *Aeneid*!

Immediately the boy looked up...and then around. Magwolf was nearby assessing the merchant's train of mules; the two guards were sitting atop their steeds watching the Jew lift himself back onto his black horse. With no one paying attention to him, Henry opened the tiny book's front cover. The first page listed 'Genoa' boldly at the top and dropped down listing numerous other towns until at the very bottom it highlighted 'Rouen.' Each town had annotations after it in very small script with a number of them being abbreviations or acronyms. As the youth looked down the page, it suddenly occurred to him that the book wasn't his and its owner might not want him to be reading it. He looked up to see if the Jewish merchant was looking at him. The fellow was sitting in his saddle and straightening his bell-shaped hat. The boy nudged his horse forward and tugged her left rein slightly to direct her toward the black-robed Jew.

"Sir," said the boy, "is this folio yours?"

Upon hearing himself so addressed, the man seemed to flinch slightly but Henry didn't pay much attention as, being now close enough to really look the fellow over, he was studying him in minute detail. His age was difficult to determine, perhaps thirty years old, certainly middle-aged. His eyes, which at first seemed to be coal-black, were actually a very dark shade of brown and his complexion was quite sun-stained, darker even than Benito. Henry wondered if the man might be wearing his black robe to make himself look paler, more like the Franks and Normans with whom he probably did business. While lacking a beard, the man's face was nevertheless sprouting two or three days of grayish growth. His hands however, gave the greatest insight into his profession. They were entirely smooth, lacking either calluses or any sign of dirt beneath the nails. All in all, the youth concluded the Jew looked a lot like Benito Tusculani.

"It certainly looks like mine," answered the merchant as he reached out for the leather-bound volume and took it. "Thank you young man. My name is Abraham Trebyianni of Genoa." The Jew leaned forward in his saddle to offer his obeisance.

The man's accent also reminded Henry of Benito.

"I am most grateful for the return of my atlas. It gives me comfort along our path and helps me with names and prices, little things which I might otherwise forget."

Henry watched Abraham slip his black book into some unseen pocket inside his robe. "I have never seen an atlas before," said Henry. "Does it have maps inside it?"

For several moments Abraham squinted at the youth before responding. "You did not look inside?" he asked.

Henry blushed and in so doing, he knew that he had shown Abraham the answer to his question. But he responded anyhow. "I did just look inside the front cover. I'm sorry. It was not my place to look inside your book."

"Ah," said the Jew, "today you are twice an honest young man for you admitted looking into my book and you returned it as well. You could have taken it and I would not have known until you were well gone. Did you not think of keeping the book?"

"No," Henry quickly replied. "I would never steal something for surely God would be displeased with me."

"So He would," responded the merchant. "So He would." Then changing his tone slightly, Abraham asked another question. "Are you wondering what the writing said?"

"Only the annotations," replied the youth. "They seemed abbreviated and I was not acquainted with them."

Showing his surprise, Abraham lifted his head slightly. "You read Latin?"

"A little," Henry replied.

The Jew gazed quizzically at the youth for several moments. "Who taught you to read?"

"Benito Tusculani."

"Tusculani," Abraham mouthed the name slowly turning it over on his tongue. "Is he of the Tusculani family just south of Rome?"

"He was," said Henry, "but he recently died."

"Oh," responded Abraham. "I am sorry to hear that."

"That is why we're going to Bec," continued Henry, "so I can continue my education."

"I see." said Abraham as he turned in his saddle to face one of his attendants. "Simon, bring me one of those good wool blankets from that first mule there." The merchant pointed with his right forefinger at the mule and then turned back to Henry. "What is your name?" he asked pleasantly.

"Henry," replied the youth, "Henry of Dol."

"I like you Henry of Dol," Abraham said proudly, "and I wish to give you a blanket to show my appreciation for you giving me back my book." Then as his attendant rode up, Abraham took a thick cream-colored blanket from the man and handed it to Henry. "If you ever need a friend in Genoa, please ask for Abraham. Any Jew will know me and many of the Christians."

"Thank you, sir," replied the gift's recipient.

Again when the boy spoke, Abraham winced. The Jewish merchant then surreptitiously looked all around to see if anyone was watching them. When he concluded no one was, he leaned in close to the boy's ear and whispered very quietly. "Henry, you shouldn't ever call a Jew 'sir.' It offends many Christians and can get the Jew into a lot of trouble." Abraham paused for a moment before speaking again. "Do you understand?"

"Yes," answered Henry.

"Good," said the merchant as he tugged on his stallion's reins to turn away. "Oh," he called back, "those 'annotations' are Yiddish. That's why you couldn't read them."

THE ABBEY OF BEC
August 1089 - December 1089

The land ahead of them had dramatically changed from a primordeal forest to a panorama of well-kept fields, some plowed but fallow and others, it being almost the Feast of Saint Bartholomew, were dense with beans, oats, barley and lentils. From still other fields, tall grass waved pleasantly. The crops were being hoed and tended by a large number of black-robed workers. No field-hand, indentured or free, would be wearing such a robe on a hot August day, so Henry knew that he and Magwolf had finally reached their objective, the Abbey of Bec. Even further ahead, he could see a high, stone tower rising amidst the tree tops. Henry and Magwolf kneed their horses in that direction.

Soon the boy could distinguish several buildings. The stone tower which he'd thought was a battlement was actually the abbey's church steeple. The church itself was not particularly large but the building beside it was. It was one story high and very long. At its furthest end, there were several chimneys rising through a roof. Henry reckoned the edifice was the monks' dormitory and the end with chimneys, their kitchen. No human beings were in sight. But since the sun hadn't yet reached its zenith, the youth surmised everyone was still in the fields. This immediately changed when two men exited from a small wooden building that stood just to the right of the dormitory. Each wore a black robe marking them, Henry knew, as Benedictine monks. The first was of average height, slender and already bald despite still being fairly young. The second followed a step or two behind and gave every appearance of being a retainer.

"Con-salutare," called out the first monk in a most friendly manner.

"Salutare," Henry replied cheerfully while trying very hard to pronounce his Latin greeting as articulately as he could.

"Ah," continued the balding monk, "you speak Latin."

"Some," replied Henry as he dismounted, "but certainly not as well as you."

The monk reached forth his hand. "Your words were correctly used and your pronunciation very good. My name is Anslem. I am the Abbot here. Do I correctly assume that you are Henry of Dol?"

"I am," said Henry as he shook the Abbot's hand, "and this is Magwolf, my father's sergeant." The youth waved his hand toward his bodyguard who remained sitting in his saddle.

Anslem turned abruptly toward the second monk. "Brother Jason, please find Peter Maillesais and bring him here." Turning back to Henry, the Abbot continued in an amicable tone. "Peter will be your mentor for your first year here. He is an oblate and thus has already been given to God by his parents. He will be helpful to you in many ways. Your situation here is somewhat different than oblates, novices and monks in that you have not yet been given to the abbey. Your status is perfectly acceptable and we are happy to have you on...what should I call it? A trial basis. But you may find that our rules apply slightly less to you in some circumstances and that Peter and others may not always understand that. To diminish any issues, it would be most helpful if you would conform to our rules unless there is some dire reason not to. This will make your life here go much more smoothly. The Benedictine Rule calls for obedience, poverty and chastity. You don't strike me as a boy who will be disobedient, nor at your age are you likely to be challenged by Satan in terms of chastity. Poverty though may be a potential problem. Did you bring any possessions with you?"

"Yes," replied Henry. "I have a copy of the *Aeneid*, a small chess game and my clothes."

"Your clothes," responded Anslem, "you can keep packed away as we shall issue you proper clothing. The chess game you may keep and play but only during undesignated times. As to the *Aeneid*, it can be put into our library or, if you prefer, kept with your clothes. Our library is a very safe place for it, as we create books in our scriptorium and therefore value them highly. Please always remember that here 'poverty' means we may own nothing. We may only use the word 'mine' in regard to our parents: 'my mother, my father.' Nothing else is mine. Your case is slightly different. Do you understand all that?"

"Yes," replied Henry, "I think so." But as he mouthed the words, he was thinking about the *Aeneid*. What to do with it? Might he one day have to give up Benito's dying bequest and also his father's game? He hadn't realized how hard it would be to become a monk.

"So much for orientation," concluded the Abbot. "Now please share with me how you learned such good Latin and at such a young age."

"Oh," said Henry, "my brother and I had a tutor named Benito

Tusculani. Perhaps you know him? Your accent is similar to his."

"Ah," responded Anslem, "the Tusculani are a noble family just south of Rome and have had close ties with the Church for many years. I believe Benito Tusculani may have been at Cluny but I don't think I've ever met him. However, your facility with the language testifies to his skill as a tutor. Is his assignment at Dol over now that you are coming here?"

"He died," replied Henry disconsolately.

"I am sorry to hear that," whispered Anslem. "Was he an old man?"

"No," responded the youth as he felt emotion rising like bile in his throat. "Some disease got into his lungs and kept him from being able to breathe. My father boiled water in Benito's room to make steam which usually helps someone breathe but it was not enough."

"Has your father knowledge of medicine?" asked Anslem.

"Yes," responded the boy. "Both my father and grandfather have had success in healing."

"That is a fine gift from God," said Anslem as he crossed himself. "Ah," he continued, "here is Peter."

Henry saw that Brother Jason had returned with a boy whom Henry judged to be about the same age as himself. Even with a robe on, the youth looked slightly built and perhaps a little out of his element.

"Peter," said the Abbot, "this is Henry of Dol whom I wish you to mentor and guide for the foreseeable future. Please help him settle into our schedule, get him proper clothes, take him to lunch, show him his place in the dormitory and answer his questions. Note that he is not yet a commit-ted member of our abbey, so he has a book and a chess game which remain his. Do you understand?"

"Yes," responded Peter in a subservient tone.

"And Brother Jason," continued the Abbot as he turned toward the other black-robed monk, "we have a guest here today for lunch and to spend the night if he wishes." Pointing to Magwolf, Anslem continued, "Please meet all his wishes and when the time comes, pray for his safe return to Dol."

Then again, turning back to the abbey's newest pupil Anslem declared, "Henry I shall see you at lunch and perhaps we can play a game of chess." Anslem turned on his heel and briskly walked back toward the little building from which he and Brother Jason had come.

With the Abbot's departure, Peter Maillesais spoke more boldly. "It's almost sext so the bell will call us to lunch very soon. But I think we have enough time for me to show you your bed in the dormitory." Peter pivoted toward the huge building behind him. "Follow me and bring your possessions. We can put them under your bed. They'll be safe there. We grow all our food ourselves. You probably came through several of our fields. Luncheon is always a salad, some cheese or eggs and vegetables just picked at this time of year. I'm certain you'll like our meals. Where is Dol?"

"Dol is about a hundred Roman miles east of here."

"Oh," said Peter. "Is that a long ride?"

"Four to six days depending on the size of the baggage train," replied Henry. "Where are you from?"

"Maillesais," responded Peter. "Do you know it?"

"No," replied Henry. "What is it near?"

"Oh," said Peter in a disheartened tone as his lower lip twitched slightly, "no one I talk to ever seems to have heard of it. When my father brought me here, I didn't pay much attention to our direction nor am I particularly knowledgeable in geography. I was only six then. Now I'm nine! I should receive my 'novitiate' when I'm fifteen and, God willing, become a monk or a priest by sixteen."

"I see," said Henry, "and what must you study to get there?"

"Well as you will see our days are very long. Usually we start with psalms two hours after midnight. But don't worry! Someone will wake you until you begin to naturally wake up on time. Brother Lester says when you wake up naturally, it is God waking you. After the psalms there's a reading and then we chant until Matins. You probably know that's dawn. Then we go back to bed until Prime when we listen to four more psalms and another reading. Of course there's regular work during the day: weeding, cooking, baking, harvesting, and assignments to the fish ponds, beehives, stable... and even construction. We have an infirmary too where we can tend the sick or injured."

"Really," interjected Henry with sincere interest. "Do you have monks whose specialty is medicine?"

"Well, we rotate through all the activities," responded Peter. "But I suppose if there was a serious injury, the Abbot would assign the monk he thought had the most experience. Our specialty is really God's lore. Each monk's closeness to God would make him a blessed messenger for an injured or sick person."

"And after work?" asked Henry.

"Oh yes," continued Peter, "after supper we all go into the church for more prayers, chanting and meditation."

When Henry saw that Peter was beginning to run out of things that the monks did every day, he asked another question. "How do you know what time it is?"

"Oh," replied Peter, "there's the church bell of course and we have hour glasses and tallow candles made to burn down over different periods of time and of course sundials, but they don't help much at night or on a rainy day."

"No," said Henry, "nor even on a cloudy day."

"Here's your bed," Peter croaked somewhat breathlessly.

Henry looked around. They were in a large, open room that was filled with wooden beds, six rows, each five deep. In the bed Peter had pointed him to, Henry saw only leather straps bound tightly from side-rail to side-rail creating a crypt-like space for bedding and blankets. There would be little privacy and not much room for him to stow his clothes, book and chess game. At the end of every row of beds sat a fat piss-pot. These nightly necessities emitted a maleficent odor, indicating that they hadn't yet been emptied. Otherwise the room was clean. Henry had hoped for a private room or at least one similar to what he had at home where only five people occupied it. But he knew he could get along here. He bent to one knee and slid his bag with the *Aeneid* under the cross-mounted leather straps. As he did, in his mind he recited a prayer to God asking for His help and protecttion in this abbey which he was now entering and as an afterthought, also for the safekeeping of his book and chess game.

Just as Henry finished this prayer and began to rise to his feet, he heard the church bell gong loudly. 'Sext,' he thought, 'time to see what the food is like.'

"Come quickly," Peter summoned with his lip quivering again. We mustn't be late." Henry's mentor began to trot toward the doorway. The very next room was filled with tables and benches just like Henry's great room in Dol. The only difference was a raised table at one end that the boy supposed was for the Abbot and visiting dignitaries.

"Come, come," Peter whispered as he wound his way toward that very table. All around them black-robed monks were scurrying to take their places at the tables. Apparently each had a designated seat. The two boys hadn't far to get to the front but no one seemed particularly willing to make room for them to pass. Nevertheless, Peter pressed forward and was eventually able to identify the correct chair for Henry. It was at the head table. The young oblate then stood behind the chair to Henry's right. However when Henry began to sit down in his designated seat, Peter jabbed a finger into his side. "Don't sit yet, not until the Abbot sits down." So Henry stood back up and waited for Anslem's arrival. At last the wiry, balding man entered the room and directed himself toward the front table. All conversation immediately ceased. But when the Abbot reached his chair which was just to Henry's left, he did not immediately sit down.

Instead Anslem paused, so long a pause that Henry began to wonder whether the respite was more to remind everyone in the room who was in charge than to simply give the Abbot time to prepare his thoughts before speaking. At last the Abbot spoke. "Dearest Lord Jesus Christ," hearing the name of their Lord, Anslem and every other person in the room crossed himself, "please bless our thoughts and actions today as we try to do Your bidding. Thank you Lord, for leading us each day toward our salvation through our prayers for others, our giving to the poor, our daily work to help each other, our abstinence from wickedness, selfish thoughts or actions and our denial of property. Please continue to strengthen us so we may maintain our purity and decline receipt of the world's temptations and other ephemeral blandishments."

The Abbot then, as if pointing straight ahead, held out both his arms and continued. "Brothers, we are blessed today by the arrival of Henry of Dol who stands beside me. He is of noble family and has been tutored by Benito Tusculani of Rome. Unlike us, he has not yet been entirely committed to God but comes here to hone his education and learn our ways. I have asked Peter of Maillesais to mentor him. Please join me in accepting Henry into our abbey. Let us show him the beneficence God has granted us and hope that His plan for this young man may ultimately bring him into our fold. But whatever the path this boy may take, may it be God's will."

"God's will be done," chanted the congregation.

"Amen," said Anslem as he lowered his arms and then sat down. Immediately all the brethren sat as well.

Henry didn't know whether he should initiate conversation with Anslem or not. He didn't ask Peter since he doubted his mentor would recommend it. The Abbot was quietly eating his bean salad and had made no verbal overtures either to Henry or Brother Jason, who sat on the Abbot's left. Nevertheless, the youth from Dol rallied his courage and spoke.

"Abbot Anslem," he queried, "how did you get your education?"

For a moment the older man finished chewing his mouthful, but when he'd swallowed he turned to Henry and replied.

"Well my mother, Ermenberga, who was from Geneva taught me logic, grammar and rhetoric when I was a child and although my father tried to prevent it, got me a tutor when I was a little older than you are now to teach me Latin, arithmetic and religious reasoning. I liked the reasoning and logic a great deal and tried to enter a monastery when I was fifteen but my father was obstinately against it. His interference succeeded but only until I was twenty-three when I came here and studied under Lanfranc. He was a wonderful mentor and taught me among other things, about the 'reform movement' within the church like clerical celibacy, the wrongs of simony, the logic of God ruling His world through His church instead of through kings and their worldly interests.

"But if you are asking me where you should start your next educational steps, I would say that you must first hone your faith in God. You cannot fully learn His mysteries until your heart is completely open to Him. Only then will He begin to show you the full breadth of His wonders. When your faith is certain, He will fill your mind and heart with His wisdom and then and only then, your life will take on direction.

"For now though, He has sent you to us. Here at Bec, just as the smith at your castle in Dol hammers a red-hot length of metal into a sharp-edged sword, your faith can be similarly edged by religious reason, prayer and wholesomeness. For one who is as bright as I believe you are, an abbey can provide an important transitional step in your development. God has surely put you here for a reason. You must make the most of it. And we here at Bec will do our best to help."

"Abbot Anslem," continued Henry, "is it logical that faith in God should come before my own reason leads me to Him?"

For several moments, Anslem stared at the boy. "That's a very good question. I have found that most men who are deeply steeped in reason and logic waste most of their lives trying to find God using those intellectual tools. If they succeed at all, it usually takes them years to get there.

Those who start by accepting God into their hearts and having faith, usually begin to see God's workings all around them.

"Most men find God in one of those two ways. The advantage of starting with faith is that it gets you more quickly into a life of harmony and love, one in which you are a better person and one from which you are more likely to be accepted into heaven. I can tell you from first-hand experience that if you truly choose faith, you will begin to see God's manifestations everywhere around you. Does that answer your question?"

"Yes," said the boy. "Thank you."

"Good," said Anslem. The Abbot then took up another spoonful of beans and lettuce and chewed them thoroughly. When he'd finished his mouthful, he turned back to the boy. "Henry, I have answered your question. Please answer one for me. Do you know how you got here?"

Henry who had finished his first course more rapidly than Anslem, looked up at the Abbot. "Do you mean by what route we took to get here?"

"No," responded Anslem. "I meant the politics of it, through whom your parents made your application and how the wheel was greased? Who spoke for you? What network came into play?"

"Oh," said Henry, "I didn't know it worked that way. I think my parents may have written some letters. Benito would have recommended me but he'd died by then. My father had great influence with William 'the Conqueror' but he has no great influence with any of his sons, so that line is unlikely. Duke William's brother, Odo, has always seemed to like us. We don't see him often but he is deemed an important friend. My mother's family is well connected in Flanders with both Roberts. Those are the only connections that might tie me to here that I know of."

The boy caught his breath then asked the Abbot another question. "Abbot Anslem why do you ask that question? Are you in some way concerned that I should not be here?"

"Oh no Henry," responded Anslem. "I am very certain that you should be here. My question was simply to satisfy my curiosity. I like to see the various ways God achieves His purposes: who they pass through, how they work, their process. His work is always masterful and, although often obscure, He always threads the needle in the most perfect way and often by means that no human could ever have dreamed up. Ah, here are our hardboiled eggs. You'll like the food here Henry."

After the mid-day meal was finished and another psalm chanted, Peter led Henry out of the dining room toward the church. "The Abbot likes you," said the mentor to his new friend. "I've never seen him talk so long to anyone here below a novice.

"But," replied Henry, "didn't he just talk to you at some length too?"

"Yes," Peter responded, "but that was just to tell me where to take you this afternoon. He talked to you about religious logic and faith. And you understood what he said. You even asked him a question."

For a moment Henry thought about Peter's comment. Abbot Anslem had shared significant insights with him at the table. He wondered if that really was unusual. Perhaps it was simply because he had dared to ask the Abbot a question. It was likely that very few youngsters had the kind of teaching Benito had given him, where asking the right question was just as important as getting the right answer. But in a way that was Peter's point. Perhaps the Abbot did think him competent enough to warrant some personal attention. Anslem had seemed interested in giving him more counseling. Henry thought he might be starting to like Bec...and the meal had been very good too.

"Peter," Henry asked, "where did Abbot Anslem say to take me?"

"To the crypt of Herluin, the infirmary and the cemetery."

~**~

As the two boys approached the entrance to the abbey's church, Peter spoke again but this time in a much lower tone. "Herluin's crypt is inside to the left."

Henry was pleasantly surprised at how cool the building was inside. Like all stone structures with very few openings through which sunlight could enter, it retained not only a degree of coolness but also a hint of dampness. The inside was quite dark, even gloomy. Ahead at the furthest point from the entry, several candles were burning and providing the building's only light.

"This way," Peter whispered as he turned sharply to his left.

Henry made the same turn and immediately saw immersed in the deep shadows ahead some sort of long, low statuary. He stopped beside Peter allowing his eyes to become better accustomed to the darkness. He'd never seen a sarcophagus before, but his mother had once described one which held her grandfather in some church in Flanders. The one in front of him outlined an ornately sculptured, life-size cameo of a mailed and helmeted knight holding a jeweled cross just above his heart. With so little light, Henry couldn't tell whether this magnificent work had been carved in stone or alabaster. In either case, the likeness presented a most worthy and pious knight.

"It's magnificent isn't it?" Peter whispered.

"Yes," murmured Henry. "It's superb."

Several moments passed while each boy assimilated the depth of devotion denoted in Herluin's image. Finally Henry spoke. "Peter please tell me about Herluin, who he was, what he did."

"He was a knight," Peter responded, "who after serving Count Gilbert of Brionne turned his life entirely over to the founding of this abbey. He was a humble and pious man who died just a few years ago. During his abbacy he induced both Lanfranc and Anslem to teach here. They elevated Bec to its current level of piety and scholarship."

"So," mused Henry, "Herluin both planted the acorn and watered the sapling."

"Yes," said Peter.

The infirmary was located in a very small wooden shack quite a distance from the abbey's main complex. When Peter had first pointed to it, Henry hadn't been able to see it due to the overhang of several trees. As the two young friends trudged toward these trees, Peter suddenly spoke. "Henry, the day before you got here I had a dream about you."

"You mean," rejoined Henry, "you dreamed about me before you even knew I was coming?"

"Oh no," replied Peter. "Brother Jason told me you'd be coming and that Abbot Anslem wanted me to mentor you. So I knew someone was coming. But in my dream you wore a chainmail shirt like the one Herluin is wearing on his sarcophagus. Doesn't it seem strange to you that my dream would portray you as a knight?"

Henry was about to ask Peter what else had happened in his dream but Peter spoke first.

"This is the infirmary. I don't know why Abbot Anslem would want me to show it to you. It's certainly nothing to show off."

In less than a moment Henry scanned the tiny, one-room building. The roof was holed, probably by a falling tree limb. There was a rickety, old bed with several broken slats, a table which showed age-old blood stains and a roughly hewn cabinet with three shelves that held only a small, rusty pot and a coil of rope... Peter was right. The infirmary was nothing to be proud of. The little medical closet on the third level of Dol castle contained much more in the way of medical gear: utensils, bandages, sutures and salves. Henry wondered why Anslem had Peter show him this abomination...unless the Abbot thought Henry could improve it.

"Seen enough?" asked Peter.

"Yes."

"Then let me show you our cemetery and reliquary."

Henry was surprised to hear that Bec had a reliquary. He couldn't imagine what religious relics might have wound their way to Bec. Rome certainly had relics: various saints' teeth, bones and sometimes even shreds of their clothing resided in reliquaries there. Benito had told him several times that real relics still carried the power of their saint and been known to have great healing power when touched. On the other hand, he'd once heard his father dismiss all relics as the work of charlatans.

Containing himself no longer, Henry burst forth his vexing question. "What relics are here at Bec?"

"Oh none," replied the youthful oblate, "but we burn a great many candles in our reliquary for our benefactors and we chant prayers for them and their family members too."

"Really," said Henry. "What do the candles do for your benefactors? And what sort of prayers do you chant for them?"

"Well," said Peter who seemed pleased to have been asked a question to which he knew the answer, "the candles are a formal way to keep the benefactor's name alive at least here among us and the prayers are usually a beseechment to one or more saints asking for intercession with Jesus on behalf of the benefactor, usually to implore Him to grant the benefactor direct entrance into heaven."

"Are you saying that the benefactor pays the abbey for these intercessional prayers?" asked Henry quizzically.

"Oh yes," responded Peter. "The benefactor not only pays us to chant prayers but pays more depending on what is asked for and how challenging the request is likely to be: how many years they want us to pray, whether there are other family members to be prayed for as well and how great their sins were. And since most of these bequests come to us when the benefactor is nearing the end of his life; many are actually made just before the last rights are administered; their desires are often very strong. And the candles can be expensive too. Often we get whole fiefs or at least large parcels of productive land...and land with tenants too. We are one of the largest landholders in eastern Normandy."

~**~

The feast day of Saint John the Evangelist that occurred just four days after Christmas happened to fall on a Sunday. Henry was making his way toward the abbey's administration building to play his usual chess game with Abbot Anslem. The youth was particularly cheerful because the church service that morning marked the end of the abbey's period of silence that always encased Christmas. No monk or servant, not even the Abbot, could talk to another without violating his oath of obedience. Henry had been surprised at how seriously this was taken. Even Peter Maillesais didn't violate it not even mistakenly. But talking could now be resumed, which meant Anslem would again be sharing his broad knowledge during their game or games if the Abbot had the time.

Recently Anslem had been talking about 'lay' investiture: how permitting kings or lesser lords to appoint bishops or even priests, in their realms lead to 'pollution of the church.' Too many of these men simply continued to lead secular lives: hunting, womanizing, drinking, eating to excess and even not sending their proper amount of tithe money to Rome. Also this sort of activity failed to set a proper example for their parishioners. Essentially a churchman must submit first to God and second to his worldly lord. Henry found these discussions fascinating and the Abbot let him ask questions that often provoked long answers with specific explanations regarding real people.

Abbott Anslem had described Pope Gregory's excommunication of the Holy Roman Emperor: how the Emperor was made to wait barefoot in the snow for three days before the Pope had finally received him back into the Holy Church and thus allowed him and the people of his realm to again take communion. Without communion of course there was no chance of getting into heaven!

Henry stepped onto the stone slab at the door to the abbey's administration building. Before knocking, he paused to focus his mind on his upcoming time with the Abbot. He knew Anslem liked him but he also knew that he didn't want to diminish himself in the eyes of the Abbot by speaking some wrong word or committing some childish gaff. Having thus focused, he knocked.

"Come in," called forth Abbot Anslem cheerfully.

Henry pushed open the door and stepped into the tiny building. To his surprise there was already someone sitting across from the Abbot at the small table on which Henry and Anslem usually played their chess game.

"Oh, excuse me," squeaked the startled youth. "I did not mean to interrupt. I'll come back some other time."

The man sitting across from Anslem was not someone Henry had met before. He was old, perhaps even in his sixties. Despite the fact that the man was sitting, the boy assessed the fellow quickly. He was tall, thin, white-haired, hook-nosed and his shoulders drooped forward. His eyes however, were his most noteworthy characteristic. They were bright, lucid and young. The dusty black robe that he wore identified him as a Benedictine monk.

"No, no," chirped Anslem as he rose to his feet, "don't go away Henry. We've just been talking about you. This," Anslem swung his left arm toward the old man sitting across from him, "is Hugh of Cluny. He is the Abbot there." The designated fellow then leaned forward and pushing his arms down on the table, stood up.

"I am pleased to meet you," Abbot Hugh said softly. "I believe felicitations are in order. I'm told you just had a birthday."

"Yes," Henry stammered. "Thank you."

Hugh smiled at the boy. It was a wide, amicable and sincere smile that showed among other things, that he still had all his teeth. "Lucifer might still win me over," the old man continued, "if he was willing to make me nine again."

"Come in and join us," interrupted Anslem as he pointed to the third and only other chair in the tiny building. "Pull that seat up here with us. I've been telling Brother Hugh how God has favored us by sending you here to Bec."

Henry clasped the designated chair and slid it up to the table and, after waiting for the two Abbots to again take their seats, he settled into his. But his chair's arms made it very awkward for him to hold his game so he placed it on the table.

Indicating that no one knew who should speak first, there was a moment of silence. Finally Hugh cleared his throat and reached out his right hand to the game box. "This must be your chess game," he said. "Abbot Anslem has told me that you play very well. Is that so?"

Trying to think how best to answer, Henry paused. In all the times he and Anslem had played, Henry had won only once and he thought Anslem might have let him win that time lest he lose interest and give up playing. "Well sir, I've only won once in all the times Abbot Anslem and I have played, so I don't think I'm a very good player yet but I think, for my age, I play fairly well."

"Would you give me the pleasure of a game?" whispered Hugh.

Henry immediately sat up even straighter in his chair then glanced at the Abbot of Bec for approval. After seeing Anslem's nod of assent, the boy turned back to Hugh. "I would be most honored," he gushed. "Would you like white or black?"

"Well," replied Hugh, "I suppose as a Christian I should pick white but today I'll take black the color of my robe...at least when it's clean."

Henry eagerly reached for the game box. He felt honored to be playing with Abbot Hugh of Cluny. Cluny was one of the two most esteemed abbies in Christendom and Hugh, as Anslem had once told him, was considered a great Abbot. But Henry also reasoned that Hugh was playing with him for a reason, most likely to measure him in some way. The boy was determined to do his best. His father had taught him against an unknown opponent to always start cautiously. Going first would allow him to do so and hopefully position him to employ his favorite tactic the 'double-entendre'—an attack that employed an apparently simple approach but also bore a more subtle and hopefully invisible secondary threat which might carry the day.

Once begun, several moves were made in complete silence. But after Hugh made what Henry thought was an odd move, the Abbot of Cluny chose to break the solemnity. "So Henry, are you the oldest child in your family?"

Wondering whether the Abbot's odd move and his question were related, the boy looked up. "I am the second of three sons in my family," he replied before turning his attention back to the board.

Quite a few more plays ensued before he saw his chance to initiate his 'double-entendre' tactic but he delayed a planned question until he unleashed the tactic's obvious threat, thus keeping the more circuitous offensive veiled in silence. "Abbot Hugh, are you on a tour of many abbeys or just Bec?" Henry did not look up lest Hugh read anything suspicious in his facial expression.

"This is actually the last stop of my tour," replied Hugh. "I've visited five other abbeys this month but I must now return to Cluny to prepare for a trip to Spain."

Henry wanted to ask where in Spain the Abbot would be going but he knew the comment was meant to distract him, so he kept his eyes on the board and played on. Many more moves went by before Henry's hidden half of the 'double-entendre' narrowly failed and he eventually found himself 'check-mated.'

"I concede," Henry stammered. Then forcing his disappointment to the back of his mind, Henry looked up at Hugh and smiled. "That was a really good game."

"Yes," Hugh replied in his usual soft tone, "it was. You played magnify-cently. You are a credit to your father as well as to Abbot Anslem. Now I want to give you one more compliment, a very important one. Please look me straight in the eye."

Henry squared his face to Hugh's and looked the old Abbot right in the eye.

"I've played chess," the Abbot said, "with my godson many times. You are without question a much better player than he is and he's the Holy Roman Emperor!"

POTENTIAL

December 1089

After Henry had left, Anslem turned to Abbot Hugh. "So, what do you think?"

"I'll take him," Hugh answered quickly. "Your assessment of the boy's potential is absolutely correct. He is well raised, bright, thoughtful, accepts authority, and is actually quite conservative for a nine-year-old. We definitely want to keep him in the Church if we can. The only negative to me taking him to Spain is that he'll be beating me in chess before we get back."

"Well," Anslem chuckled, "he's already beating me. How long do you think you'll be?"

"Six months," replied Hugh, "give or take a little allowing for the unexpected. But we'll have to leave for Cluny tomorrow. Can the boy be ready?"

"Oh, I think so," responded Anslem. "I'll have to find a horse for him but that shouldn't be too difficult."

"I have some extra horses in my train," interjected Hugh. "You know we breed them."

"Other than that," continued Anslem, "Henry has a book, the *Aeneid*, but I think I can get him to leave it here in our library. That would be safer for it than going on a trip to Spain."

"Good," concluded Hugh. "I shall begin my preparations for departure. But one thing more before I do, did you see how he timed his question about my tour in order to obfuscate his 'double-entendre?"

"I did," replied Anslem. "He hasn't done that before. I mean the talking while playing."

"No," said Hugh. "He learned that talking gambit when I asked him about his family. He's a quick learner! Surely God has sent him to us so we can encourage him into the Church. But of course only time will tell."

COINDICENCES

December 1089 – January 1090

With his coat and saddlebags in hand, Henry stood at the entrance of the Abbey of Bec's stable looking for Jonathan the stableman whom Anslem had said would provide him a horse. The stable itself was a large facility built sturdily with wooden sides and a thatched roof. But with Hugh's departure at hand, it was now crowded with bustling men and mounts.

There were Hugh's three monks in their black habits, four rough-looking fellows who were probably servants or perhaps guards, and a great quantity of capering horses and resisting mules. The equines were kicking up clouds of reddish dust which, hanging in the air, attached itself to everything: man, mule, watcher and wall. Tethered on the far right were four mules with their crosstree saddles already strapped on their backs. Amidst the din, they seemed to be the only creatures in the entire stable that appeared ready to leave.

Turning his gaze back to the midst of the fray, Henry saw a squarely built man leading a brown mare through the confusion. Seeing the boy's eyes upon him, the fellow waved his free hand as if to indicate he was bringing the horse to Henry. Henry watched as the burley handler, whom he assumed must be Jonathan, wound his way through the hubbub.

"I'm Jonathan and this is Meredith," the man said as he reached Henry. "Anslem suggested she would suit you."

"Thank you for bringing her to me," responded the boy. "Does she have any quirky characteristics I should be aware of?"

"Her best attribute," responded Jonathan, "is her speed. She can outrun almost any stallion or gelding. But," he continued after a slight pause, "with a weak-willed rider she can have a mind of her own. I suggest you establish command early or risk being taken advantage of later."

"Thank you, Jonathan," responded Henry. "I shall do my best to communicate with her in a most unequivocal manner."

The youth took the horse's reins from the stableman then stepped directly in front of the equine; immediately he drew down the reins intending to make the animal lower her head to his. There was, based on Jonathan's warning, a hint of resistance. "My name is Henry," the boy whispered softly to the mare. "I shall be your master for the next several months." Then without warning, Henry violently jerked down the reins and simultaneously bellowed. "Lower your head!"

Meredith complied.

Turning back to the stableman, Henry spoke again in a soft tone. "Thank you Jonathan."

"You're welcome," replied the smiling horse-tamer as he turned back toward the pink cloud of swirling dust.

Once under way, Henry at first tried to keep Meredith beside Abbot Hugh but he quickly found that when riding, the Abbot was neither talkative nor gregarious. Instead he seemed lost in his own thoughts. So instead of vexing his mentor, Henry let Meredith fall back to where Brothers Paul, Raymond and Bruglio were riding.

After introductions all around, Brother Bruglio spoke first. "So you are from Dol. That is somewhere to the northwest I believe."

"Yes, it is," Henry replied, "perhaps a hundred Roman miles."

"And," continued Bruglio, "did you have a Roman tutor to teach you Latin?"

"I did," replied the youth, "Benito Tusculani. Did you know him?"

"No, I don't think so," answered Bruglio. "Of course I know the Tusculani. They hold estates south of Rome and are a politically powerful family in Rome both in local elections and also when it comes to picking new popes. Is your tutor deceased?"

"Yes," replied Henry. "That's why I was sent to Bec...to complete my education."

"You are not an oblate?" asked Bruglio.

"No," responded the boy. "I'm not yet committed."

"I see," mused the monk. "Now I understand why you were picked."

"What do you mean?" asked Henry in a tone which bordered on irritability. "I don't know why I was picked." Then after taking a moment to regain his composure, he continued. "I'd appreciate it if you would tell me."

For a moment Bruglio stared at the boy's facial expression, then apparently seeing only sincerity, he continued. "Well of course it is not my place to tell you, but I might be within my parameters to ask you a question." For a moment, Brother Bruglio's lips formed almost into a grin. But whatever it was, it was gone immediately. "Do you think you will be more likely or less likely to become an oblate once you have been treated so specially with this trip to Spain by an Abbot of such distinction as Abbot Hugh?"

Henry digested the monk's question before responding. "Thank you Brother Bruglio for sharing your question with me. I think I understand its point. But it leads me to ask you another question if I may."

"Of course," said the monk.

"You see, I've been thinking that I'm unworthy of being chosen but...that it must be God's will that I go." For a moment Henry stopped speaking, glad that he had finally been able to express his feelings of self-doubt and confusion regarding his going to Spain.

"Ah," interjected Brother Bruglio, "God's will is everywhere around us and yet it's so difficult to discern. In my experience it is often clearest in hindsight but usually not very discernable in the present. However, and this is the most important point, it doesn't matter. You can only put your trust in Him and do your best. That is all any of us can ever do."

A long pause followed before Henry spoke again. "Brother Bruglio, I heard someone say that you are the 'bursar' at Cluny. But I don't know what a bursar is."

"Oh," replied the older man as he twisted in his saddle and again looked at Henry, "I was hoping you might know and tell me." The monk smiled at his companion then continued in a more serious tone. "I believe the term derives from the word 'purse' which is a name for a little bag one keeps coins in. Accordingly, a bursar is one who keeps the coin. So as bursar, I am responsible for the coin at Cluny. And your quick mind is already wondering what that means, which is the part I don't know. Does it simply mean to keep and protect the abbey's coin? Or might it have a broader meaning, such as raising more coin, keeping track of income and expense, projecting annual revenue over expense, knowing what quantity of tithes, donations and benefices we must raise in order to build a larger church, determining how much coin and goods we should extract from our sister abbeys, churches and parishes, knowing how much charity we can afford to give the poor, how many hostels we can create for pilgrims and how much income they must produce to become self-sustaining.

"Ah Henry, the answer to the question 'what is a bursar' is an endless one. And still worse, it is a perilous job as well. Many of these functions I just mentioned, if pursued with too much zeal, may be sinful. There is a constant struggle to balance our giving to the needy against expanding our fiefs and therefore having even more to give in the future. How much should we take from our freemen and our serfs? And how should we adjust our takings for the all-too-prevalent droughts, floods and famines that can make our best paying tenants suddenly as needy as the poorest serf? How many lands, tenancies and fiefs should we attempt to squeeze out of some lord when he lies dying on his bed and hopes that our chants and prayers will gain him entry into heaven? How does one distinguish at what point 'God's work' becomes simply avarice on behalf of ourselves? All these are issues on which a bursar constantly prays for insight. And since he must make decisions of degree regarding these issues, a bursar like a boy, often wonders where 'God's will' ends and sin begins."

"That was well said." It was Abbot Hugh who spoke. He'd slowed his horse in order to let his entourage catch up. "Brother Bruglio and I some-times disagree as to how much we should ask from our tenants and donors. On occasion we may take too much. But Brother Bruglio isn't the one who has to make that decision. I do. This I point out because it relieves him from the burden of the decision at least most of it. We Benedictines have only three rules: poverty, chastity and obedience. Following these rules protect a man from sin as much as is humanly possible. No rules how-ever are perfect or so clear as to never leave some room for doubt. When a man becomes a monk, he gives up family, titles, possessions, freedom, the hope of children and the supposed 'pleasures' of sloth, fornication and various other excesses. These 'give-ups' allow him to clear his field-of-vision of the distractions which can lead to sin. However these removals do not guarantee him a seat in heaven. They only make the path easier to see and follow. Additionally, our regimen at the abbey purposely focuses on only prayer, work and study. Free time is not permitted lest it lead to sin. Becoming a Benedictine monk is a choice, one which can improve a man's chance to have his soul live everlastingly in heaven. It is not however, a choice that should be entered into lightly. First the man must be certain of his belief in God. A man gains this strength in youth, learned from his parents, his priest, or perhaps from his own intuitive grasp of the world around him. For others the process can be long and difficult, filled with doubt and a need for proof."

For a moment Hugh stopped speaking but then, as he pointed his long, right forefinger directly at Henry's nose, he continued. "You my son, do you believe in Him?"

Henry's shoulders jerked back as he realized that Hugh's discourse had suddenly departed from its esoteric scope. Now the Abbot was staring expectantly at him. For just a moment the youth hesitated, then stuttered his reply. "Yes... Yes I do."

"Well, good," said Hugh as he lowered his finger. "But you are still too young to know how firm your faith will be. A person's faith, like a tempered blade, must be further hardened. You must take heed of miracles, signs and coincidences. These are means by which you can actually see His hand at work, proof of His actions, veritable proof!"

After several moments passed, Henry began to wonder if Hugh was expecting him to respond in some way but the Abbot was no longer looking at him. Instead he was staring ahead as he usually did when in the saddle. Hoping for some direction, Henry glanced toward Brother Bruglio. The bursar, reading the boy's expression perfectly, lifted a finger to his lips to indicate a need for silence. And shortly thereafter, the Abbot continued his discourse.

"God does display His intentions for us to see. Let me recount a story for you from my own past, which I believe validates this point. It goes back more than twenty years when I was traveling with a small contingent to the great Abbey of Monte Cassino. We were crossing the Alps through the Mount Cenis pass, the one which comes out just above Turin, and had stopped for the night at a woodcutter's cottage where there's now a Cluniac hostel. We were just preparing for our meal when I was stricken with a pain in my side so powerful that I doubled over and began rolling on the dirt floor. The pain was so severe that I was moaning and had to gasp for every breath. I was certain I was dying and had only moments left in which to give my last confession. Fortunately Brother Simon, a most devout colleague of mine who himself died only a few years ago, was there to hear my last words and give me absolution. Once my confession was completed, on his knees beside me Simon implored God to grant me entry into heaven and then, leaving no stone unturned, he asked Jesus, should it be His will, to send someone to save my life that I might continue to save the souls of others here on earth. I had no expectation of surviving for more than another moment or two. But almost immediately there came a knock on the cottage door and in walked a Jew. I never saw any attendants, although I can't imagine he was there by himself. In any case, the fellow looked at me writhing on the floor and asked if I wished his assistance.

Brother Simon explained that he'd just completed the last rites but then, probably recalling his prayer, told the fellow that any help would be gratefully appreciated.

"The Jew bent down beside me and lightly touched the spot in my side from which the pain emanated. He asked if it was there that it hurt. I told him it was. He said that was good because it probably meant that he could heal me. This man sat me up and directed one of my attendants to bring water. When this was done, he told me to drink it all and after that, he had my attendant bring more. Only a little time went by and just as suddenly as it had come, my pain was gone. And so I was cured by God through a Jew, a Jew very knowledgeable in medicine."

Having completed his recollection, Hugh again turned to Henry. "This story, while quite true, has been called a miracle, a coincidence, a sign of God's love for those who do His work, a sign of the devil's work done through a Jew and simply 'luck.' I myself do not believe in luck, nor coincidences nor that the devil would save a Benedictine monk. However I do believe that God shows Himself through these acts, acts which most humans choose to ignore.

"Henry, when you encounter such an event, you must press yourself to look more deeply. Don't just pass it off as luck or coincidence. Deeper thought will turn up questions: Why is God communicating to me? What is He saying? What must I do? How will I know I am responding to His wishes? These Henry, are constructive questions. But you must always remember that you won't understand everything that happens, nor will you like everything He does. You can only fall back on your faith and trust in Him. For many of us that is the most difficult thing to do, to trust in Him when everything going on around us seems senseless, wrong and unfair. This is when you will learn whether or not you are really a soldier of God. It is also when God will learn how faithful you really are.

"So," Abbot Hugh continued as he turned in his saddle to look at his bursar, "Brother Bruglio is right to think you were chosen to go on this trip because of your potential to the Church. But God's plans for you may be quite different...or not."

~**~

We'll be staying at an inn tonight," called out Abbot Hugh.

In his mind, Henry had been planning how to draw out Abbot Hugh as to the purpose of their upcoming trip to Spain. All the youth knew was that Hugh, Bruglio and he would leave Cluny for Spain a couple of weeks after they'd reached the abbey.

The inn was small but the odor from its chimney promised good food. The inn itself had only two rooms: a kitchen and a dining room separated by a large fire place. In the dining room, there were five small tables each circled by three chairs. Seeing a possible opportunity, Henry quickly went to the furthest table and stood beside it hoping Abbot Hugh and Brother Bruglio would want to sit with him. Hugh was the second to enter. Seeing the boy, he immediately wound his way to Henry's table. When Brother Bruglio finally entered, the empty seat at Henry's table was the only one left!

The three assaulted their meals without a word spoken. Finally though, the Abbot put down his fork and turned toward the boy. "Henry, what would you like to discuss tonight?"

Henry had expected that he'd have to somehow take a topic of Abbot Hugh's and bring it around to Spain. Hugh's offer to him to pick any topic he wanted was a surprise...but not one he couldn't rise to. "Abbot Hugh, have you ever been to Santiago de Compostela?"

"Sadly I have not," the Abbot replied. "I have been to Spain once before. Let's see, that was in the year of our Lord 1077. Of course King Ferdinand and I began communicating long before that. He, like his father, was a wonderful supporter of our abbey. You probably know of his kingdom in northwestern 'Hispania,' which includes Castile, Leon and Galicia, all Christian lands that he constantly defended from the profane hordes which the Muslim Almoravids kept hurling at him. I visited Ferdinand's son Alfonso, when I went there. He, with the help of a mercenary named Rodriego Diaz, had recently cobbled his father's kingdom back together and wished to continue supporting Cluny as his father and grandfather had before him. His need to redeem himself in God's eyes was greatly elevated by the manner in which he...overwhelmed his brother Sancho during this period of consolidation."

"He murdered Sancho," Brother Bruglio interjected.

Hugh snapped his head around to face Brother Bruglio but he paused before speaking. "Sadly, that is true," the Abbot murmured, "but he has shown his contrition for committing that deed by the great quantity of gold he sends to Cluny. You see, he attributes his success in consolidating his kingdom, particularly his more recent acquisition of Castile, to the daily prayers our monks make on his behalf, and he also believes that our prayers may to some degree assuage the penalty he will receive in the hereafter for his sin. Additionally he seeks atonement through the very large subsidies that he donates through Cluny to build hospitals, hostels and churches in northern Spain. Unfortunately, he has recently suffered a defeat at Sagrajas, which has diminished what he feels he can contribute."

"Even the prayers of our brotherhood, no matter how beseaching," interrupted Brother Bruglio, "are insufficient when the plaintive has murdered his own brother."

With great irritation in his voice, Hugh again turned to face Brother Bruglio. This time he spoke sternly. "Please do not interrupt me Brother Bruglio. I can convey these points myself."

Bowing his head to his Abbot, Brother Bruglio's response came in a whisper. "My Abbot, I beg your forgiveness. It is my Italian temper flaring up. Please forgive me."

Hugh nodded. "I accept your apology."

Then the Abbot turned back to Henry. "Alfonso and Cluny have been making great strides on behalf of the pilgrims who go to Saint James' shrine to seek remission of their sins. There are many thousands every year who travel from as far away as England and the Holy Roman Empire. We have been erecting hospitals along the Camino de Santiago, which put up pilgrims overnight and can provide them succor including protection from thieves and rapists as well as food and medical assistance when needed. Shortly after my first trip to meet with him, Alfonso gifted us the ancient Abbey of Sahagun, which lies between Burgos and Leon. There are now some fifty other monasteries and priories dependant on Sahagun. It was even awarded a special degree of self-control by Pope Gregory, somewhat like Cluny, which his eminence conferred personally to Abbot Bernard in Rome. And only five years ago, when Alfonso conquered Toledo, he doubled his contribution to our worthy endeavors from one thousand pieces of gold a year to two. And that benefice has allowed us to start the construction of a grand new church at Cluny.

"So you see, the answer to your real question, Henry, is that we go to visit Alfonso to encourage him to again elevate his payments to their previous high. At that level, his tithe will keep the pilgrim hostels, monasteries and priories fully functioning, help Cluny build a great house of worship, and encourage God to forgive him for his brother's death."

CLUNY

January 1090

Hugh, Bruglio and Henry only stayed at Cluny for a fortnight. During this time the bursar had begun to show Henry the processes the abbey used to track their revenues and expenses. In only a few days the youth learned the overarching methodology as well as 'the concerns', the term Brother Bruglio used, which identified likely problems.

"The most interesting reports," the bursar said, "are those which compare similar church's income and identify 'outliers'—those that produce less revenue than we would expect. Of course there could be very logical explanations such as a small war between local lords, perhaps a flooded river which destroyed most of the region's crops, a priest having died and no one yet covering his parish. Also a parish's numbers might be skewed by unusual donations in recent years. But more often than not, the numbers are off because something is amiss. These cases could be as simple as someone stealing or the result of simony in which the recipient, a priest, vicar or even a bishop, had to pay off his 'obligations' for getting his new position! Or it could simply be that the priest was unable to do sums and the reports were wrong. All of these cases warrant follow-up. And none of them can be quickly fixed. The purposeful ones undertaken by a wily sinner are the hardest. It's often incredibly difficult to remove a priest particularly if his bishop is in on the skullduggery. We have to send a person out to perform a review and that person has very little impact when confronting a knight, lord or bishop. And of course even if we do get some coin out of them, it mostly goes to Rome."

Since no one had assigned him any specific work functions while at Cluny, Henry sought out the bursary where Bruglio's two clerks worked. Brother Bruglio had told them that if he wasn't there which was quite often, that they should share their work and their conclusions with his young protege. Henry discovered from Joslyn, who was not a 'brother' but a 'secular,' that there were, in addition to financial reports on outliers, additional files that included additional detail on 'persons of interest.' Fascinated, the boy read through several of these files before he was interrupted by Brother John.

"Ah Henry, there you are," heralded the monk. "I've been looking all over for you. Abbot Hugh has sent me to tell you that his entourage for Spain will be leaving at Prime tomorrow. Don't be late."

~**~

Hugh's entourage left shortly after sunrise. Other than Brothers Paul and Raymond who were staying at Cluny, the traveling group was exactly the same as those who had ridden from Bec.

"Henry," called out Hugh from the front of their tiny company, "please ride up here with me."

The boy clapped his knees against Meredith's flanks and quickly cantered up beside the Abbot.

"We have a long trip ahead of us, perhaps six or eight weeks depending on the vagaries of travel and the possible needs for my attention at any of our stops along the way. So, while we're riding I want to use some of our time to educate you on some essential topics. I'm sure you've noted that when I'm riding, I focus on whatever subject I feel I must be preparing for. During the next several days my topic will be your erudition."

The Abbot glanced toward the boy. "Do you know what 'erudition' means?"

"I'm not sure my lord. Does it derive from the Latin word 'erudio?"

Hugh smiled. "Yes. I think it does."

"Then I believe you intend to educate me on some subject."

"That is correct Henry. I shall try in some respects to pick up behind your tutor Benito. That was his name wasn't it?"

"Yes," answered Henry.

"We shall be riding south-westerly," continued the Abbot, "with an eventual destination of Sahagun; but more specifically we are going to Claremont, Bordeaux and Bayonne. Cluny has an attachment to religious houses in those places and I like to visit them occasionally to be certain everything is going well."

'Bayonne' resonated in Henry's brain. There was a church there that was on Brother Bruglio's outlier list and it also had a supplementary file detailing the communications that had already been undertaken regarding its recent decline in revenue. The boy started to open his mouth but stopped when it occurred to him that he might be aware of events which he shouldn't know.

"Did you wish to speak?" asked the Abbot.

"Well, yes I suppose I do. How do you go about checking up on these churches? Do you have a list of topics to review? Does the priest know you're coming and what the topics are? Or are there certain issues you already know exist which need... illumination?"

Hugh frowned. "Have you by chance been reading some of Brother Bruglio's 'outlier' files?"

"It wasn't Brother Bruglio's fault. I spent most of last week in the bursary learning what clerks do. I did see the list of outlier churches and I also read several of the 'action' files. I did not knowingly exceed my place. I apologize if I did."

"You needn't apologize," responded the still smiling Abbot. "You have not exceeded your place. Quite the contrary, you have met my highest expectations. And Brother Bruglio is not in trouble for sharing his information with you. I told him to give you all the water you could drink. I believe my exact words were 'to put your head into a rushing river and see if you could drink it dry.' Did you read the action report on Bayonne?"

"Not all of it," replied Henry. "It had a lot of information which seemed unimportant, at least to one who is not yet well versed in these things."

"Ha, ha," chuckled the Abbot. "Those clerks write reports as if parchment were dung. What a wonderment a succinct report would be... What conclusions did you reach in regard to the diminution of revenue?"

In order to organize his thoughts, Henry paused for a moment. "Well," he finally replied, "the priest is new and was recommended, perhaps I should say 'pushed,' by the local lord who contributes nothing to charity that we know of, pays no tithe to the church and doesn't attend services there either. And the Bishop seemed not to have yet met the priest, which suggests he doesn't go to that part of Gascony very often. What I didn't find in the report was how much revenue the church was getting during the previous priest's incumbency. So despite all the potential issues, we don't even know if the church is out anything." Then, looking up at the Abbot, Henry whispered. "Did I get most of the important points?"

"Oh, yes my boy," chortled Hugh. "All of them!"

The Abbot twisted in his saddle to face forward. "Henry, we'll talk more about Bayonne but for now I want to talk about some other things.

"I had just become Abbot of Cluny. I believe it was in February of 1049 when a German bishop by the name of Bruno of Egisheim was enthroned in

Rome as Pope Leo. He was appointed to the papacy by the Holy Roman Emperor Henry and, being a descendant of Charles the Great, the first Holy Roman Emperor, Henry believed it was his God-given right to appoint all the Church's bishops; and that the bishopric of Rome was no different than any other. Accordingly the Emperor expected Leo who was also his cousin, to be appropriately subservient to his wishes. In this assumption the Emperor was mistaken. Leo believed that God intended to oversee mankind through His chosen churchmen not through secular lords whose views lacked religious insight and often conflicted with the Church's priorities because the lay-lords usually put material and political goals ahead of the need to be saving men's souls. And to make his point preeminently clear, upon his appointment Leo immediately sought out the various other bishops and high churchmen of Rome to see whether they too wanted him to become pope. Of course this action directly refuted the Emperor's authority to decide who should become pope. It essentially created a discordant theorem: which states that God speaks not through a lay-man in this case the Emperor, but rather through the Pope. Leo was correct when he asserted that lay princes have multiple priorities that often conflict with religious principles. Take for example our 'Peace-of-God' initiative, which tries to limit local lords from feuding with one-another by forbidding acts of violence between Wednesday evening and Monday morning. It's a worthy concept but unfortunately not one taken up by most waring nobles.

"This Churchly perspective of Leo's has spawned other discordant concepts as well. There is now a raging battle over who, Churchmen or lay-lords, should appoint local church priests. There is even debate over what attributes should be valued when choosing among candidates: celibacy is an example; simony, which is purchasing an appointment, is lambasted by Rome but considered quite acceptable by local lords; marriage for priests is definitely unacceptable in Rome but is usually overlooked when the priest is doing a good job in his parish." Halting his discourse in order to catch his breath, Hugh turned his head toward his acolyte. "Did you follow all that Henry?"

"I think so, but...I'm not quite certain whether you believe God speaks to us through the Pope or through the lay-lords." With great trepidation the boy turned his eyes to the Abbot.

"Henry, I believe that God speaks to each of us individually. Very few choose to listen and of those that do, many confuse their own certainty with that of God's will. It is always important for us to remember that we are human...and thus capable of error!

Hugh again turned back toward the boy. "So Henry, who do you think should speak for God here on earth?"

The boy sank slightly into his saddle. "Are you asking me?"

"Yes, you Henry." The Abbot's question seemed to arc toward the youth like an arrow in flight. There could be no avoiding it.

"I don't yet feel qualified to know," Henry finally gurgled. "I mean I'm only nine years old."

"That really doesn't matter," the Abbot responded. "I'm sixty-something years old and I don't feel qualified yet to know the answer to that question. But I can share a story that I believe has helped me at certain times answer who might be correct and who might not be. Would you like to hear it?"

Henry felt a great weight lifting off his shoulders. "Yes, my lord."

The Abbot smiled at his protégé. "Long ago when I was an oblate at Saint Marcel's, a wise old monk named Brother George asked me if I had any values. Of course I told him I did. But then he rejoined me by asking specifically what they were. I stammered for a while trying to think what values I thought I stood for, but no specifics were coming quickly to my mind. Finally I realized that George had made his point. A value should be deeply ingrained in your heart and leap forth in your brain the moment it is called for. It is like the northstar always telling you which way you're going, be it the right way or the wrong way. Think on that Henry and we'll talk tomorrow of what value, or values, you might wish to put into your personal constellation. Ask God for His help in making your choice. For me, my values help me decide what to do and whose advice to take. Your values when well chosen, will keep you prepared for difficult questions such as this one we've been talking about."

"But for now, let me share with you where these battles between the Emperor and the Papacy have taken us. Despite his contrition and pleas for relief from excommunication, the Emperor in his heart remained intransigent. This became visible to me the very night at which Pope Gregory accepted the Emperor back into the Church after he'd publicly promised to recognize the Pope's authority and give up his practice of appointing bishops. I sat beside Henry at dinner in Canossa's great room. He never spoke a word, didn't eat and loudly drummed his fingers on the table in front of him. It didn't surprise me when Gregory less than three years later again excommunicated him. But by then Henry had planned for it. His nobles were in check and the German church, particularly its bishops, supported him. Accordingly, I think it was in June of 1080, Henry declared the Pope deposed and appointed the archbishop of Ravenna in his place under the name Clement. Then the Emperor led an army into Italy where after defeating Matilda's forces, he took Rome and had Clement crown him 'the affirmed' Holy Roman Emperor with all the sundry powers and privileges. I was called by Gregory to come to Rome to mediate, but my efforts were to no avail. I had to return to Cluny and leave Gregory to his fate. And the man then made his ignominy even greater by calling Robert Guiscard to rescue him. Guiscard, always an evil man, came up and sacked Rome which made the Romans so mad that Gregory had to flee. He went to Salerno where he died an angry, old man who, I should point out, brought almost all of his bereavements upon himself through his own obstinacy.

"So Henry, what do you think of all these musings?"

"Well," mulled the youth, "I should like to talk more about values. Would you please share yours and why you chose them?"

"I suppose I could," replied Hugh, "but ultimately you must choose your own, ones that fit you personally the best."

"Yes," said Henry. "I understand that from what you've said but I thought I might be better able to pick my own if I first heard how you went about choosing yours."

"I suppose that makes sense," said Hugh. "Let me try and remember how I did it. Let's see... Oh, I remember. After considering many different values, I concluded that respect and integrity were the two most important to me: respect because I believe each of us should assume that everyone we meet is one of God's creatures, at least until they show they aren't. The giving of respect to others will gain you their respect in return and it will quickly show you the 'trim of their sails.' Of course you don't have to continue to respect a person who doesn't warrant it. Many people will deservedly lose your respect either quickly or over time but guessing whether to respect a man before you know him is a foolish way to judge."

"My lord," interjected Henry, "what does it mean to learn 'the trim of someone's sails?'"

"Oh," said Hugh, "you're not a sailor are you?"

"No," replied the boy, "I can swim but I've never sailed in a boat."

"Well," replied Hugh, "a boat can be directed across the water according to the degree to which its sail is set facing the wind and its speed can be modified by trimming, that's reducing or expanding the amount of sail catching the wind. So, to learn 'the trim of a man's sail' is to learn in what direction he goes and how fast."

"That would be to know the man quite well," interjected Henry.

"Yes," replied the Abbot, "quite well indeed."

"And integrity?" asked the boy.

"Oh integrity is honesty, to be morally straight, to be a man of honor. It is a particularly difficult standard to attain and hold on to. There are often benefits derived from lying or just misleading someone. Most challenging is to speak up when, by holding one's tongue, you might benefit or not be hurt in some way. Integrity, when lived up to, is a value that permits you to look in a mirror and know the person you are looking at is 'worthy.' Be certain that your friends have integrity. Then you'll know they can be counted on."

Perhaps thinking that Hugh had completed his discourse, Henry interposed again. "Do you have any other values?"

"One other that I shall name today. I do not want to tell you all of mine because I want you first to think on the subject of what your own should be. My third value is 'stewardship.' It means to watch over something, to preserve it for the future. For me, my abbacy over Cluny is a stewardship. I do my best to sustain the abbey and to grow it in a manner pleasing to God. It is a great responsibility and one I prioritize daily. Now that's enough of my values for now. Please use some of your time on this trip to think on what your own values should be. I'll be happy to discuss them with you and help hone your choices but I want you to pick some first. That way you'll get the idea about how to do it. And you needn't hurry. It will be a long trip."

At Bayonne, Hugh's entourage laid-over for five days. The Abbot personally and solely interviewed the priest, the bishop and the local lord. On the morning of the sixth day, which was misty and damp but showing some signs of clearing, Hugh and his group departed with no apparent action taken in regard to any of the three people with whom Hugh had met. Henry was aching to ask Hugh what he'd done to alleviate the outlier. So having waited until mid-morning, the youth finally kneed his horse up beside the Abbot.

"In regard to the apparent disparity of income, were you able to determine the cause of the problem my lord?"

"No," replied Hugh. "They each carried their 'fasces' of excuses well bound and well rehearsed."

Several moments passed before Henry realized that Hugh might not be going to explain any more about his meetings. "Then what will you do?"

"Oh," replied the aged Abbot, "I explained their Christian duty to them and finished by telling them that I would see to it that the two churchmen would be replaced and the noble excommunicated if the situation didn't improve immediately."

"But how," blurted forth the boy, "can you do that? You don't know if they're all guilty."

"Quite so," replied Hugh mildly, "but they do." The Abbot turned toward his acolyte and smiled. "How are you coming with your values?"

"Oh," murmured Henry who gathered that the conversation about Bayonne's outlier was now over, "I have thought quite a lot about what my values should be. I like integrity and respect and, if it's alright with you, I shall enroll them as mine too. Respect will guide me in how I meet and treat people, and integrity will obligate me to hold the highest standards, being honest, speaking up and following Christ's teachings

"Each is a good choice Henry, and I consider you're picking two of mine to be a compliment. Have you thought of more?"

"I have thought of one more... 'others'. To me it means helping, serving and watching out for other people. But I don't yet know quite how I might go about exercising this value in the future." The youth stopped speaking and again, hoping for affirmation, turned his head toward Hugh.

"That is an excellent choice Henry, excellent indeed! And not knowing yet quite how you'll carry out your values, particularly your commitment to others, is entirely understandable given your age."

~**~

"Anyhow," said Hugh, "it's at Sahagun that we shall meet Brother Bernard. He has been an agile supporter of Pope Gregory's reform movement and is now the archbishop of Toledo as well as the primary of Saint Facundus at

Sahagun. You will like him Henry; he is bright, energetic and devoted to the Church. Like all of us, he has some weaknesses but I prefer to overlook the imperfections of men who do so much good. We shall meet him at Sahagun and ask for his help in bringing Alfonso around. I am certain he will know all the best approaches to use. Oh, I almost forgot to tell you, he is a Gascon from Sedirac and before becoming a monk he was a knight, a calling he has not entirely forgotten judging by the assault he led on the mosque in Toledo shortly after he was promoted to Archbishop there. He is an interesting man."

Sahagun was a lonely Christian sentinel in the midst of a vast, barren plain. But at the entrance to the monastery, Hugh's group was well met. Several black-robed brothers, who had obviously been assigned to await Hugh's arrival, rushed forth to help the visiting envoys with their baggage and mounts. Almost as quickly a tall man dressed in black also leaped through the doorway.

"Abbot Hugh, how good to see you." Then rushing forward, the churchman clasped his long arms around Cluny's Abbot and administered what Henry's mother had always called a 'bear hug.'

"It's been much too long since I've seen you," Bernard continued. "I had to look it up to see when you were here last. It's been thirteen years! Welcome. Welcome."

Hugh, who may have had too little breath left with which to give much of a response, whispered softly. "Thank you Bernard. You are so generous."

"Oh," responded the monk, "it is you who are generous to come all this way."

Henry judged Bernard to be still in his thirties. He had black hair tonsured in the old-fashioned manner, a broad smile which showed flashing white teeth, was very closely shaven and, just as Hugh had described, extremely energetic. All in all, the man was immediately likable.

"Ah ha," exclaimed Sahagun's Abbot as he turned toward another of Hugh's retinue, "you have brought Brother Bruglio." The tall Gascon then rushed to Bruglio and swept his arms around the bursar just as he had Hugh. "Welcome bursar of bursars. I shall now not have to strain myself for any financial answers as I know you will already have them right on your tongue. Welcome, welcome... Oh, and who is this?" he asked as his eyes fell on Henry.

"This," replied Hugh who appeared to have caught his breath, "is Henry of Dol who is a young student at Bec whom I have whisked away from there to accompany us on our trip to Spain."

"Ah," said Bernard as he stared at Henry, "neither an oblate nor a novice! Abbot Hugh must really want you to join the Church for him to have brought you on such a wonderful trip." Bernard leapt forward and clasped the young man in yet another bear-hug. "You are welcome here," he gushed as he released the boy.

Henry gasped air back into his lungs before replying. "Thank you Abbot Bernard. Thank you for your greeting."

"You may want to play some chess with Henry," said Hugh. "He's just a beginner but you may still find him a challenge."

"Oh a chess player, are you?" chortled Bernard. "I'm only moderately skilled in the game and may not be much of a match for you but there are two young Arab boys who live nearby who may compete effectively. Did you know that chess is an Arab game?"

"No," said Henry who was quite surprised to hear such a pronouncement. "I didn't know that."

"Oh, yes," replied Bernard. "God has not withheld from our Muslim brothers a thirst for learning and knowledge. I shall introduce you to them. But for now, follow me please and you can all cleanse yourselves before prayers and dinner."

Sahagun's dinning room was exactly like Bec's except the tables and benches were more darkly stained and the lighting was brighter due to several wall torches. The principal difference though was Bernard. The Bishop was genial, loquatious, humorous and full of levity. His smile and gayity filled the room. But after the main course was over, the tenor became more serious.

"Abbot Hugh," said Bernard, "I know you are expecting me to go with you to meet with King Alfonso but that is no longer a good idea. You see he and I have had a falling out. Hopefully it is only temporary but with Alfonso one never knows. You see we have disagreed over some church appointments. He feels they fall within his jurisdiction and I believe they fall within mine. I cannot elevate the quality of the Church if I can't pick the right men. Anyhow as you know, Alfonso has a temper and at this moment, he is very angry with me. You will do better without me along."

"But," responded Hugh quickly, "Bruglio and I can't go without you. Etiquette would be trampled and, as you know, they take etiquette very seriously here."

"You could tell the King that I'd been called to Santiago on urgent church business and had already departed when you arrived."

Hugh seemed to be considering the efficacy of that gambit when Bernard spoke again. "I can leave immediately to make it true…and I'll take Henry with me to show him the shrine and get him his 'compostele.' And we'll be back in less than two weeks."

~**~

"**H**enry… Henry my boy," harangued Bernard as he leaned across their table and poked his young friend with his forefinger, "you're falling asleep again."

Henry's head jerked up and he looked around. They were in a small, well-lit building. It was crowded with people; people making lots of noise: laughing, drinking, cavorting, calling out, waving their arms, slapping one another on the back.

"Henry," giggled a female voice from just behind his left ear, "is my service not keeping you awake? Perhaps I shall have to tickle you."

The boy's head jerked as he felt the tingling sensation of a finger softly sliding up the side of his neck.

"Rosalette, stop that," Bernard chuckled. "He's only a boy."

Henry twisted around in his chair to see his tormenter. Rosalette was a young woman with black hair, huge brown eyes and a laughing smile which showed off her perfectly aligned white teeth. She looked Henry squarely in the eye, batted her eyelashes and giggled again. Instinctively Henry knew she was flirting with him but he couldn't decide whether she warranted reproof or appreciation.

"Rosalette," continued Bernard, "he's too young for you."

"But," she smilingly replied, "he is so handsome. I just can't help myself. But if you wish it, I shall treat him like a member of the church." With that said, the beautiful young woman pirouetted toward the kitchen. "I'll get some more wine," she trilled, "something to loosen you all up."

"Henry," continued Bernard, "before you go to bed, I want to review our agenda. Tomorrow you will get your compostele. But first let me share Saint James' story. He, as you know, was one of Jesus' disciples and also his cousin. You probably also know that Jesus' last command to his disciples was for them to spread out across the land and evangelize wherever possible. James came to Spain for an unknown length of time and then returned to Jerusalem where he was martyred by a Roman sword. Two of his most loyal followers from Spain brought his body back here for burial. Since then the exact location of the grave was lost until God sent a star to shine on it and celestial music to ring above it. This miracle was witnessed about two hundred years ago by a local hermit who of course told the king the good news. The king immediately built a church and a monastery at the site and named it 'the field of the star'—'Campus Stellae.' Since then Saint James has appeared on numerous occasions usually helping our Christian soldiers fight back the Muslim hordes."

Henry was considering how difficult it must have been to bring a dead body all the way from Jerusalem to northern Spain when Bernard continued his discourse.

"You know, Henry," the Abbot continued, "it is a shame we don't have more time. I'd love to take you to Cordoba.

"Have you actually been there?" interrupted Henry with great interest.

"Oh yes," responded Bernard.

"The Arabs let you in?"

"Of course," replied the Abbot. "Muslims respect both Christians and Jews as people who worship the same God they do. But they think we have failed to hear the words of their great prophet Muhammad and therefore we don't understand God's intentions as well as they do. They refer to us as 'dhimmis' and treat us as second class citizens: not able to bear arms, required to keep silent during Muslim prayers and having to pay a special head tax. But we certainly are permitted to move freely within the city and to pray in our own churches and synagogues. And the more educated we are, the more quickly we are permitted into their circle of great scholars. Actually the greatest doctors are almost all Jews and the Muslims know enough to go to them when they're ill."

"I didn't know that," whispered Henry.

"But back to the agenda, tomorrow at first light we shall tour the entire facility: the shrine, the church, the shops, purchase some cockle shells, get your compostele and see all the sights. Then first thing the next day, we're back for Sahagun and double quick we'll have to go. Now my compatriots here will take you to our inn and put you to bed. We have a big day tomorrow."

"Abbot Bernard," asked Henry as he rose from his chair, "what is a compostele?"

"Oh, didn't I mention that? How silly of me. A compostele is a certificate attesting that you've been here. It is merely a piece of paper. But when you pray at the shrine tomorrow, you will actually receive remission of your sins, at least remission for those sins you have already committed. I shall join you there and seek redemption too. Good night, my boy."

As Henry turned to leave, he almost bumped into Rosalette who was returning with more wine.

"Good night Henry," she chirped as they passed. "May God grant you safe passage back to Sahagun."

"Thank you," replied the boy. "May He also watch over you."

THE ROAD HOME
April 1090 – December 1091

It was April first when Hugh's train started back north from Sahagun. In Dol Henry had always found April to be windy, wet and chilly. On the plains of Spain it was windy, wet and warm, so warm that George, Randulf and John chose to tie their conical helmets to their belts rather than wear them. Fortunately Henry still had the wide-brimmed hat that Anslem had given him. It was light on his head and shielded his eyes from the direct rays of the sun.

"Henry," asked Abbot Hugh, "how did you like Santiago de Compostela?"

"My lord, to be purged of my sins certainly made the trip worthwhile. The shrine was elegant, perhaps as Saint James was himself. The church was small but sufficient for the number of pilgrims who pray there."

"So," concluded Hugh, "you didn't like it."

At first Henry was taken aback by the Abbot's remark but as he thought about it, he realized Hugh was right. There was something he hadn't liked at Santiago but he couldn't quite put his finger on what.

"I think," the boy finally replied, "that it wasn't what I expected."

"Do you know what it was that you didn't expect?" asked Hugh.

"Well," said Henry as he thought about it, "I think all of the shops and general hubbub diminished my sense of being close to Saint James. I mean he was one of Jesus' apostles and spent most of his life with Him. But there was so much noise and commotion from all the stall-holders hocking their wares: the wine-skins, cockle shells, leather bags and purses, medicines and potions, things that James supposedly touched, even the composteles had to be paid for!"

"Did you buy one?"

"Yes but I don't value it highly. It's only a piece of paper."

"That is true," said Hugh, "but the coin you bought it with is only a piece of metal." The Abbot glanced at the boy to gauge his reaction to such a comment.

For a moment Henry stared at the old man riding in his travel-worn black robe. "I'm not sure I understand your point."

"Well," continued Hugh as he smiled, "you cannot take either of them with you to heaven, nor to hell I suppose."

"No," mused the boy. "I suppose not but it still didn't feel right, all that buying and selling, yelling and shouting."

"I know exactly what you mean," Hugh interjected. "The activities of God's hands are often cloaked by the habitual hubbub and humdrum of humanity. At first glance, His efforts are often obscured. But when you look really hard for Him, you will find His workings all around you: His signs, His coincidences. One of my greatest pleasures is to study a place, a situation, something that I don't understand and look very carefully until I find Him. Think on it for a moment Henry. Amidst all the chaos and the noise at Santiago, what may you have overlooked?"

For several moments Henry consciously recalled his visit to Saint James' shrine: the church, the shops, the yelling, the noise. Then quite suddenly he remembered the young woman and child. He'd just risen from praying at the shrine and was turning to depart when he saw them approaching.

The little boy was perhaps two or three years old and quite thin. The young woman looked to be fifteen or sixteen years old and was pulling the boy along by one hand. Whether she was the boy's older sister or mother, Henry couldn't tell. But what was evident beyond any doubt was her focus. Her eyes were set on the crucifix which hung just above Saint James' sarcophagus. Her sole objective was to reach it. She was oblivious to anything else: the noise, the crowd, the rush...all unnoticed.

As Henry reviewed this recollection in his mind, he noted something else he hadn't identified before. Her skin was oddly...ashen. She was ill, critically ill. And then it dawned on him that she wasn't there to assuage her sins but rather to find succor for the boy. For a moment Henry couldn't draw a breath...as if he'd been stabbed in his chest. When he'd first seen the young woman, he'd missed all the signs: her condition, her predicament, her need and he'd walked right past her without even a nod. How thought Henry had he been so negligent, so unaware?

Hugh stared at his acolyte's expression of bewilderment. "So," the Abbot murmured, "you did see His hand amidst the throng...something of note, something meaningful?"

"Yes," stammered the young man, "I saw someone who needed my help...but I failed to realize it until just now." Henry's countenance showed a stricken sense of pain.

"And what did you see?"

With his feelings of remorse overwhelming him, Henry stared blankly at the Abbot. Several moments passed before he spoke. "A dying woman bringing her young brother or perhaps her son, to the sarcophagus in hopes that Saint James might intercede on the boy's behalf and find someone to care for him."

"Ah," replied Hugh softly, "amidst all the human noise, tumult, confusion and chaos, God showed you a person with real need and now you berate yourself for not recognizing it at the time and doing something to help her."

"Yes," said Henry in a quivering voice.

"But," said Hugh, "I don't think God showed you that woman and child hoping you would help them. If He had wanted you to be their salvation, He would have caused you to understand their need then, not days later. What I think God really wanted was for you to learn to see within the rush of daily life those things that are truly important and those that are not. He has shown Himself to you and shared with you how to distinguish in the future what is really important and what is not. You have been blessed Henry."

Henry contemplated Hugh's words. It was certainly too late for him to help that woman and child. Perhaps God had taught him a lesson. And with that in mind, Henry promised himself to keep his mind more open in the future: to see God's meaning in all the things, little or large, which went on. Hugh was right! God had given him a gift. Now he must be worthy of it.

Quite a bit of time passed before Hugh finally broke their silence. "So Henry, let me share with you how Brother Bruglio and I fared with Alfonso. The king has rehired Rodrigo Diaz to lead his troops, so he is again thinking he can drive the Muslims out of his southern territories. This will of course allow him to refill his treasury and, thank God, make good on his tithe to Cluny together with all the concurrent subsidies for hostels along the Camino Santiago de Compostela. We had much less difficulty than I expected. It seems the King has recently been having chest pains which have caused him to contemplate meeting God sooner than he previously was planning to. Accordingly his desire to be prayed for, his soul to be prayed for, is again very important to him. This of course favors Cluny because he continues to think that our prayers have been the most important cause of his success. Brother Bruglio told him that 'with so little time left', it was essential that he procure even more prayers and chants on his behalf if he really wants redemption to come before he dies. And Bruglio said it so well. I was proud of him.

"Now when we get to Cluny, I'm going to have George and Randulf take you on to Bec. They as you probably know are younger brothers from Chalon. Hence, they are knights with little hope of estates. They have been serving God, Cluny and me for several years now. Each is entirely trust-worthy and a good Christian. You will be in good hands. Of course if you wish, you may stay over at Cluny for a few days to rest. Having been away so long, I shall be quite busy. I do want to thank you Henry for going to Spain. You are a fine young man and I most sincerely hope that God's plans bring you into the Church. But whatever path you eventually take, Jesus will be watching over you. He has shown Himself to be interested in your welfare."

The Abbot of Cluny then clapped his knees against the flanks of his horse and returned to his accustomed position at the head of his retinue.

Henry decided to stay one night at Cluny. He hadn't made a lot of friends there and he didn't have much interest in the daily routine. He did stop to converse with Bruglio's two clerks and to thank the bursar for being such a good companion. He also gave Hugh a thankful 'good-bye,' but he didn't talk with the Abbot long because he knew Hugh had intended his parting words during their trip to be his final comments. They separated with a simple 'Pax vo biscum.'

George and Randulf were brothers. Neither was particularly talkative. They were friendly enough, they just didn't talk much. George was the second oldest of six children, Randulf the fourth and each was a knight.

At first Henry queried one or the other about Chalon, his family and his religious beliefs. Their answers were always succinct and without reference to anything else which might have led to other topics. However in Randulf, Henry did uncover one subject of interest. He was bi-lingual. Chalon, it turned out, was in Champagne, which was beside Upper and Lower Lorraine where German was spoken. Accordingly both brothers spoke German as well as French.

So Henry set about learning some German from Randulf. While it was quickly apparent that the young knight was not a skilled teacher, Henry made a point of accosting his new instructor in a pleasant and humorous manner. The boy would ask what a certain word was in German and then search Randulf's answer for its Latin roots. Quickly they progressed to verbs and were soon making short sentences. Often Henry's attempts produced raucous rounds of laughter on Randulf's part as the boy's 'sentence' had turned out to mean something entirely different than what he'd intended. The two got on very well playing this 'game' and passed their time quickly while riding to Bec.

~**~

"**Y**ou missed the funeral," said Brother Jason off-handedly.

Thunder-struck by the portent of the monk's comment, Henry immediately responded. "What do you mean? What funeral?"

The corners of Jason's mouth were slightly inverted which made his smile apparent but not pronounced. "You haven't heard?" The monk's question served only to prolong Henry's concern as to who had died.

"No," barked the boy. "Who died?"

With his lips still slightly inverted, Brother Jason discharged his news. "Peter Maillesais, your mentor."

Henry paused as he digested Jason's words...not Anslem, not his father nor his mother but Peter Maillesais, his kind young friend who had been assigned to be his guide at Bec...but he was too young...

"What happened?" Henry finally asked.

"Well," responded Jason who obviously enjoyed his importance, "his eyes were watering, he was blowing his nose a lot and then he began to have trouble breathing."

"Did you boil water to create steam for him?" interjected Henry.

"Oh," responded Jason whose lips were no longer inverted, "I don't know about that but of course we prayed for him."

In his mind Henry was forming a foul curse to be directed at Jason but before uttering it his mind jumped to another subject, his own absence. He was the 'prefect' of Bec's infirmary. He would have known to boil water and put Peter's head above the kettle to breathe in the hot moisture. Had he been at his job, he might have saved his friend.

"Henry," it was Anslem's voice calling out breathlessly, "we did try steam and some herbs which relaxed him some but God must have wanted him because nothing we did seemed to help. I'm so sorry."

With tears running down his cheeks, Henry turned to the Abbot. "I should have been here to help him."

Anslem advanced and put his arms around the boy. "No," he whispered, "it was God's will and certainly not your fault."

So Henry resumed his participation in Bec's routines: the readings, prayers, chants, gardening and bee-keeping. But Abbot Anslem assigned him two additional functions that were well outside the norm, the infirmary and clerking. The infirmary 'prefecture' meant that Henry was to learn about healing, medicines, illnesses and cures. Books were to be loaned from other monasteries. Henry's friend, Abbot Bernard in Sahagun, even routed him some Arabic volumes on various healing methodologies which Henry was able to have translated by Brother Minolo who had grown up in central Spain and somehow matriculated his way to Bec. Minolo was bald, aged and incredibly serious. He allocated his time with Henry generously but in return expected complete focus and concentration. Conversation on other than the Arabic books and Arabic topics was bluntly rejected. "We haven't time for that" the old monk would say. However within the circumference of those accepted topics was Arabic, the language. So Henry was able to add a limited grasp of Arabic to his linguistic skills. He and Minolo even played a game of questioning each other on Arabic medical terminology. The content came from the books they studied and Henry enjoyed the competition.

It was late in the afternoon and being late December, quite dark when Brother Minolo lit a second candle. Henry and the Spanish monk were organizing a new medical folio which would do four things: list various symptoms, identify the possible illnesses causing said symptoms, offer the most likely remedies and describe how to make and apply them. Their work, which they'd just begun, was intended to amalgamate both Arab and Christian sources. It would be a very significant work and in Henry's mind, be a force majeure on behalf of 'others.'

Suddenly the door to Bec's little library opened and Brother Jason burst in. "Henry are you here?"

"Yes," replied the boy.

"Ah," said Anslem's assistant as if he were greatly annoyed, "I could hardly see you in this awful darkness." Taking in the tiny room with its three shelves of books and simultaneously nodding to Minolo, Jason continued. "Henry, our Abbot wants you to attend him in his office immediately."

"Oh," said Henry who was straightening his back which was stiff from bending over the reading table for so long. "Do you know what he wants?"

"No," replied the martinet, "although it probably has to do with the messenger who just arrived from Dol."

Instantly Henry completed his rise from the table. A messenger from Dol...probably with bad news but what? "Thank you, Brother Jason," the youth mumbled as he bolted out the door.

Magwolf's horse was tethered outside Anslem's office. Henry took a deep breath and then knocked.

"Come in." It was Anslem's voice responding in a subdued tone.

Henry entered quickly. The little room was brightly lit by several candles. He first saw Magwolf who was standing on his left near the wall. Hoping for some sort of information, the boy immediately glanced into the eyes of his father's knight. In response, Magwolf tipped his head toward the Abbot who was standing behind the table. Henry stepped forward. "My lord, Brother Jason has sent me in response to your request."

"Yes," replied Anslem very solemnly, "please sit down. I have sad news."

Henry glanced again at Magwolf and then sat down in one of the chairs. 'Sad news,' he thought. 'My father or mother has died.'

"Your father has sent me a letter," Anslem began. "Your brother William has died."

William! Henry's mind leapt...not his father, not his mother but William. How could that be? He was too young. "William?"

"Yes," whispered the Abbot gently, "apparently of a fever. I am so sorry Henry."

It took Henry a moment to focus his thoughts. All he could see was William's broad smile as he'd entered the great-room on the day he'd brought down his first deer. Such a happy smile...William with whom he'd shared a bed, learned Latin, gone in tandem up and down the castle stairways protecting their father... Henry felt tears welling up in his eyes.

Anslem waited until the boy had composed himself. "Henry, your father wants you to return to Dol. You are now the heir apparent and I believe he wishes you to prepare for that. I know this is a great shock. All I can say is that you have our heart-felt support and, if you'll allow me, I would like to lead our prayers tonight to honor your brother William."

With tears on his cheeks and a pained expression on his face, Henry looked up at Anslem. "Thank you," he whispered, "that would be very kind."

The next morning, low clouds drizzeled a mixed substance, half rain and half snow. Henry's broad-brimmed hat repelled most of the icy droplets but not all of them. Those that made it past his hat seemed unerringly to hit his neck and then drool their way beneath his clothing and down his back. He was riding with Magwolf back to Dol. There wasn't much conversation. Henry was still digesting the news. He couldn't understand why God would take William at such a young age. He had so much ability. It didn't make sense. And Anslem had said his father now wanted him to prepare to become the Lord of Dol. But what did that mean? Was he no longer to study at Bec? Was he to become a knight? There were so many questions.

Henry and Magwolf arrived at Dol castle just as they had left Bec...in a freezing rain that chilled to the bone. But great warmth greeted them in the castle. And after a brief flurry of hugs, tears, handshakes and kisses, the two travelers were whisked out of the rain, put into dry clothes and served mulled mead in front of a crackling fire. A young woman, whom Audrey introduced as Mildrid, was playing a harp. The music and the mead quickly relaxed Henry and soon he found himself playing a sort of 'hide and seek' with his younger brother.

Since it was one day before the extended family would arrive for Christmas, the group in front of the fire included only the staff, immediate family and a handful of Walter's liegemen, about fifteen in all. Walter and Audrey gave a brief summary of the events that had happened at Dol during Henry's absence which kept the occasion fairly cheerful. For his part, Henry reviewed his activities at Bec and his trip to Spain with Hugh. Other than Audrey, Walter and several of the liegemen who'd been to Hastings' field, no one there had been anywhere outside of Brittany. In fact, most of the servants and staff had never been more than a mile from the castle. Accordingly, Henry's telling of his trip to Spain kept the group enthralled from beginning to end...and even after the end because there were questions.

This assemblage lasted well into the evening until Audrey finally asked one of the maids to bring Magwolf some blankets so he could sleep next to the fire. Recognizing their cue, everyone then rose to leave. Henry retired to his and William's bed on the third floor. After sliding under the covers, the boy thought about the evening. It had been very pleasant, one he knew he'd never forget. Shortly his thoughts turned to William and how much his brother would have enjoyed being there. Then, seeking the warmth of William's body, Henry slipped the fingers of his left hand toward where his brother had always been. There was no warmth...William was gone.

At sun-up Audrey departed and Walter asked Henry to remain in the family room so he could present 'what comes next.' So father and son, each atop his bed, sat facing one another.

Walter began. "Henry, losing William was the saddest event of my entire life. He was a fine, young man and I miss him greatly. But life presents us with many sad events and all we can do is accept them and move on. You also are a fine young man, one whom your mother and I love deeply just as we did William. You are now the heir apparent at Dol, the one who will succeed me when I die.

"Accordingly your course must change from training for the church to training to become a knight and a lord. Your mother and I had already begun this process for William by engaging your mother's cousin, Count Robert of Flanders, to oversee his training. His son, also named Robert, oversees an academy that trains young men to become knights. It is a very fine school with an outstanding group of experienced sergeants to bring you to knighthood. So now, instead of sending William, we intend to send you to Flanders. Robert is expecting William sometime in January, but I'm sure he will accept you in William's place. Your mother has a letter prepared for him that explains everything.

"I know this entire event is a shock to you. Clearly you were excelling in your academic pursuits. Nevertheless, our primary duty is to Dol. Do you understand what I'm saying?"

"Yes," murmured the boy.

"Good," said Walter. "I'm holding Magwolf here through Christmas so he can take you to Flanders. All our family will be here from today until the second of January. Then you can ride for Flanders. Meanwhile," Walter continued in a more vibrant tone, "we can celebrate your birthday a few days late. You are I believe ten years old, practically an old man. Magwolf told me that you never even mentioned your birthday on your way here. Did you forget it or just not want to celebrate?"

"I didn't feel like celebrating."

"I know," whispered Walter, "but it's important to keep your mother in good spirits and this may be the last time she sees you for several years."

A KNIGHT'S TRAINING
January 1092 – December 1095

Robert of Flanders' Knights School was a quarter mile beyond his castle. There were two buildings each made of wood and each quite large. There was only one odd thing about the school. The wide fields around the two buildings were not plowed. Instead they were beaten down like a well travelled road. Henry steered Meredith toward the front entrance of the dormitory and dismounted.

Immediately a young boy, perhaps six or seven years old, burst out of the doorway and ran directly to the new arrivals. "Be you William of Dol?" the boy breathlessly asked.

Henry pivoted to face his questioner. "No. I am Henry of Dol here in place of my brother William." Henry felt a twinge of pain as he referenced William but he cleared his throat and continued. "William died this past November, so I am here to take his place."

The little boy obviously hadn't expected this response and didn't know what to say next.

"Perhaps," continued Henry, "you could take us to Count Robert and we can complete our introductions with him."

For a moment the boy stood absolutely still obviously trying to determine what he should do. He didn't have to resolve his dilemma though because just then, a man exited the dormitory and took charge of the conversation. "Did I hear you say your name is Henry?"

"I did," said Henry. "Henry of Dol and this is Magwolf a trusted knight of my father."

The man looked to be in his thirties, was squarely built, about average height and had a muscular physique which promised strength. He was wearing a chainmail hauberk which split at his crotch and continued down to his knees. His head was thinly topped with graying blond hair and his eyes were pale-blue and probing. "Welcome to both of you. I am Robert 'the younger.' My father is the Count but unfortunately cannot greet you today as he is ill." The man then stepped up to Henry and reached forth his hand. "You are Henry, not William?" he said.

"I am," replied Henry. "My brother William, whom you expected, died this past November. My parents have sent me instead."

"I am sorry to hear of your brother's passing," murmured Robert. "May he rest peacefully with Jesus." Robert crossed himself then looked up as if seeing God somewhere in the clouds. At last Robert lowered his stare and continued. "Your mother and father are well?"

"Yes," answered Henry. "And your father, is he combating an illness which challenges him?"

"He is," said Robert. "I shall be most happy to take you to him. First though, we shall get you settled here. The knight swung his right arm toward the little boy who had so recently come out of the dormitory. "This is Johnnie. He is one of our charges here at the school. He is a sturdy young man of good parentage who will one day become a fine knight." Robert smiled at the boy. "Isn't that so, Johnnie?"

"Yes, my lord."

"Tell Reynauld," continued Robert, "that his new student has arrived from Dol and that we wish to meet him in the dormitory."

Again the boy hesitated as if awaiting further instructions.

"Dismissed," said Robert.

Johnnie immediately leaped back through the dormitory entryway.

"There," said Robert. "Now let's get your gear and we'll take you to your room."

Henry's mind raced, a room. Could he be going to get a room of his own?

"Magwolf," said Robert firmly, "you are welcome to stay the night or longer if you wish. We eat well here which is appropriate because Reynauld works the boys hard. Is this Henry's equipment?"

"Aye," replied the knight from Dol as he dismounted and began to unbuckle the strap on the mule holding Henry's few belongings. The two men quickly divided the items between them: two blankets, assorted clothes and Walter's mail shirt, sword and shield. Bringing up the rear Henry carried his chess set and the *Aeneid*.

It turned out the dormitory did not have individual rooms but rather 'cubicles' with a wall around each individual's section that was about four feet high. Each space, there were twenty, was about seven feet long and four wide with a bed and a small wooden box to hold clothing or other belongings. Johnnie had beaten them to the cubicles and was eagerly pointing to one that was empty of any equipment or personal items.

When the three bearers of Henry's possessions entered the large dormitory room, there were two young men standing just inside the doorway. Each was significantly bigger and older than Henry, perhaps twelve years old. Seeing Robert carrying a shield and chainmail shirt, each took one of the items and put it on Henry's bed. Once Magwolf and Henry had also deposited their items, Robert cleared his throat to speak.

"This," he said as he waved a hand toward Henry, "is Henry of Dol."

Henry nodded his head to Robert and then to each of the two young men.

"He," Robert continued, "is the oldest son of Walter the Lord of Dol and Audrey his wife who is my cousin. Dol is in Brittany." Robert turned slightly to his left and pointed to each of the two young men who, having put down Henry's shirt and shield, now stood silently facing Robert. "This is Ludolf and his brother Bartholomew both from Tournai. Each is a junior prefect here at our school."

Henry assessed the pair. Ludolf had black hair down to the back of his neck and a stern, almost sullen, expression. Bartholomew was pale-skinned, freckle-faced and had a thick mop of orange hair. His expression was also stern but not unfriendly.

"Ah," continued Robert, "here is Reynauld our Master of War-Craft."

A large man strode through the doorway. His bulk barely allowed him to fit through the portal. He was tall, muscular and red haired, though dark red unlike Bartholomew's orange, and beginning to grey at the temples. This was clearly a knight past his prime but still a man of tumultuous strength, size, and, Henry assumed, skill.

"Reynauld," said Robert, "this is Henry of Dol and this is Magwolf, a knight of Henry's father the Lord of Dol." Turning back toward Henry, Robert went on. "Reynauld is a knight who has served my father loyally and skillfully since before my father became Count, which was after a prolonged and contentious series of battles. He has most recently returned from Jerusalem and Constantinople to which my father went as a pilgrim. He now serves as the Master of War-Craft here at our school."

Henry bowed his head to Reynauld, the 'El Cid' of Flanders the boy presumed, a man who could teach him to become a knight.

"Would you like to speak?" asked Robert of Reynauld.

"Certainly sir," replied the 'Master' as he stepped forward and turned to face his new student. "Henry, you are welcome here. We will teach you to become a knight. You will learn to fight with lance, sword and bow, how to ride, follow commands and understand strategy and tactics. But most importantly, we shall teach you the values of a knight: faith, obedience and honor." With those brief remarks stated, Reynauld acknowledged Henry with a quick nod and stepped back beside Robert.

"Johnnie," said Robert who apparently had more to say, "I want you to become Henry's batman: help him know where to go and when, introduce him to his mates and help him at the stable with his horse. Yes?"

"Yes, sir," responded the little boy.

"All right," said Robert. "Henry, after you and Johnnie take care of your horse, please find me and we'll visit my father."

So after Johnnie had sufficiently assured Henry that his possessions would be safe in his cubicle—a discourse recounting a knight's honor to his fellow knights—the two took Meredith to the stable. There the stableman directed them to an empty stall and firmly stated 'that all grooming would be done by the horse's owner.' Henry had been expecting to take care of Meredith. It was a duty his father had told him always came first. Johnnie was eager to help though so Meredith lacked for nothing. As soon as they were done, Henry dismissed his young friend and went looking for Count Robert.

Due to the oncoming darkness, Robert and Henry walked to the castle at a very fast pace, so fast that the boy was breathless by the time they got there.

"You'll find," Robert said, "that part of the school's regimen is to run from the dormitory to the castle and back every morning. The boy who finishes last must run the course again in the afternoon. A knight must be in excellent physical condition because fighting requires both strength and stamina."

Henry understood the logic of such conditioning but wasn't certain he'd enjoy the actual effort.

Somewhat later, Henry exited the room with a feeling of deep sadness. Robert's father had clearly been a vibrant human being only a short while ago. Now he was a mere shadow of his former self. Briefly Henry wondered why God let this sort of thing happen but then he put his mind to what he could do to ameliorate the old man's situation.

"Sir Robert," Henry queried the Count's son, "I have a book with me, the *Aeneid* by Virgil. Perhaps I could occasionally read a page or two of it to your father. I know I cannot cure him but I might be able to give him some respite from the disease."

"What sort of book is it?" asked the Flemish knight.

Henry was surprised that Robert wasn't acquainted with the *Aeneid* but he hid his surprise with a quick response. "It is about Aeneas' founding of Rome. Aeneas was the great Trojan warrior who came to Italy and laid down the values upon which Rome was built. Your father has been a warrior most of his life. He will like the story. I'll read only a page or two a day so as not to tire him."

"But," responded Robert, "is the book in Latin?"

"Yes," answered Henry somewhat confused by his cousin's question.

"My father can neither speak nor read Latin," said Robert coolly, "so he won't understand you reading it."

"Oh no," interjected Henry. "I'll translate it. I'm sure he'll understand it."

"You can do that?" asked Robert in a doubtful tone.

"Yes," replied the boy, "and I'll review the pages the day before I recite them so I'll be well prepared."

So Henry read the *Aeneid* two or three times a week to Robert 'the elder.' To his surprise and to everyone else's, these readings, or perhaps it was just the attention, kindled a fresh spark in the old man's eyes. In turn the cheer in the father created cheer in the son. All this also pleased Henry because it showed him that his efforts on behalf of others were working not just on the recipient but on more people as well.

Meanwhile with the objective of attaining knighthood, Henry took up the regimen of his new school. He was at first the youngest and least physically developed of his mates. Accordingly Henry ran the foot race against his peers and lost, thus having to run the course again that afternoon. He was of course greatly embarrassed. But his legs and stamina improved with repeated efforts putting him into closer and closer finishes. Eventually a new boy joined the school and provided Henry his first finish not in last place. By then though, Henry had come to see the benefit he was receiving from running, so instead of giving up his afternoon run he continued it.

A greater challenge for Henry to overcome was one he had not foreseen, his education. Once it became known that he was reading Latin to Robert 'the elder,' he instantly became a pariah among his schoolmates. Several of the older boys began derisively calling him 'the bishop' a term picked Henry assumed, because a bishop could read and speak Latin. His biggest disappointment was that most of his 'mates' simply stopped talking to him. The one notable exception was Bartholomew who cheerfully continued to play chess with him and be his friend. And of course Johnnie was a friend as well. Henry understood that none of his school mates had ever had the opportunity to learn Latin but he couldn't understand why this caused them to ostracize him the way they did. He'd had to catch up to them running so why didn't they just ask him to teach them Latin?

This issue plagued Henry for almost a year until Johnnie, his young batman, inadvertently provided a solution. On a quiet Sunday afternoon the boy who was obviously bored, asked Henry if he would read to him. Of course Henry was happy to do so since Johnnie helped him with all manner of things. The setting for this reading naturally became Henry's cubicle which since its walls were only four feet high, excluded no one. Within a week there were seven attendees, within two, twelve. And during the third week, Reynauld sat in and declared it 'a wonderful story.' Thus Henry was anointed.

Only a few days after this, Reynauld and Henry had what the Master of war-craft later called a 'skirmish.' Reynauld was lecturing about the 'values' of a knight: that every true knight ought to have a very concise set of values, beliefs and characteristics. They included bravery, loyalty, generosity and most of all keeping one's word. The Master elaborated on each value at great length. But when he finished, Henry asked a question.

"Master Reynauld, may a knight have other values as well?"

"No," the huge warrior brusquely responded. Reynauld had spent years choosing these specific values. They were now inexorably woven into his very fiber. He had no intention of letting some boy, some educated boy, contradict what had taken him years to learn. This boy was bright but experience hadn't yet tempered his blade.

"But what about 'integrity?" continued Henry.

This set Reynauld back. "Well... well, it's part of honor," he stammered in a much softer tone.

"And would 'respect' be part of honor too?" Henry queried in a very serious tone.

"Yes... yes it would," responded the Master as he realized the boy was simply defining 'honor' more specifically. "That's a very good point Henry. A knight must respect other knights. Having integrity is just like honor."

"Thank you," the boy pensively responded. "May I ask one more question?"

"Certainly," replied Reynauld who was no longer feeling threatened.

For a moment the youth paused. "One of my values is 'others,' as being interested in other's well-being or helping others in trouble or...those less fortunate."

At first Reynauld wasn't quite sure where Henry's 'others' fit within his list of a knight's values. But then the Master's mind leaped forward. "We've been talking about how knights must fight as a team, 'cover each other's backs.' That's thinking of others...helping others."

After being in Reynauld's school for almost a year, Henry thought he'd figured out the priorities and subjects which his teacher was presenting. Every day except Sunday, there was physical exercise: running, riding, boxing, mock combat and some unusual activities like ladder-climbing and balancing. On Mondays, Wednesdays and Fridays, there was offensive weapons training and defense against the same instruments. Every conceivable weapon was studied and used: sword, lance, knife, crossbow, longbow and even composite bow. All of these had to be mastered for use and recognized from afar in order to properly defend against them. Siege weapons were also reviewed as a need might arise where their weapons' handlers might be dead or wounded and a knight have to step in to operate them. All sorts of heavy equipment, none of which Henry had ever dreamed of, was rolled out of the castle and put into action. These included ballista, catapult, mangonel, mattocks and trebuchet. Tuesdays and Thursdays were usually devoted to knowing all about one's own equipment, how to use it as well as how to fix it.

And there were stories from Reynauld or 'special' guests like Robert 'the younger.' These stories were first-hand accounts of combat situations and covered both valiant and fearful moments. One of Robert's knights named Courtney, whom Henry hadn't met before, described his first combat in '71 against knights and foot soldiers from Bouillon, a place somewhere to the east. In this battle recoiling from the blood and gore in front of him, Courtney had hesitated for a moment opening a space ahead between his best friend and himself. In that moment an enemy stepped into the void and slew his friend. Twenty three years later, Courtney's eyes were tearful as he still blamed himself for his friend's death.

Saturdays were reserved for strategy and tactics and were presented by Robert the Younger.

"In the German King's case, it's usually more of a game than a war. So our objective is to avoid a decisive battle and get into the fall so he'll have to start paying his soldiers. Against someone our own size, a count or a duke, our goal would be to acquire lands with some rich towns or ports. But we try very hard not to anoy our smaller neighbors." Henry was taken with how rational Robert was in determining his objectives. The goal was to achieve the possible. But Robert made a second point as well. "It's best to know your opponent personally. If you don't, find out all you can about him and I don't mean after the war starts. Do it now. You must know whether he'll attack, hole-up in his castle or worst of all, do something unexpected. Will good men follow him? Is he an honorable man or a 'nithing?'

"I always remind myself," said Robert, "of the Conqueror's reference to castles. 'That they are the bones of the kingdom.' But you must remember that a castle is not a place to hide. You must think offensively. Oh, a castle can provide safety from a larger force but its real role is to allow you to sortie forth and ravage the enemy. A castle is the focal point not only of your defense but of your offense as well. Offense is the basis of victory. Against an aggressive foe, no one can win a war simply by hiding in his castle. On the other hand when investing a castle, you may need to starve out the garrison and thus ravage the surrounding countryside. Such actions may bring forth the castellan, at least it will take food out of his mouth. Without food or better yet water, no enemy can fight for long. Besiege him, starve him, kill his peasants who produce the food, make wider alliances against him, do everything you can to wear him down. But at all costs avoid a pitched battle. Large battles are always chancy. The bigger and better force often loses. Nothing is more capricious than a battle. Even if your 'knights' service' is up, the forty days gone by and you can't afford to keep them any longer, do not seek salvation in a major battle. It's better to use sappers, trebuchets, disease, counter-castles, starvation, siege towers, kidnapping his family, tortoises, battering rams, or treachery than a pitched battle."

During his time at the school, Henry grew both intellectually and physically. His acuity of mind which had always impressed others but less so himself, took a great leap forward as he began to see how appearingly disparate actions, ideas and events often came together in a reasonably predictable manner. In combat he learned to make certain thrusts or parries that would eventually lead to his adversary presenting an opening which he could take advantage of. In debate, he learned to listen carefully to his antagonist's argument and then, using a carefully chosen analogy, he would turn his opponent's words upon themselves. Predicting the evolution and final outcomes of events, Henry learned most poignantly from Robert 'the younger' who always was able to distill the moving parts of any event into two or three base ingredients and, after studying them carefully, would announce the most likely outcomes which, when he explained his reasoning, always seemed obvious.

Henry's physical growth needed no interpretation. In three years, he grew to be the tallest, the fastest and the quickest of all the students in Reynauld's group. He attributed his height to his father and mother who were both taller than average and he'd been told his Uncle Henry was even taller than his father. His speed and endurance he attributed to his running around the castle every day. For his quickness, he simply thanked God.

On Sundays, Robert and his wife Clem, Reynauld and all the students together with many of Robert's household knights, castellans and staff attended mass at a nearby stone church. After mass, they all repaired to lunch in Robert's great-room where the meals were always excellent. Sunday afternoons were 'free,' which meant each young man could do as he pleased. Henry had taken to currying Meredith, his horse, and so trekked to the barn where she was stabled.

When he arrived, he was surprised to find a young woman there patting a pony he'd seen before. Since she was facing the horse and obviously hadn't heard him, lest he startle her he spoke before getting too close.

"Good day."

"Yeee," she shrieked as she swiveled quickly to see who was behind her. "Oh," she gasped as her right hand rose to cover her mouth, "you startled me." Then before Henry could utter any response she began to giggle.

~**~

It was sometime in the spring after Henry's fourteenth birthday when Robert sent for him and Reynauld to come to the castle. This instruction was a command, not a request, because it was accompanied by the word 'urgent,' which Robert's seneschal Rudolf, personally delivered. So Henry, who was executing 'team' maneuvers on horseback in one of Reynauld's heavily trodden fields, turned Meredith toward the castle and accompanied Rudolf and his teacher at a trot.

Robert met them just inside the castle wall near the stable. "Thank you for coming so quickly," the Count said earnestly. "We've received a letter from the Emperor, the Greek Emperor Alexius. It bears his wax seal but the letter is written in Latin, several pages of it. Henry, I'm hoping you will read it to us. I have a clerk who can read a little Latin but not nearly as well as you. "

"Of course," said Henry.

"Thank you," said Robert as they hurried toward the twisting entryway to the inner castle. "I cannot imagine why Alexius would be writing to me. Perhaps it is his condolences on my father's passing or perhaps he doesn't know about my father's death and the letter is actually to my father. Reynauld, thank you for coming. You too may be able to verify the seal or the contents in some way."

"I shall do my best," replied the knight.

Robert took them to the little room in which his father had resided before he died. There was a fire burning in the fireplace but the real light in the room came from two torches that were ensconced upon the wall and were brightly burning. Robert's wife Clem, was there holding their new baby Baldwin in her arms while simultaneously clasping several pages of thin white paper between two of her fingers. She stepped toward Henry and leaned her head as if pointing to the pieces of paper. In response Henry nodded and carefully took the pages from her hand. The paper, Henry noted, was not the kind used by Rome for dispatches and filings. It was much thinner, almost transparent. The youth stepped toward the wall where the brightest light would illuminate the writing. When he got there, he looked back to Robert for permission to begin. The Lord of Flanders nodded his head affirmatively.

Henry cleared his throat. "To Robert, Lord and glorious Count of the Flemings, and to all the princes in the entire realm, lovers of the Christian faith, laymen as well as clerics, the Constantinopolitan Emperor extends you greeting and peace in our same Lord Jesus Christ, His Father and the Holy Spirit.

"Oh most illustrious Count and special comforter of the Christian faith, I wish to make known to you how the most sacred empire of the Greek

Christians is being sorely distressed by the Patzinaks and the Turks, who daily ravage us and unintermittently seize our territory, and dispense promiscuous slaughter and indescribable killing of Christians. They circumcise the boys and youths of the Christians over the Christian baptismal fonts, and in contempt of Christ, they pour the blood from the circumcision into the said baptismal fonts and compel these youths to urinate thereon; and thereafter they violently drag the boys around in the church, compelling them to blaspheme the name of the Holy Trinity and their belief therein. Noble matrons and their daughters, they defile in adultery...and there are matters of even greater depravity. Men of every age: boys, adolescents and alack, what from the beginning has never been said or heard, even bishops whom they defile with the sin of sodomy. They desecrate and destroy the holy places in numberless ways, and they threaten them with worse treatment.

"For almost the entire land, from Jerusalem to Greece, has already been invaded by them, and now almost nothing remains for them except Constantinople, which they are threatening to snatch away from us very soon, unless the aid of God and the faithful Latin Christians should reach us swiftly. Accordingly, for love of God and out of sympathy for all Christian Greeks, whatever faithful warriors of Christ you may be able to enlist in your own land—those of major as well as those of minor and middle condition—with whom you may fight with all your strength, you and they shall joyfully receive in heaven a glorious and ineffable reward.

"Do not let the precious Christian relics here in Constantinople be lost to these heathens: the pillar to which He was bound, the lash with which He was scourged, the scarlet robe in which He was arrayed, the crown of thorns which circled His brow, the larger part of the wooden cross on which He was crucified, the nails with which He was affixed, and the linen clothes found in the sepulcher after His resurrection.

"However, if the Latin knights should be unwilling to fight for these, the holiest of relics and their love of gold be greater, they will find more of it here than in all the world. The treasure vaults of the churches in Constantinople abound in silver, gold, gems, precious stones and silken garments. We shall pay princely sums to princely warriors.

"Therefore, lest you should lose the kingdom of the Christians and, what is greater, the Lord's Sepulcher, act while you still have time; and then you will have not doom, but the reward of heaven!"

When Henry finished reading the Emperor's letter, he looked up to discern its affects upon his audience. Robert's cheeks were wet with tears, Clem's too. Reynauld and the seneschal were dry-eyed, but the knight's jaw was set so tightly that the muscle just below his ear was twitching. There was a long silence while only the fire crackled.

Finally, Robert raised his gaze and spoke very softly. "If we leave now with a significant following, the German Emperor will take our lands as soon as he can muster a force. His father tried. He will too. But," the Count mused, "there might still be a way." Robert turned to the 'Master of war-craft.'

"Reynauld, perhaps you could take a letter from me to the Pope. Henry could write it. And we could ask if Urban would guarantee the safety of our lands by means of a papal fiat threatening excommunication for those who wickedly attempt to steal our property. Pope Gregory certainly set the Emperor back with that before. On the other hand, the Emperor may not feel so encumbered now that he has his own 'anti-pope.' Nevertheless, we can ask Urban about the efficacy of this sort of guarantee. I want to think on this a little longer but time is very important.

"Henry, you come back here after your afternoon session is over. I'll be ready by then to recite the letter. And Reynauld, you make arrangements to have your best knight-in-training take your place at the school as I shall have you deliver this letter to Pope Urban. You may be gone for as long as three months tracking down Urban. I'll want opinions from you both about what I should include in the letter. At least now Urban is back in Rome. That should save us some time."

"So," said Reynauld as he and Henry exited the castle, "who would you pick to oversee the school while I'm gone?"

Henry had not expected to be asked but he had been thinking about who Reynauld would pick. In his mind there were really only two candidates, the brothers Ludolf and Bartholomew. Ludolf was the older. He was not Henry's favorite. Being taciturn and prickly, he was hard to like. Bartholomew, on the other hand, had become a close friend. Like his brother he too was quiet, but unlike Ludolf he was friendly and a thinker. He even beat Henry at chess occasionally. But still Henry wasn't sure that Bart could hold the students' attention the way Ludolf would.

"I think Ludolf or Bart would be the best to choose between, probably Ludolf since he's older and has more experience. But you'll have to be clear with him what you expect: what classes, speakers, topics, those sorts of things."

"I thought you'd choose Bart."

"I would have," replied the young trainee, "if I thought you'd be gone longer than three months. But Ludolf has earned the opportunity and it's more important to him."

As it turned out, Ludolf did a good job overseeing the aspiring would-be-knights. In a way, Henry thought Ludolf's aloofness helped him teach effectively. He didn't get off-topic with stories and he didn't let up on any student no matter their age, size or status. He was an unyielding task-master.

Reynauld was back in slightly less than three months. His challenge had been determining the Pope's itinerant schedule. But once he'd gotten that, he tracked down Urban, delivered Robert's letter and brought back a response. Accordingly Henry was again called to the castle to read it. Unlike the letter from Alexius, the Pope wrote on thick Roman paper and was very brief. It simply said that he, Urban, had received a similar letter from Alexius and would be discussing it at an upcoming synod at Piacenza in March. It seemed to Henry that Urban's letter hadn't really answered Robert's question about protecting his lands but Robert seemed happy enough with the reply so Henry, thinking that Robert perhaps didn't really want to go, said nothing more on the subject.

But in the early fall, Robert received another letter from the Pope and Henry was of course called in to read it. His Holiness was in Toulouse and wanted Robert to know that he would be in Reims in February to conduct a most holy mass. He hoped 'very fervently' to meet Robert there and discuss 'protections' he was considering for Christian lords and knights who, by making a pilgrimage to Jerusalem, might leave their lands and fiefs less protected until their return. Robert considered the invitation to Reims neigh-on to a command from God and immediately announced that he'd take the whole school and as many of his liegemen as possible. Henry was ecstatic. He'd never dreamed of meeting the Pope.

KNIGHTHOOD
November 1095

Surveying his youthful protégés, Reynauld stood spear-straight. His students were arrayed before him dressed like him in their best regalia: chainmail shirts, leather pants and boots. Their clothing had been burnished or oiled to a glistening sheen. Each stood in phalanx formation with the oldest Ludolf, on the left and the youngest Thorvald, on the right.

Reynauld liked lining them up this way because it showed how immensely they'd matured. Ludolf was a full-grown man. At his neck and chest, his muscular physique pressed forth his hauberk, attesting to his years of exercise and training. His hair, dropping to his shoulders, was black and straight and framed his face which, as always, was serious and set. One look was enough to warn anyone that he was not a man to trifle with.

Next to him stood Bartholomew his brother, who'd obviously tried to damp and pat down his unruly hair. With his helmet on Bart looked just like Ludolf, strong and quiet. With it off one could see immediately that the brothers' personalities were not the same. Othocar and Hugh stood next beyond Bart. Each of them could be counted on in a tight spot.

The last of the five to be knighted was Henry who also stood slightly in front of the others. He was the tallest of the group yet still only fourteen, the youngest of those to be knighted that day.

Had Reynauld made the final decision, he probably would have held him back a year longer but Robert had suggested that knighting the boy before their trip to Reims would be a good idea. It was unusual for Robert to express an opinion on who should be belted but Reynauld didn't contradict his lord. In fact he really liked the boy. At first he'd been a little put off by his education but when Henry had stood right up for his values and articulated their importance, the 'Master' had changed his mind. It was a rare thing for one of his students to address him so boldly. But he had done it respectfully and he'd been right.

So Reynauld thought Henry had earned his place among the honored this day. Reynauld continued to move his gaze down the line until his eyes finally fell on the youngest. Thorvald was seven, one of their orphans. For his age, the boy was not particularly small, but compared to the five standing a step forward, he looked, nay he was...tiny. The five who would be knighted had trained for years. They were grown men and could prove it on the field of battle.

The 'Master of Warfare' lifted his stare to the crowded great-room. It was packed with people. To make room for the event, the benches and tables had been removed save the one directly in front of Robert and Reynauld. There were upwards of a hundred onlookers, many of them knights themselves, including Raymond of Laon and Hugh of Avesnes-Rochforte, who were the fathers of Othocar and Hugh, respectively. Behind the multitude and propped against the great room's walls were displayed the shields of all the knights who were present as well as the shields of the would-be five. There were more people present than at Christmas or Easter, which Reynauld thought was not that surprising since there was no higher honor for a living man than knighthood.

Next to Reynauld stood his lord, Robert Count of Flanders, wearing a scarlet robe over his hauberk and cauf. It was his best robe, the one he wore solely for a knighting ceremony. On the table in front of them were the five fresh, leather belts that, when buckled on and accompanied by the blessing and swearing in, would forever designate these young men as knights. Reynauld reminded himself it was not the sword but the belt which signified knighthood. A sword was the sign of a 'freeman,' the belt was the sign of a knight. The 'Master' remembered his own 'belting,' which had occurred in this very room almost thirty years before. Robert 'the elder' had girded it around his waist. Robert had been a fine lord. Reynauld was only five when his father was killed. He didn't remember much of his father, just a big man on a horse—a knight of course. Nor had he ever learned how his father died. But he did remember Count Robert coming to their little fief and telling his mother that her husband was dead. His mother had cried. But when she'd stopped, Robert said something which Reynauld never forgot. 'When a knight has died, it is the lord's duty to care for his vassal's family.'

Robert took Reynauld with him to his castle and brought him up as one of the family. And for the boy's mother, the Count found a castellan to marry her. Reynauld was given his knight's belt by Robert when he was fifteen and fought for his lord in the wars against the German Emperor. Later Reynauld went to Jerusalem with him on pilgrimage. They'd hunted, hawked and chased behind Robert's greyhounds and brachets many times.

Oh, he'd had a chance to marry but it was a small fief miles away from the goings on at the castle. At best he would have only been back during his annual forty day 'call-up.' He didn't really mind being a landless knight because he knew Robert would always keep him fed, clothed and horsed. Of course he had day-dreamed about some great victory bringing Robert vast estates and Robert giving one to him. But Flanders was predominately surrounded by great lords with enormous resources, so Robert's military exploits were primarily defensive, which naturally didn't acquire much in the way of vast estates. But he'd been loyal to Robert just as Robert had been loyal to him. That after all, was how vassalage was supposed to work. And there was one more thing. Robert was a man of God. He never asked nor expected, his men to do anything sinful.

Again Reynauld looked up and down the line of young men before him. These were good men, men with values, men of honor, men who would be brave in battle and support one-another no matter what. They could ride, attack, defend, hit a moving target with an arrow from a hundred feet away and even play chess.

Then just for a moment, the 'Master' turned his thoughts to himself. He had grown old. He felt it in his bones: his body ached, his endurance had lessened, he limped slightly from an old wound, his eyes weren't as good as they once had been. 'Jesus,' he intoned, 'I know my time is coming. I believe I have led a good life and I thank You for it. Please grant me one favor when You take me. Do it quickly. Please don't let me linger as my lord Robert did.'

'DEUS VULT'
February 1096

"**A**rgh!" Fagen's sleep-befuddled mind groped its way out of oblivion into a semi-wakeful state of confusion and fear. He was in his hut but it was too dark to see what woke him. Quickly he drew the back of his hand across his face. Water! He could hear rain pouring on the thatch roof above him. Another leak! He hadn't replaced the thatch last summer. He knew he should have but with his wife dying and then his son, each with that fever and not being able to breath, he just hadn't the time. His mind whirled through the usual questions. 'What did I do Lord to offend you so? Left like this, how can I ever do all the work? And Johnson and his wife gone too, their east furlong hadn't even been plowed, just went to weed. And their daughter Jan, left for me to take care of. Not enough hands and too many mouths to feed. At least she jumps when I tell her to and keeps me warm at night, but there's just too much to do.

Fagen sniffed the scent of fresh dung coming from the cow's stall behind him. The odor was blowing along the narrow walkway where the mud wall had cracked open last fall. The dim gray light outside just permitted Fagen to discern the outline of the fissure. With this heavy rain falling, it suddenly occurred to him that it might be later than he'd first thought. He pushed himself up off the dirt floor. The effort provoked a groan as he felt the muscles in his lower back complain. He had to be in Reims with those six grommets so the smith's son could swap him new ones. It would cost him one of the two pennies he still had from last fall's fair. Too much he thought, but there was no one else who could make new ones. He had to replace those grommets every year or the plow would break.

He kicked his dirty sheepskin blankets onto Jan. She needed to be up and collect that dung before the stupid cow stepped on it. Manure was useful in the field not where they slept. He was wearing his leather tunic but he had to search for his boots. Despite the holes in the walls it was still dark. The fire in the middle of his little hovel had burned down to only a couple of visible embers. He knew though, that beneath that heap of soot, there were still hot coals which would reignite when Jan put on fresh kindling. To prod the girl, Fagen poked the pile of skins with his foot.

"Wake up," he growled. "I need to be fed. I've got a half day's walk to town ahead of me." As he waited for Jan to show some sign of rising, he wondered what else he might take to the smith. Did his sickle bar need new grommets? No. He couldn't afford all that. His whetstone was worn down but it probably had a year of life left in it. With his plow regrommeted, he planned to swap some time plowing on the lord's fields. That would give him some favor with the steward which he could use for most anything later on.

Suddenly a strong gust of wind ripped across the thatch roof above and noisily squeezed through the cracks in the hovel's walls, causing the fire's smoldering pile of soot to swirl up. As he breathed in the contagion, Fagen choked and began to cough. The cough continued until he finally cleared his throat and spit phlegm onto the dirt floor. Recovered but still irritable, he kicked the the heap of worn skin blankets again but this time much harder and with result as the blankets moved noticeably. Finally Fagen stepped to the wood pile and lofted two rotten but fairly dry, sticks of kindling atop the pile of embers. The coals scattered, bringing into view several pulsing red fagots. As Jan rose from amidst the skins, the coals' dim light played upon her face painting it a dark red. Her countenance reminded him of the gargoyles that hung above the entrance of the church, threatening yet not.

Her nose was thin and when she smiled her teeth were black in places. He couldn't remember how old she was, probably ten or twelve. He hadn't fucked her yet. Within himself it was a close-fought battle. In the reddish light, she looked old not becoming. For a moment, Fagen wondered what she might think of him. Her father's friend? The neighbor who'd helped cut hay and stack it? An old man? When he thought about being old, he realized he couldn't remember how old he was.

His oldest son had taken on a tenancy, said he wouldn't wait for his free-hold inheritance since it was too small for a family anyhow. Before he was fifteen, he'd fathered three children by the widow there. So he'd been right that Fagen's little piece of ground would have been too small for him. Fagen's daughter got pregnant right after she'd begun to bleed. The priest married her to Ted and then she went off to Ted's father's tenancy which was so small that a May frost would starve them all to death. But Jan's parents' property was large enough to feed five or six mouths. Fagan wondered why he hadn't thought about trying to get hold of it... Now that was a good idea. He'd stop by to see the steward on his way back from

Reims. Yes, this very day. Then he'd ask his daughter to come back. Her husband was a real worker.

By mid-morning Fagen had reached Reims. He'd worn his straw hat to deflect some of the downpour. But shortly after he'd left, the hard rain let up and was replaced by a dense, chilling mist. In a way it was worse. It seeped beneath his tunic and made him shiver. For a winter weekday, the town was much busier than usual. Coming from the north, he hadn't noticed any travelers. But once he'd gotten into town, he saw lots of people and not all peasants either. There were several knights with their sergeants and attendants, a couple of burghers wearing wool coats and funny-looking hats and, strangest of all, a churchman in a red robe with several servants following him. Fagen was mulling over the oddity of the churchman when he finally got to the smithy. It was really a very small smithy: a couple of horse stalls, a forge, numerous tools laying about, and a pitched wooden roof, which Fagen knew was purposely not thatched for fear of a fire caused by sparks from the forge. The smith's son was already there. He was beating on a sickle-bar with a large hammer. The bar was a dark orange and the boy was hammering upon its left side as it lay on the anvil. Fagen could tell by the darkness of its color that the iron had cooled considerably from its most heated state. There were no other people about, which was surprising since he'd assumed that the abundance of people he'd seen elsewhere would mean a long wait at the smithy. He couldn't imagine why else they'd all be in town.

"Hullo," called Fagen to the young smith who he assumed hadn't heard him coming due to the loud clanging noises he was making.

The smith looked up and then put his hammer down. "Fagen, here with your grommets are you?"

"I am," the older man wheezed.

"None too soon," said the smith. "I've got the new ones right here somewhere." The young man started to wander about looking among his tools, wooden chests, metal bars and various parts and pieces that were scattered throughout the shop. "I'll be closing up right after I find them."

"Closing up?" Fagen asked. "Are you giving up your trade?"

"No, no," replied the youth. "I meant closing for the afternoon. I'm going to hear the Pope."

Fagen laughed loudly. "The Pope!" he giggled and then laughed some more. Finally he had to breathe and so was able to speak. "Am I... am I to believe you're making a pilgrimage to Rome?" Several more guffaws followed.

While patiently waiting for Fagen's laughter to cease, the young smith stared at his customer. At last he got a chance to speak. "You haven't heard about the Pope coming?"

"No, no," chortled Fagen while his straw hat bobbed up and down as he continued to laugh. "I haven't heard but I suppose he's come here to say mass for us."

"Yes," replied the smith, "and when you stop laughing, you can go see him. It's a noon service, and right now they're setting up a platform for him to stand on in the field beside the church. There are too many people coming to fit them all inside."

Fagen's giggles ceased. "You're serious?"

"Ah, here they are," the smith said as he bent to pick up several metal objects. "It's six you want, isn't it?"

"Yes," replied Fagen, "but tell me true. Is the Pope really here?"

The young smith smiled at his grizzled customer. "Yes," he answered, "and we can go together if you'll let me just put this sickle bar into the water trough first. Have you got your penny?"

Never in his entire life had Fagen seen so many people. He heard one of the knights standing near him say there were at least a thousand people there. Fagen didn't know how many a thousand was. He could only count to ten. But he knew there were a lot. The entire field was packed with onlookers. Set up in the middle was a wooden platform perhaps six feet above the ground. There was no one on it yet, but there were four black robed monks keeping a path open back to the church's side entrance. Fagen assumed the Pope would come from there. Standing right in front of the platform, there were several men in scarlet robes whom Fagen supposed were church officials of great importance. Each wore a tall, white, conical hat and held a long crook. Behind these men there were about twenty horses each tethered by some means, which Fagen couldn't see. Near on his left there was a banner atop a long pole that had been stuck into the ground. Around it there were knights in their chainmail armor, foot soldiers, archers and entire families, some even with young children. For just a moment Fagen wistfully thought how wonderful it would have been if his wife could have been with him to see all this.

At that moment, a murmur began to spread through the throng of spectators. At first Fagen wasn't sure what was happening, but when he glanced toward the path the four monks were keeping open, he saw a procession of scarlet issuing forth from the church. Six churchmen were marching out. Like their brethren in front of the platform, they also wore scarlet robes, tall hats and carried crooks. But the last one's hat, while appearing the same, was somehow different. It had some substance circling it that cast off a yellowish hue. Even through the thick mist, Fagen could discern...

"Gold!" he heard someone say.

Yes, thought the rustic, it is gold. He'd never actually seen gold before. But this was it. He heard the crowd issue a soft 'oooh.' This really was the Pope and gold too, just like the three kings had brought to Jesus in Bethlehem. Perhaps the very same gold!

As the man with the golden hat approached the platform, Fagen watched him split off and begin to climb the wooden steps. Once he reached the top, he stopped and waited for complete silence. Finally he lifted his arms to indicate he was about to speak.

"Oh, race of Franks, race from across the mountains, race beloved and chosen by God as is clear from many of your works, set apart from all other nations by the situation of your country as well as by your Catholic faith and the honor that you render to the holy Church, to you our discourse is addressed and for you our exhortations are intended." Despite the distance, Fagen could hear the pontiff quite clearly. "We wish you to know that a grievous cause has led us here, for it is the imminent peril threatening you and all the faithful, which has brought us hither.

"From the confines of Jerusalem and from the city of Constantinople a grievous report has gone forth and has repeatedly been brought to our ears; namely, that a race from the kingdom of the Persians, an accursed race, a race wholly alienated from God, has violently invaded the lands of those Christians and has depopulated them by pillage and fire. They have led away a part of the captives into their own country, and a part they have killed by cruel tortures. They have either destroyed the churches of God or appropriated them for the rites of their own religion. They have destroyed alters after having defiled them with their uncleanness. The kingdom of the Greeks is now dismembered by them and has been deprived of territory so vast in extent that it could only be traversed in two months' time.

"On whom therefore is the labor of avenging these wrongs and of recovering this territory incumbent if not you? You upon whom, above all other nations, God has conferred remarkable glory in arms, great courage, bodily activity, and strength to humble the heads of those who resist you? Let the deeds of your ancestors encourage you and incite your minds to manly achievements—the greatness of King Charles and his son, Louis, and your other monarchs who have battled the heathens in Spain and have extended the sway of the Church over lands previously possessed by the pagan. Let the holy sepulcher of our Lord and Savior, which is possessed by unclean nations, especially arouse you, and the holy places that are now treated with ignominy and irreverently polluted with the filth of the unclean. Oh, most valiant soldiers and descendants of invincible ancestors, do not degenerate but recall the valor of your progenitors.

"Let none of your possessions retain you, nor your family affairs. For this land you inhabit, shut in on all sides by the seas and surrounded by the mountain peaks, is too narrow for your large population; nor does it abound in wealth; and it furnishes scarcely food enough for its cultivators. Let those who have formerly been accustomed to contend wickedly in private warfare against the faithful fight against the infidel and bring to a victorious end the war which ought already to have begun. Let those who have hitherto been robbers now become soldiers. Let those who have formerly contended against their brothers and relatives now fight against the barbarians as they ought. Let those who have formerly been mercenaries at low wages now gain eternal rewards.

"Let hatred, therefore, depart from among you, let your quarrels end, let wars cease and let all dissentions and controversies slumber. Enter upon the road to the Holy Sepulcher, wrest that land from the wicked and subject it to yourselves. That land which, as the scripture says, 'floweth with milk and honey,' was given by God into the power of the children of Israel. Jerusalem is the center of the earth; the land is fruitful above all others like another paradise of delights. This spot the Redeemer of mankind has made illustrious by His advent, has beautified by His sojourn, has consecrated by His death and has glorified by His rise into heaven.

"However, the people of this royal city are now held captive by the enemies of Christ and are forced to worship a false god. They cry out to you to deliver them from their bondage, they implore your aid. From you especially they seek succor because God has conferred upon you above all other races great glory in arms. Accordingly, undertake this journey eagerly for the remission of your sins, with the assurance of the reward of imperishable glory in the kingdom of heaven."

When the Pope finished speaking, there was a moment of complete silence. Then a voice from just behind the wooden platform called out. "Deus la volt!"

Fagen didn't catch the words until a young knight on his left raised his voice. "God wills it." Immediately, a thousand other voices joined in. "God wills it... God wills it. God wills it.. ."

Eventually, His Eminence the Pope raised his arms for quiet. "Most beloved brethren, the Lord has said 'where two or three are gathered in my name, I too shall be there.' Although this cry issued forth from all your mouths, the origin was clearly Him. He alone could implant this magnify-cent outcry in your breasts and then pull it forth so wondrously all at once. Therefore, let this be your war cry in combat against the infidel because it has been given to you by God Himself... God wills it!"

The crowd immediately picked up the call, "God wills it. God wills it. God wills it," Finally the pontiff raised his arms again.

"Whoever of you shall commit to this holy pilgrimage and shall make his vow to God to that effect, may wear the sign of the cross on his forehead or on his breast. When he shall return from his journey having fulfilled his vow, then let him place this cross on his back. My churchmen here have cut crosses from their robes to give to those of you devoted enough to undertake this great pilgrimage."

The Pope's words may have continued but Fagen couldn't hear them over the tumultuous uproar as the crowd surged forward.

FAREWELLS
February 1096 – March 1096

It was noon when Henry and Johnnie arrived at Dol. Of their ten days traveling, the first and the last were exactly the same—gray, wet and thick with heavy mist. Having arrived fairly early in the day, Henry had a chance to greet his parents, turn over his and Johnnie's horses at the stable, eat a little at the kitchen and hand his young friend over to his younger brother Edmond. With all these things attended to, he repaired to the great-room and its fire. His father had gotten there ahead of him, which at first led Henry to think this might be the right moment to talk to his father about going to Jerusalem. But before he could begin, his mother came in and immediately asked him if he would recount all his adventures to the household at dinner. Accordingly Henry postponed his talk with Walter.

After dinner, Henry was called upon to recount his experiences in Flanders up to his becoming a knight. The audience included several of Walter's knights, so the designated relater decided to tell stories he thought they'd like to hear. He began with Reynauld's experiences in Constantinople, Robert 'the elder's' receipt of John the Baptist's left hand from Alexius, explanations of the various siege weapons he'd been taught to use, the theory of coordinated horse warfare and finally a description of the ceremony used when he had been knighted. With all that completed, Henry raised his cup of mead and issued a salute to Count Robert, Reynauld and all the speakers and teachers who had helped him and his fellow students toward knighthood.

But just when Henry was thinking he could relax for the rest of the evening, his brother Edmond loudly interrupted. "Aren't you going to tell us about meeting the Pope and the great pilgrimage?"

Henry's stomach sank as he realized Johnnie must have told Edmond about their meeting with Pope Urban and also about the planned pilgrimage to save the eastern Christians. Apparently he would have to immediately share those events but he wouldn't allow himself to be baited into having to ask his father and mother for permission to go to Jerusalem while sitting in front of the entire household—knights, attendants, servants and other help. He'd tell them of his meeting with the Pope and of His

Holiness' call for a great pilgrimage to save Christians, particularly in Jerusalem, from the cruel horrors being forced upon them by the vicious Turks; tell them of the torture, rape and even sodomy of innocent women and children. All this he would describe just as Urban had in his speech. And then he'd take his father and mother up to the battlements where they could talk.

"Yes," responded the young knight as he raised his voice. "Let me tell you of Pope Urban's sermon at Reims, of the infamous goings-on in Jerusalem and of His Holiness' call nay, his mustering of all good Christians to defend the holy land and its people."

~**~

When Audrey, Walter and Henry stepped out onto the castle's roof, it was cold and clear. The sky spread forth black above them yet it was sprinkled with thousands of far away, tiny lights which collectively shone brightly enough to make the castle walls clearly visible. Henry's father and mother made their way to their wooden beam and sat down. Audrey drew her coat around her shoulders and Walter leaned his crutches against the nearest parapet. Facing them, Henry sat down with his back against the wall.

Henry was the first to break the silence. "Robert has asked me to go with him to Jerusalem. He's taking three thousand men and plans to meet other lords on the way."

Audrey's gasp was audible but Walter was the first to speak. "Do you want to go?"

"Yes," Henry replied. "I feel compelled to go. I'm not exactly sure why I feel so certain but I do."

Walter looked his son directly in the eye. "Henry, you are now a man and a knight and therefore are ready to set your life's direction. Robert would not have asked you if he didn't think you were ready. Your mother and I shall pray for your safe return."

When Walter finished speaking, Audrey thrust toward her son and dropping onto her knees, clasped his legs in her arms. "May God be with you," she whispered. "May God be with you."

The following afternoon Henry was seated next to his father in their great room. They were awaiting a chapel service at which all those who wished to come could pray for Henry's safe return. Despite the fire being close at hand, the great room was a little chilly.

"Henry," said Walter in a serious tone, "I have something of importance to discuss with you. Some of my men have asked me if they can go with you: my squire Bart and both of Manion's sons Alfred and Glendon. Given the military nature of your pilgrimage, I assume that Robert would like to have as many good men as possible. Is that your belief?"

"Yes," Henry replied. "Robert is taking all the fighting men whom he feels are competent and trustworthy."

"So," continued the crippled knight, "what do you think of the three I named?"

For a moment Henry paused while he digested the merits of the three men whom his father had mentioned. "I believe they're all worthy," he finally said, "but I'd keep Alfred here. He is the oldest son, and therefore the one who should oversee his fief. He is capable enough to go but so is Glendon. Bart is a good man and has only the stable and your personal needs to oversee. If you can do without him, the pilgrimage will be well served."

"I agree," said Walter. "I need to keep Alfred and a few of the other knights to protect us from the unforeseen. Glendon however, has no prospects and Bart is too able to be held back. You'll particularly like his foraging skills. He can fill the cooking pot when others are going hungry. I'll tell the two of them to be ready to go right after the service. I received one other request regarding you leaving. Do you remember Mariteth, the midwife?"

"Of course," responded Henry. "I have not seen her for years but I remember her well. She's always been interested in my welfare. What did she want?"

"To see you for a moment," replied Walter. "I don't think she'll come into the chapel but I told her she could wish you well after the service."

"Good," said Henry, "I've always liked her."

"Well," said Walter, "hers were the first human hands to touch you."

"Yes," replied the young knight. "Mother told me that too, that she was the midwife at my birth."

"Yes," said Audrey who had quietly entered the room, "and a hard birth it was, you being so big."

Henry smiled and beckoned his mother to come and sit down. Once she'd done so, Henry cleared his throat and spoke again. "Just in case," he murmured, "I want to thank you both for being my parents, for the job you've done raising me and…I love you."

"We love you too," whispered Audrey. "We love you too."

LEADERSHIP

September 1096 – October 1096

Robert of Flanders ascended the narrow, circling stairway toward the roof and ramparts high atop his castle. Despite his square physique, his strides were long and rapid. Every inhabitant in Flanders knew their liege lord to be a man of drive and determination. For months he'd planned every aspect of this great pilgrimage: the goal—Jerusalem; the route—to Italy, across the Adriatic, the Via Egnatia, Constantinople and finally the Holy Land; the schedule—to reach Constantinople in time for the Spring fighting season and therefore Pontarlier in upper Burgundy by October 15th where they would meet Robert of Normandy and Stephen of Blois and cross the Adriatic before the winter weather shut off passage; who'd go—as many fighting men as possible but only those committed and reliable; rules – their mission had been ordained by God. Therefore there could be no looting, raping or sinful acts commited along the way; these men were God's soldiers and must be worthy of Him. And he'd planned the victualing—Robert had sent ahead as far as Pontarlier for provisions to be acquired and stocked. He would also take with him, as should each man according to his means, sufficient wealth to acquire supplies along the way. By means of loans collateralized against three different monasteries, he'd amassed a large sum of coin. Additionally he'd scavenged through his castle and loaded his train with gold and silver challises, rings and belts, many of which were inlaid with valuable jewels and precious stones.

This meeting atop his castle would address the 'who would stay' part of his plan. When Robert exited the stairwell, he saw his two most trusted supporters waiting for him: Clementia his wife and John his head castellan.

"Good day," the Count pronounced powerfully as he looked squarely into the eyes of Clementia and then repeated this personal form of connection with John. "I wish to review with you some important points regarding the oversight of things here while we're gone."

Robert paused for a moment to see if either his wife or his knight had any preliminary questions. Clementia already oversaw all the castle's activities as well as the bookkeeping for the county's agricultural and financial goings-on. She was intelligent, educated and well-born. Robert had complete confidence in his wife's abilities. John was an older knight who had served as castellan during Robert 'the elder's' sojourn to Jerusalem and Constantinople. He was loyal and would follow orders.

When neither responded to his pause, the Count continued. "Clem will be in charge."

Turning to John, Robert spoke just as assertively. "John, I'm sure you would like to go to Jerusalem with us but I need you here. Your responsibilities will include command of all the remaining knights and foot soldiers as well as handling my judicial duties whereever needed throughout the county. Please consult with Clementia regularly on all things so you both know everything that's going on and nothing will go astray. Do you each understand your roles?"

Robert looked at Clementia and then at John. As he did, each answered, "Yes."

"Good," said Robert, "If I were less certain of either of you, I would spend more time reviewing the details but I know I don't need to. There is however one thing more. I think you both know we'll be traveling with Baldwin of Alost, Count of Ghent and a good friend. He's mustered five hundred men so together we'll have over twenty-five hundred. This will leave Flanders with so few trained men that we shall be at risk to enemies who may choose not to go on this pilgrimage. I have received guarantees from Pope Urban that the Papacy will protect our lands from any such interlopers should they attempt an invasion while we're gone. But the Pope hasn't soldiers with which to make good his promise, only his God-given power to withhold from the perpetrators the eternal glory of heaven: to excommunicate a count, duke, king or emperor, particularly Emperor Henry who might try to take Flanders from you while we are in the Holy Land. So if the Emperor should raise an army and thrust it upon you, here's what I want you to do. Establish a defensive posture within this and other castles and do not provoke him. Certainly there will be an opportunity to parlay. When it comes, show him this." The Count reached inside his surcoat, upon the breast of which was woven a bright crimson cross and pulled forth a thick piece of vellum that he proceeded to unfold. Robert then handed it to Clementia.

"This you may show to the German Emperor if merely telling him is insufficient. Should he still hold to a sinful course, give up those castles you must. Such action on your part will not be shameful but will save lives and be reversed later by God and the Pope. Be very certain though that you not give the Emperor any sign of fealty; don't make any promises or give him any permission whatsoever. Do you understand?"

"Yes," replied Robert's commanders.

"Good," said the Count. "Now one more thing... If for some reason God should find us unworthy in our effort and we should not return, Clementia you will likely have to find a husband, more likely you will have a great number of suitors. Our duty as always is to God and to those who serve us," Robert smiled broadly, "so pick the very best."

Clementia stepped forward and clasped her arms around her husband. Robert powerfully returned the hug. When the two separated, the Count of Flanders smiled again and reached his hand to John.

The next morning, Robert's force began to move out. It was certainly large enough to be unwieldy but due to its high proportion of veterans and their ubiquitous leader, it commenced its journey in good order. Robert expected nothing less. His plan called for a march to Pontarlier in two weeks' time with leeway of two days to cover the unexpected. During this estimated fortnight Robert intended to meet all his men. He'd establish himself personally, assess the leaders, reiterate the rules of travel, review the flag and horn communications and if time allowed, begin to identify potential leaders from among the novices. Knowing who to promote was important as there would surely be casualties. Most important was that he establish reciprocal trust and respect with his men. There would come a time when his soldiers' faith in him would either hold their ranks together or break them into little pieces. That personal bond, not friendship but respect, would then make all the difference.

Shortly Robert found himself riding beside a group of foot soldiers, none of whom he recognized. Looking down at the nearest man, the Count spoke. "Good man, where are you from?"

The young soldier wore a thick leather shirt, a conical metal helmet and, strapped to his side, bore a sword encased in a roughly crafted scabbard. "Cambray, my lord."

"Ah, Cambray," Robert called out quite loudly, "I thought you had the look of a soldier about you. Cambray has always produced fine soldiers. Did you make that scabbard yourself?"

"No, my lord. T'was my dad made it."

"It looks quite sturdy." Robert swung his right foot back over his mount's rump and lowered himself to the ground. "May I walk with your contingent while my horse rests?"

"Certainly," replied the young soldier. "We'd be honored."

"What's your name?" asked the Count.

"Gerald."

"And are these your friends?" continued Robert as he looked beyond Gerald at the group marching beside the would-be warrior. "I am Robert of Flanders. Please tell me your names."

"Bob, Josh, Frankson, Bart, Jon, Matthew."

"And you are all from Cambray?"

"Aye," the group chorused in response.

"Now," continued Robert, "it's been some time since I was in Cambray. Have they finished repairing the church steeple yet?"

"Yes," replied the group in perfect unison.

"Good," replied the Count, "then we are twice blessed: the steeple fixed and God's certain promise to us of eternal life in heaven should we fall in this battle against the heathens. The Pope himself told me that: eternal life in heaven. Well, my horse has probably regained his wind by now so I shall be off. Oh, Gerald after you camp tonight, find my bivouac and tell someone there that I said you were to be given a shield. We have a few extra and the Persians are archers." Robert remounted his horse and continued forward in search of another group of young soldiers.

Two days later Count Robert came on Henry of Dol who was easy to recognize due to his height and walking next to him was Bartholomew of Tournai displaying a great swatch of orange hair. "Henry, Bart! I've been expecting to see you. Where's Ludolf? Isn't he with you?" Robert dismounted beside his graduates.

"Reynauld appointed Ludolf to be the coordinator of our unit" responded Henry. "So he is acquainting himself with the leaders and coordinators of our brother units."

"Good," said Robert. "I'm glad to see that Reynauld is properly overseeing this group's welfare just as I would expect. You and Bart look well." Then, recognizing a young face amidst the throng, the Count burst forth "Johnnie!" The boy was holding the reins of three horses but dropped them when he heard the Count's boisterous greeting and ran forward to embrace his lord. Robert lifted the boy into the air but obviously found him heavier than he'd expected and put him down quickly.

"Johnnie," the Count exhaled employing an exaggerated breath, "you've grown to be quite big." The boy's grin spread from ear to ear.

Robert glanced beyond his young charges to several other men he hadn't seen before. "And who," he asked Henry, "are these fine fellows?"

"My lord," answered Henry, "this is Glendon, a knight of my father; and this is Bart, my father's squire."

In deference to the Count each of the men lowered his head.

"Welcome," said Robert loudly enough so all nearby could hear, "welcome to you all. I am greatly pleased that you have joined us on this most worthy pilgrimage. The crosses that you wear on your breasts reflect your commitment to God's will: that you will take Jerusalem and free its inhabitants from the cruel persecution put upon them by the awful Persians. Our mission is a most worthy one. But I must warn you that we may all suffer grievously, for our task is not just to defeat the heathens but to do so in a manner worthy of God. We must not be sinners while serving Him. We must not loot, rape, steal, or otherwise disregard His teachings. Your crosses represent your pledge to Him that you will act honorably and without sin. I commend you for your commitment and I honor your comradeship. Thank you for joining us in this great effort."

A brief silence followed before Robert spoke again, this time in a shrill yell. "Have you each committed yourself to the man beside you?"

"Yes," roared back the men around him.

"Will you protect his back?" Robert screamed.

"Yes!" shrieked back the crowd.

As the roar lessened slightly, the Count of Flanders raised his arms to quell the sound. "Before God I promise you that, though I shall be at the very front, I shall cover your backs as well."

Once more the soldiers roared but this time Robert mounted his horse and as he did, waved to Henry to follow him. Henry scurried to mount Meredith and, having done so, quickly caught up with the Count.

"Ride with me Henry for I wish to ask something of you. As we join other lords with many troops who speak many languages, I may need a coordinator of my own. The role will be different than Ludolf's in that I shall need someone who can speak Latin with these other lords' coordinators, to be a translator. Also, since you will mingle with these people and get to know them and the men within their retinues, I shall wish your counsel and advice. We may need to write in cases when we haven't time to call in a scribe. My peers will often have churchmen for their coordinators. I do not. But I have you Henry and I trust your judgment and abilities. Not all churchmen are as honorable as you. Your role will require that you keep near me at all times. It is not a promotion in that you will oversee other knights, but rather an opportunity for you to employ more of your skills and education in a way that will greatly help our cause. May I count on you?"

"Of course my lord," replied the young knight. "When shall I start?"

"Well," responded Robert, "are you overseeing Johnnie?"

"Yes," answered Henry.

"And your father's knight and squire too?"

"Yes," said Henry.

For a moment Robert thought. "See if Bart will take charge of them. You may tell him that I asked to have him do so. I sense your father's knight, Glendon I think you called him, may need some help getting acclimated. Take a day or two to help your people transition to Bart then report back to me. And thank you Henry. You will be a great help to me and to God's cause. Oh by the way, do you know that there's a little sprig from a fir tree on the shoulder of your surcoat?"

"Oh," said Henry as Robert began to turn his horse, "that's a sprig of spruce given to me by an old friend. She said it would bring me luck."

"Good," said Robert as he kicked his horse. "I hope it works for all of us."

CURTHOSE AND THE POET
October 1096

Robert of Flanders was conversing with a knight Henry didn't recognize. The man was tall, lithe and had gray hair setting in just above his ears. Additionally he was dressed very casually. He hadn't a helmet or a shield and appeared not even to be wearing chainmail under his surcoat. But what was most startling, Henry didn't notice until he got quite close. The man didn't have a cross on his surcoat. Henry knew that a few men had their crosses sewn on their cloak's shoulder and a handful of them had branded a cross on their foreheads but this man apparently had none anywhere.

"Henry, you're back," hailed Robert who had obviously seen his young knight approaching.

From the tone of Robert's voice, Henry instantly discerned that Robert was agitated over something. But before Henry could even quicken his pace, Robert waved his left arm toward the graying knight in front of him and called again. "Come and greet Count Stephen of Blois."

Henry trotted forward and bowed his head slightly as he introduced himself. "Sir, I am Henry of Dol. Count Robert has kindly allowed me to travel with his group to Jerusalem."

The Count of Blois bowed to Henry. "Well met good sir. I also have the pleasure of joining Count Robert enroute to Jerusalem. Robert has been telling me that you are his coordinator and are well lettered too. I look forward to talking with you further." The Count turned back to Robert.

"I can't give you any solace in regard to the Duke of Normandy. I assume he left around the first. That was what his last message said he planned to do. Our contingent sent out no riders as we didn't know what path he'd take. But regarding our food supplies, John of Chartres has been overseeing that for me. I have heard no complaints, so I assume he has it well in hand. We can ask him when we see him."

"If it meets with your approval," interjected the Count of Flanders, "may I ask Henry to seek John out and have the two of them determine our current supply situation and make plans for the acquisition of additional victuals between here and Rome if appropriate?"

"Of course," replied Stephen, "a very good idea."

"Henry," growled Robert, "John of Chartres, find him. Learn the status of Count Stephen's foodstuffs, their quantity and suitability and return here with the man so the two of you can give the Count and me a full report." Robert turned back to Stephen. "Where should Henry look for John?"

"Oh," replied Stephen, "I imagine amidst the supply trains. They're toward the..."

"I know where they are sir," interrupted Henry who was just starting to turn away.

"Good fellow," interjected Stephen, "please take my coordinator with you. This is Alexander my chaplain." Stephen waved his hand toward a short, round fellow of perhaps forty who was totally encased in a brownish robe made of sack cloth. "He has been a student at the Benedictine abbey at Vezelay and a tutor there as well. He knows John of Chartres and I'm sure he can help the two of you with your food computations."

Henry wasn't sure if the man was a monk or something else. His face was round but not as round as his belly which pushed the front of his robe out in front of him. The young knight glanced to Robert who in turn lowered his chin slightly. Henry took that as a sign of approval at least in terms of taking the man with him.

Henry's search to find John of Chartres was not enhanced by his having to take Alexander with him. The chaplain was neither talkative nor fast. To make matters worse, the monk's mule was ornery. It resisted all commands particularly those calling for speed. Quite suddenly a great gust of wind buffeted Henry and then, rushing beyond him, lifted the limbs of an old maple tree, turning its leaves over and exposing their silvery underbellies.

"A sign," shouted the youth as he turned in his saddle to look for the raindrops that would surely follow.

Alexander was riding just behind Henry. "Not a sign," the monk yelled back, "an omen...another omen!"

Henry's brow furrowed. He wasn't sure he'd heard what Alexander just said. "I said a sign," repeated the knight.

"Yes," responded Stephen's chaplain, "but it was an omen. A sign signifies something coming of relatively little importance. This was an omen because it portends a great calamity."

Still holding his gaze on Alexander, Henry reined in Meredith so the monk's mule could come up beside him. "What are you talking about?"

"I refer," replied the chubby chaplain whose mule had just of its own volition stopped beside Meredith, "to your improper use of the term 'sign' when you should have used the word 'omen.'"

Henry paused for a moment to ponder what this odd fellow was trying to communicate. He'd said practically nothing since they'd met earlier in the day and now he was splitting hairs regarding the definition of the word 'sign.' In regard to word definitions, Henry couldn't remember anyone correcting him before except Benito Tusculani. This fat monk in his sackcloth robe was becoming an irritant. But the youth reminded himself that his role as Robert's coordinator required him to get along with other lords' coordinators. With that considered, Henry tried to advance the conversation politely.

"I don't understand," he began, "why I should have used a word signifying something of great importance when I was only expecting rain to follow the wind. Have I missed something?"

Alexander was shorter than Henry in height and was seated on an animal considerably smaller than Meredith, so he was looking almost straight up as he answered. "Yes, but it's probably not your fault. I expect you are not trained in identifying the significance of signs, omens, portents, symbols, signals, guideposts or clues. Is that the case?"

Taken aback, Henry again paused before replying. Was this little, round fellow serious? Trained in signs, omens and portents? "No," the knight irritably responded. "My training has been in the Trivium and Quadrivium but," he added with a tinge of insincerity, "I'm sure I have more to learn."

"But you do believe in signs, don't you?" asked the suddenly loquacious monk.

"Yes, I suppose I do."

"Good," chortled Alexander almost triumphantly. "If you're willing to concede that one kernel of corn, I can take you to an entire field of it. There have been numerous signs and omens leading up to this pilgrimage. The floods, droughts and famines were probably the most dramatic harbingers. Sadly we have become so used to them that we no longer recognize them as omens. But the meteor and eclipse of the moon were unusual and clearly eye catching. Henry, the magnitude of a portended event can be quantified by the number and rarity of its harbingers. This gust of wind causing those maple leaves to turn up their undersides is not itself startling. But when one puts all these things together, the magnitude of the coming event grows. I've been assessing these omens for months... Have you followed my explanation so far?"

"Yes," replied the still irritated knight.

"Good," said Stephen's priest as he smiled up at the youth. "All these omens regard our great pilgrimage and promise great losses of men and even some of our leaders. Those leaves turning up their bellies like fish being caught in a net are our men. A huge number of our pilgrims are going to die." Alexander halted his lecture and looked at his student to gauge the impact of his words.

For a long time Henry stared directly back at Alexander. Finally he spoke. "Even if you are right that we shall lose a lot of our men on the way to Jerusalem, that doesn't mean we won't take the city and free the Christians there from Persian tyranny. Your omens don't say we shall fail do they?"

The pudgy monk cocked his head to one side for quite a while before responding. "My son, I cannot be certain of anything. I only identify these signs and omens as they happen and try to piece their meaning together. It is clear to me that many of our men will suffer and die on this pilgrimage. But despite this, if we press on I suppose victory may still be possible. I have not yet seen a sign or omen that speaks to victory or defeat. I only know our cost in lives will be immense. My lord, Stephen saw the meteor. Does that mean he will die on our trip? I don't know. The eclipse, which I also did not personally see, was reported to me through several intermediaries. I don't know if the moon was full, which way it faced or if perhaps it was in its crescent shape. An eclipse of a crescent moon would be a clear omen portending the fall of the Islamic Persians. Oh that that might be. But I have not yet heard or seen anything which suggests victory or defeat. Without a clear sign as to our outcome, I remain in doubt."

"Then I shall call you Thomas," responded Henry, "until you regain your faith in Him."

THE GREEK EMPEROR ALEXIUS
April 1097

"Well, they're finally gone," growled Alexius.

At Blachernae castle, which perched just inside the northwest corner of Constantinople's massive walls, the Emperor and his prime counselor stood in an elaborately decorated reception chamber. The room was magnificent: mosaic walls depicted Christ bearing His cross up Calvary Hill, green marble floors were inlaid with biblical quotations; finely crafted wooden chairs with soft embroidered pillows were set out for groups of four or five to converse together; plumper pillows were arrayed across the floor for anyone's convenience; the finest vases and pottery reposed upon thick oak tables and intricate ornaments adorned wooden wall cases.

Niketas' appearance matched the room. He wore a beautiful gold-embroidered, white tunic; his hair was dyed orange and held in place with numerous gold ringlets; his neck, arms and legs displayed a pudginess that denoted a person with no history of physical activity. The Emperor, to a superficial observer, also matched the room. Although he was not a particularly big man, his hair was stylishly graying, his skin was sun-bleached to a golden brown and his teeth were strikingly white. But contrary to the room's accoutrements, he wore a simple cloak which, hanging from his shoulders, left his arms and lower legs exposed. Those extremities were muscularly defined and revealed a physically active man.

"Yes, your highness," responded Niketas, "and it was mightily well done, turning a horrible threat into a potential beneficence."

"Yes Niketas, you're advice may save us again. This was our second monstrosity in just six months, and both from the north. Pope Urban never said any of his... his inductees would be coming through Belgrade. All our preparations, food and escorts were placed westward along the Via Egnatia as far as Dyrrachium. That imbecile preacher Peter, who came last summer had almost twenty thousand vulgus, 'pilgrims' he called them. They plundered, raped, murdered and pillaged from Hungry to here: endless thefts, broke into palaces and villas, even stole the lead off church roofs. And after we got them across the Bospherus, they slaughtered Greek Christians near Nicaea. And against my prefrence, I took your advice and forgave that idiot

Peter. If he'd been only a little less stupid, I'd have hanged him. You were right though. Now he's almost eager to sing our praises.

"But this Duke of Bouillon, this Godfrey fellow and his two brothers, they were a real threat: living off the land, pillaging is what I call it. But you were right about them too. 'Treat them carefully,' you said. And we did. I sent forth two of my best Norman soldiers, Rudolf and Roger. And Godfrey told them his men were misbehaving because we were imprisoning Hugh of Vermandois. Imagine after all we did for Hugh who was ship-wrecked and washed up on shore practically dead. We nursed him back to health and treated him like a king. But you were right on that one too because when we sent Hugh to allay Godfrey's concerns, things settled down; at least until I asked Godfrey to swear the oath to give us back any Greek cities or territories he captures from the Turks. Oh, didn't he splutter over that. 'No!' He'd already sworn to his own emperor. So when I twisted him some by withholding provisions, his men went to looting and then esca-lated by attacking our very own Pege Gate right here in Constantinople. It wasn't till our soldiers pushed them back that he finally came around and took the oath. Of course we did have to change the oath's wording, again per your suggestion, to subvert it to all previous oaths. When he finally agreed though, we had him out of here and across the straits in a flash. Good riddance!"

"A truly great challenge," offered Niketas, "but now they'll have to deal with Kilij Arslan and perhaps take Nicaea for you. Godfrey has twelve thousand men, mostly veterans, with a large number of knights on horse-back. Don't forget how well those Normans fight, my lord."

"Oh, I won't. But I still might have put Godfrey in his place if it hadn't been for that rumor you heard about Bohemond being near with his army and the possibility that he and Godfrey were contemplating joining forces to attack us."

"Niketas, think of all the challenges we've had: the Petchenegs in the north undone by a timely bribe to the Cumans; Canka and his fleet in Smyrna undone by a well placed rumor delivered to Kilij Arslan; Robert Guiscard in the west stealing Apulia and Calabria from us and then invading the Dalmatian coast; the Seljuk Turks pressing us constantly in the east; and conspiracies here in Constantinople too. All those we've defeated or held at bay with your advice Niketas, your very good advice."

"Thank you my lord but we haven't time for compliments. Bohemond,

Guiscard's oldest son and general of his army when they were beating us in Dalmatia, is only days away; and we know his lands in Italy aren't enough to suit him since his uncle and younger brother grabbed the most valuable territories before he could get back to defend them. All this considered I doubt that he's coming east for only religious reasons. Most likely he will be a Norman opportunist similar to Roussel of Bailleul. You remember him, the Norman who turned traitor after our loss at Manzikert and tried to set up a kingdom of his own in Rum."

"You're right Niketas. Bohemond's likely to be just the same: two-faced, self-seeking, capable and very, very dangerous. He'll be our greatest challenge; ironic that our friends should turn out to be even more threatening than our enemies. All I asked of Pope Urban was to send a few mercenaries like the five hundred Robert 'the elder' sent us from Flanders. How does that saying go? 'Be careful what you wish for."

"But first my lord, Robert 'the younger' is less than a day's ride from here. What think you of how to handle him?"

"I think Robert will be both a friend and a soldier. His father was a good friend, sent us five hundred horsemen, rode with me skirmishing in Anatolia and prayed with me in the Hagia Sophia. If his son is half the man his father was, and I've been told he is, he'll be a stalwart ally that we can count on."

"Good," responded Niketas, "then I'll send a linguistic Proedros trained in diplomacy to meet them and bring them here. We already have fields west of the city to camp Robert's army in. Am I correct to do that or should we move them quickly for embarkation across the Bospherus?"

Before replying, the Emperor thought for a moment. "Place Robert's troops in those fields for now. We can always press them forward if our meeting doesn't go smoothly. But assuming we get his oath and find him to be friendly, we can keep him and his army nearby. I expect Robert will be a calming influence on the other Latin leaders. We know he's acquainted with Robert of Normandy and with Count Stephen of Blois, the Conqueror's son-in-law. Right now I think Robert can do us more good if he's nearby than he can if he's across the Bospherus. What do you think?"

"I agree, my lord. A friend among the Latin leaders will certainly increase the likelihood of a positive reception for our ideas and strategy… particularly in regard to oaths. Should we plan to share our strategy with Robert?"

"Let's measure him first," replied Alexius. "If he's weak or not the supporter I expect, we can hold off sharing our strategy lest it be conveyed piece-meal. If however, he is a man we can trust, we'll treat him like a brother and apprise him of all our plans so he can articulately support them. I had hoped for a few thousand good soldiers from the Latins to help us save our city and the hinterlands in Rum. Now my hope is to supply and guide these western armies toward Nicaea, Antioch and perhaps Jerusalem—their objective not ours. I think their chance of reaching Jerusalem is at best unlikely. They will surely draw Muslim armies from Nicaea, Damascus, Aleppo, and even Bagdad and Cairo are possibilities. They may take Nicaea but Antioch and Jerusalem are major fortifications very unlikely to fall to a siege before relief arrives. We shall cover their flank though, by thoroughly investing Galatia and Caladonia, which, as you know, are our principle priorities. We may want to send a communication to our Fatimid friends in Cairo to assure them of our good intentions. They're a major trading partner and also an enemy of the Seljuk Turks. Anyhow Egypt is well beyond the Latin's goal and certainly beyond their reach."

CONTANTINOPAL
April 1097

Since landing at Dyrrachium on the west coast of Dalmatia, Henry thought the trip had been long and generally uninspiring. They'd been immediately met by John Comnenus, a relative of Emperor Alexius who had known Count Robert's father. There were sufficient food-stuffs along the way, particularly in Thessalonica, but hay, oats, and grain were less plentiful and the local populace, if willing at all, would only part with what they had at ridiculously high prices. Meredith seemed to be doing better than most of the animals. Henry attributed that to his squire Bart, who was more proficient than almost anyone else at both negotiating prices and 'finding' things. Nevertheless, Meredith's flanks were thinner than they had been when they'd started their trip.

About an hour's ride out of Constantinople, Henry was startled out of his 'nap' in the saddle by a horn blowing. Fortunately it wasn't a signal announcing an enemy nearby. Insead it was announcing the arrival of a young diplomat dressed in clothes of the brightest colors: his shirt a rich purple and his leggings polished leather. His hair was his most distinctive attribute. It was yellow, not natural blond as many of the Normans were, but a gaudy, bright almost iridescent yellow; and within its locks, it somehow held a score of golden ringlets.

One of Robert's knights pointed the fellow toward Henry.

"Good day Sir," said the young dandy to Henry in perfect Latin. "My name is Angelos Choniates. I have been dispatched by my Emperor Alexius Comnenus to bring Robert the Second of Flanders, a Count held in the highest regard by my Emperor, to the most magnificent city in the entire world...Constantinople."

After introductions were made and a billeting site for Robert's men identified, Robert, Henry and Angelos set off for the city. Almost immediately Robert asked Angelos which of the Christian armies had already arrived and how many men they had.

Angelos' reply was at best halting. "Ah... well... Hugh of Vermandois is here. He is the King of France's brother. His ship was wrecked on an island just south of here. He is now recovering in Constantople… Otherwise… not too many…"

Henry finally interrupted. "Angelos, what about other Latins? Are there other armies here yet?"

"Well," responded the stylish translator, "there has been an unusual group that came here last fall, mostly poor pilgrims. Their leader is an unwashed, itinerant preacher without training in arms. Peter they call him. And there were a few knights and soldiers too…perhaps a thousand."

"A thousand!" interrupted Henry in a startled tone, "How many were there all together?"

"Twenty thousand," replied Angelos peevishly.

"Twenty thousand!" gasped Henry, "and are they all still somewhere here by the city?"

"No," replied Angelos.

Henry waited for the Greek to continue his response but, after what seemed like a very long time had gone by, he pressed Angelos again. "Then where are they?"

"They're dead," blurted out the Greek, "at least most of them."

"Dead!" gasped Henry. "Twenty thousand dead!"

"A few survived," whispered Angelos, "Peter and a few others."

"How did they die?" asked Robert after he'd heard Henry's translation.

"They crossed the Hellespont and attacked Nicaea," replied the young Greek. "The Emperor told them to wait for the trained soldiers but they wouldn't wait and the Turks massacred them."

~**~

"Robert, please accept my condolences. Your father was a good friend of mine," said the Emperor as he rose from his gilded throne and stepped toward his guest. "I am so glad you have come," continued the Emperor as he reached forth his right hand and clasped Robert's.

There were perhaps thirty other people in the room. Almost all of them were Greeks. Each wore a white, light-weight frock accented with colorful lapels and ribbons. Each had his hair done up into swirls and waves held in place by silver or gold pins. The entire room reeked of perfume. Two other men stood atop the dais. One was a guard and, judging by his real blonde hair, Henry guessed he might be a Saxon. In any case, he stood in uniform:

tall, straight and inscrutable. The second man standing on the dais looked entirely different. He was medium in height, overweight and lacking any noticeable musculature. Interestingly his most prominent feature was also his eyes. They were practically black and certainly furtive. Instinctively Henry didn't trust him. The room itself was gaudy. The furniture was gilded with gold; the wall-hangings bedecked with jewels; the sculptures in their half-round crevices adorned with gold and jewels; and the panoply of pillows on the floor were all silk-covered. Henry had never seen anything like it. But he wasn't impressed. It was simply too 'ostentatio.'

Alexius then nodded to his entourage and all but Niketas and the Verangian guard left the room. Next Niketas pointed toward the numerous silk-covered cushions on the floor. "Rest yourselves upon these cushions and we'll talk."

Henry noted how much less formal everything became once the perfumed gaggle had left the room.

"Robert," began the Emperor, "you look just like your father. Surely though he has passed into Jesus' hands. He and I had many a fine time together both campaigning and wintering over here in the city. Did he show you the hand of John the Baptist? It talked to him you know. Robert actually felt it reach out to him, certainly a sign of great import. Alas I don't know how to read signs. Here that science has fallen into disrepute. Those who try to employ it are usually accused of being charlatans. Anyhow thank you for your letter regarding your coming. And on schedule too! Your father was a stickler for being on time. But before we talk about the upcoming campaign, we have one piece of business to transact. I must ask you to swear allegiance to me in regard to only your actions while here on this campaign. In your case, I know you are already committed to Christ. I really only ask it because several of the places you hope to take have been Byzantine possessions for hundreds of years and have only recently been rudely grasped from our 'Oikoumene' and put under the most brutal control of the Seljuk Turks who have defiled...well, you got my letter."

"I swear," declared Robert. "I know you have worked to treat the Christians in the Levant civilly and worked with various Muslim leaders to see that they treat Christians well. That is why we're here. We have already sworn to God. Now I swear to you."

"Thank you," responded Alexius. "Robert you probably already know this but we have a practice here, part of our 'Oikoumene,' to recognize and thank those who work with us to spread our Christian beliefs, values and culture. Niketas please call in your steward."

The near black-eyed man suddenly clapped his hands together creating a resounding 'crack' which was so startling that Henry inadvertently snapped his head back. Immediately two attendants who had apparently been waiting somewhere just outside the room, came limping in carrying a large cloth bag of great weight. Seeing three men they didn't know, one of them looked to Niketas for directions. The minister pointed to Robert and the two bearers summarily dropped their load directly at the feet of their designated recipient. The heavy bag thudded on the floor and simultaneously emitted a tinkling sound that could only denote coins.

"These are gold coins," continued Alexius, "that are meant as a token of our thanks for your help and aid in the Levant."

"Thank you," replied Robert. "We shall do our best to be worthy of your trust. May I be so bold as to ask for your thoughts on how we should proceed from here?"

"Certainly," replied Alexius. "No more small talk. You are a man of action as am I. While it is not for me to say exactly what you and your Christian brethren should attempt, I do have some strategic thoughts and some tactical advice to offer. First to the strategy, the Seljuk Turks our enemy are a nomadic tribe that flows toward us from the open steppes, a grassy plain that goes on to the east for perhaps a thousand miles. They are horsemen and herdsmen whose weapon is primarily the bow and they are courageous unless taken completely by surprise. Niketas, the map."

Again the black-eyed councilor clapped his hands together. "The map," he called without raising his voice. Again two bearers entered the room but this time with a large map which they immediately laid out on the floor beside the bag of coins. Once done, the servants looked up at Niketas for further direction.

Pointing at the map with his finger, Niketas swiveled his digit. The servants, then seeing their mistake, rotated the parchment half way around so that it faced Robert. They then left the room.

Bending onto one knee, Alexius continued while pointing to various places on the map. "Rome is on my right. Constantinople is here and over here is Jerusalem. The Seljuks have come from here and have gotten as far west as Nicaea, which is here less than a hundred miles from where we are right now."

The Emperor looked up to see whether his three guests were attending and had grasped the magnitude of the Turkish threat. Concluding that they had, he continued. "Now as I understand your Pope's directions, you are to move southeast from here to take Jerusalem. Therefore in order to protect your supply lines, you will have to take at least Nicaea here, and Antioch here, and simultaneously subdue any Muslim armies which may be thrust against you. Such armies might come from Damascus, Aleppo, Mosul or elsewhere. As you progress, your left flank will be increasingly exposed to the Seljuks. I propose to move my army across Bithnia, Galatia, and Capadocia thus clearing your flank and repatriating a vast number of Christians who have been lost to our Church. Comments or questions?"

"Yes," Robert quickly responded, "the strategy is sound but will we have enough troops to take Jerusalem?"

"I don't know yet," replied Alexius. "I have been told to expect contingents from southern France led by Bishop Adhemar of Le Puy with a Count Raymond of Toulouse, yourselves from northern France with Duke Robert of Normandy and Count Stephen of Blois. Are they coming?"

"Yes," said Robert. "Robert and Stephen wintered over in Calabria but should be here shortly."

"There are two other groups coming," continued the Emperor, "one from Germany and one from Italy but I know little about them in regard to leaders or numbers. If you are to successfully make your way to Jerusalem, you will need ten times the number you now have. If you get much less, we shall have to combine with you and move on Nicaea and perhaps Antioch. More may not be possible."

Robert nodded his head. "We shall wait to see how many come. Unfortunately it seems that's all we can do for now. But Alexius, please share your thoughts on tactics. Very few of us have fought Turks before."

"Gladly," responded the Emperor. "The Muslims are divided into two primary parts: the Sunni and the Shia as well as numerous splinter groups. They constantly fight among themselves which is our greatest advantage. This weakness we can fertilize by sowing seeds of mistrust and playing one group off against another. Their tactics are universal: they are bowmen, lightly armored with fast horses. They will ride up to you, discharge their arrows and ride away. If you send some of your knights after them, they will try to cut off your sallying group and annihilate it piecemeal. Their foot soldiers tend to be mustered out of the fields and are neither well-trained nor reliable. The Seljuks have hardly any foot, the Fatimids in Egypt a lot. The Egyptians are usually reasonable to deal with. You may be able to turn them through some political arrangement that benefits you both. In any case I shall supply you with guides and engineers to help you along the way. What more should we talk about?"

Again Robert spoke but this time less boldly. "We have been told about a large group of Christian pilgrims who preceded us here last fall and may have been wiped out. Can you tell us what happened?"

Alexius glanced at his lace clad councilor and then back to Robert. "My friend this is a sad story which I attribute to inexperienced leadership and naivete. Last fall a huge number of Christian pilgrims led by an itinerant preacher named Peter wound their way to us through Hungry from the provinces of the German king. The rabble was so vast and so poorly led that they caused trouble everywhere they went—looting, raping and murdering. Eventually I had to have my soldiers contain and feed them. Their leader Peter wanted us to cross them over the Hellispont so they could move on to Jerusalem. I put them in Civetot and counseled them not to move against the Turks but to wait for the van that was scheduled to arrive in the spring. But Peter couldn't control them and some of their leaders split off to take on Kilij Arslan in Nicaea. There they were slaughtered."

"All dead?" Robert queried.

"No," answered Alexius. "There were perhaps a thousand survivors whom we were able to rescue. Peter himself was here in Constantinople during the battle."

"What could have led them to such a needless end?" mused Robert more to himself than to his host. "Did they have any real soldiers?"

"Oh yes," replied Alexius, "perhaps two or three thousand but they had no experienced leaders. The vast majority were just simple folk: serfs, laborers, woodsmen, farmers, even a great number of women and children. But Robert, Angelos told me that you want to be back with your soldiers by dusk and, if you are anything like your father, you probably would like to pray at our Hagia Sophia. Is that the case?"

"Yes," said Robert, "praying there would be a great opportunity. Can we do so today?"

"Surely," replied Alexius as he turned toward his counselor.

~**~

The next morning as Henry rode back toward the city, he was thinking about the value of his knowledge and what he could get in return for it when talking with Niketas. Certainly he wouldn't give up insights that could be used against Robert or others who might eventually be involved in this great pilgrimage. He was not so naïve as to not grasp that the Byzantines might have different goals and motives than the Latins. But he thought he might still be able to parry Niketas' questions in a way that would gain him similar information about the Greeks. He could certainly ask the minister the same questions he was asked. But what did he really want to learn? What unique questions should he ask?

"So Henry, tell me about your trip to get here," asked the Greek Proedros.

"Well," responded the young knight, "you know that I'm from Dol and Robert is from Flanders. We left Flanders on October first and met Stephen and Robert in Pontarlier and then..."

"Before you go too far Henry, please tell me a little about about the Duke and the Count of Blois."

"I shall if you will share similar information with me," responded the boy who had determined to set ground rules for their information sharing.

"That's fair," replied Niketas. "We are allies Henry; I will not abuse your confidences nor must you share with me anything you don't wish to. I'll start with Tatikios. He is an experienced soldier of ours and a man of tempered disposition who can deal well with all sorts of other people. He has broard experience in tactics against the Turks and a great deal of knowledge in engineering. He will likely be in charge of the liason group that the Emperor will give you as guides through Rum. He is a good choice and should be consulted before your group rashly undertakes any illadvised initatives. Does that description meet with your expectations?"

"Yes, thank you Niketas. Stephen of Blois is a poet, writer and good Christian. He is unlikely though to receive a leadership role in the fighting. His father-in-law was William the Conqueror. His men and Robert's have fighting experience, although they're probably less disciplined than Count Robert's. Robert of Normandy is an able fighter but not a dedicated leader. All together the northen Normans will number over ten thousand and are mostly veterans.

"We came across the mountains north of Italy and met the Pope at Lucca. Urban gave us his blessing there but we didn't stay long. Oh, Urban is a tall man with a reddish beard and has the ability to convince you to undertake almost any enterprise. He spent time at Cluny and is well regarded in the Church."

"Is he a reformer or one of the old school?" asked Niketas.

"Before I categorize him," responded Henry, "let's first define our terms. What do you mean by 'a reformer?'"

"I would say that a reformer sees the Pope somewhere between God and the world and accordingly believes that most all decisions must be channeled through him. The old school was much more flexible realizing that all humans are subject to error and therefore they were much more open to compromise and delegation. Does that suit you for a definition?"

"Almost," responded Henry, "but the venal weaknesses exhibited by the old school—simony, nepotism, the outright sale of salvation, excessive drinking and fornication – these are why the reformists must prevail."

"But look on the other side Henry. Pope Gregory, the most recent one, he was so willful, so obstinate and so benighted that he confused himself with God. And that sort of thinking may have done the world of Christendom more harm than all the simony, nepotism and excess drinking undertaken by all its habit wearers. All people are human Henry even a pope. A wrong by one does not make the other right!"

For several moments the two men stared at one another. Then simultaneously each began to speak. "I think I see your point," acknowledged Henry as Niketas apologized, "I did not mean to argue with you."

Each man stopped. Then Niketas repeated his comment. "I did not mean to harry you Henry. You are entitled to your opinion."

"No," said Henry, "I see your point. Neither is absolutely right. I hadn't thought about it that way before. Is that why your Church and mine combat so over excommunications and convoluted interpretations?"

"I believe so," smiled the Greek, "but I'm sure there's more to it. Anyhow, back to your time with the Pope. Did he talk to you about becoming a Fidelis?"

Henry was thunderstruck. How could this Greek know of his discussion with the Pope? It had been a conversation in which Pope Urban had explained to him that there was a chosen group of Christians commited to supporting his reform efforts and that he hoped Henry would give consideration to joining them.

"I see from your expression," said Niketas, "that he did. That is not an unforgivable thing but it does politicize the Church which will have a long term negative impact. Most pleasing is that you listened to my point of view and gave it consideration. With a mind that open, you may find your Church even less perfect than I do. God bless you though. I do like a man who really listens."

"But if you don't mind, continued the Proedros, I have one more question. Why are all these men coming? It's expensive, they may die, it will take years out of their lives. What motivates a man to do that?"

Henry was set back by the question, powerfully set back. For a long time he stared at Niketas trying to determine if the man was serious. The Greek certainly looked sincere. His eyes were staring fixedly back at Henry. There was no hint of insincerity. So Henry finally responded. "I talked to a knight not long ago named Stephen of Neublans who told me this and I remember his words almost exactly. 'Considering how many are my sins and how our lord Jesus Christ has given us His love, clemency and mercy, I have determined to repay Him in some measure for everything He has given me freely, although I am unworthy." Henry choked slightly as he iterated these last few words.

"I see," whispered the Greek. "Thank you for sharing that."

Henry nodded.

"Now," asked Alexius' counselor, "what questions of yours may I answer?"

"I think I'd like to know about your people," the youth responded, "what you believe in, what you value, what your challenges are and where you see yourselves going."

"Oh," laughed Niketas, "only that."

"I think so," answered Henry quite seriously, "but if you think I missed something important, please add it to my questions."

"Ah, where to start?" murmured the Greek. "Let me begin with Constantine. He moved the center of civilization from Rome to Constantinople in 324 Anno Domini and transferred the imperial scepter, the senate and all the Roman knighthood and left in Rome nothing but slaves, fishermen, confectioners, poulterers, bastards, plebians and underlings. Since then, our fair city has been favored by God: our great church, the Hagia Sofia, was clearly built with God's help, our 'God Guarded City' whose walls by His hand have withstood so many sieges, our 'special protection' abetted by the Virgin Mary, our numerous relics laid here to protect us by their power, our Proedros by whose hands the city and empire run smoothly no matter how great the level of chaos, our honors, wealth, and principles—all God given.

"Now let me elaborate on each point. Constantine: He took from Rome everything of value and left nothing of importance. And God came with him Who has shown us all His favors: He has helped us build our Hagia Sophia. His touch is palpable within the Sophia's domes. He has helped us locate our Saintly relics and enjoin them to our places of worship. And of course, God has helped us defend our walls. His power and those of the Saints radiates throughout this city. Henry you have been to Rome. It is merely a city of ruins. You have seen it. Did you sense the hand of God? No. You saw only the rot of hedonism. It is our Emperor here who reaches his hand into distant lands to protect Christ's people. It is our Church here that shines amidst His works. And His hand has caused the magistery of Christendom to expand and linger far and wide by means of our Proedros, the most intelligent and educated class of people in the entire world, those families who actually hold the reins of government through their administration of taxes, trade, culture, courts and even the military. Those people, the brightest of the bright, cause their wisdom to flower near and far, all for the good of Christians.

"And how do these few do all this? That too is extraordinary. The Proedros are entirely flexible as to their means. We buy whole countries, their armies and their people. When the Pechenegs threatened us, we bought the Cumans. When Guiscard challenged us, we bought the Venetians. When we were short on soldiers, we hired your Flemish knights. Others we calmed with treaties. And for yet others, we give honors and titles. With the Arabs, we divide them, we sprinkle rumors, we hire assassins. They don't even know we're the ones doing it. Take the Paulicians who, although citizens of the realm, we deemed a threat. We cajoled them into trusting us and then arrested their leaders, displaced their people and took their lands. You have studied Homer Henry. Remember crafty Odysseus, the wily Lord of Ithaca? In the arts of war and politics, we are like him, a crafty people who win no matter what it takes! Do you understand better now who we are?"

"I do," stammered the young knight who was aghast at what he'd just heard. Henry's mind stammered forth questions: What values do these people have who act so dishonorably, so deplorably, so dishonestly? Such deceit and selfishness! These were not the values he had chosen... Not Abbot Hugh's nor Abbot Anslem's... nor his father's or mother's.

"I can see by your countenance," Niketas continued, "that you are dismayed by what my candor has revealed. But you should not judge us by your standards Henry, partly because you are young and not yet experienced in the ways of the world and partly because your world and ours are very different. Our values, like yours, have been chosen to allow us to function in our world. Be open to our ways for you will see this eastern world is far more complex than yours. Your values would not work here."

"I shall do my best Niketas. I do appreciate your candor."

"That is why I have been so candid Henry because you, unlike most of the others in this world, will give our ways consideration, for which I thank you."

Two days later, Henry toured the great city with Angelos. The young Proedros was as colorful as ever. But now that Henry had talked with Niketas, he saw his blond friend differently, as if the dandy's ringlets were more of a disguise than a defining feature. Beneath the cheeriness, there was a vast unknown. Nevertheless the tour was pleasant and expansive.

The Hagia Sophia, 'the Holy Wisdom' Angelos called it, was incredibly impressive. It was hundreds of years old and did give off an intense sense of God's handiwork, a sort of aura that Henry hadn't felt anywhere else. From this wondrous church, Angelos took him to the Hippodrome, an immense chariot racetrack four hundred meters long entirely surrounded by rising levels of seats, a hundred thousand Angelos said, a number greater than Henry could conceive until he looked. Next there were two forums each with immense space inside for great assemblies; then the monastery of Saint Mamus, a place at which Henry wished to talk with the Orthodox monks but couldn't because they were at prayers. After that the two young men walked north atop the west wall which was, Henry estimated, thirty feet high and fifteen feet thick—a mighty barrier that had, he was told, a long, successful history of holding back sieges. There were, Angelos proffered, nearly a million people who lived or worked within the walls.

When they got to the Blachernae Palace still atop the wall, they turned right, which faced them northeast looking out over the Golden Horn. There they walked a mile or two before Angelos pointed out the Venetian Quarter, which was quickly followed by the Amalfian, Pisan and Arab Quarters. Here the press was the greatest. The Greek tour giver identified barrels filled with eastern spices, packs of porcelain, racks of tile, bales of wool, crates of Italian tin, small boxes of amber carried by slaves and guarded by Russ, more barrels but filled with wax and honey and finally more bales of hides and furs.

"We receive a customs tax of ten percent from all of these," said Angelos.

"What does that mean?" asked Henry.

The young Greek Proedros stared at his companion in apparent disbelief. Finally he responded. "Henry, every item which passes through our port, be it from the Black Sea or the Med, is subject to a ten-percent customs fee. These merchants pay us ten-percent on their entire cargo. It is a passage fee that permits them to come and go, to use our city for warehousing and distribution and to be protected throughout the civilized world by our navy. Think of it as similar to the taxes you place upon your serfs who labor in the fields. They pay you don't they?"

"Yes," responded Henry, "but they pay mostly in produce."

"Ah," responded Angelos, "ours is a more coin-oriented economy. We take occasional payments in product but we prefer coin. It is far more liquid and its value is certifiable."

"But," responded Henry still in awe, "you must get an incredible sum from all this trade!"

"Oh," replied the golden haired youth, "we do but that's the point. Now follow me, we still haven't gotten to the trademen's shops: the smiths of gold and silver, the cabinet makers, jewelers, clothiers, candle makers, bankers and lenders. Come Henry. You will be impressed."

MOTIVES
April 1097

Henry surveyed Blachemere castle's crowded meeting room. Very shortly the Emperor would conduct another oath-taking ceremony. The young knight assumed it would be similar to the one on Easter three days ago, at which Alexius took oaths from the three Lorrainian brothers—Godfrey, Baldwin and Eustas. To Henry these oaths seemed reasonable enough. They directed themselves primarily to returning any captured Christian lands and cities to Alexius on the basis that the Greeks had held them for hundreds of years prior. Henry hoped to meet the three brothers so he could establish his 'bona fides' as Robert's coordinator and if he got the chance,to ask them why they thought the oaths were so unacceptable. From what he'd heard, Godfrey had resisted the oath very pugnaciously, even initiating a brawl at the Adrianople Gate against Emperor Alexius' castellans. Of course Henry had learned not to believe all the rumors that swirled through Constantinople. The most virulent and ubiquitous of them were often the most likely to be untrue.

The room was large and ornately decorated with mosaic tile floors, hanging tapestries and numerous clay and alabaster art works. Despite all this, the day's swearing-in would be less pompous than Easter's at which the process had started in the Hagia Sophia, 'the Holy Wisdom' the Greeks called it, and culminated with the oaths themselves followed by Alexius giving out expensive and lavish gifts to his new vassals. Henry had never realized there was so much gold in the world until he witnessed this part of the swearing-ins. Alexius gave it forth as if he had an endless supply. Various lesser nobles and knights had apparently been straggling into the city for several days. Among them was Rainald the Count of Toul, who was also one of Godfrey's vassals but he had, like the northern Franks, taken the southern route through Italy to Constantinople. Henry noted that the Greeks, following correct protocol, had brought Godfrey and Baldwin back across the Bosporus for this occasion.

Since there seemed to be no specific function going on at the moment and there was a great quantity of food and drink being set out by numerous, crisply outfitted attendants, Henry began to work his way through the crowd toward Godfrey and Baldwin.

Godfrey was only an inch or two shorter than Henry. His most noticeable attribute was his blond hair and beard. Henry judged him to be about forty, which made sense since he knew from Reynauld that the Lorrainian leader had fought for the German Emperor in the wars of the eighties.

"Good day my lord," said the youth. "I am Henry of Dol, Count Robert of Flanders' coordinator."

"Hail and well met," declared the blond knight, his blue eyes shining amidst his blond thatches of hair. "Your Count told me you'd introduce yourself."

"Well," said Henry, "I wanted to meet you before we got into combat so you'd recognize me if I had to communicate with you."

"Yes, yes," replied Godfrey, "a wise preparation. You surprise me though. You are quite young to be a coordinator."

"I am only recently knighted," Henry replied. "I think Count Robert chose me more for my knowledge of Latin and languages than for my experience as a knight."

"Then he made a wise choice. We will have an army that speaks many languages. I can hardly understand your accent and you're speaking one of my native tongues! Where is Dol?"

"In Brittany," Henry answered.

"Ah," responded Godfrey, "you've come a long way."

"As have you," said Henry who was feeling that he was settling in well with the Duke.

"How is it that you speak German?" asked Godfrey.

"I rode for a couple of weeks with two brothers who were from Chalons. One of them, Randulf, taught me just enough German to get by."

"That will do you well. Many of my men speak only German but I'm sure they'd be happy to teach you more if you'd like."

"Oh, certainly," Henry responded cheerfully as he contemplated meeting more people and expanding his linguistics.

"Were you perhaps trained by Reynauld?" asked Godfrey.

"I was."

"He was a worthy adversary when we fought in the eighties. If you learned from him, you have been well trained... Do you believe in God?"

Henry was surprised by the question.

"I do," he answered, "but why did you ask me that?"

"Because," responded the Duke, "it is He who gives a soldier courage and protection in battle. He watches out for people who believe in Him."

Then apparently having heard someone speaking behind him, Godfrey turned. "Baldwin, you will need to know this knight. He is Count Robert's coordinator, Henry of Dol, a fine young man who believes in Jesus."

Henry turned to greet Baldwin. The man was about the same height as Godfrey but otherwise the two men could not have been more different. Baldwin's hair was black, his chin shaven, his complexion pale and his expression cold.

"Good day."

A moment passed before Henry realized the Lorrainer had completed his greeting.

"I've heard," said Henry, "that you attended the great school at Reims. I visited the church there when we heard Pope Urban speak last winter. It's where I received my cross."

"Good for you," muttered Baldwin as he turned away.

Anger was not an emotion that rose quickly in Henry but he knew he'd been snubbed.

"Please excuse the rudeness of my youngest brother," interrupted a man whom Henry hadn't seen before. "My name is Eustace, Count of Boulogne." This speaker was taller than Baldwin but soft-spoken and thinner. "You see, Baldwin being the third brother, did not inherit any of our father's lands, so he bears the world a grudge. Did you receive your cross directly from the Pope?"

"No," replied Henry, "from one of his bishops."

"You were still honord," Eustace agreed, "both to have heard the Pope speak and to have received your cross from a bishop. Our crosses were cut from a piece of red cloth Godfrey acquired from the abbot of a Cluniac monastery at Brogne. Despite his crossbow, Godfrey is a very devout man who has always been close with a number of priests, abbots and bishops all around Bouillon and Lower Lorrain."

"Eustace, I don't remember seeing you at the oath-taking ceremony on Easter. Were you there?"

"No," replied Godfrey's older brother. "I came with Rainald the Count of Toul through Italy and just now got here. I shall be sworn in today."

"Ah," exclaimed the young knight, "that explains why I didn't recognize you. If I may though, I have another question." The coordinator paused to be certain that Eustace wasn't in a rush to break off their conversation as Baldwin had been. Then seeing the Count seeming to wait for him, Henry continued. "Please tell me about the swan on Godfrey's shield. I've been told that it has something to do with Charlemagne being an ancestor. Is that true?"

"That is correct," replied Eustace. "Charlemagne was a progenitor of ours, something our family is very proud of. The story of the swan is most likely hypochrophal but the ancestry part is real."

Glancing at Godfrey who was not too far away, Henry had another thought. "Eustace, I don't mean to be impolite but how is it that your younger brother became the leader of your contingent and not you?"

"Oh," replied the older knight who appeared not to feel at all abused by Henry's question, "that was simple enough. Godfrey recruited many more men than I, so we thought it made more sense for him to be the leader. My estates are partly in England, so I had a harder time recruiting and, in fairness, Godfrey has always been much more committed. He raised much more coin and could therefore raise and outfit a much larger force. You know, we have over thirteen thousand soldiers."

"But how," asked Henry, "could he have raised so much more coin than you?"

"Let me think for a moment how best to answer that," responded Eustace. "He was able to...ah...encourage his Jews to contribute a great deal of gold and silver."

"But nothing untoward?" Henry queried.

"Oh no," Eustace replied. "No one was killed or held hostage. Godfrey simply offered to continue extending their current tax rates, trading privyleges and use of various business sites. He has long treated his Jews very generously which has accrued them great wealth."

"I see," said Henry, "but I have one more question if you don't mind."

"Certainly," replied Eustace.

"I know now that you came by a different route, so you may not know the answer, but why did Godfrey refuse Alexius' request for an oath?"

"Oh that's simple to answer," responded the Count. "It comes from him being so devout. You see, he's given his allegiance to Emperor Henry and believes by doing that, he has made a sacred commitment before God to give his loyalty to only the Emperor. Any second oath or pledge could potentially bring him into a conflicted position. We have seen this happen at home when a civil war broke out and various lords were committed to opposing sides. Godfrey would never put himself into a conflicted position, not even a potential one. He feels the second oath might compromise his promise to God. He's told Alexius he doesn't intend to acquire land anyhow."

"But," interrupted Henry, "I thought he'd finally given in and agreed to take the oath."

"Oh, he did," responded Eustace. "I talked to him about that. All he wanted to do was get his men on the road to Jerusalem. But the Emperor wouldn't give him food if he wouldn't take the oath. So thinking he might get his men fed if he pushed a little, Godfrey initiated a little fracas at one of the city gates. Alexius sent out half his army. He was willing to have good Christian soldiers dying over an unnecessary oath. So my brother prayed to God imploring Him for direction and after a great deal of thought, he finally relented and agreed to take the oath. Now he lives in fear of becoming conflicted by it."

"Thank you, Eustace, for sharing that insight. I did not understand God-frey's perspective. Perhaps you could tell me a little more about Baldwin as he was not very forthcoming."

"Certainly," replied the Count of Boulogne, "Baldwin, as I have already stated, was left no lands as inheritance. Instead, at an early age, my father set him on a path toward the Church. He went to Reims as an oblate. They gave him an education and taught him to be cultivated with a taste for fine things. Then there was some falling out. I don't know the details but he came home looking for some station—a clerkship, a bookkeeper, some-thing that would employ his education."

"I see," said Henry, "but he brings his wife Godvere and their little chil-dren on this pilgrimage?"

"Yes," continued Eustace. "He has no intention of returning home from the Holy Land. He really hasn't much to return to."

There was a pause in the conversation before Henry spoke again. "But what of you, Eustace? Do you intend to return to your lands in Boulogne and England?"

"If God wills it, I shall. My lands are rich in produce and my wife has given me three children."

"Ah," said Henry, "boys or girls?"

~**~

Blood red on the horizon, the sun stippled its domain. In high relief, a golden fringe tinged a series of gray-bottomed clouds; to the south, a scrubby cypress tree atop a granite outcropping shimmered orange. Even Henry's chainmail coat, usually a dull gray, was compelled by the mighty orb's rays to cast back a brighter hue. The young knight was riding south keeping Nicaea's eastern wall clearly in view. He was accompanied by two sergeants, Aubrey and Everad, whom Reynauld had assigned as his escort. The youth's thoughts had wandered back to Constantinople. By the end of April, all the expected western armies had arrived except Robert and Stephen's northern Normans.

Not wishing to miss the prime fighting season, the Council of leaders decided to march on Nicaea, which was only a hundred miles to the southeast and their obvious first objective. 'Curthose and the Poet will just have to catch up' Robert of Flanders said. Robert's force together with Godfrey's departed in late April followed closely by the southern Normans who were led by Tancred, Bohemond having stayed behind to coordinate with the Greeks regarding supplies. Count Raymond of Toulouse's soldiers lagged behind. To Henry's surprise the lead van had neither been attacked nor scouted as best anyone could tell. Accordingly on May 6th, they reached Nicaea without incident. The city's walls stretched more than four miles and had two hundred and forty towers. Capturing it would be a formidable challenge. Undaunted, Godfrey's and Robert's men invested the northern section of the walls while Tancred's settled in along the eastern side. The south was left for Raymond whose men arrived on the 16th. The city's western walls pressed so closely against Lake Askanius that a total investment was possible only with boats.

During the advance toward Nicaea, Henry encountered two sights that he knew would be etched in his memory for the rest of his life. The first of these was the bones, the decaying remains of the thousands of pilgrims who had followed Peter the Hermit on their way to Jerusalem. They'd been surprised by Sultan Kilij Arslan's army and been systematically slaughtered. Henry had been told that many of the women and children had been carried off to Muslim slave markets but he'd still seen hundreds of bodies among the dead that, despite their black, swollen and rotting remains, were clearly women and children. The Christian armies marched more than two miles amidst this carnage. At its easterly end, they found the bodies of approximately two hundred fighting men together with the bloated remnants of their mounts. Several of these men still had as many as seven or eight arrows protruding from their bodies. Most however had none, a sign a veteran soldier told Henry, that their armor and other belongings had been stripped from them after they died. Even after six months, there was still a nauseating odor floating in the air. Many of the Christian knights vomited, some like Henry more than once.

The second experience that Henry knew he'd never forget was the chain of crosses. Alexius had assigned a detachment of engineers under the command of Manual Butumedes to guide the Franks. The engineers' secondary assignment was to place large wooden crosses into the ground every mile as they went. These were intended to guide future pilgrims to Jerusalem. But to Henry, these markers were not just a measurement of their army's progress but a quantification of the Christian Church's literal return to its roots...to the land of Jesus, to His teachings, to His sacrifice, to Him. Every time Henry passed one of these large wooden emblems, the significance of this thought poignantly moved him. He felt profound warmth. And he knew he wasn't the only one who felt it. When he approached a cross, he saw the men ahead of him touch their forehead and then their chest. And after passing a cross when he looked back, he saw those behind him cross themselves as well. It didn't matter whether the man was a lord, knight or foot soldier. All were now one, soldiers of Christ! Every man crossed himself every time he reached one of those crosses... hundreds of times. But no one ever mentioned it aloud or referred to it in any way and somehow that made it the most powerful commitment any of them had ever made.

Henry rode past the southern Normans who were spread outside Nicaea's eastern wall. Bohemond's banner had replaced Tancred's several days earlier after their tall, handsome leader had completed his victualing coordination with Alexius. Bohemond was the tallest man Henry had ever known. His ice-blue eyes were fully two hand-widths higher than Henry's. His hair was darkly blond and his face cleanly shaven. He was a man of great personal presence which was best shown by the high regard his men showed for him. Henry's meeting with him had been brief but poignant. Bohemond's handshake was like a vice and his eyes seemingly pierced past

Henry's face right into the young knight's head. Instinctively Henry knew this man was a leader whose every order would be obeyed.

Tancred, Bohemond's nephew, also had presence but it hadn't yet congealed into that of a man who truly knew himself. Accordingly Tancred's personality still had a need to prove itself. In any case neither of these southern Normans was likely to be shy in battle.

Not long after passing the south Normans, Henry saw ahead of him Raymond's pennant limply hanging from its pole. The young knight gently tugged on Meredith's reins to guide her toward the lord's tent which had been erected just beyond the pennant. There Henry and his bodyguard were greeted by a boy of perhaps twelve.

"Welcome," chirped the boy in French so badly pronounced that even his simple one word greeting was hard to understand. "Is one of you Henry?"

"I am," replied the young knight as he dismounted.

The boy leapt to take Meredith's reins and in so doing left Aubrey and Everad to fend for themselves.

"My lord Raymond awaits you," said the boy very cheerfully although still in his thick accent.

"Thank you," said Henry as he wondered whether the boy would lead him into the tent or he was to enter by himself.

Almost immediately a smiling man in a black robe exited the tent speaking understandable French with only the slightest accent.

"Welcome Henry of Dol. I am Adhemar of Monteil, Bishop of Le Puy. Please come in and let me introduce you to my friends Raymond, Count of Toulouse and Saint-Gilles and my colleague William, Bishop of Orange and Gaston of Bearn."

Henry's assessment of Adhemar was immediately positive. The bishop's voice was soft and reassuring, his beard neatly cropped and his eyes inquiring. The color of his robe marked him as a Benedictine.

"Thank you," replied Henry, "but do you wish me to bring in my escort," Henry waved his right hand in the direction of Aubrey and Everad, "or shall I bid them return to the north wall?"

"Please invite them to come with you," replied Adhemar. "We are all equally committed."

The tent was quite large, not that Henry considered himself a judge since he'd seen very few tents before he'd gone to Flanders. The first person they came upon was an attractive, middle-aged woman whose black hair and brown eyes reminded Henry of the women he'd seen in Spain. She bowed her head as they passed. Henry surmised she was Raymond's wife but no introductions were made. Instead, Adhemar took them directly to a bed where an old man lay with his naked left foot propped up on several cushions. A vermillion scar furrowed across his forehead reappearing just below his left eye where it continued down his cheek. The eye was entirely opaque. Otherwise the man wore leather leggings and a red tunic made from an unusually fine fabric. His cheeks were neatly shaven and his hair was turning white but his jaw was tightly clamped shut as if in pain. Looking down at the man's elevated left foot, Henry saw the source of the pain. His ankle was severely swollen.

"Gout!" spit out the Count in French only slightly better than the boy's.

"Yes," Henry immediately responded, "most assuredly. Have you altered your consumption of liquids to only water?"

For several moments Raymond glared at the young knight. "How old are you boy?"

"Sixteen," responded Henry, "but I know that Arab doctors have found that drinking only clear water lessens gout attacks."

"Humph," murmured the Count. "My wife's been telling me the same thing. Have you two been joining the devil at séances or do you have something more substantial to base your opinion on?"

Henry noted that the pitch in Raymond's voice had dropped an octave. "My sources were two books loaned to me from the library at Sahagun by Bishop Bernard in which two renowned Arab doctors advocated the solution. Each wrote if used over several weeks it cured most, though not all, of their patients. If this clear water prescription is what your wife told you to do, then I suggest you take her advice."

For what seemed like quite a long time Raymond continued to stare at Henry. Finally he spoke. "You know Bishop Bernard of Sahagun?"

"Yes," said Henry, "he is a friend. I travelled with him to Santiago de Compostela. I got my compostele there."

Again Raymond appraised the young knight. Then he turned his head toward the entry through which Henry had just passed and spoke in a much softer tone. "Elvira, please come here."

The dark-haired woman whom they had passed coming in immediately stepped into view.

"Come in, come in," said Raymond in a much softer tone as he pointed to a location near Henry.

Elvira stepped to her designated spot.

The Count of Toulouse and Saint Gilles then continued. "Elvira, this is Henry of Dol."

The woman turned her head toward Henry and lowered her gaze as she had when the young knight first entered the tent.

"Henry, this is my wife, Elvira of Aragon. By blood she is related to both royal houses in Spain. I met her on one of my campaigns in Spain and, as you can see, it was a very propitious campaign. She is quiet in front of strangers but in addition to her native Spanish, she speaks both French and Provencal quite well."

The Count turned his gaze back to his wife. "This young knight has been to Sahagun and is a friend of Bishop Bernard."

Immediately Elvira elevated her head and looked directly at Henry.

"Truly," she asked, "you have been to Spain?" Her emotion was so strong that she nearly gurgled.

"Yes," replied Henry. "Your husband and I were just discussing a possible cure for his gout which you apparently have already recommended."

"Yes," she replied in excellent French. "Hopefully now he will try the 'clear-water' prescription and his affliction will diminish. But I must note an important point that you did not mention. The clear water should first be boiled and then cooled before drinking. The Arab and Jewish doctors with whom I am acquainted have all emphasized this point not just for gout but at all times to avoid some of the very worst diseases." She turned her head back toward her husband. "I sincerely hope that now, with this knight's corroboration of this prescription, you will try it and, God willing, overcome this debilitating malady."

Henry liked this woman. She was willing to press her overbearing husband in hope of doing him some good. And seeing this opportunity to help, Henry spoke again. "I have not previously heard of boiling all drinking water before ingesting it, but I shall initiate the practice immediately as you have suggested. When we get a chance we must share other medical prescriptions and techniques. You have undoubtedly had access to sources that I have not and perhaps I may know some things that you have not yet heard as well."

"I would be most pleased to talk with you more," replied Elvira. "But you are likely to be busier than I, so I shall leave the day and time of our next discussion up to you and our place can be here."

With Elvira's and Henry's discussion over, Raymond spoke up in a very cheerful manner. "Henry, I believe God has sent you to me with this medical prescription. I shall pray my thanks to Him but first let's get to business. I know you are Robert of Flanders' coordinator and I now have cause to be certain that he has chosen a good one. You have already met Adhemar of Monteil. He is an unassuming man very much as Christ Himself was. He is the Bishop of Toulouse, a close confidant of Pope Urban and the Pope's designated representative for this pilgrimage."

Henry acknowledged Adhemar with a nod and the Bishop nodded back.

"I wish also to introduce you to my good friend Gaston of Bearn who I have campaigned with in Spain and with whom I also share membership in the 'Faithful of Saint Peter,' which is a federation of Christians dedicated to supporting the Pope. Perhaps you know of it?"

"I do," replied Henry. "Pope Urban asked me to join the Faithful when he blessed us at Lucca. It is a fine group of people devoted to extending God's reach over mankind. I commend you both for your allegiance." Henry and Gaston exchanged nods.

"Ah," responded Raymond who was obviously impressed by both Henry's connections and knowledge, "you have again impressed me young man. Now, let me introduce you to William of Orange who is the Bishop of Orange. He is my coordinator with whom you may share all issues regarding supplies, equipment and logistics. But come directly to me with anything more compelling, such as surprises or strategy."

Henry turned and saw a slightly built, older man standing just beyond Adhemar. He also wore a black robe but unlike the papal representative, his face was closely shaven.

"Lord Raymond," interjected Henry, "before William and I repair for our discussion, I should share one important piece of news. My lord Robert, has agreed that his force, about thirty-five hundred knights, foot soldiers and archers, will be our army's mobile unit to provide emergency back-up anywhere we are attacked. Accordingly if you are attacked and wish assistance, please dispatch a rider, or riders, to our location which is currently at the north end of the city. We shall come immediately and are prepared to do so. Thank you for your time."

Henry bowed to Raymond and turned toward William who in turn stepped toward a far corner of the tent. There the two coordinators, together with Aubrey and Everad, set about their exchange of logistics, details and processes. By mid-morning they had completed their task.

"*If* you have a little more time William, perhaps we could share some more information before I have to leave." Henry then turned toward his two escorts. "William and I are going to take a walk. We shouldn't be very long." And so the black-robed bishop and the young knight stepped out of Raymond's tent and began to meander through the bustling campsite.

Henry was the first to speak. "I'm hoping you might give me a better understanding of who Raymond is: his values, beliefs and why he is here. I shall be happy to share the same about Robert."

"Of course," replied William. "Raymond is a very great and powerful lord. He is the Count of Toulouse and Saint Gilles and Marquis of Provence. He effectively controls all activities in south-eastern France. He was the layman Pope Urban sought to lead this great pilgrimage. Raymond commited himself fully even before Urban's invocation at Claremont. He very strongly believes that the Pope picked Adhemar to be the spiritual leader and himself to be the military commander of this expedition. You see, the Pope was aware of Raymond's previous campaigns in Spain against the Moors and of his experience fighting there. That's how he lost his eye. The Count has explained many times how the Muslims fight...archery and speed mostly. And of course campaigning in Spain is like campaigning in the Holy Land. You have to learn how to deal with the sun, the heat and no water. Raymond is our only military commander with such experience. Of course Adhemar went on a pilgrimage to Jerusalem ten years ago and he is experienced in warfare but not as much as Raymond. Most of all, Raymond is really committed to taking Jerusalem." William lowered his voice. "You know, Godfrey just attacked the Emperor's troops at one of the western gates and Bohemond, who led Robert Guiscard's troops in the eighties against the Greeks, rushed forward from Thrace to join him. But he got there too late." William furtively glanced over his shoulder then lowered his voice to a barely audible whisper. "You know they may be plotting to overthrow the Emperor."

"You really think so?" Henry whispered back.

"We're not sure," responded William, "but we do know that Bohemond asked Alexius to make him the 'Grand Domestic' in the east. That's the title the Greeks have for the senior military commander who oversees everything east of the Bosporus."

"But Alexius didn't give Bohemond the job, did he?" Henry asked.

William looked over his shoulder again. "No. He told him he'd think about it. But we know from the Emperor that Bohemond will never get it. Alexius doesn't trust him."

"I see," said Henry, "but Raymond is bringing Elvira and the little boy. Is he not intending to return to Toulouse?"

"His son's name is Alfonso. But Raymond intends to die in the Holy Land. I don't mean he expects to be killed. It's just that he's over sixty and a realist. He hopes to establish a county or dukedom if things go well but his primary goal is to free Jerusalem."

"That's very helpful William. Let me now share what I can about Robert..."

~**~

Almost immediately the Seljuk Sultan, Kilij Arslan, unleashed his army against the Christian armies investing Nicaea. Perhaps the Sultan expected another easy go of it. In any case, coming up from the south, the Turks attacked Raymond's force of Provancals. Fortunately, the attack came the day after Henry had visited Raymond and communicated Robert of Flanders' readiness to be the army's reserve. One of Raymond's knights, his horse white with lather, had ridden into Robert's camp to notify them of the Turkish onslaught. Robert's men, having trained several times for just such a moment, immediately marched and attacked the Turks' flank. The Turkish horsemen fought just as Reynauld had always said they would: riding up, loosing their arrows and then riding away to reload. Given the chainmail the Franks wore, the risk from the arrows released at more than short range was minimal. The horses Henry concluded were the enemy's real target. Many of them fell leaving their riders exposed to future shafts which could, due to the horseless knight's immobility, be loosed at close range with penetrating affect. Conversely Henry learned, if a knight could get close enough to a Muslim warrior to use his sword, there was near certainty of success. In this exact manner, he killed three Turkish riders, his training in horse and swordsmanship directing him through the process. In the midst of combat there was no time to think beyond the scope of give and take. At the moment of greatest peril, Reynauld's training kept him alive.

Once Kilij Arslan realized his opponents were not unarmed men, women and children but trained Christian knights, he withdrew.

When the sun came up the next day, the Christian soldiers discovered that the Greek's pennant was flapping above Nicaea's battlements. During the night the Greek liason, Butumedes, had negotiated a peaceful surrender of the city. Henry learned that a few of the Latin leaders had known these negotiations were going on but it was very apparent that the rank and file neither knew nor appreciated the outcome. Most of the foot soldiers had counted on pillaging the city. Accordingly, resentment toward the Greeks was no longer limited to only those from whom Alexius expected an oath.

A week after the fall of Nicaea as the Franks approached Dorylaeum, the lead section of the army under Bohemond's command and with Robert's men attached, was set upon by Kilij Arslan's remaining army. The Turks were howling, gabbling, hooting and loosing clouds of arrows. A pitched battle followed in which Henry found himself in the midst of the action.

It was immediately apparent to the young knight that Bohemond and his soldiers were well prepared for an attack. Their leader instantly issued orders: non-combatants to the middle of camp, women to bring water forward and watch over the children, foot soldiers and archers to take up defensive positions around their outside perimeter and knights to dis-mount and protect their horses. Several riders, who apparently had a pre-designated role, rode off immediately to call forth the rest of the Christian army. In clear view of the enemy Bohemond called out directions calmly and concisely. He paid no heed to the hissing arrows that flew into the camp nor did he hesitate in his zeal to keep everyone on task. Once Bohe-mond had his charges as well protected as possible, he transitioned his efforts to the psychology of waiting for the rest of the army to arrive. It was a long wait.

The Sultan's men had attacked at sunrise and relief didn't appear until noon. Meanwhile, Bohemond reminded his men of their duty and, with what Henry thought was real humor, the Norman leader discussed their 'promised' benefits in heaven should they be killed, but then went on to dissuade them from being killed foolishly, lest that not qualify them for God's pardon. Bohemond also went on even further to remind everyone that Sultans carried their gold, silver and jewels with them when on campaign. So, for those who kept themselves alive until the van of the Christian army arrived, there would likely be a significant financial reward.

As soon as the rest of the Christian army appeared, Bohemond leapt up and called his knights to action. "Mount up men. It's time for us to search out the Sultan's treasure chest."

ANTIOCH

November 1097

Henry trudged across the rain-soaked ground. They'd been in this camp for more than a month and over that time the fields had become a wet patchwork of slippery slopes and muddy morasses. Slick lanes wound among dripping tents and lean-tos cobbled together out of sticks and cloth under which two or three men would try to find shelter from the rain, snow and cold.

Robert's coordinator was seeking Raynauld, his teacher, mentor and friend. Henry had heard that Reynauld's horse had died, the very worst thing that could happen to a knight. For a moment Henry wondered how God could let this happen to someone so devoted, someone with such clear values and someone who actually lived by his values. But before his mind had time to contend with such a philosophical question, he saw two soldiers cutting horse meat into chunks and tossing them into a kettle. Henry knew their camp, in fact the entire army, was again falling into starvation. Only a month ago, everything had been so plentiful: grain, fruit, squash, meat, beans, even wine and mead. Now there was nothing.

On Henry's right were the walls of Antioch. When he'd first viewed them, the city had seemed immense: miles of high walls, hundreds of towers, thousands of defenders, larger than Nicaea by a lot. Count Stephen had dubbed Antioch 'nearly impregnable.' Henry himself remembered thinking that only a fool would try to assault such monstrous walls but Reynauld, apparently reading the young knight's mind, had quietly whispered. 'That which man can put up, he can take down.'

The south Normans had been the first to arrive, so Robert's van passed Bohemond's blood-red banner near the city's Saint Paul gate and settled down just to the southwest. Those who followed went further along the western side of the city to the Dog gate where Raymond placed his banner and eventually Godfrey's men settled outside the Gate of the Duke.

After setting up camp, the leaders held a council to determine what strategy they'd use to take the city. It was clear to everyone that bypassing Antioch wasn't an option. The city was simply too big and too powerful to leave in their rear. It would constantly threaten land communications with the Greeks and wreak havoc on the most fertile land available for supplies. A frontal attack was considered foolhardy by all except Raymond, whose only specific argument regarding how to take it was 'to trust in Jesus.' This was deemed insufficient.

So their only remaining option was to invest the city. But because Antioch's garrison was estimated to be over five thousand, the Franks thought they hadn't sufficient men to safely block off six different entrances. Furthermore the east portal, the Iron Gate, was a twelve mile ride from any of the other gates the Franks would be blocking. This was because the eastern part of the city rose precipitously up the sides of two mountains. The Iron Gate actually allowed the city an exit between these two mountains, thus the twelve mile ride around one of the mountains necessary to rescue investing Christian soldiers there. Accordingly the initial investment did not include blocking off the Iron Gate, which of course left the city open on its eastern side to receive food and supplies. All the Christian leaders knew this solution was woefully inadequate. But for the moment, all they thought they could do was call for Alexius' army and pray for more volunteers from the west whom they'd been told, were on the way.

Their Council meeting ended with all the leaders and their liegemen taking an oath not to desert the siege. Henry thought the oath was taken because it was obvious to everyone that the investment strategy without significant improvements simply wasn't going to accomplish anything. Meanwhile their most pressing issue was food.

Henry finally spotted Reynauld only a little ahead of him lying on a bed of small rocks beneath several shredded pieces of clothing that he'd hung above him by means of sticks and strings.

"Reynauld, is that you?" called out the knight in a tone he tried to make as cheerful as possible.

The Flemish knight turned his head revealing a broad smile and simultaneously lifted his left arm, which in turn knocked his make-shift tent asunder.

"Henry, how glad I am to see you." With one great sweep of his arm, the knight flung the remaining shards of his domicile aside and with a groan, elevated himself to a standing position.

"Oh," said Henry, "I didn't mean to cause you to break up your...your tent."

"Oh, don't be concerned about that," replied the Master of War Craft. "It falls apart like that whenever I get up, or even roll over for that matter. But how are you?"

"I'm a little hungry but otherwise well. And you?"

"The same," replied Reynauld. "I am neither sick nor wounded and I am among some very valiant warriors, both knights and foot soldiers. We are a determined and very able group. But please tell me of the strategies and larger plans of which we hear very little."

"Oh," responded Henry who wanted very much to offer a vibrant response, "our investment strategy is coalescing particularly with the advent of Malregard, our little fortress by the Saint Paul Gate."

"I've heard of it," replied Reynauld, "but how will it help us close the Iron Gate?"

"Well," said Henry as he noted that his teacher was just as perceptive as ever, "we hope we'll be able to close off the Iron Gate in much the same way, in which case the hunger within the walls should become greater than ours outside."

"Wonderful," said Reynauld. "We can all hope for that. Have you heard whether the Turks have any relief armies on the way?"

"No," responded Henry, "none that we know of."

"That's good," said Reynauld. "At least it may be good. What else is going on?"

"Well," replied the youth as he mustered his courage, "I've heard that you lost your horse."

"Ah," sighed Reynauld, "sadly that is so. He died a week ago. He never really recovered from that famine in Anatolia. What an awful place that was."

Henry nodded. "Meredith is skinny and winded easily but she's still alive thanks mostly to Bart who is a marvelous forager."

"I'm glad for you Henry. There can't be more than a thousand horses left. Many of my comrades here are unhorsed knights. We make good foot soldiers. We just cover less ground."

"Would you take Meredith?" blurted out the pupil.

Reynauld stared at his now knighted student. His hesitation however was brief. "No," the 'Master' replied in a tone which left no doubt. "Meredith is your horse. You need her to do your job as coordinator. Nor would Robert permit it... Henry, your offer is most kind betokening your selfless value of 'others.' I appreciate it for I know you truly mean it. But we both know it cannot be. In fact it is probably God who keeps your horse alive so that you can do your duty. You wouldn't want us to contradict God's will would you?"

Henry stared at the ground. "But Reynauld, what of you? You know a foot soldier is much more at risk than a knight. The Turks can ride up close to you and loose their arrows and penetrate your mail."

"Henry, I'm old for this bloody business. I don't want to die an old soldier's death sitting beside Robert's hearth not even being able to put a log on the fire. I may well die from a Turkish arrow but I'll fight as my father did and die like a knight. And on this pilgrimage, I'll die in the best of company with my sword in my hand and heaven ahead. What can be better than that!"

With tears in his eyes, Henry looked up at his friend but before he could speak, Reynauld continued.

"Henry, you still haven't gotten an aventail to cover your neck. I want you to promise me that you'll take mine when the time comes." The Master then raised his voice an octave. "Swear it to me now Henry, right now."

"I swear," sniffed the youth.

"You can do better than that," growled Reynauld.

Hearing the tone of command, Henry lifted his eyes to look directly at Reynauld. "I swear it to you," the erstwhile student growled back. "Should that sad day come, I shall take your aventail as a gift from my mentor, the Master of War Craft."

ANTIOCH
December 1097 – January 1098

On December 28th, Robert of Flanders and Bohemond of Toranto set out on a sortie with four hundred knights and a thousand foot soldiers in search of food. They went south into the Ruj Valley which promised opportunity. On the second night out, their resolve was tested by a combination of unusual phenomena: a comet was spotted coming directly at them, the Aurora Borealis shone so brightly that many of the soldiers fell to their knees and prayed for forgiveness and then the very earth beneath their feet started to shake. Everyone believed these portents combined with snow, hail, downpours and powerful winds, signified God's displeasure.

Henry regretted that William, the Bishop of Orange, hadn't come with them, as he was the only person Henry knew who was trained in the interpretation of unusual phenomena. Henry himself tended to dismiss interpretations of such events. But all these occurrences together at the same time were just too much to have no meaning. And no one was interpreting their meaning to be positive. Several of the men near Henry began to rail loudly about all the sinful actions they'd been seeing which in their minds constituted cause for God's anger. These included lack of prayer, exhibits of pridefulness, brigandage, theft, cheating at cards, avarice, dissipation and numerous examples of fornication and adultery. Henry thought it a very complete and accurate list, although in his mind he did add their act of beheading prisoners and catapulting their heads over the walls at both Nicaea and Antioch.

His failure to further confess his own sins gnawed at him as well, so much so that he finally promised God that he would confess as soon as they returned to camp. His immediate concern though was less about past transgressions than what God might exact next upon them; and whether He would exact His retribution from the entire army or just Bohemond's and Robert's contingents. Having no immediate answer to that question, Henry wondered what Reynauld would advise. His mentor was somewhere in their van but Henry had no idea exactly where. The young knight finally settled on one of Reynauld's general exhortations: 'Never worry about what you can't do anything about.'

As it turned out, Henry didn't have long to fret about what might go wrong. At first light they were attacked by an immense force of Turkish horse archers. The Franks were surprised, separated, surrounded and infiltrated. Swarms of arrows hissed at them as the Muslims recurrently charged, retreated and charged again. Immediately Henry was in the midst of swirling confusion. He did his best to stay close to Robert or at least Robert's standard bearer.

Then Count Robert's voice rang out above the fray. "Rally to me... Rally to me. I'll call out what direction and when to charge. The sun's to our east."

In his heart Henry rejoiced. Robert would lead.

"South...now!"

Henry charged and was immediately in the midst of more enemy horsemen. He thrust and parried...parried and thrust, cutting down two Turks before they'd even been able to rein in their mounts. The two groups, Christian and Muslim, mingled for what seemed like a long time. Swinging and cutting, Henry killed more. Then he heard Robert again.

"Back to the infantry. North...now!"

The turmoil continued. Henry knew they were killing great quantities of the enemy but all he could see around him were thousands more. They darkened the landscape.

"South...now!"

The knights charged into another swarm of enemy horsemen... the slaughter continued.

Henry's right arm began to ache from the constant swinging of his sword. He found himself out of breath and sweating profusely, so much that sweat was getting into his eyes and blurring his vision. More charges followed. Henry lost count. But just as Reynauld had taught him, he concentrated on maintaining his focus and not making a mistake.

'Dear God, please watch over us.'

Suddenly, there was a great gush among the enemy as if something was pushing them all in one direction. Then in the very midst of their ranks, Bohemond appeared riding at full gallop battering Turks off their horses left and right. When the son of Guiscard reached Robert, he reined in and called out above the din.

"Robert, follow us. There are too many of them. If we stay here, we'll all be killed." Bohemond then wheeled his horse and called out once more.

"Follow me!"

When the Norman knights finally broke free from the Turkish host, Henry glanced back over his shoulder to assess the infantry's situation. There was a great, dark mass of Arab horsemen still dashing about. Amidst this swarm, he couldn't see the Frankish infantry but he knew they were there.

Henry kneed Meredith next to Robert and called out. "Our infantry, we must go back for our infantry."

"We can't go back," yelled Bohemond. "There are too many of them."

Henry looked at Robert. The Count's face was filled with anguish. "We can't help them Henry. Follow Bohemond."

The next day Robert took a small contingent back to look for survivors. On their way they were very cautious lest they run into the whole Turkish army again but that didn't happen.

There were bodies everywhere, mostly Arab but plenty of Franks too. The corpses were thickest where the Norman infantry lay. Although not yet blackened and bloated, they looked like Peter's dead followers, awkwardly twisted bodies with numerous arrows protruding from them. A few had their chainmail and weapons stripped away but most were untouched. Apparently the Turks had departed quickly.

Even before Henry found Reynauld, he was crying. The 'Master of War Craft' lay on his back with the feathered ends of three arrows rising from his chest. His expression seemed almost calm as if, Henry thought, he was already in heaven.

The youth drew his right leg back over Meredith's saddle and dismounted. For a long while he stood looking at his mentor. Finally he bent down onto his knees and with effort slipped off Reynauld's aventail and placed it over his own shoulders. Then he unsheathed his knife and cut the knight's crimson cross from the breast of his surcoat. This he put into the inner pocket of his own surcoat. Last, Henry bowed his head and whispered a prayer.

"Dearest Lord, please accept this man's soul into Your castle for he has certainly been a good Christian."

After a slight pause, the young knight continued speaking but this time no longer to God but to Reynauld. "Goodbye my friend. Thank you for watching over me. I'll do my best to make you proud of me and I'll look forward to seeing you again when I die."

"Aye," joined Robert's voice from behind Henry. "God willing may we all rest in heaven together."

Their sortie to lay in food was aborted. It was going to be a very hard winter, very hard indeed. And when they got back to Antioch, the morale there was very low too.

While they'd been gone, the Christians investing Antioch had also experienced the comet, aurora and earthquake. Their conclusions were the same: God was displeased with His soldiers. And their retribution had come on the night of the 29th. Yaghi-Siyan, the Turkish overseer of the city, obviously knowing that a large number of Christian soldiers outside the gates had departed, initiated a major sortie sending out almost the entire garrison upon Raymond's forces at the Dog Gate. Raymond's men reacted quickly and decisively; so effectively that they might have entered the city but for the bad fortune of a rider-less horse charging back through the Christian ranks in near total darkness. They also lost a number of men, one of whom was Bishop Adhemar's standard bearer, a brave young knight named Bernard of Beziers. Adhemar's standard now hung atop the city walls where the Turks had placed it.

All this bad fortune caused the clergy, headed by Adhemar and Fulcher of Chartres to initiate corrective actions in hope of regaining God's favor. Intense liturgical observance was believed to be the only way to bring God back to their side. Accordingly in order to reduce sin, dissipation, avarice, pride, and rapaciousness, extreme austerity and Christian ritual were employed. Regular fasts, praying and giving of alms was required and even monitored.

ANTIOCH
June 1098

Tancred's tent held only three men. Henry of Dol and Roger of Barneville were sitting on the ground leaning back against a large wooden chest while Tancred sat on a wooden plank facing them. The three had been drinking since dusk.

After it became completely dark and the stars were visible, Henry noted that his two companions were responding to their liquor quite differently. Roger, who usually spoke abruptly and succinctly, began to say nothing. Tancred on the other hand, who was usually very direct and never talked on any subject for very long, seemed to have found a subject, Godfrey's younger brother Baldwin, about whom he had a lot to say.

"Henry, in September when I sortied south out of Heraclea with Roger and my brother-in-law, Richard, I only took a hundred and fifty men. We had the blessing of the Council and an Armenian guide to take us to Tarsus, a fine port city through which I knew we could acquire supplies from Cypress, Constantinople or even Genoa. That was the plan and I did it...cowed the garrison and even had my banner atop the citadel. I was working out the details of exchanging control when that son-of-the-devil Baldwin appeared with three hundred men. Naively I invited him to join us at the feast we were having. Well all the time we were breaking bread together, he must have been plotting how to undo us. The next morning I arose to find his banner flying over the city and mine awash in a peat bog! As he had twice the men I did, I couldn't do anything but leave. The rotten son-of-a-whore...may his soul burn in hell!"

Tancred turned his head and furiously spit.

"But did you hear what happened a few nights later? Three hundred men, Henry, three hundred fine Christian soldiers! Because they were Bohemond's men, Baldwin wouldn't let them inside the city walls. He made them sleep outside. Well the Turks, they have spies everywhere, dispatched a party of assassins to murder those poor men and they did, every one of them! All because that devil-incarnate wouldn't let them into the city! Three hundred men of the cross! May Baldwin's soul burn in hell!

"Meanwhile my men and I went to Adana where we helped an

Armenian named Oshin take back control of his town from the Turks and then with his support we took Mamistra, a prosperous little city on the banks of the Pyramus River. Well of course Baldwin showed up two days later and wanted us to give him that town too. But the situation was different: there were my men, two hundred of Oshin's, and several hundred more from Mamistra. So when Baldwin pressed, we didn't give in. The brawl was so violent that two men were killed, killed Henry! All for Baldwin's greed and ambition. Anyhow he had to depart without sacking the city. Ha, ha. He didn't win that one.

"I haven't seen the asshole since but I've heard what he did next. He got an Armenian guide, a fellow named Bagrat, who took him east of the Euphrates to Edessa which was overseen by a local lord named Thoros. Edessa is a big city. Anyhow you've probably heard the story, how he plotted with the locals there to murder Thoros and got himself made lord of the city. Him! A supposed Christian pilgrim sworn to take Jerusalem. Henry do you know how far Edessa is from Jerusalem? Three hundred miles! The conniving son-of-Satan, completely off the path he'd sworn to take and...and all for his own personal ambition. Oh, I almost forgot. He's a venal monster too. Apparently his guide had a pretty wife, so in Baldwin's comings and goings, he accused Bagrat of plotting against him and had the poor fellow beheaded. I'm told though that Bagrat's wife was kept on...in Baldwin's bed chamber."

"Tancred," growled Roger, "the keg's empty."

Momentarily interrupted, Tancred waved his arm toward the open chest behind Roger and Henry. "There's another one in there."

Henry thought Tancred was beginning to slur his words slightly. But Roger took action and was shortly filling Tancred's cup and then Henry's too.

"You know," continued Tancred in a milder tone, "I've been getting Roger to ask some of the Arabs we come upon about the Muslim military, their leaders and their politics. Not about their tactics. I think we've all learned what those are, but who we're up against and how coordinated they are. Alexius got me thinking about all that when he said we might want to talk to the Egyptians because they don't like the Turks. Well do you know Henry that their religion is divided into all sorts of separate groups, like our Roman and Greek churches, only with much more hate. They have 'Sunni' Turks and 'Shia' Arabs, something about Muhammad's descendants.

But the point is they really hate each other. Their sultans are scattered all over the place: in Egypt a fellow named Afdal, in Damascus Duqaq the one we squashed when we were foraging, and in Mozul, that's somewhere east of here, there's a fellow named Kerbogha. Anyhow it's very possible they won't help each other. That's their weakness!

"Of course they have strengths too. We've seen they're good fighters not afraid to die. But their other strength that we don't think about enough is their spies. My uncle learned about them in Italy. The Arabs and the Greeks, it must be an eastern thing, have all sorts of spies. They just pay people to get them information.

"Now Henry, where you live all the people are Christians. No one would betray another Christian for a handful of coins. It would be like being Judas Iscariot! But here all the Armenians and Arabs who sell us food, rob us is a better term for it, they're all spies! My uncle Bohemond learned this when he was fighting the Greeks. 'Once you know they're all spies,' he told me, 'you can use them.' And not just to get information, you can give them false information which they'll sell to the enemy. And if you make it sound reasonable, something they want to hear, they'll take action on it. When he was fighting the Greeks, Bohemond even gave useful information to one fellow several times so the Greeks would trust him. It takes time but you can set up an entire network. That's how Bohemond connected with this Firuz fellow, the Armenian convert who's betraying the city tonight. My uncle's been talking to him for weeks...right over there at the Tower of the Two Sisters."

Tancred waved his arm toward one of the city towers just a short distance away. "That's where we'll climb up but not till after the late watch goes by. Actually," contiued Tancred in a whisper, "it shouldn't be too long now."

Henry knew about the plan because it had just been discussed at the Council. He glanced at Roger to discern whether Tancred had told his liegeman. Roger was nodding his head in affirmation, so Henry was certain that he too already knew.

"Deception," chortled Tancred, "it's such a sweet thing when it's being deployed by us. Henry, did I ever tell you how Bohemond got rid of that Greek, Taticius?"

"No," said Henry who was quite taken aback by the question. "Bohemond had something to do with Taticius' leaving? I thought he went to Cypress to improve our supply situation."

"Ha, ha," laughed Tancred. "Not even close, not even close. No. That's just what he said when he left. It was really that Bohemond got tired of having him around always pleading Alexius' case at our Council meetings. You know the Emperor really just wants us to take cities for him. He's a coward Henry, not a real Christian here to restore Christianity to the land where Jesus walked and taught."

"But," stammered Henry, "how could Bohemond have gotten Taticius to leave? It doesn't make sense."

"Oh yes it does," snapped Tancred who didn't like having people contradict him. "Bohemond told Taticius that some of our leaders thought the Greeks were intentionally delaying our progress to Jerusalem and even inciting the Turks to move against us and that those leaders were plotting to kill him if there were any more delays. My uncle can be very persuasive. You don't see Taticius around anymore do you? Didn't you wonder why he left so quickly?"

"Anyhow, my uncle ferreted out this fellow Firuz. He's an Armenian who's now a Muslim but hates the Turks. You'll get a kick out of this Roger; some lusty Turk is bedding his wife. Anyhow his only real interest in life is how high the pile of gold we give him will be for betraying the city. Obviously he's been living here in the east all his life, no real values."

"Tancred," gurgled Roger, "have we another keg?"

"No," whispered Tancred, "but I think I hear something."

Henry reached for his sword. Someone was entering the tent from the side away from the city. As he rose to his feet, Henry felt his head swim. It had been a long time since he'd had so much wine.

"We're back," whispered Bohemond. "Has the late watch come by yet?"

"No," replied Tancred as he rose from his plank. "Is everyone with you?"

"Yes," replied Bohemond, "all in their places, the orders given, the secret still intact and sixty of my best men ready to go. We'll wait right here till the watch passes then we'll go forward. Has anything significant happened while we've been gone?"

"No," said Tancred. "It's almost been too quiet."

"There's the watch now." Bohemond pointed toward the Tower of the Two Sisters.

In the dark, Henry could hardly make out Bohemond's arm. But when he turned to look toward the towers, he could discern two torches bobbing their way forward atop the battlements.

"Tonight by God's will we'll take this city," whispered Bohemond... And only a short time later he whispered again. "Follow me."

Henry had put his helmet on but not yet drawn his sword. He reasoned if they were detected outside the walls, they'd have only a short run to escape missiles. But once on the walls, it would be a life or death situation. He hoped every one among them realized that between the time they mounted the wall and a gate was opened, silence would be essential. As he followed Tancred and Roger, Henry wondered if his father would be proud of him. Audrey would certainly be aghast.

As they approached the wall, Bohemond called out softly. "Drop the rope."

Henry forced himself not to think of all the ways their surprise could go wrong. Instead he willed his mind as Reynauld had taught him...to focus solely on the immediate objective, the very next thing that must be done, nothing else.

A rope dropped down from an opening high in the wall. It occurred to Henry that the hole from which the rope hung must be their way in. He'd thought they'd be going over the wall onto the battlements. After a moment of thinking though, he concluded this might be better...at least he hoped so.

Three knights trotted forward carrying an ox-hide ladder. They bent and tied their rope to the ladder. Almost immediately, one raised his arm and Bohemond quietly called out again. The long, twined ladder quickly rose toward the window above. A few moments later a voice called down in a language Henry didn't recognize.

Fulcher Fitz-Gerard of Chartres was the first to climb. Henry knew him to be a canon of Notre Dame and a man of God. Just as this thought passed through the youth's mind, the ox-hide ladder broke and several men tumbled to the ground. As they hit, Henry could hear their 'umphs'. But not one let forth a cry. It seemed as if an eternity passed before the rope came down again. Meanwhile, Bohemond's men repaired the ox-hide ladder and quickly tied it to the rope to be hauled up again. Henry was pleased to see Fulcher take his place again as 'the first man up.' All the men going up had specific instructions as to their order and tasks. On several occasions, Bohemond encouraged his men with whispered reminders. It all seemed to be taking a great deal of time but, when Bohemond pointed his finger at

Tancred, Roger and Henry, the young knight was startled. Nevertheless he fell right in behind his two friends. The climb itself was awkward and slow. There was enough time for Henry's mind to fleetingly wonder if the entire affair might be a trap: Turks waiting inside that little window to kill them as they entered. But Reynauld's training returned and Henry focused.

Once Henry was through the high window on the wall, he was glad to see Tancred and Roger waiting for him. They each had their swords drawn and their shields held on their left arm. Henry twisted his shield off his back, drew his sword and nodded to his companions. Roger smiled at him and winked. Henry couldn't really tell what sort of room they had entered. There was a tiny candle burning but its band of light barely illuminated his two friends. Tancred turned away and Roger and Henry followed. They exited onto a stone stairway, which appeared to lead up to the battlements as well as down to the ground. Henry hadn't any idea which way they should go but Tancred had either been given specific directions or was quick making decisions. They went up. At the battlements, Tancred turned right along the wall toward another tower. When they reached it, the entry door was ajar. Tancred clasped the door handle and glanced back at his two compatriots. Then he jerked open the wooden door and sprang into the unknown. As third man in, Henry expected little resistance. Ahead of him within the milky glow of another candle's light, two dead Turks lay on the floor. Two black pools of blood were spread around them. Beyond there were footsteps in the blood where Tancred and Roger had not yet reached, so they knew these two dead had been killed by a prior team of Christians.

Tancred waved them toward the next tower. The scene was the same. The three knights never spoke a word but this time Tancred changed direction. With his sword, he signaled they would go down. Again Henry followed Roger. It was very dark. Deftly they descended a narrow, curving stairway to what Henry guessed was the third level of habitation in the tower. From ahead the young knight heard Tancred whisper. "A door."

Then Henry heard a loud crash and saw a glimmer of light. Roger was a short, squarely built man of obvious strength but most importantly he was quick. The knight from Barneville went through the broken doorway in an instant. Henry followed. A lantern lit the center of the room; the room's edges, though, were still heavily shadowed. Ahead of him, Henry heard a thump as if a body had fallen, but he couldn't make anything out yet because Roger was in the way. As Roger continued forward, Henry saw a half-naked man slumped upon the floor. He was emitting odd gurgling sounds that were mixed with shallow gasps for air. Beneath him a pool of blood was rapidly spreading.

Henry saw Tancred begin to step over the dying man, when a piercing screech from just behind Henry's his right ear broke the silence. Immediately he felt a pointed blow behind his right shoulder. His reaction was ingrained in him just as Reynauld had intended it to be. The young knight pivoted on his right foot and savagely sliced his sword up and across. Even before he saw his attacker, he felt his blade cut into its target. As his eyes caught up with his spiraling weapon, Henry saw a woman! Her expression of anger and surprise was palpable: her jaw hung agape, her frenzied scream hung in the air, her hate and fury were etched across her face and then in an instant, her eyes lost their focus. Still holding her knife above her shoulder, her body crumpled to the floor.

"Oh God!" At first Henry's voice came to him from a great distance but, almost immediately he transitioned out of his instinctive mode back into his sentient self.

"What have I done?"

"Are you all right?" Roger asked. "Did the knife penetrate?"

Henry stood stock still; he was only aware of the woman's facial expression which still floated in his brain. Then he felt a hard blow on his shield and for a moment, his visceral personage retook control. His body began to pivot left.

"Come on, Henry," called a familiar voice...it was Roger's voice. "We've got work to do. You didn't kill her on purpose."

Somewhere deep in his head, Henry assessed Roger's call to action. 'Yes,' he thought, 'I must continue. Our objective is yet ahead.'

REDEMPTION
June 1098 – January 1099

The Christians took the city but on the morning of the 7th, Kerbogha's army arrived and began to invest the gates. Various Christian leaders estimated the size of the Muslim army to be between thirty and fifty thousand men. It was clearly much larger than the Franks' remaining army. To make matters even worse, the Franks were extremely low on food and had only about a thousand horses left.

Henry, whose mind was constantly reviewing his slaying of that woman, did find time to ask Bishop Adhemar to meet with him in order to hear his confession. The Papal Legate agreed and set a time for Henry to come to his tent.

When Henry arrived, he found another young knight, Hugh de Payens, also waiting to see Adhemar. The two men quickly fell into conversation.

"The Bishop has been kind enough to agree to hear my confession," said Hugh.

Henry noted that the knight's equipment was old and outdated, but he spoke in a calm voice which Henry thought portrayed a certainty of inner self. He appeared to be a man one could trust, a good man to go into battle with.

"The Bishop called me here for just the same reason," responded Henry and then without thinking, he continued. "I killed a woman by mistake." Henry watched Hugh closely to gauge the man's reaction to his statement. It was the first time he'd told anyone.

Hugh's expression remained calm and after a while he spoke. "This pilgrimage has not been a pleasant experience. We've seen bloated, black corpses of men, women and children littered across the plain for miles; we've seen men and women starve to death, die of disease, fall off mountain sides. I've killed so many Turks that I've stopped...feeling it. I don't even know how many I've killed. Arrows swarm at us and I am spared while my best friend was killed and he a better Christian than I. All I can conclude is that God's will is very hard to understand. I'm told I must have faith but... What I come back to is that I must set my goal on something just, something unselfish. Rescuing the Christians in Jerusalem is a worthy objective as is opening the pilgrimage routes to get there. But what I fear is that in so doing, we become more and more like the butchers who now murder the pilgrims along the way."

Henry thought on Hugh's words. He knew he wasn't yet the same as those Turks who'd purposely slain women and children. But like Hugh, he knew he was closer to being like them now than he had been when he left Flanders... At least he hadn't killed that woman on purpose.

Meanwhile through Count Robert, Henry learned of two quite different occurrences which if true, might prove to be enormously uplifting. Two men in the Christian camp had seen a vision. The first, a rather disreputable fellow named Peter Bartholomew, told Bishop Adhemar that Saint Andrew had come to him in a dream and told him that 'the Most Holy Lance' which had been used to pierce Jesus' side when He was on the cross, was buried nearby in the cathedral of Saint Peter. The second man, a priest named Stephen, had met a mysterious visitor in the Church of Our Lady who, after some thought, he recognized to be Jesus by the halo surrounding his head. Christ had then told Stephen that He would forgive His soldiers for their lust, fornications and other sins if they immediately repented and again took up true Christian righteousness.

That night a hurtling meteor was seen which seemed to fall directly on the Turkish camp. Immediately the next morning the Council of leaders was convened. The visions were discussed and the meteor's flight assessed. The conclusions from the Council were two-fold: All the nobles in the army were to immediately swear an oath stating that none of them would desert; second it was decided that a team of twelve, including Raymond of Toulouse, Bishop William of Orange, Farald of Thomars and Raymond of Aguilers, would accompany Peter to dig up the floor of the cathedral in search of the Lance. The digging continued most of the day leaving all but Peter disillusioned and disappointed. Finally Peter, clad only in a shirt, leapt into the hole crying out, "I see it." Forthwith he reached into the dirt and withdrew a shard of iron. The discovery produced immediate rapture and ebullience among the Christian forces. The Holy Lance had been found! God's favor had been restored.

Despair was replaced by enthusiasm. The Christian leaders immediately began planning an attack. Bohemond was appointed to be the architect of the plan and also to become its executer. He divided the army into six parts, reserving all the horses for the final unit that he intended to use as 'shock' troops to break the enemy's resolve by means of a valiant charge into their midst. This he believed would be their best way to throw Kerbogha's vast army into confusion and retreat. Meanwhile, the bishops and priests collected alms from the wealthiest members of the army thus allowing them to repent by giving to the needy. Also, a holy celebration recognizing the discovery of the Lance took place with great fan-fare on the 21st. All leaders, high and low, were bidden to 'buck-up' their men with the knowledge that in the battle ahead, they would be acting as God's right hand.

June 28th was set as 'the day.' The three days prior were devoted to fasting, prayer, confession and absolution. Each man thus received his for-giveness and was reminded of God's promise to accept him directly into heaven in return for his full effort to carry out his promise to reach and take Jerusalem.

The next day, the Christian army exited the city gates and formed up in their new component units. Hugh's Franks and Robert's Flemish were at the front; behind them, Godfrey's Lotharingians; third, Duke Robert's Nor-mans; fourth the Toulousans and Provencals under Adhemar of Le Puy; fifth, the south Normans under Tancred, and last led by Bohemond, all the mounted knights on whatever beasts they could find. Henry, serving on foot, kept as close to Robert as he could.

The role of the infantry was to march directly toward the center of Kerbogha's army while ignoring the hoards of Arab horse-archers who swarmed on their flanks. Just before reaching the Turk's main force, the foot soldiers were to split apart in order to make space for Bohemond's mounted knights to charge through and crash directly into the Arab infantry who, until that very last moment, would not be expecting mounted knights.

When Henry first heard Bohemond present his plan, the youth had been very impressed because it allowed the Franks to employ a mounted frontal assault against foot soldiers, which was where knights functioned preeminently well. Also the plan protected their small band of horsemen, about seven hundred, until they were right into the enemy. Going at the Turks in any other way would have mixed the Christian knights in with the Muslim horse archers and diluted the attack.

The third part of Bohemond's plan was to focus their offense by having all the arrows in the Christian camp, given to Hugh's archers, so they could be loosed at the Arab infantry just before Bohemond's cavalry emerged, charging from the midst of the Christian army. And overlooking nothing, Bohemond placed the Holy Lance in the hands of Raymond of Aguilers who carried it high on a pole so everyone could see it. Raymond had proven many times that he would take himself to the heart of the battle. And every Christian knew the closer he was to that lance, the safer he would be. The entire plan rested on perfect execution and an all-in effort at the very beginning.

After the battle, Henry thought that their victory against such overwhelming odds reflected the actual intercession of God. Several of their soldiers had even seen a troop of white knights chasing Kerbogha's horsemen off to the horizon. Henry had seen some low-hanging clouds but, at the time, he hadn't deemed them to be God's knights. Nevertheless, the soldiers who reported having seen this sign of heavenly intervention wouldn't accept any concessions to their story. Henry had little doubt that God's hand had played a decisive role: from the beginning by inspiring Pope Urban to propose the pilgrimage, along the way by reinforcing God's will in regard to having righteous soldiers and now here at Antioch by helping the soldiers overcome an enemy two or three times larger than themselves.

ANOTHER CHESS PLAYER
June 1099

From atop the walls of Jerusalem, Ali Abduli Kafa squinted through the night's partial darkness. He thought he saw a group of riders a mile or so away but the moon was too new for him to be certain. If there were riders, they could be either Muslims or Christians. Just that morning, his scouts had reported that the Christian army would arrive the next day or at most, the day after. This night though, he could still get some sleep without being urgently awakened.

Ali was the commander of the elite Sudanese cavalry unit sent just ten weeks before from Egypt to bolster the defense of Jerusalem. At the time, it seemed as if it would be a quiet post. The Greeks were considered friends if not allies, and the Christians were fighting the Turks who were the Egyptian Shiites' only identified enemy. But two weeks after he'd arrived, all that changed. A member of an Egyptian delegation that had been meeting with the Greeks and Christians near Antioch was dropped off at Jaffa to give Iftikhar, Jerusalem's governor, important news. The Christian army would shortly march against Jerusalem! This information certainly startled Iftikhar. Ali was less surprised because at his previous assignment in Cairo, he'd become aware of a letter from the Greek Emperor to Al-Afdal, the boy Caliph's Vizier, which stated quite simply that Alexius would not be responsible for future actions taken by the Franks. The Vizier had concluded from this that the Franks were now an independent force to be reckoned with. Ali had served in Cairo long enough to accept this sort of bedlam calmly. In his eight years there, he had experienced assassinations, plots, spies, coups, uprisings, traitors and rapists. Accordingly he'd learned never to trust anyone or any group until he or they had been carefully watched for a significant period of time, and even then he always retained a seed of doubt in the back of his mind just in case.

Ali always found the careers of fighting soldiers like himself to be somewhat humorous. During less threatening times, they were honored but ignored and definitely not promoted. He thought if the real motives for that could ever be sifted out from all the rhetoric that deep down the politicians feared and despised soldiers due to their predilection to tell the truth and make decisions, each of which Ali thought would eviscerate the smoke upon which the politicians rested their laurels. His own sudden rise in Jerusalem was a comic example. Without so much as a single question, Iftikhar, a very well connected political appointee, had assumed that Ali since he'd been in several battles and knew everything military.

Ali remembered how he and most of the male members of his family had been inducted ten years before. An official had shown up on their lord's plantation deep in the delta and announced that the Sultan was preparing for war and it was his job to induct men into His Magnificence's army. At the time Ali was only fourteen but since he could ride he was taken. His father, older brother, three cousins, six horses and three mules were also inducted and all taken to Cairo. There the men were each given a sword, a small round shield and put into units of about two hundred. There was no training, just mass confusion and rotten food. However Ali was lucky. One day at the food wagon while he was holding out his cup to receive its usual heap of gruel, a big, older man beside him called out to an equally large fellow nearby.

'Hakem, I can't find anyone here who plays chess." The other fellow had simply shrugged and turned away.

"Not a brain in this entire mob," the first speaker growled as he turned from the food wagon and bumped into Ali.

Fondly Ali remembered his response. "I play chess."

Haru became Ali's best friend and mentor, at least until he was killed a year later. But he taught Ali a great deal: how to attack with his sword, how to defend with his shield, how to direct his horse with his knees and how when on horseback, to gain a favorable position against an opponent. Most of all, Haru taught Ali how to follow the Qur'an, living by one's word and thus pleasing Allah. Having grown up in a Christian family, Ali didn't know much about the teachings of the Qur'an. But Haru was a patient man who took the time to teach his pupil about Jihad: that there were two elements of which the 'greater' was the overcoming of one's own 'lower' self-immorality and sin. And there was the 'lesser Jihad' which called upon Muslims to spread their beliefs and bring over unbelievers.

In ten years Ali had been in three battles, two uprisings, and several tussles arising while he was on guard duty. Of the others he'd been inducted with, three were dead, one severely disabled and the last one back on the plantation. More than anyone, Ali understood that rising in the military had less to do with skill and insight than survival, a thought that took his mind back to the caprice of being appointed the military headman in Jerusalem. No one had ever given him any training on how to prepare a city for a siege. So when he was assigned the role, he'd quickly set himself to thinking and asking. His thinking got his brain to envision what it would be like to be surrounded without access to provisions or communications. His asking he directed to an Imam with whom he'd recently played chess. Ali-Selami suggested that he first throw all the Christians out of the city: 'fewer mouths to feed and entirely untrustworthy.' Also Ali-Selami continued, 'Poison the wells outside the city as far as you can so the Christians will have as little water as possible and drive all the livestock into the city so you can be feasting while they are starving.' Ali followed all this advice to the letter. Additionally, all supplies of wood that could be found were brought into the city lest the Christians be able to build scaling ladders. And with the wood, Ali's men were able to construct forty mangonels in forty days. He knew these would prove useful to destroy siege towers, support equipment, and human beings should they group together within range. Also the heat would be on their side. The sun was already baking clods of mud into bricks. These Franks wouldn't like the heat. They were soft creatures used to living in a fat land. And while the Christians suffered from thirst, the good people within the walls would be awash with the cool waters of the huge Hezekial pool and the Jewish Pool of Israel.

The only mistake Ali thought he might have made was in not delaying the Christians' arrival more than he had. This however would have required that he allocate resources to distant ambuscades, which in turn meant his men would have done less in Jerusalem. Nevertheless, not having done it still concerned him. He'd expected the Christians would devote their summer to pillaging the wealthy towns along the coast: Tripoli, Tyre, Acre, Haifa and Jaffa. But they had not. They had skipped right past them ignoring all of their gold and silver. He was certain they knew those towns were rich. So why hadn't they stopped? It got them to Jerusalem a lot faster. But not fast enough to catch Ali unprepared. And this rush forward left their east flank and rear unprotected, a point that could become quite important if their siege lasted into the winter. Ali wondered if the Christians somehow knew about al-Afdal gathering a relief army in Cairo. If they did, they would know they did not have much time to take the city and accordingly, hurry to get over the walls as fast as they could. If they didn't know, they might procrastinate and get caught between the garrison and Afdal's army. That would be very good. In either case, Ali thought he would learn what they knew based on how quickly they worked. Ali smiled. He was glad his men had rounded up all the lumber outside the city and brought it inside the walls. The Christians would not have anything with which to construct ladders, towers or mangonels.

JERUSALEM

June 1099

Henry was riding his new horse. Robert had given him Pegasus as a replacement for Meredith who had died just after her charge into Kerbogha's army. She had been sturdy, reliable and, with Bart's help, a survivor. The Christian army was now down from seventy thousand before Dorylaeum to only twenty thousand: twelve hundred knights, twelve thousand foot soldiers and archers and about six thousand camp-followers who were a mixed bunch including women, children and assorted smiths, armorers and herdsmen all of whom were poor.

As they approached Jerusalem, there was a new moon in the sky but it was wafer-thin and cast hardly any light on the Christian troop. There was however one notable event. The crescent moon passed through an eclipse. When the members of the Christian troop realized this, they halted. An eclipse was always a meaningful event.

"A very good omen," Baldwin of Le Bourcq said to Tancred.

"Yell it out," said Tancred, "so all the men can hear you."

"Aye," replied Baldwin. "The crescent moon is the Arabs' sign. This eclipse foretells their time is up!"

"Aye… Aye," rejoined the following knights.

Arriving on a hill top which pilgrims called Mount Joy, Tancred reined in his horse and quickly dismounted. Arrayed before him was Jerusalem, the center of the earth on every Christian map in the last thousand years. Their leader then sank to his knees. With tears welling up in his eyes and emotion roiling his voice, Tancred took a moment before he spoke. "I shall willingly give my life for the opportunity to kiss the Holy Sepulchre."

By the evening of the 7th, the lords and their armies had all settled into camp sites outside the city wall. Raymond was located on Mount Zion, a hill on the southwest side of the city. He was joined there by the poorest of the poor, the Tarfurs. The rest of the armies settled in along the north side of the wall, which promised level ground suitable for a siege tower. The west and east sides of Jerusalem were traversed by the ravine of Kedran and the Vail of Gehenna. Each was composed of very rough terrain unsuitable for anything military. Along the northern and southern locations though, there were outer walls that would first have to be broken down and, once past them, there was a ditch in front of the main wall that would have to be filled before a tower could be put across to the wall. These sites would surely be well defended. But with proper equipment and committed soldiers, the Christian leaders thought they were assailable.

Henry's duties were numerous. He had to establish communications with all the other coordinators, determine food and water sources and aquire opinions from the more astute leaders as to strategies for their siege of the city. Also he intended to locate Bartholomew of Tournai to find out how Bart of Dol and Johnnie of Flanders were doing. The army's overall situation was very similar to that at Antioch, too few soldiers to totally invest the city, a likely relief army coming and therefore, a need to move quickly. That and all the details—food, water, animals, equipment, siege towers, mangonels and ladders—would be subjects for the Council. And Henry thought if he already knew they had to move quickly, the leaders would know that too.

As Henry rode from camp to camp, he found little disagreement among the lords. A classic attack was called for: towers, catapults and ladders. Fortunately the leadership had extensive experience along these lines. Robert of Normandy had fought his father, William the Conqueror, for three years investing castles; Godfrey had defended his castle in Bouillon early in his career and laid siege to castles elsewhere; Tancred had left an ongoing siege at Bari to join their pilgrimage, and Gaston of Bearne had laid siege to several Arab cities in Iberia.

The issues were speed and the acquisition of lumber. Unfortunately, the local topography was barren of trees, and most of the buildings outside the city had already been plundered for their timber by the Egyptians' siege of the city the previous fall. Accordingly, Robert of Flanders volunteered to ride to Nablus with two hundred men, enough to deter robbers or small units of Fatimids but not enough should they run into an entire Muslim army. Nablus had a forest which was known for its excellent cypress trees but was over a hundred miles north in the direction of Damascus.

Despite the risk, Robert left with a number of woodcutters as well as his own soldiers. Propitiously Tancred, who was patrolling a wide swath south of Jerusalem with forty knights hoping to get early knowledge of any Fatimid military sorties out of Egypt, happened onto a magnificent cash of four hundred pieces of timber. He'd been suffering from dysentery and was making a stop at a convenient cave when he came upon the lumber.

Lumber was not their only need. Iftikhar's poisoning of the wells forced the Christians to travel six miles for good water. Also the supplies of food were short. Henry had learned that hardships came in groups. In addition to the lack of water and victuals, there was an abundance of heat, sun and dust, which were all made more painful by the ever-blowing siroccos. There was one unpolluted spring nearby, the Gihan, but it was within bow shot of the city's walls. The Fatimid archers enjoyed dispatching speculative shots toward those Christians who were dehydrated enough to make visits to the spring. Most of the knights' horses were kept at a well eight miles away so their water was assured. Accordingly transportation near the city had changed from horse to camel. Despite the privation, the Christian army persevered and prepared.

On the 17th six Christian ships put into Jaffa with a cargo of food, rope, nails, bolts and lumber. All this material was quickly brought to the besieging army together with many of the ships' crew who were skilled craftsmen and, due to the Fatimid navy's sudden blockade of Jaffa, free to aid the effort to take Jerusalem by building towers, catapults and ladders. Two of the sailors from Genoa, brothers named Embriaco, led the crews in these endeavors. So with lumber from three different sources, there was more than enough for two towers, forty-some mangonels and numerous ladders.

What Henry hadn't anticipated was another vision. On July 6th, Peter Desiderius, a well-respected priest, came to William-Hugh of Monteil, the brother of the deceased Bishop Adhemar, conveying Adhemar's wish beheld in a dream that the Christian army give up selfishness, repent sins, fast and walk barefoot in procession around the walls of the city. If they did, Adhemar had said, they would capture the city in exactly nine days...on the 15th! This message was accepted as real as Peter was a devout member of the Church and because in less than a week, the towers and ladders would be ready.

Raymond of Toulouse dipped into his treasure chest and hired William Embriaco and most of his sailors and craftsmen to erect a tower that

Raymond intended to roll down from Mount Zion and abut to the city's south wall. The plan for the tower called for a height of more than fifteen meters to assure that the tower's top floor would be well above the city wall, giving Christian archers and crossbow men an ideal position from which to loose their shafts and bolts.

With similar intent, Godfrey of Bouillon hired Gaston of Bearne to oversee the erection of a second tower to be directed against the city's north wall. From his numerous sojourns into Iberia, Gaston had extensive experience with towers. And despite being a Provancal, he was quite willing to hire on with Godfrey. Henry found him to be one of the most pleasant and outgoing knights in the entire army and had little doubt that he would build a fine tower. Through his coordinator's role, the young knight also knew that Gaston's tower was designed to be taken apart quickly, moved and reassembled. This was a technique Gaston said he'd learned in Spain and saw used to great advantage when the tower's first targeted location had to be changed. 'Flexibility,' Gaston called it.

The other secret that Henry learned was that 'Greek fire,' which the Muslims would surely employ in hope of setting the two towers ablaze, could be quelled by vinegar. The Council had learned this from some of the Christian inhabitants of the city whom the Fatimids had expelled as untrustworthy prior to the Franks' arrival. Thus the towers were stocked with casks of vinegar, and their front-facing sides hung with animal skins and wattle to protect the towers' wooden sides from catching fire.

A huge crowd gathered on Friday the eighth of July. The barefoot procession of penitents wound around the city following the bishops and clerics. Knights, soldiers, Tarfurs, women and children followed. It was a brutally bright day with heat so great that the horizon shimmered. The siroccos lifted dust into the devotees' eyes and the baked hard pack beneath them scorched the bottoms of their feet. At the front of the column were a series of banners, crosses, relics and cherished items. Standing atop the city walls, the Muslim enemy hooted their derision, called out blasphemies and urinated on crosses. No degree of disparagement diminished the Christians' uplifted sense of comradeship, devotion and purpose. They were one…and they knew it!

From the 9th to the morning of the 14th, Henry was kept close to the activities around the north wall. It was a beehive of activity and needed every pair of hands available. On the late afternoon of the 13th, moving the tower to a better site was presented to their leaders silent acclimation. At dark thousands of men, women and children immediately set to work acquiring and carrying thousands of small stones with which to fill the dry ditch just in front of the main wall. It was a dangerous job but was protected by the darkness of the night. Simultaneously, hundreds of men helped carry the huge timbers of the tower to its new location. The mangonels, catapults and trebuchets, together with the large rocks they would throw, also were relocated.

In the morning, the Fatimids discovered to their dismay that the additional defensive works they'd created opposite the tower's original position were no longer of any value and that the dry ditch opposite the newly targeted site had already been filled in. All they could do was realign their catapults to target the tower's newly projected path.

Meanwhile the Christians waited for the morning of the 14th, their time to assault the city. Finally the sun rose sufficiently to cast its rays off the chain-mailed row of knights who stood shoulder-to-shoulder facing the wall. As the light reflected off their coats of metal ringlets, their phalanx glistened and glinted. Henry stood beside Robert of Flanders. Behind them were a myriad of knights, foot soldiers, archers, old men, women and children...all veterans of this nearly four-year armed pilgrimage. Among the camp-followers were some without weapons, mostly women and children, who carried buckets or hide stitched pouches with which to carry water. The rest held knives, swords or clubs. Their facial expressions were mixed reflecting inner resolve, fear and relgious belief. All of these soldiers, serfs, wives and laborers had long ago committed themselves before God to capture this holiest of cities. The day to do so had finally arrived.

Henry's mind was assessing his own feelings. Long ago he had reached an agreement with God. When Jesus called, he would go. Meanwhile he intended to exact God's will. That part he reasoned was simple enough and settled. But he hadn't previously realized that in the heat of battle, he might err as he had with that woman in Antioch. But now that he'd had time to think about it, he'd concluded that he must redouble his efforts. God had set a higher bar than he'd expected. He would have to do his very best to live up to it.

The tactics for taking the city were straight forward. A huge battering ram would be pushed forward against the wall and there pound the barrier until it was so holed that the Christian army could rush in. The contraption itself was an immense wheeled devise with a reinforced, upward-pointing v-shaped roof to protect the men under it from dropped stones or liquid fire. Beneath the roof swung an eighteen-foot long, giant tree trunk with a pointed, iron cone attached to its nose, to be drawn back and, when let go, swing forward against whatever it faced, in this case the stones in Jerusalem's north wall. It was a mighty weapon and should produce the desired outcome if it could be swung enough times.

Henry's thoughts were interrupted when a knight standing quite near him whispered, "God's will." Henry's mind jumped back to the long line of Christian knights standing shoulder to shoulder beside and behind him.

"God's will," called forth another knight.

"God's will," called out Henry with several other knights who'd caught the cadence.

"God's will," barked a hundred men.

"God's will," roared thousands of God's soldiers.

"To your tasks," yelled Robert.

Henry barely heard his lord amidst the roar of another 'God's will,' but he trotted forward to Godfrey's tower. He'd been assigned to stay near Godfrey who'd be atop his wooden castle directing the attack. He was to bring Godfrey's orders back to the two Roberts whenever appropriate. The tower rose ahead of him with its east-facing wall painted a bright orange by the sun's early light and its west side still a dark grey, almost black. On its south side, the side intended to be pushed against the city's wall, a great number of cattle and camel hides had been nailed to the wood to protect it from bomblets of Greek fire. Henry knew there were many wooden kegs full of vinegar within the tower waiting to counteract the liquid fire. It struck him as interestingly odd that the city walls against which they were aiming their ram and tower had been similarly adorned with protective layers of cotton layments and wattle. These the Fatimids apparently thought would diminish the impact of the huge stones thrown against the walls by the Christian mangonels, catapults and trebuchets. Whether the cotton bales would save the walls or not, Henry had no idea. It was clear the Fatimids thought they would because they were frantically hanging the layments on their newly threatened section as fast as they could.

Several days earlier, Henry had inspected Gaston's tower. When he was through, he was certain that whoever had recommended Gaston was incredibly insightful. The wooden castle was a masterful piece of work. It stood over forty feet high, was protected from enemy archers on three sides, rolled forward or back on small wheels, could be broken down, moved and reconstructed in less than twelve hours by an experienced crew, had a fifth level battlement that provided ample space for archers, crossbowmen, stone throwers and had exits on the fourth level where two front-facing wall planks could be laid out onto the adjacent city wall and used to cross over.

The ram and the tower advanced in much the same manner. Each had haulers who went ahead of their ordinance and hauled on ropes which were attached to it. Conversely each had pushers who pressed their cargo forward by hand while other pushers, who couldn't get close enough to employ their hands, pushed with poles. Once the tower got close enough to the wall, many of the pushers climbed aboard and took up their primary role as archers, crossbowmen, rock droppers or wall rushers. Henry helped push the tower until the ram was squarely up against the massive stone wall, which it had been designed to hole. The very sound of the huge, iron-tipped tree trunk slamming against the stone was sonorous to the young knight's ears. He could tell from the tenor of each thud that the mighty battering ram was pulverizing the stone into gravel. Within the tower, smiles showed forth from under every helmet. And there was more good news. The tower was now close enough to the city wall to allow archers, crossbowmen, and stone throwers to rain down their missiles upon the hapless Fatimids. The pulley on the back side of the tower was squeaking constantly as it lifted rocks and other ammunition to the fifth level.

Henry thought he ought to check-in with Godfrey, if for no other reason than to see the action from above. He clambered up the successive ladders and had almost reached the top when he heard his name called out.

"Henry!"

Despite the shadows that obscured the closely packed-in knights all around him, Henry immediately identified his friend Bartholomew of Tournai whose unruly mop of red hair was at the moment uncovered.

"Bart, is that you?" Henry's response expressed both surprise and pleasure. "I thought you and Ludolf were with Godfrey's knights."

"We are," bellowed Bart. "These are Godfrey's knights all around you."

"Oh...of course," responded Henry sheepishly. "Is Ludolf with you?"

"I am," said a big knight who'd been peering out through a small hole in their tower's front-facing wall.

Henry carefully stepped between two knights who were sitting on the floor and shook Ludolf's hand. "I'm glad to see you, Ludolf."

"As I am to see you Henry." Ludolf's tone was as dead-pan as always but Henry had trained with Ludolf long enough to know that his tenor reflected no animosity.

Henry turned back toward Bart. "If I'd known you two were here, I'd have come up to be with you."

"Well, join us now," responded Bart.

"Thank you. I will. But first I must check in with Godfrey as I am a runner for Robert."

"We'll hold a space for you," said Bart as his smile exposed his teeth.

Henry then climbed the last ladder to the 'roof.' When he poked his head up through the hatch hole, he still had to take two more steps up the ladder before he could see over the three foot wooden wall the tower had around its three frontal sides. When he finally saw the city's stone wall, it was well below him and only twenty-some feet distant. There Fatimids there bobbing up to shoot arrows at the tower's men and then dropping back to reload. Quickly the young knight lowered his head and looked around. Just in front of him sat Eustus, Godfrey's older brother, who was winding up a crossbow. Beyond him stood Godfrey, standing straight up like a church spire amidst all the missiles. The Duke was apparently waiting for Eustus to pass him his reloaded crossbow. Meanwhile with his blond locks flowing out beneath his helmet, Godfrey was surveying the battle. Eventually Eustus completed his task and, holding forth the loaded weapon, prodded the Duke's leg with it.

As Godfrey turned for the crossbow, he saw Henry. "Henry, come here my boy. Don't be afraid. They've slowed firing their mangonels, too likely to hit their own men on the wall. You can get a good view of the situation from here." As he spoke in his German accent, Godfrey's fingers clasped the crossbow and began to raise it to his shoulder.

Henry leapt to his feet if for no other reason than to dissuade Godfrey from thinking he was afraid. Quickly he stepped up beside the Lotharingian. "I've come to see if you have any directions for me to take to the Roberts, my lord."

"Yes I have." Godfrey raised his bow and took careful aim at a location just above the city wall. "I believe you could give them an update. The ram is making good progress at creating a hole. Once it actually holes the wall, we will have to reposition it slightly so it can widen the circumference of the cavity. When that is done, we can put the tower against the wall and then simultaneously send men through the hole, onto the wall from the tower and up the walls with ladders. God willing by late afternoon we'll be ready for all that. Tell the Roberts that when I stand up and blow my trumpet, they should bring their men forward with ladders. And you come back here right away Henry, even with God on our side, there are still many things that can go wrong. Now excuse me for a moment while I try to send another Fatimid to where ever their dead go." The Duke lowered his right eye to the sites of the crossbow.

Henry quickly searched the wall for Godfrey's target. There was none, at least not yet. Both knights watched patiently while they waited for Godfrey's quarry to lift his head above the wall. Several moments passed while the Duke's concentration never faltered. Finally a Fatimid's head popped up and, swinging his loaded bow toward the tower, the archer rose into a firing position. Godfrey didn't hurry his shot. He took careful aim. Henry heard the snap as the crossbow released its quarrel. He hadn't been watching Godfrey or his bow. His eyes were locked on the Arab. The man's expression seemed to be just registering concern when the Duke's bolt penetrated his left eye. As it did, the quarry's head jerked violently back and his entire body fell away behind the battlements.

"Finally I got him," growled Godfrey. "Praise be to God." The Duke passed his bow back to Eustus.

"That was a perfect shot," said Henry with complete sincerity.

"Thank you," replied Godfrey. "I like the crossbow. I know some think it un-Christian to use a weapon that can penetrate armor but most of those who say that sort of thing have never been in combat. And of course, we're not killing Christians... God has given me a steady hand which is well suited to this weapon. So I use it."

Henry nodded. "Well, I'll be off to tell the Roberts to await your horn and, God willing, this afternoon your ram will hole the wall and we can charge through the opening. I should be back quite quickly and I'll be on the floor just below you with Ludolf and Bartholomew of Tournai."

While the Roberts were glad to get an update, they already knew, as did all their men, that the airing of Godfrey's horn would mean his ram had broken a big enough hole through the wall so an all-out assault could commence. Accordingly Henry didn't have any really significant information to share other than the ram was doing its job and might hole its way into the city at any moment. After sharing his update, Henry returned to his spot on the fourth floor of the tower with his two friends. Not surprisingly, Ludolf was still peering out his peephole near one of the exit planks. When he poked his sword through the hole and jostled the hides hanging there, he could see some of what was going on. As the leader of the knights on the fourth floor and the only person who could see out at all, he was regularly conveying status reports of anything noteworthy in his usual stolid and unruffled tone.

The first time Ludolf said, "Greek fire on our hides," Henry felt a man beside him start to move. Everyone could see flames licking brightly through numerous cracks and openings in their front wall, but before concern could transition into fear, Ludolf spoke. "Don't worry. The men above us are already splashing their vinegar on the flames."

A moment later, Ludolf's men heard hissing and the visible sparks of flame immediately diminished. Another time there was a mighty crash. A boulder had hit the front side of the tower. "Ah," muttered Ludolf, "I knew those mangonels couldn't miss forever. Now we see why they call this a wooden castle. The men who built it surely knew their business. I think it hit that beam right there." Ludolf pointed as he rose to his feet. "Here, let's have a look. If need be, we can shore it up." The knight stepped forward between two of his men. "Ah ha," he finally said in his impassive tone as he drew his head back from the beam, "she's not done yet. These beams were cut from green wood. They'll take a hundred of those little bumps before we have to shore them up." Several of Henry's cohorts laughed.

A short while later, another dousing of Greek fire splashed across the tower's front-facing wall. Little licks of flame again investigated each tiny hole among the timbers and outside hanging hides. Again footsteps above were heard and a second dousing of vinegar was delivered. The flames diminished. Between these points of high challenge, Ludolf continued to gaze out through his little opening. "Those poor bastards are taking an awful beating from Godfrey and our archers…simple, short shots and they haven't chain mail to protect themselves. If the ram doesn't hurry up, there won't be any left for us. Too bad we're behind the ram. If we were twenty feet to the right, we could push right up to the wall and drop these two planks of ours. As we are, we're about two plank lengths from the wall. The good news though, is that the ram is still thumping away below, and they've pushed it forward twice so there can't be much wall left."

Not long after Ludolf had uttered those words, Henry heard a cheer from below. It could only be the ram's crew celebrating the breakthrough of the wall.

"It won't be long now," said someone.

Time passed. Neither Godfrey's horn sounded nor did the ram's jarring thuds recommence. Henry glanced at Ludolf. Recognizing Henry's unspoken question, Ludolf again poked his sword through the peephole and squinted down at the ram.

"They're trying to pull the ram back," the floor leader finally said. "To widen the hole they need a different angle but they seem to be having trouble pulling the fucker back."

"Should we go down to help?" asked someone.

"I don't know," replied Ludolf. "Henry go down and see if they need any help."

Henry rose quickly. He was glad to have an ambulatory assignment. His legs were stiff from sitting. It was easy to see that things weren't going well below. There were tears in the eyes of several of the ram's crew. All were pulling on ropes attached to the batterer but the mighty mechanism wasn't moving away from the wall. The ram's front legs were about five feet inside the wall; so far in fact that Henry could see a little daylight shining through just beyond the ram's iron head. But the crew's efforts to reposition the wooden monster were not availing. Despite the danger from dropped boulders and flying missiles, Henry raised his shield and trotted forward to enter the cavern that the ram had so far created. There he could see the problem. The small wheels under the front end of the ram were broken and, to make matters worse, the lowest frontal crossbeam had dropped into a slight depression, which made their pulling effort much more onerous.

"I can get more men to pull," Henry yelled at one of the crewmen. "Have you got more ropes?"

"Yes," cried the fellow who was naked and almost completely black from the amalgamation of his sweat and the rock dust the ram's head produced. "They're straight back just beyond bowshot, but we'll have to prize up the front of this piece of shit before it will move. See if there are any long crowbars. I don't know where they'd be but someone will."

Henry re-climbed the tower quickly. He updated Godfrey first then got Ludolf's men after the ropes. Finally he went looking for Gaston of Bearne as he thought he was the most likely to know where to find long crowbars. This all took time. Fortunately Gaston was nearby waiting. He immediately dispatched some of his men to get the crowbars and then joined Henry to supervise the repositioning. It was growing dark when Gaston finally admitted defeat and changed the strategy completely.

"Burn the ram so we can push the tower forward," he yelled.

The nearby squad of women, children and old men who had spent their entire day putting out Greek fire in order to protect the ram, now changed their role and began stoking fires beneath their mighty mechanism. It was a dangerous job. In moments Henry saw two women killed by arrows from above. Simultaneously the Arab fire mongers atop the wall switched their ware from fire to water. For a moment Henry's mind clasped the irony of this change in roles; then his eyes halted on the ram's tree-like back end. It was sticking out of the city's damaged wall some twelve feet and would, he thought, not burn sufficiently to permit the tower to get within their plank's length of the wall.

Henry ran to Gaston who was doing his best to direct the various crews.

"Gaston," yelled the youth, "I don't think that tree-trunk will burn away enough in a week. Perhaps we should be repositioning the tower, get our men over the wall instead of through it."

Gaston stared at Henry for a moment. Then he looked at the ram's mighty trunk.

"You're right," the accented Provencal proclaimed. "It's getting dark too, so we'll only have time tonight to pull the tower clear and then bring her up again tomorrow. Leave the fire burning though. It will give the Egyptians something to do. Get the pullers. We'll get her clear as fast as we can and do repair work tonight. Yes, yes. Repairs tonight and over the wall tomorrow! Good thinking Henry. Good thinking."

Gaston of Bearne and his men got very little sleep that night. First they had to withdraw their tower to a point out of range of the Muslim man-gonels; then slightly redirect it so in the morning it would roll forward to the right of the damaged ram. Furthermore Gaston gave a lot of thought to how, since the tower had become their only means of putting men over the wall, they could protect or obfuscate their effort and thus improve their chance of success. And just as the rosy fingers of dawn began pressing away the darkness, the Provencal knight had an idea. He immediately went looking for several of his friends who had served with Hugh Magnus. Finding them, he explained that once the tower had been set against the wall, he wanted them to shoot flaming arrows at the cotton padding the Egyptians had hung to protect the wall from the Christian mangonels. Gaston hoped the cotton would catch fire and create enough smoke to make the attackers crossing over their planks to the wall less visible to the defenders. His friends agreed to shoot flaming arrows at the bales of cotton, if for no other reason until the walls were breached, they had little else to do.

In his sleep, Henry sensed a stirring and was awake instantly. There was hot food available but he didn't eat much. He wondered how Raymond's troops were faring. He'd heard that their tower had been badly mauled but he was certain that Raymond, who was a haughty man, would have his men back at the wall in their tower no matter how damaged it might be. Henry's own tower, looming ahead in the predawn light, looked grey and foreboding. For a moment the young knight wondered if this great wooden castle might soon become his own coffin...but he consciously swept that thought from his mind. 'Though I walk into the valley of death,' he whispered.

Godfrey was at the tower ahead of Henry. The Lotharingian lord had his page with him. The boy was barely big enough to heft the bucket of crossbow bolts he was carrying. As Henry stepped up beside Godfrey, Gaston was speaking.

"My lord," growled the Provencal in his thick accent, "I'll have men firing flaming arrows at those cotton bales the Egyptians have hung over the wall. They'll start shooting just as the tower touches the wall. At that moment, hold back your assault for two reasons: first, the Arabs will swell forward as the tower reaches the wall. This will be the time for your archers to rive their ranks. Second, give the fire archers a chance to set the cotton bales ablaze. If they can, it will give your men some safety as they cross. Do you understand?"

"Of course I understand," chirped Godfrey irritably. "I'll give your archers some time but understand we're crossing over that wall today no matter what. I've not spent almost four years getting here to miss the opportunity." Godfrey lowered his voice to a more civil tone. "We are God's soldiers Gaston. It is He who wills it."

"Yes," replied the Provencal as he turned with a broad smile on his face. "Pullers forward," he yelled. "Pushers take up your poles, knights behind the tower. Remember we're taking her to the right of the ram. Commence when I say now."

"Henry," said Godfrey, "come up inside the tower with me. I want to fill you in on what I expect when Ludolf and his men cross over onto the wall."

Godfrey then hopped up onto the slow moving castle with his page, Randolf Vulphy, and two other knights. Henry clambered aboard behind them. The group followed their leader up the rough-hewn ladders to Ludolf's floor. Henry slowed to help the boy with his bucket of crossbow bolts but Godfrey must have seen him do so.

"Siegfried," called back the Duke, "put the pail down for now and just come up yourself."

When they'd all congregated on the fourth level, Godfrey issued clear directions. "Henry when several of Ludolf's knights have crossed, I want you to cross over but hang back in order to determine whether our sally will succeed. Do not make your decision hastily but wait until there can be no doubt. If you see that we shall succeed, come back and report to me, then run to your horse and ride to Raymond at his tent and tell him that we've breached the wall and to put all his men over as fast as he can. The Muslims will be running everywhere except to the walls."

Suddenly Henry felt the tower tip beneath him; splinters of wood flew past his nose; the sound of a huge crash roiled into his ears; spontaneously his hands rose for balance. He sensed something pass in front of him from left to right and then he saw Randolf's head disappear. He heard a metallic snap, a squishing thud and saw a cloud-like mist of particles hanging in the air where Randolf's head had been less than a moment before. Within this mist were colors: red, grey and purple, all floating above the knight's body which still stood straight up. His neck was cleanly severed but, just for a moment, it continued to pump blood...one, two spurts and then stopped. Another moment passed before the torso crumpled to the floor.

Henry's first thought was one of surprise that Randolf's body hadn't been thrown backward by the impact. In an instant though, his mind leapt out of its paralysis. He looked to see if the others were all right. Godfrey had globules of blood and brain tissue smeared across his face but he was turning toward his men and page. Henry also turned his gaze back to the other knights and boy. Each man's face held a glazed expression, mouth still open, eyes wide, jaw slack. Henry looked down at Siegfried. The boy's eyes still stared straight at where Randolf had been standing. The boy's face was completely devoid of expression and he seemed not to be breathing. Henry stepped in front of the youth, knelt down so he could look straight into the boy's eyes and put his hands on his shoulders.

"Siegfried, do you hear me?"

The boy rotated his eyes slightly so they met Henry's. "Yes," he murmured.

"That was an awful thing we just saw, how Randolf died. Have you seen a man die before?"

"No," whispered the boy.

"I have," said the knight. "And I want to share something about it. Is that all right?"

"Yes," replied Siegfried faintly.

"God decides when He wants us to return to Him. Our minds haven't the capacity to know when or how death will come. But Randolf's was a quick death. He hadn't time to know what hit him. He felt nothing, no pain, no fear, nothing. It is the kind of death we all hope for. I believe God calls us back to Him when He feels we have accomplished here on earth that which He wished us to do... Do you remember a time when you saw Randolf laughing and cheerful?"

For a moment the boy seemed nonplussed. Henry fervently hoped he had such a memory. These Germans seemed more reserved than most people at least until they'd had a few drinks.

Henry whispered again, "Perhaps some time around Christmas in front of a great hearth with a mug of mulled mead?"

The boy's frozen expression suddenly melted into a smile. "Yes," he replied. "We were all laughing about the time the snow slid off the roof and fell on Brother Manfried's head. Randolf was telling the story and..." Siegfried's voice suddenly fell away and he began to cry.

Henry wrapped his arms around the sobbing youth and whispered in his ear. "Randolf would want you to remember him then, not as you just saw him. Do you think you can do that Siegfried? For Randolf."

For several moments, Siegfried's sobs continued. But eventually he spoke. "Yes," he murmured, "for Randolf."

Again Henry looked the boy squarely in the eye. Siegfried's mind had re-centered. Henry knew the boy would be all right at least until the battle ended. After that, no one could ever be certain.

Henry returned to his position as a pusher. It was hard work. The pace of the tower's advance was incredibly slow, reminding him of the times he'd followed his father up Dol's winding stairways to the battlements. Here though, it was not only slower but more risky. Each time he heard the 'thwumph' of an Egyptian mangonel launch a boulder, Henry would silently count to three. If he was still alive after 'three,' he knew the giant rock had missed. Eventually as the tower got close to the wall, the mangonel fire ceased due to the city's wall having risen into the path of the thrown stones. There was a shared sigh of relief among the Christian soldiers as they realized the tower would now make it to the wall. Of course they'd still have to cross to the wall.

"Belay below," called down Godfrey who'd just moved to the back of the tower five levels above. "The damned Arabs have hung down a burning log in front of us. If we push any closer, it will set our tower ablaze. Hold for now while we see if we can put out its flames. Oh, we're about six feet from the wall now and our archers are starting to take a lot of them out. I'll be right back."

After Henry had gotten his breath, he turned around and eased his butt down onto the tower's open-backed first floor. As he did, he saw that a great many of the Roberts' knights and soldiers had advanced using wicker mantelets to protect themselves. These brave men obviously intended to go up the tower and cross over the wall as soon as they possibly could.

"Down below!" called out Godfrey. "We're putting out the flames with vinegar but we're going to need you to grapple onto the chain holding the log and pull it out of the way. There are some grappling hooks in my tent. Ludolf, send some men for them; then come forward to assess the task. We'll put down suppressing fire to cover you. After you've seen what needs to be done, do it!"

"Fourth floor to me," bellowed Ludolf.

Henry twisted on his floor seat. "Shields first," he yelled as he completed his swivel and clambered up into the tower's first floor where the knights' shields had been stacked. In a flash, the screens were handed out and Ludolf's floor was ready.

"Second floor, to Godfrey's tent at a trot," yelled the taciturn knight from Tournai. "Get the grappling hooks and rope if you can find some. Go!" Ludolf twisted back toward his hand-picked fourth floorers. "Bart, Henry, come with me to assess what we've got to do. You others think how you can best protect the grapplers when they get back. We'll only be a moment."

Leaving the rest of the knights in the back of the tower, the threesome sprinted out from behind their wooden castle and, holding their kite-shaped shields above their heads, raced forward to see the obstacle they were supposed to remove. Henry's first impression came when he saw the front face of the tower. It looked like a hedgehog with its quills all raised. There were hundreds of arrows stuck into its wooden face. Eight feet above the ground against the city's stone wall hung a large smoldering log. Henry's first thought was that the enemy had dropped it too soon. The Christian tower was still some six feet from the wall, so the huge firebrand hadn't been close enough to cause any real damage. The log hung from atop the wall by two chains, one attached to each end of the log. These were presumably to be grappled and pulled along the face of the wall to allow the tower to move forward, abut the wall and dispense its warriors. Henry noted in his mind that the grapplers' chance to pull the log aside really depended on how the chains had been hung. If they'd been lashed behind the wall to each other, then the grapplers would be pulling against themselves. If not, it would become a tug-of-war with the Christians pulling one way and the Arabs the other.

"Ready?" called Ludolf.

"Yes," replied Bart and Henry at once.

The three trotted back behind the tower.

"What do you think?" queried Ludolf in his stolid tone.

"We can grapple it," said Bart, "but I have no idea whether we can move it."

"Henry?"

"We can try grappling. If it doesn't work, we can try to push closer. Those planks are long enough to reach the wall right now. It would be dangerous but as a last resort it could be tried."

"I agree," muttered Ludolf. "We'll take them in that order: grapple, roll closer or just lay out the planks and crawl for it."

At that moment the second floor knights returned with grappling hooks and several lengths of rope.

"All quiet," bellowed Ludolf. "Second floor, make teams for each hook and teams for ropes. First and third floor, use your shields to protect the second and take out wounded when necessary. Bart, you direct the hookers. Henry, you go up and tell Godfrey what we're doing. Go!"

Henry leapt up onto the tower's first floor, swung his shield over his back and climbed the ladders as quickly as he could. When he reached the top, Godfrey was waiting for him.

"Good work," said the Duke. "They've already hooked the chains and started to pull the log away."

"My lord," croaked Henry breathlessly. "Our plan is to try grappling first. If it doesn't work, we'll try to push our castle closer. If that doesn't work, we'll just lay out the planks and crawl over. The last will be the most dangerous for our crossers but we can do it with suppressing fire and hopefully those cotton bales alight and smoking."

"That's the spirit, Henry. We'll cross no matter what." Godfrey then hauled the coordinator up through the entry hole. "Come and look," he ordered.

Henry twisted his long shield off his back and placed it ahead of him. Godfrey didn't use his shield. He just leaned out over the front of the tower and pointed.

"They're making progress, Henry. Look! The log is moving." The Duke glanced back. "You don't need your shield Henry. They're all pulling on their damned chains."

From his high vantage point, Henry could see that Godfrey was right. The Arab defenders had put down their bows and taken up the chains. There really was a tug-of-war!

"Siegfried, bring me my crossbow and more bolts." Godfrey turned away from the enemy to search for his bow. As he did, he spoke to Henry again. "We're really taking them off the wall now. Them all pulling that chain out exposed like that! No suppressers at all. We're going to take them Henry. Throw one of those rocks if you want." Godfrey bent down behind the floor's shallow wall and began to wind his crossbow. Siegfried, having delivered the bow, was skittering back across the floor in search of more quarrels.

Had it not been for the withering fire which swept their ranks, the Arabs might have been able to hold their log in place. But they couldn't and the log was pulled clear to make room for the tower's advancement. Ludolf's men then ran back behind the tower and again took up their pusher positions. Still other knights picked up poles or pressed in where they could to push the tower forward. However, for what to Henry seemed like a very long time, the tower didn't move. Henry watched closely to determine what the problem was. Finally, Henry saw Ludolf and Bart directly below him huddle for a moment and then, with their shields over their heads, trot forward to where the tower's front wheels were. Almost immediately, Ludolf lifted his gaze to Godfrey and Henry.

"We'll go to plan three Henry," the squarely shaped knight called up. He and Bart then trotted back behind the tower but Henry could still hear what Ludolf said next. "Into our castle, knights; we're going to cross the hard way."

Knowing what that meant, Henry turned back toward Godfrey who was already waving at the archers who would loose their flaming arrows. Very quickly everything began to change! Thick, black smoke billowed up between the tower's front face and the city's stone wall. Gaston's plan to set the hanging cotton bales ablaze was working.

"My lord," gurgled Henry, "this smoke will hide us from the Arabs. We must cross immediately."

"Look," hooted the Duke, "the infidels are falling back. God's will Henry! God's will! They can't breathe. The smoke's too thick. Tell Ludolf to go immediately. Don't wait...and tell me when you're sure. Go."

Henry twisted his shield back over his shoulder and lowered his foot for the highest rung on the ladder. He could already hear his floor-mates banging the two crossing planks out from their places in the tower's front wall. Henry got to his place just in time to see Ludolf with his shield on his back commence his crawl into the thick black smoke.

Bart went second, Henry third and Bernard, the Advocate of the Monastery of Saint-sur-Somme, would follow him. Keeping his head as low as possible so he could see the plank, Henry held his breath and shuffled his hands and knees forward as quickly as he could. At the wall, the smoke swirled over and down making it impossible to see where Bart had gone or, for that matter, whether Fatimid soldiers lay in wait. Henry didn't slow down though. He needed to breathe. He clambered across the wall but the plank only extended two feet beyond, so he had to slide his feet over the side of the board and lower them into the swirling black smoke. Thank God! His toes touched the stone walkway. Immediately he twisted his shield onto his left arm and ducked under the plank in order to move to his left as Ludolf had previously directed. As he did, he sensed Bernard above him.

"It's me," Henry called in a hushed voice.

"Good," choked Bernard.

Henry put his shield out to his left so he could feel where the wall was and diminish his chance of falling forty feet to the ground below. He was coughing almost uncontrollably and his eyes were streaming tears. With his shield scraping the wall and his sword in his right hand, he moved blindly forward through the swirling black smoke. He knew he needed better air quickly or he would pass out. 'Dear God, please help me.' In only ten steps, Henry's eyes saw daylight. He breathed in a great gulp of air. "Thank you Lord! Thank you."

Bart and Ludolf were just ahead. The walkway behind the wall was no more than three feet wide. Accordingly the two knights were striding forward with Ludolf in the lead pushing fifteen or twenty Arabs ahead of him. The Arabs wore hardly any armor and had discarded most of their bows. Had they been able to surround their opponents, they might have had a chance but the width of the walkway forced them to fight one-on-one against a ferocious, trained and well-protected Norman knight. It was slaughter.

Henry was certain that this left side of the wall would be secured. With Ludolf in the lead, he'd never really had any doubt. He turned and looked back at the oily, black smoke still swirling up over the wall. An amorphous shape seemed to be forming from within the writhing billows. Another knight stepped out of the caldron into the clear air. Henry waved him forward. Everyone knew their role and Henry's too. Going back through the smoke would be a risk. He didn't know how far he would have to go before he reached clean air and he didn't know how many knights he would encounter who might mistake him for a Muslim. With these concerns foremost in his mind, the young knight did his duty and stepped into the smoke. He slid the butt of his sword handle along the wall and held his shield close in front of him just in case.

"Coming through," he rasped as loudly as he could.

Suddenly the smoke began to thin, cleaner air entered his throat. "God's will!" the young knight shouted. "God's will."

"God's will to you," said Baldric of Boulogne who, striding up just in front of Henry, was the fifth in their group of left turners to cross over.

Henry darted through the thinning fumes and was at the plank to help another knight find his footing on the walkway. The second plank lay across the wall only a few feet beyond. Henry could see two knights ahead of him and another just exiting the tower. He ducked under the overreaching plank and rushed forward to see how the right turners were doing. Occasional waves of smoke still billowed up over the wall, but they weren't thick enough or sequential enough to blot out his view. The right turners had already fought their way through the first guard tower.

"Yes," said Henry as he pivoted and almost sprinted back to the Christians' crossing point. Despite intermittent swirls of smoke, the Duke stood tall atop his wooden castle.

"My lord," yelled Henry, "send everyone every way possible. We've cleared the wall from guard tower to guard tower."

Godfrey saw Henry gesticulating and called back. "Did you say everyone, every way?"

"Yes," shouted back Henry while he nodded his head affirmatively.

Godfrey raised his horn and blew it. Then he went to the back of the tower and winded it twice more. After that, the Duke returned to the front of the tower and again called across to Henry. "I'll interrupt the crawlers for a moment to let you get back and ride to Raymond. Someone crossing will tell you when."

As Henry trotted toward the Christian tents where the wounded were, he knew Johnnie was waiting for him with Pegasus. But he stopped just once to look back. The billowing smoke from the hanging cotton bales had diminished to only an occasional puff or two, which allowed the young knight to see the soldiers of Robert of Flanders and Robert, Duke of Normandy, swarming up ladders which had been laid against Jerusalem's wall. He thought there must be thirty ladders in use and each with two or three climbers on it. And best of all, there wasn't a defender in sight. July the 15th...Peter's prophesy was right!

INTEGRITY
July 1099

Once in the saddle, Henry pushed Pegasus hard. Raymond's tent, from which the Provencal lord directed his campaigns, was about a mile away. Henry knew his new mount could handle that distance easily. As he got near the hill the Provencal camp rested on, Henry waved frantically, hoping his meaning would be apparent. He couldn't tell but it didn't matter much because he reined in beside Raymond's tent only moments later.

As he swung down from his saddle, he yelled out as loudly as he could. "We've taken the north wall. Send your men forward. The city is open!"

A large number of Raymond's highest lords were already departing from the tent. Raymond was right behind them.

Seeing the Provencal leader, Henry breathlessly called out again. "My lord, we've breached the wall, the north wall. Send your men forward as fast as you can. Ladders should be enough as the garrison's in turmoil."

Raymond yelled back to his liegemen. "Bear left to David's Tower. We'll converge there. Go!" Then the Count turned back toward his tent and yelled again. "Raynald, come take Henry's horse for him and tell Elvira we're taking the city." The Count turned back to Henry. "Good work my boy! Will you join me now as we take the south side of Jesus' city?"

"Certainly, sir," replied Henry who'd regained his breath. "It will be an honor."

Raymond didn't rush for a ladder. Instead he walked to the large Zion gate and waited for his men to get over the wall and open it. It wasn't a long wait. Inside the city, pandemonium prevailed. Citizens were screaming, crying, and running every which way. Some carried babies, some belongings, some nothing at all. Along the way, Henry saw several of the Provencals bear off toward wealthy looking buildings and one knight veer away behind a young woman who seemed bereft of direction. Raymond didn't seem to notice. His objective was clearly the Tower of David, Jerusalem's citadel. The massive structure was surrounded by a dry moat and a high wall. It was a formidable redoubt.

Iftikhar and a number of his men had already reached the citadel. There, riderless horses were wandering near the main gate. The

Provencals were quickly rounding them up and marking them with various cloths, strings or personal identifiers. Horses were very valuable.

Seeing that the citadel was occupied by an unknown number of the Fatimid garrison, Raymond convened an immediate conference of his liegemen. Henry recognized Raymond Pilet, William Sabran, Peter Narbonne and Isoard the Count of Die, who had taken over the leadership of Adhemar's troops after the Papal legate had died at Antioch. The conference was brief. Raymond wanted the citadel as fast as possible. Henry concluded that, just as at Antioch where Raymond had occupied the most defensible part of the city and used his possession of it to promote 'his right' to become the overlord of the city, he was planning the same tactic here. Henry didn't say anything though. It wasn't the right time.

"Do we rush it or parley?" asked Raymond of his lords.

"We don't know how many men they have my lord," responded Isoard. "Rushing them could take the rest of the day assuming they're numerous and prepared. They'll certainly be motivated."

"Yes," added Raymond Pilet, "if you want this place quickly my lord, you'd best try parleying first."

The Count of Toulouse turned to Henry. "Henry, I believe I've heard you speaking some Arabic with Elvira. Would you go to David's Tower with Isoard and translate while he parleys?"

"Yes, my lord," responded the coordinator, "if they'll give us safe passage."

"John," growled the Count as he turned to a knight who Henry didn't know, "get a white cloth, tie it to a stick and start waving it so the Fatimids can see you. Then wait for Isoard and Henry. Do you understand?"

"Yes, my lord," replied the knight as he turned and ran off. Raymond turned back to Isoard. "My terms will be whatever it takes to get them out and gone: safe passage to Ascalon for them, their families and whoever is with them. Tell them that Raymond, Count of Toulouse, guarantees their safety. Tell them we'll take them out tonight and they'll have to go on foot. Their horses aren't theirs anymore. Questions?"

"No, my lord," replied Isoard. "John is coming back with his flag so we can start."

"God be with you," said Raymond in a low voice.

Henry walked slightly behind John, who was waving his white flag as rapidly as possible. Isoard walked beside Henry.

"Henry," said the Lord of Die, "if you have suggestions or thoughts, please utter them to me in French and I'll agree or not before you translate."

"Certainly my lord. I've not done this before, so I may not have any suggestions."

"I'm not dissuading you from proffering any. I'm just making sure we speak as one."

"Someone's leaning over the gate," stammered John. "I think he's going to talk with us."

"Let's stop here for a moment," said Henry, "and be sure before we get into range."

"A good idea," commented Isoard.

Henry stepped up beside John and cupped his hands around his mouth. They were about a hundred feet from the gate. "Do you wish to parley?" he asked in passable Arabic.

"Yes," called back the Fatimid above the gate. "We'll hold our arrows so you can come closer."

Henry turned to Isoard and nodded his head affirmatively.

A few moments later, the threesome stood below the gate looking up at the man who'd called them over. He was young, brown-skinned and had wavy black hair.

Henry looked to Isoard for direction. "Tell him Raymond the Count of Toulouse, whose word is impeccably good, offers those within safe conduct to Ascalon. They may take they're women, children and possessions but must be ready to go right after dark, carry no weapons and walk. As further guarantee, we shall exchange hostages."

"How do you propose to determine the hostages?" asked the Fatimid.

"Tell him that you and John will take them to Ascalon and that when you get safely back to Jerusalem, one of Iftikhar's sons will be released."

"Me?" questioned Henry.

"Well," smiled Isoard, "they'll need an interpreter."

"Alright," murmured the coordinator.

When Henry turned to relay Isoard's message, he saw that the dark-haired Fatimid had been joined by a shorter, older and more grizzled figure. Henry assumed it was Iftikhar.

"How may we be sure that it is Count Raymond of Toulouse who gives these assurances?" asked the older man.

"He stands three hundred feet behind me," replied Henry. "These are all his men. What further proof do you need?"

A moment or two passed while the two Arabs talked. "Who will you give as hostages?" the younger man finally called down.

"Myself and this knight," replied Henry as he pointed toward John.

"Iftikhar has no children but he will exchange his wife. Will that do?"

Henry turned to Isoard. "A Muslim man does not keep a wife who does not bear him children. We should press for a son. By doing so, they will learn that we are not simpletons and act correctly toward us."

"Try," said Isoard, "but give in if he balks."

"We know that he has at least one son," called back Henry, "and Iftikhar will be holding two sons of fathers who also care for their children. We're wasting time and we won't be able to get you out later than tonight. Raymond is extending this kindness while the other Christian lords are sacking the city. When they are done, they may not agree with such kind terms."

More conversation transpired between the two Arabs. "All right," said the older man. "One son only and we are agreed. I shall leave this draw bridge up and exit by the west gate right after dark. We shall be unarmed. Also I would like to personally thank Count Raymond of Toulouse for his generous terms. His name will be widely recognized as an honorable foe. Is it all right that I meet with him...briefly of course?"

"Yes," said Henry. "We shall meet you after dark at the west gate and we shall have Count Raymond with us. Is there anything else?"

"Call for Ali," said the young Fatimid, "and we will know it is you."

Henry waved his hand and turned away. He wasn't certain whether Raymond would personally meet with Iftikhar or not. But he spent more time wondering whether it had been Isoard or Raymond who'd offered him up to be a hostage.

~**~

After Henry, John, and their motley group of some three hundred transitioning Fatimids, a third of whom were women and children, had passed out of Jerusalem, the translator realized that his position as a 'hostage' wasn't as risky as he had first thought. He and twenty of Isoard's knights were riding fully armed while their flock was walking without weapons of any kind. Iftikhar had left one of his sons, Nur, with Raymond together with several leather bags of gold which Henry reasoned would liken the boy to Raymond. In any case Henry had no doubt that Raymond would keep his word. The Count was in many respects an odd man, but no one doubted his religious zeal or his word. His arrogance, 'timidity' and pride exceeded all the other lords but his word was good.

Soon Henry found himself riding beside the black-haired, young soldier whose words he had translated for Isoard in the city.

"Do you have a family Ali?" asked Henry.

"Yes," replied the Fatimid. "Allah has favored me. Do you?"

"Not yet," said Henry. "I hope to som e day, God willing."

"What is your name?"

"Henry, Henry of Dol," responded the young knight.

"Henry, may I ask you a question?"

"Of course."

"What will become of the inhabitants of Jerusalem?"

"Well," replied Henry hesitantly, "I suppose some will be ransomed, some sold into slavery and others put to farm work. Why do you ask?"

"I saw some being killed...women and children."

Henry looked away. "Perhaps just in the initial frenzy?"

"Perhaps," replied Ali who was watching the Christian knight intently.

A few moments passed before Henry violently twisted back toward the Arab. "Ali, I too fear that pent up hate and frustration may lead to slaughter. I saw it happen in Antioch. I pray it will not happen in Jerusalem but I fear it may. It is one of the reasons why I agreed to take you out of the city."

For several moments Ali assessed his counterpart. "Henry, I sense your sincerity. You are a well meaning man but a young one. I felt as you do when I first entered the wars. I think I was fourteen. I vomited when I saw so many die in combat and I threw up again after the battle was over when I watched our surviving enemies being decapitated. I could not understand why those...those defenseless prisoners should be killed. I still don't understand it but I have come to expect it. Even Mohammad at Medina had the heads of seven hundred Jews chopped off."

"I see," said Henry, "So how did you recently treat the Christians and Jews in the city?"

"Oh quite well," answered Ali. "Iftikhar and I are Shi'ah Muslim not Sunni Turks."

Henry stared coolly at the Fatimid. "We have long heard stories of robbery, murder, and other brigandage as well as desecration of holy places perpetrated by Muslims both in and around Jerusalem and I know you ejected the Christians from the city just before we arrived!"

"Oh yes," Ali quickly replied, "but only because they couldn't be trusted. As to your references of earlier abuses, we only wrestled the city from the Turks nine months ago. The stories you heard were probably true but done by the Turks, not the Fatimid Shi'ah. We would do none of that. We do however have rules for non-believers but only mild ones. They may not pray aloud in the city, nor ride horses, nor bear arms. They are subject to a head tax and must wear identifying insignia. But they may live within the city and keep their synagogues and churches. To abuse them is not permitted."

"So, you let pilgrims enter freely to the holy places: the Church of the Holy Sepulchre, the Mount of Olives, the Dome of the Rock?"

"Most assuredly," replied Ali. "Visiting the Dome of the Rock is sometimes contentious. But that is only because Mohammed together with Gabriel ascended to heaven from there, so we've had to assign certain days of the week: Thursday Christians, Friday Muslims. That particular example is often complicated by how many different Christian sects there are: Armenians, Greek Orthodox, Maronites, Jacobites and Nestorians.

"Oh," said Henry who was warming to this Arab soldier who seemed quite forthright. "I am interested in medicine. Where do the Nestorian doctors put up their signs?"

"Their sign?" questioned Ali. "You mean where do they practice?"

"Yes," responded Henry. "Where would I find them?"

"Just inside the Josaphat Gate," responded Ali. "There is a Christian hostel there overseen by Brother Gerard. He is a fine man who devotes his life to helping others. May I ask you another question?"

"Of course, I'll answer it if I can."

"I have been told that most of your Christian army are from a tribe called Norman. Is that the case and if so, who are they?"

"Well," answered Henry, "I've never thought of our forefathers as a tribe but I suppose in some respects that may be true. The name Norman derives from 'Northman.' Several generations ago our grandfathers and great grandfathers migrated from Scandinavia into northern France, Germany and England. We were and I suppose still are, a warlike people. Since then we've converted to Christianity and taken the language of the

Franks whom we conquered. Nevertheless a number of us still have a thirst to rove and many of our men are good fighters."

"So you Normans are like the Turks," pronounced Ali. "They have recently invaded civilized lands in Anatolia even down to Damascus and Jerusalem. They also are recent converts to the Muslim faith and are fearsome warriors, horsemen and archers. We, the Fatimid Muslims, consider ourselves more civilized than the Seljuk and perhaps less warlike. I do not mean to offend," Ali continued, "but I do see some similarities between the Seljuk Turks and you Normans."

"Henry, you are an interesting man. You look at your religion and consider where its words and its actions differ and you ask yourself why. I have noticed your distaste for unnecessary slaughter. You find it abhorrent and cannot match it to your god's teachings. We may be more alike than one might think. When I learned to read, which was quite recently, I began to investigate some of the great religious teachers and their profundity. I was shocked by a story, supposedly true, about a decision Calif Umar once made in response to one of his generals. The general had just taken Alexandria with its great library of antiquities and wrote to Umar in Damascus to ask what he should do with the library. I haven't the text, so I may muddle the Calif's response somewhat but only slightly. Umar answered, "if the books in the library agree with the Qur'an, they are not required; if they disagree with the Qur'an, they are not desired. Therefore destroy them."

DEEDS IN THE HOLY CITY
July 1099

At dusk on the 20th, Henry, John and their twenty-knight vanguard arrived back in Jerusalem. The smoke rising over the walls of the city had been discernable from a great distance. The stench of death wasn't palpable until they were quite close. As Henry breathed in the odor his heart sank. Not a man among them spoke.

At Ascalon, Henry's tiny vanguard wasn't permitted through the gate. The Fatimid garrison obviously didn't want the Christians to learn anything about the town's defenses or see any revealing signs that might suggest how soon the Egyptian relief army would be arriving. Outside the wall, Henry saw no signs indicating herds of cattle or sheep that might suggest Egyptian efforts to amass food for an arriving army. But as their rescued hodgepodge of Sudanese cavalry, Jews and Muslims streamed through the town's gate, Iftikhar together with Ali stopped one more time to implore Henry to quickly rescue Nur from his imprisonment. Henry reasoned that Iftikhar knew the relief army would arrive soon and that if it did, it might interfere with Raymond's efforts to return the boy. When the Egyptian lord had completed his beseechment, Henry promised the regent that he would return the boy. But he then went on to ask Iftikhar to alert all the Egyptian soldiers, scouts, spies and others to be aware that a Christian knight would be returning Nur to Ascalon in the next few days under a safe passage granted by the regent.

Iftikhar immediately promised to issue such an order, after which Henry kneed Pegasus and rode off. As he did, it crossed his mind that Christ might be pleased that someone in this great battle was looking out for a child.

When he arrived at the Tower of David, Henry immediately went looking for Raymond.

"Ah Henry," the Count of Toulouse uttered most cheerfully, "you are back safely. Did everything go well?"

"Yes," replied the young knight. "Iftikhar, Ali, their Sudanese troops and the flock of refugees have been delivered to Ascalon. But I must take Nur there quickly before al-Afdal arrives with his army."

"Did you hear anything about them coming? See any signs?" The tone of the Count's voice revealed anxiety.

"No," said Henry, "but his desire for haste suggests their army may be close."

"Yes," murmured Raymond. "Yes, it probably does. But you said you'd take the boy yourself?"

"Yes, I promised Iftikhar that I'd do my best to get his son to Ascalon by late tomorrow and he promised to immediately send out word that his son would be returning with a Christian knight under a safe passage."

"Good," said Raymond as he smiled. "It is both a brave and a worthy thing that you do. I shall pray tonight at the Holy Sepulchre for your safe return. Will you check in with Robert or head right back?"

"I shall leave the moment the boy is ready."

"Good," the Count responded as he turned his head toward an open door. "Philip, get Henry whatever food and drink he wishes, refill his water jackets, attend to anything else he wishes and get him a fresh horse. He'll be leaving right away."

"Thank you, my lord," interjected the knight, "but I'll ride Pegasus back to Ascalon. He'll need fodder and water but otherwise he'll be ready."

"You're certain? That's a lot of riding without a fresh mount."

"Yes, I'm certain. He's got stamina and real speed."

"Henry this is Nur."

Henry turned and saw a boy about six years old. He had black hair and was wearing a white shift which made his skin look quite dark. The knight nodded to the boy. To Henry's surprise, the child stepped directly behind the aged Count so that only his head remained in view.

"Nur," scolded Raymond, "Henry is a man of God whom you can trust. He will not harm you. He is the one who will take you back to your father."

For a long moment the boy stared at Henry. Finally he twisted his head around so he was looking directly back into the room he'd just come from. "Is this really a man of God," he called out in Arabic, "or just another bloodthirsty infidel?"

Elvira stepped out of the shadows and responded in Arabic. "He is a Godly man who will take you safely to your father."

The boy turned his eyes back to the Christian knight but his glare displayed continued mistrust. "Does he speak Arabic?"

"I do," interjected Henry before the Countess could reply, "and I have given my word to your father that I shall return you to him as quickly as possible."

The boy continued to stare at Henry before finally responding. "Did you partake in the burning of the synagogue or the slaughter at the mosque of al-Aqsa?"

Henry's brow furrowed. He looked up at Elvira and still speaking in Arabic asked, "To what does he refer?"

The Countess lowered her eyes and replied in a whisper. "Many of the Jews sought refuge in their synagogue and many Muslims in their mosque at the Dome of the Rock. They were all killed."

Anguish traced deeply across Henry's face but he eventually spoke."No, I did not partake in any of that. I was taking your father and Ali to Ascalon to safety which is what Count Raymond promised. And I have promised your father to bring you safely to him. My word, like Raymond's, is good. You may trust me but we haven't much time. I am sorry the Jews and Muslims were slaughtered but I cannot do anything about it. I can however still save you but only if we leave right away."

Again the boy glanced toward Elvira. She nodded her head affirmatively.

Nur looked back at Henry. "I am ready!"

~**~

Sitting atop two wooden crates, Tancred leapt up. "Henry! I've been worried about you. I haven't seen you since before we took the city. How are you?"

"Very well...and you?"

"Oh, quite well, quite well," Tancred replied in a slightly distracted tone. "I've been hiring some knights and been quite busy paying off old debts and purchasing arms, horses and equipment. Where have you been?"

"Oh," answered Henry who wasn't certain how some of the Christian lords would feel about Raymond's issuance of safe passage to Iftikhar, "mostly I've been doing my coordinator role. But you must have done very well to be acquiring so many new knights and horses."

"Oh, very well indeed," interrupted Tancred. "Let me tell you my friend but first look at all this gold and silver! It took six camels just to carry it all. Sit down Henry." Tancred pointed toward several more wooden crates as he eased back onto the two he'd been sitting on. "You know how I've worked the local Christians for information, gotten intelligence on the Arabs' use of Greek fire and its antidote vinegar?"

"Yes," replied Henry who knew that Tancred had always been very deft at gathering information.

"Well," continued the south Norman, "long before we breached the walls, I made a point of finding out where in the city the most valuable stashes of gold and silver were. So Gaston and I were ready with seventy knights and two local Christians to lead us when the opportunity presented itself. Using Godfrey's tower, we went over the wall and then ran through the crowds to get to the Haram es-Sharif complex where the Dome of the Rock and the al-Aqsa mosque are. We were delayed by the iron gates of the Haram but we finally broke them using a crowbar and got in. Henry, you should have seen it! Hanging from the ceiling by silver chains there was a monstrous gold vessel and around the walls forty large silver lamps, and inlaid in the wall all around the room was a band of silver a hand's width high and a thumb-length deep and lots of precious stones and jewels too. Six camels Henry, six camels to carry it all!"

"What will you and Gaston do with all this...this wealth?" queried Henry who didn't prioritize the acquisition of gold and silver very highly.

"Well," replied his friend, "as you know I'm planning to stay here in the Holy Land and defend it against whatever hosts the Muslims throw at us: Sunni Turks, Shi'a Fatimids or any other faction, cult or mullah. To do that I'll need to keep a lot of knights armed, horsed and ready." For a moment Tancred paused and stared at his crates of gold and silver. "Actually I acquired a lot more than this, more than three hundred wealthy Jews and Muslim merchants. I'd left my banner protecting them but the stupid Tarfurs slaughtered the lot." Tancred's voice quivered with rage. "Those damned Tarfurs defied my banner! If I'd been there, I would have killed them. If I knew which ones they were, I'd kill them now. I could have ransomed those prisoners for ten thousand dinars!" The south Norman paused and then turned back toward Henry. "Of course, I'd probably have had to kill those prisoners anyhow. We couldn't have kept them in the city with al-Afdal investing us, too much risk of betrayal. But ignoring my banner! That's not pardonable!"

"I've already given a tenth of this treasure to Godfrey, who is now my overlord. And naturally I've given a tenth to Peter Desiderius to distribute to the poor. Even so there are still envious voices calling for me to give more away, all so self-righteous! Of course they just want it for themselves. To be specific Arnulf of Chocques, Duke Robert's chaplain, has been talking behind my back. I'm sure there are others too. Deep down they're just angry they didn't think of going after all this themselves. Henry after we defeat al-Afdal, do you plan to return to Dol? I know Count Robert intends to return to Flanders."

"Oh," responded Henry, "Yes...I mean I haven't really thought about it. Mostly I've just been focusing on taking Jerusalem and now defeating al-Afdal. But I'm the eldest surviving son so I should go back to Dol and settle down."

"You have a younger brother don't you?"

"Yes," replied Henry.

Tancred quickly continued. "Henry, there's going to be tremendous opportunity here: rich land, trade, more towns to take and so few of us left to take them. That's why I need all this gold and silver, to hire more knights and equip them. Right now I have eighty knights. I know that sounds like a little but think on it. Three years ago we started with twelve thousand knights. Now we have at best twelve hundred, and after we defeat al-Afdal, most of them will go home. I estimate eighty knights will be the fourth largest military force in all of Outremer. Henry, don't go back right away. Stay here for just a year or two and see what happens. Will you think on that?"

"Well, I don't know," Henry heard himself say. "I'll probably go home but I'll think on it."

"Good," said Tancred cheerily. "Do you need some coin?"

Robert of Flanders was contemplating the upcoming Council meeting which the leaders had called to determine who among them would rule over Jerusalem. He himself planned to join Robert of Normandy, Eustus of Boulongue and Gaston of Bearne to head home after, God willing, they'd overcome al-Afdal's relief army. It was clear that most of the army's knights and foot soldiers intended to go with them. Robert thought this would leave about three thousand Christian soldiers to protect Jerusalem, a woefully small number! And worse still, there were only three potential candidates—Raymond, Godfrey and Tancred—to rule over this revivified Christian Holy land. And of the three, Robert thought two were poor choices and the third not interested.

Raymond had ceded all his holdings: Toulouse, Saint-Gilles and Provence to his son Bertrand; which strongly suggested he had no intention to return to France. He'd also brought his wife Elvira. The Count had consistently argued that Pope Urban had intended Bishop Adhemar to be the Papal representative on the great pilgrimage and himself to be the secular leader. Additionally, Raymond had attempted to become the ruler of Antioch both before and after they'd taken it. When that hadn't worked, he'd shown interest in Tripoli which failed to materialize. Raymond did have some strengths for the job: he led a large number of soldiers and was pious and wealthy. His negatives included: overbearing arrogance, a regular tendency to be sick when called on to fight and, when his men were fighting, to lead from his tent. This 'shyness' was contradicted to some degree by his missing eye and advanced age.

Godfrey also commanded a large following and his personal fighting skills and bravery were legendary. He'd once cut a Turkish horse archer clean in two, a feat no one in the Christian army had ever heard of before. And his bravery atop his tower had been seen by every knight and foot soldier on the north side of the city. His leadership skills were excellent as shown by his soldiers' execution of his expectations and the amount of time he spent in prayer was renowned. Before leaving Lorraine, he had sold all his estates, castles and holdings and he had no living wife. Despite all this to Robert's knowledge, he'd never shown interest in command of more than his own army. All this information left Robert very doubtful as to whether Godfrey would be interested in ruling Jerusalem.

Tancred in the past week had raised his following from forty knights to eighty, an accomplishment unmatched by any other lord. By any standard Tancred was brave. But he was also young, rash and unpredictable. Not yet, Robert thought, was Tancred someone whom he'd promote to lead an army or oversee a city.

Robert had even heard rumors that several of the leading clergy might propose, Jerusalem being Jerusalem, that a representative of the Pope should rule the city. Robert knew the lords would have to be careful how they responded to such a preposterous proposal. Jerusalem was a city completely surrounded by Muslims, with armies coming at it from Damascus, Rum, Mosul and Cairo.

~**~

Henry of Dol had been shaking down Geoffrey, one of Count Robert's cooks, when his liege lord entered the kitchen.

"Ah, ha! Henry, you're up. We need to take a walk," proffered the Count. "Load up that plate and follow me."

Once on the street outside, Robert began to catch his coordinator up on the process the lords and leaders were going through to determine who should rule Jerusalem. The Count finished his status report as Henry was just swallowing his last spoonful of beet-greens.

"So," summed up Robert, "we have Raymond seeming to waiver over the priest's issue of the title 'king'; we have Godfrey who has expressed no interest at all; and we have Tancred who I'm sure would love to be king but none of us think he's ready."

"Are you asking for my opinion, my lord?"

"Yes," replied Robert. "We seem to have run out of candidates."

"Well," responded the young knight, "Tancred isn't ready. I think he may eventually rise to that level. But right now he keeps trying to show he's there which only proves that he isn't. Raymond has come east looking at least for a county—Antioch, Ma'ara, Tripoli or Jerusalem. It doesn't seem to matter which. He left his oldest son, Bertrand, in Toulouse overseeing all his estates there and of course he's brought Elvira and his younger son with him here. His arrogance can be very abrasive but, in my opinion, the biggest problem with putting him into the kingship is that most of his men won't stay. Almost all the Provencals, particularly Adhemar's men, are chaffing to return home. It's actually good that al-Afdal's army is coming fairly soon. If it weren't, we might lose the Provencals which would be more than a third of our knights and foot soldiers."

"Yes," said Robert, "that's my biggest concern about putting Raymond in charge. I don't want to have to come right back here to do it all over again. But that just leaves Godfrey and he doesn't seem interested."

"Ah," whispered Henry, "I read Godfrey differently. It is true that he has not expressed an interest in becoming king. But Godfrey is not a man who promotes himself. He's not like Raymond or Tancred. He doesn't see himself as a king or even a leader for that matter. He sees himself as a servant: a servant to his men, his people and most of all to God. If you sit down with him quietly and explain our dilemma for leadership in Jerusalem and present it not as a 'king-ship' but as a position which God needs filled, he'll take it...and do it well."

"You really think so?" asked Robert.

"Well," responded Henry, "try it. If he says no, you'll be no worse off than before. But I think he'll say yes, which is good because if you have to go deeper, there will be problems."

"But," asked Robert, "what about Peter Desiderius' issue of calling someone king in Jerusalem? A lot of our army will see that as offending Christ."

"That's one of the best reasons for choosing Godfrey. He won't care what his title is. Call him..." Henry paused for a moment to think up a title, "call him 'Protector of the Holy Land."

~**~

On the 22nd of July, Godfrey of Bouillon was officially affirmed leader of Jerusalem with the title of 'Advocate of the Holy Sepulchre.' As such, he conceded to the sensibilities of the Church while retaining all the powers of kingship. As a man of clear and decisive action, Godfrey immediately moved to consolidate his power and prepare for al-Afdal's arrival. Among his first initiatives was taking control of the city's citadel, the Tower of David, which Raymond's soldiers still held. Upon hearing that Godfrey was to become ruler of Jerusalem, Raymond was immensely disappointed and initially refused to hand over David's Tower, saying that his men would continue to live there until Easter when they planned to return to Toulouse. A compromise was eventually reached in which Raymond agreed to have his own Bishop of Albara make the decision of who should get the Tower. The Bishop immediately handed the Tower over to Godfrey.

On August 1st, Arnulf of Chocques was provisionally promoted to become the Holy City's new church leader. The Greek Patriarch, Simon, had long ago escaped the Turks in Jerusalem and reached the more pleasant surroundings of Cypress. On several occasions, he'd sent the Christian leaders supplies and fresh fruit. These gifts were happily received but not so appreciated that any of the Christian leaders gave thought to having a

Greek Orthodox Christian lead church services in their newly freed city. Arnulf, amid rhyming, ribald verses and hooted heckling, was appointed not as Patriarch but as 'Chancellor of the Church of Jerusalem, Protector of the Holy Relics and Custodian of the Alms of the Faithful.' Like Godfrey's title, Arnulf's titles purposely implied less than his predecessor's but still granted all the actual functions, significance and remuneration of a recognized Patriarch. The only thing that diminished the priest's appointment was that it was subject to papal confirmation. Henry wondered whether Pope Urban, whose ears as Pope were all-hearing, would confirm Arnulf.

On August 4th, word came that al-Afdal's army was at Ascalon! Godfrey immediately dispatched instructions for Tancred and Eustus to reconnoiter to the south in order to determine the size and make-up of the Egyptian force. Meanwhile The Advocate of the Holy Sepulchre collected every fighting man he possibly could and, after a prayerful and barefoot march past the Holy Sepulchre, set out for Ascalon leaving only Peter 'the Hermit' behind leading several priests and monks in organized prayers of supplication. Fortunately for The Advocate's army, Tancred and Eustus were able to capture several Fatimid herdsmen who were driving a huge herd of cattle and sheep toward Ascalon. Useful information was wrung out of these drovers and passed on to Godfrey. Accordingly by the evening of the 11th, Godfrey's army lay just out of sight of Ascalon making their final plans for an attack at dawn the next day.

Henry was riding with Robert's contingent from Flanders. He thought Godfrey's plan of attack was somewhat dangerous because Tancred's intelligence suggested the Arab army was at least twice as large as the Christian's. But the young knight also understood as did Godfrey, that most of the Christian soldiers intended to return home in the immediate future and therefore wouldn't be available after another week or two.

The Christian army rode forward at dawn with no certainty that the Egyptians wouldn't be waiting for them in prepared positions. Godfrey's final words were simply 'let God's work be done.'

Henry was joyfully amazed to find himself and his compatriots charging a foe that had not sent out scouts, had not placed skirmishers, nor yet awakened its soldiers. The Christians were falling upon a completely unprepared enemy. It was bedlam and slaughter.

OUTREMERE

August 1099 – December 1099

After their stunning rout of al-Afdal's Egyptians, the Christian army was riding back to Jerusalem with their wounded and their booty. Henry was marveling at yet another miracle that God had given them against an enemy force twice their size.

"Henry, may I speak with you?"

It was Godfrey who'd just ridden up beside the knight and was now slowing his horse in order to maintain his position. Only a few miles back, Henry had just witnessed the newly dubbed 'Advocate of the Holy Sepulchre' let the capture of Ascalon slip through his fingers—a walled port town that would have had real value to the Christians in Jerusalem – and all because, having seen the safe passage given to Iftikhar by Count Raymond, the town's negotiators would only give themselves up to Raymond. Godfrey's response to this, which he'd apparently taken as a personal affront, had been angry, direct and negative. Henry had seen Godfrey irritable before, perhaps on the edge of anger, but never so angry as this...and the price was Ascalon!

"Yes, my lord," replied the young knight.

"Do you intend to return to Dol with the Roberts when they leave?"

Before answering, Henry paused for a moment. He'd been contemplating whether to return immediately or stay a while as Tancred had asked him to. But the potential opportunities that his friend had referred to weren't really as high in his mind as was the simple thought that, having committed so greatly in lives, time and hardship, the Christians should be certain their tree had taken root before they left it behind.

"I have not yet decided, my lord."

"Then please let me encourage you to stay on as my coordinator," said Godfrey as he looked Henry squarely in the eye. "I'll need someone I can trust to translate all these languages and I'll need a few liegemen with whom I can discuss priorities and strategies and know that they'll be giving me their opinions without concern for what they think I want to hear. I believe you will do that. I do not ask you this expecting you to stay the rest of your life but only to commit for a year and then you can stay or go with my complete support. It's important though that you stay at this very crucial juncture. I'm estimating by Christmas we'll have only three hundred knights and twelve hundred foot soldiers left. I've asked both Roberts to send back all the fighting men they can. But this first year, we'll be mightily challenged to hold Jerusalem."

"My lord," stammered the young knight, "you have been most generous in what you have said about my willingness to speak my mind. May I ask you a question?"

"Certainly," replied the Advocate. "What is it?"

"My lord, this is not intended to be rude but why did you not let Count Raymond take Ascalon?"

For a moment Godfrey stared at the young soldier then his face broadened into a smile. "Ah Henry, you are willing to be direct, just as I thought." Quickly Godfrey looked around to see who might be listening. No one was particularly close. Nevertheless the Advocate lowered his voice. "Henry, Ascalon would have been nice to take. But after most of our army has departed for home, and if Raymond is in Ascalon, he'll have three times as many men as me. He has always considered himself Pope Urban's choice to lead our pilgrimage and he craves lands similar to those he had in France. I feared to embolden him only thirty miles from Jerusalem. If he goes back up the coast, there are several cities there that will meet his needs and not threaten Jerusalem. I simply could not take a chance placing a hungry prince so close to a sweet meat."

For a long moment Henry stared at Godfrey. "Then you weren't really angry?"

"Well, a little," the Advocate replied. "I'd hoped we'd get Ascalon without Raymond's name coming up but once it did, I knew we'd have to leave Ascalon to the Egyptians."

"Then it wasn't just your anger at a personal affront?"

"No," smiled Godfrey, "but I thought it better to have it look that way."

"Then I apologize," said Henry.

"Why do you apologize?"

"I thought you'd let your personal feelings come ahead of your duty."

"I shall consider that a compliment," responded the former Duke of Lower Lorraine. That's exactly what I'd hoped people would think and having them think I can get angry occasionally can help too."

Henry's voice became serious, "My lord, I shall stay on with you at least for a year."

"Good," said Godfrey definitively. "Please start doing for me whatever you did for Robert as soon as he releases you. Let me know when that is and I'll have you join my liege lord meetings. Thank you Henry." Godfrey kneed his horse and trotted off.

While Pegasus continued walking, Henry's mind turned to his new role. He felt honored to be asked by Godfrey to join him at the level of a liege-man. And after their discussion about Ascalon, he felt certain the Advocate would listen to his thoughts and advice. Additionally he felt good about staying because it was the right thing to do; and, after a year, he could choose whether or not to leave for Dol.

Godfrey had specifically mentioned his language skills. The breadth of languages spoken on their pilgrimage counting Latin and all the various dialects, he'd once calculated to be nineteen. He considered himself pass-able in only French, German, Spanish and Latin. Fortunately many of the other languages had their roots in Latin which helped. He knew he'd never know them all. His travels in the east had also taught him that, if he were to stay for long, he would have to learn Arabic. In Outremere, there were numerous religious and ethnic groups: Armenians, Greek Orthodox, Marinites, Jacobites, Nestorians, Sunni Muslims, Shi'a Muslims, the Nizari, and of course Jews and Zoroastrians. Almost all of them spoke Arabic either as their first or second language. Henry set his mind to thinking whom he could get to teach him Arabic. Suddenly he had an idea... a very good idea. There were a number of orphaned Arab children scavenging about the streets of Jerusalem. He'd find one to live with him and have the boy speak Arabic to him all the time. In return, Henry could provide him food, shelter and...and an upbringing. Perhaps he'd even find two or three orphans.

Of course he'd have to see whether Johnnie was going to stay or go back to Flanders. Up until the last year or so, Henry would have assumed the boy would stay with him. But Johnnie was now fifteen and their rela-tionship didn't seem as strong as it once had. Of course Bart would stay; at least he thought he would. Another thing that Henry would have to do right away was write a letter to his mother and father to tell them he'd been asked by the Advocate to stay for a year. He had sent three letters to Dol since leaving and received no responses. One could never be sure that a letter would get through. But if he sent this one with Count Robert, it would be very likely to reach Dol. With these thoughts jostling for position in his brain, Henry kneed Pegasus. Robert would be somewhere up ahead.

When Henry finally found his overlord, he told Robert of Godfrey's offer and explained why he'd accepted it. He'd feared his Count would resist but that turned out not to be the case.

"Henry if you're going to stay, you should start with Godfrey right away. His new organization is setting up as we speak and his need for help will be greatest at the beginning."

So Henry reported to Godfrey the very next day. The Advocate gave him a house in the city and allocated him a monthly stipend.

"This will allow you to maintain yourself and still be close at hand should I need you. Set yourself up in your house today and come to the Tower for my liege lord meeting at sunrise tomorrow. I think you know all the men. We'll discuss your role and responsibilities so that everyone will know yours as well as their own."

Henry found the house quite easily. It wasn't large but would accommodate Johnnie if he chose to stay, Bart and two or three Muslim boys as well. He decided to leave Pegasus stabled where he already was. The horse's stable master was attentive and the cost, given Henry's new income, was quite manageable. With his duties done, he set about looking for an Arab orphan or two. This task turned out to be more difficult than he'd expected. Every time he sighted a prospect or two, the young boys would run off. Eventually he tried a different approach. Carrying a large clay vessel, he went to Hezekiah's Pool, an open cistern, and waited. Several young boys came into view but they quickly halted and, after a brief wait ran off. Finally Henry gave up and initiated a search for Peter Desidarius. When he found the priest, he asked him to help.

"Ah," responded Peter, "I may be able to be of some assistance." The priest placed two fingers between his lips and issued forth two sharp whistles. Almost immediately two dark-skinned boys came running up. Peter spoke a few words of Arabic to them of which Henry understood enough to grasp that Peter was presenting him as someone who could provide food and shelter.

The older boy stared at Henry in a very untrusting manner. So the priest turned to the smaller boy, a youth of about six and asked him something about his sister. The little boy glanced appraisingly at Henry and answered so quickly that Henry didn't grasp his meaning. Peter then went on at great length. When he finished, the boy looked Henry up and down again but still very carefully. Eventually he turned to his taller Arab compatriot obviously soliciting his opinion.

The older boy shook his head negatively but Peter interrupted. "I'll go with you to Henry's house." The priest reached his hand out to the boy. After a slight hesitation, the youth took it.

"Take us to your house Henry," directed Peter. "This is Ezekial who is fluent in both Arabic and Yiddish. He and his younger sister are Jewish. I trust you will take a Jew into your house in place of an Arab?"

"If he will teach me Arabic, I will. And I'll be doubly indebted if I can learn some Yiddish too."

At the house, Henry showed Ezekial and Peter the rooms and the outhouse and explained that they might also have another young man staying with them. Then Peter talked to the boy about respect and integrity which Peter had remembered were two of Henry's values. Apparently Peter was explaining what would be expected of Ezekial. Henry watched closely as Peter and the boy discussed the two values. The knight sensed the values were having a positive affect.

Eventually, Peter turned to Henry. "Ezekial will get his sister and move in with you. I have promised him that I shall visit occasionally to make certain that each of you is adhering to God's rules."

"Thank you," said Henry. "But before you go, I wish to give Ezekial some coin so he can buy us food and drink for dinner." Henry reached into his surcoat's pocket where he'd put Godfrey's stipend. When he pulled out a silver penny, the boy's eyes widened. Henry reached forth his hand. "Ezekial, this should be enough for our food for quite some time. Let me know when you need more."

Not understanding Henry's 'Frange,' the boy turned to Peter, who repeated Henry's words in Arabic.

Ezekial looked back at Henry and tentatively reached out to accept the coin.

Henry smiled as the boy took it. This caused the edges of Ezekial's mouth to spread into a grin.

In the next several days, Henry settled into both his new work schedule and his new home. Godfrey was accustomed to regular meetings at certain times on certain days. So much so that Henry thought his new lord could have fit right into a monastery. At the house, Ezekial proved capable of overseeing the kitchen and trustworthy of being the bursar. His younger sister, Rachel, was at first quite shy but as the days passed, she became talkative and even began to hide behind Henry if someone stopped by. Their conversations were usually in Arabic although the children were eager to learn 'Frange'; and, if no one else was there, Henry found he could draw forth a little Yiddish. Ezekial also took to playing chess regularly and after a few weeks began to press Henry.

The night before most of the Christian army departed for home, Henry visited Robert. He asked the Count if he'd please take the letter he'd written for his parents, which Robert promised to do. They also discussed Johnnie who had decided to stay in the Holy Land. This surprised Henry as he'd had a sense that his relationship with the young man was diminishing. Robert thought the boy's staying out late in recent evenings probably had more to do with his decision. Henry made a mental note to set clear rules for Johnnie when the youth stayed at his house. Most importantly, Henry thanked the Count for his many kindnesses: the knight's school, the opportunity to be his coordinator, including him in all that was going on during the pilgrimage and letting him participate in the early entrances of Antioch and Jerusalem.

"Henry, you're a fine young man with whom I am glad to have served God. We helped each other in many ways and most of all we helped Him. You will note that I have my palm frond and that I have moved my cross from the chest of my surcoat to the back shoulder. So I am ready to go. If you do return to Dol, please visit Clem and me in Flanders. By then our children may have stopped believing my stories so it will be good to have a witness to confirm them. May God be with you."

The two men hugged.

When Henry had spare time, he went to visit Gerard, the Christian monk, who was the guardian of the Benedictine hospital in Jerusalem. The monk was a serious and sincere man whose highest hope was to serve, protect and give succor to Christian pilgrims. Despite his predilection to Christians, he was renowned for never turning away any 'child of God.'

On one of his visits, Henry met a young woman who was hauling piss-pots out of one of the hospital's small buildings where the invalids resided.

"Good day," the woman whispered in perfect French as she stepped aside to let him pass.

Immediately recognizing her accent as Bretton or Norman, Henry stopped. "Are you from Normandy?" he asked.

The woman winced then, bobbing her head in some sort of deference, mumbled, "Caen."

"I'm from Dol," Henry responded ecstatically. "What's your name?"

"Brinette," the woman answered as she held her eyes to the ground.

"Mine is Henry," proffered the knight as he swallowed deeply. He'd not met her before...but Caen. She was practically a neighbor. "How did you get here?"

"I came with the Christian army," she answered cautiously.

"So did I," Henry responded jubilantly, "but I don't think I've met you before."

Brinette raised her eyes and looked directly at the knight. "I was a Tarfur."

Not having noticed the descent of the woman's tone, Henry rushed on. "I was with Count Robert of Flanders. We must have travelled together for four years and never met. Of course there were thousands of us. But you didn't go back. Didn't you want to go home?"

"No," Brinette answered bluntly. "I didn't."

"No parents or relatives?"

"No," repeated the woman.

Finally catching Brinette's mood, Henry tried to reverse course. "Well," he pronounced, "I chose to stay too, at least for a year until Godfrey gets things settled in. What do you do here at the hospital?"

"I clean up after the patients," she murmured.

"Oh," Henry mused, "does Gerard pay you?"

"He gives me food," she replied.

"But where do you stay?"

"I survive," Brinette answered sullenly.

"I have a house," blurted out the knight. "We haven't much space but there's room enough for another."

The woman cocked her head sideways and stared at Henry appraisingly. "And what would you want in return?" she asked.

"Oh," answered Henry, "I hadn't thought of payment. But if you wish, you could help cook our food and clean the house." Henry smiled. "I'll not take advantage of you if that's what you're afraid of."

Brinette's suspicious stare did not diminish. "How many of you are there?"

"Four," Henry replied, "myself, Johnnie, he's about fifteen, and two children who are five and six."

The woman's stony expression lost a little of its edge but she offered no response.

"Look," said Henry sternly, "you can live on the streets if you wish. My offer is well meant. Ask Peter Narbonne. He knows me, my family and where we live. He can vouchsafe our intentions." Then Henry turned on his heel and stomped out of the hospital.

Henry found his role as Godfrey's coordinator quite different than it had been for Robert. After Robert of Normandy, Gaston of Bearne, Raymond of Toulouse, and Robert of Flanders departed with their knights and foot soldiers, there were only three hundred knights and two thousand infantry left. This eliminated a great deal of running around for Henry. Godfrey simply held weekly communication meetings with his liegemen. The Advocate did need counsel and advice in regard to the administration of his lands. In the desmenes of France and Germany, the lords provided justice and protection for their freemen and tenants and in return, took about one tenth of the crop, wood, hay, honey, herd and time from their subjects. In Outremere the agricultural outputs tended to be 'money crops.' The farmers, be they Arab, Armenian, Jacobite, Zoroastrian, Nestorian, Greek, or Maronite, simply produced particular crops, herds, spices, wheat, and sundries and sold them either to local merchants or tradesmen who shipped the goods across the sea to foreign ports.

Godfrey and his liegemen quickly concluded that taking one tenth of their farmers' income instead of one tenth of their produce was much simpler for everyone. Of course justice still had to be provided but it functioned quite smoothly in essentially the same manner as it had in France and Germany. In fact Henry learned that the Arab tenants found justice under the 'Frange' fairer than under the Muslims because there were no issues of Sunni judging Shi'a or Shi'a judging Sunni. These changes had several immediate impacts. Foremost was that the lords no longer had to live on their estates. They simply paid an administrator to keep the books and collect the taxes.

Henry's top priority turned out to be the establishment of an alarm methodology. The risk of Muslim armies attacking at any moment without much warning created a need for Godfrey to call up his knights and foot soldiers instantaneously. What was put into place primarily by Henry, was a system of twelve principals each having to contact five others who in turn would contact five more and so on. The initial riders would convey the location of their meeting place and each recipient of this information would be expected to arrive on location in a specified length of time fully armed and on horseback if appropriate. This system was regularly tested until it worked flawlessly. The key was having responsible riders and holding them accountable for the timeliness of their arrival. Not being found or being late was severely penalized.

There were other issues too. One had to do with marriages between Roman Christians and Armenians or Nestorians; the latter while Christians interpreted various doctrines differently than their western brothers. Accordingly, some of the Roman priests thought such unions were a sacrilege. After asking Henry for advice, Godfrey settled the issue. 'A Christian is a Christian and a Christain marriage will produce more Christian soldiers.' As it turned out, Henry experienced a first-hand example of this when Johnnie announced his plan to marry a young Armenian woman. When Henry shared this with 'the Advocate', Godfrey's only comment was to 'add all the men in the woman's family to the call-up list.'

At another of Godfrey's sunrise meetings, Henry had a very odd personal experience. He was sitting amidst the usual thirty or so lords, knights, soldiers and administrators as Godfrey was discussing the need to assign someone a relatively unimportant job. Suddenly Henry felt himself rise from his bench to a fully standing position. He hadn't any reason to stand up nor had he consciously decided to do so. Then Godfrey, who was not facing him at that moment, and therefore couldn't have known he was standing, called out Henry's name for the job he'd just been describing. Henry was mortified by the oddity of the event. The men around him seemed to take little notice of it, but to Henry it was as if somehow he'd been communicated to prior to the event. It reminded him of the time he'd been hunting in Dol and had called out 'two' before the second person appeared.

Of other note and to Henry's surprise Brinette, having asked Peter Narbonne about the efficacy of Henry's offer, moved into the knight's house.

A week before Christmas, at one of the liege lord meetings, Henry noticed that Godfrey had lost weight. The Advocate's face was thinner, his cheek bones more prominent and the flesh under his jaw tighter. Upon further perusal, Henry concluded his lord's skin color was grey where it had been ruddy. When the reports were over and the meeting concluded, Henry delayed his exit so he and Godfrey would be alone together.

"My lord," queried the knight, "are you feeling well?"

For a moment Godfrey stared at his coordinator. "I've been having some difficulty shitting," he finally answered with a broad smile filling his face, "but," he continued as the smile diminished, "I've been thinking of asking your opinion."

After three meetings over three weeks, Henry concluded that his lord was dying. By then Godfrey had concluded the same outcome. The Advocate only asked two questions.

"How long will it take?"

"Between a month and six months," replied the coordinator.

"Will I have great pain?"

"I do not know," responded Henry. "Sometimes there is pain, other times not."

"Well then," responded Godfrey, "just in case, I shall keep my knife nearby."

"My lord," asked Henry, "should we tell anyone? The kingdom will be both at risk and in play."

"Not yet Henry," answered Godfrey. "God will replace me with whomever He thinks best. I have been blessed to serve Him and, now that we have achieved our goal, I do not fear dying."

Henry didn't share his knowledge of Godfrey's illness but he knew well enough that there would soon be signs too clear to miss. By May, Godfrey was being visited by more members of his family than Henry had ever previously known existed. Tancred visited too.

On July 18th, Godfrey passed away quietly in his bed, his knife unneeded. Henry thought his lord's lack of suffering reflected God's grace given to a loyal supporter. So when the subject of his burial arose among Godfrey's liegemen, Henry recommended that the Advocate's body be interred in the Church of the Holy Sepulchre. This proposal received no opposition from the lords and was quickly followed. Accordingly, when a rumor resonated that Godfrey's dying wish was to have his brother Baldwin brought south to become ruler of Jerusalem, Henry did not contradict it.

As it turned out, the only other candidate for sovereignty over Jerusalem was Bohemond whom Tancred promoted. And Bohemond might well have become ruler had he not managed to get himself captured by the Danishmed Turks during a minor skirmish in August. Accordingly, Baldwin of Edessa rode into Jerusalem in November to a cheering crowd of Lotharingians. Baldwin was accompanied by a bodyguard of no less than four hundred and fifty knights. So on Christmas day, in the Church of the Holy Sepulchre, the darker, younger brother of Godfrey received his coronation as 'King' of Jerusalem. Pope Paschal's newly appointed Patriarch, Daimbert of Pisa, performed the ceremony. He was a short, officious fellow who'd been to Spain and just the day before the ceremony in a particularly arrogant way, had described Abbott Bernard of Sahagun as a 'womanizer.'

Following the coronation, Tancred sold his estates in Galilee in order to leave for Antioch where he was the obvious candidate to succeed his uncle Bohemond. Henry, who'd never liked Baldwin and expected little kindness from him, rode north with Tancred. He took Ezekial, Rachel and Bart with him and left his house to Brinette, Johnnie and Johnie's wife. Like Robert of Flanders, Henry removed his cross from the front of his surcoat and stitched it instead onto his back right shoulder. In his leather packet behind his saddle, he carried his wool blanket, wide-brimmed hat, chess game, book, Reynauld's cross and several minor items.

THE ROAD HOME
January 1101

"It's hard," said Tancred, "for me to see God's hand behind Baldwin getting the throne."

"I agree," responded the knight from Dol, "but God's hand is often hard to discern."

"He's a totally selfish person," continued Tancred. "I mean it's always about what benefits him. How could God entrust a man like that to rule over the world's most holy city? I just can't understand it."

"That's why we're riding north with you. I don't want to serve him either."

"The very first thing he asked me after we'd heard about Bohemond's unfortunate situation was whether or not I'd be going to Antioch to take over the city...and that if I did, I'd first have to swear fielty to him and then release my little piece of Galilee to him. He didn't even ask how I was, just told me what I'd have to do for him before I left."

"You're right," said Henry, "but..."

"I can't see how he can hold onto his knights," continued Tancred. "I mean, how can they trust him?"

"Tancred," said Henry much more forcefully, "what will you do if Bohemond is ransomed, if he comes back and wants to rule Antioch again? I mean you haven't got any other place to go now that Galilee and Bethlehem have been taken by Baldwin."

"That's why I wanted to keep Galilee, but that's why Baldwin wanted it, so I wouldn't ever come back. I threaten him Henry. He doesn't want anyone strong around him...like me with eighty knights. If he were thinking about Jerusalem's safety first, he'd want my knights on your call-up list."

"But what about Bohemond?" asked Henry. "What will you do if he comes back?"

"Well," Tancred replied, "I don't know that they'll even want me in Antioch. I expect they will but I don't know yet. The Turks may present us with a ransom offer but I don't know that yet either. My uncle could die in prison before payment is completed or the Turks may realize that he'll always be nibbling at their heels and decide not to offer him up. I don't know how long it would take us to raise a ransom. But to answer your question, if my uncle returned, I'd have to turn the city over to him. I'd still have these eighty knights and the camel-loads of coin. Perhaps Tripoli? But it's all just speculation until I get to Antioch and feel out the situation. At least it will be better than serving Baldwin."

"Amen," murmured Henry. "Amen."

~**~

After Henry's group and mounts disembarked at the southern Italian town of Bari, the knight stood on the pier and considered their situation. He felt as if he was swaying slightly. Suddenly the realization that he was no longer in the Holy Land rushed into his brain. He'd known they were leaving but somehow the reality had just sunk in. He looked back across the green sea water. Would Jerusalem be safe? The Holy Land continue to be Christian?

Then Henry turned his gaze toward Bari. It was a prosperous looking port. Could he see a church? Yes. He would go there first to thank God for His help and guidance in getting to Jerusalem and to ask for His help in the future to keep Jesus' city safe for Christian pilgrims.

As it turned out, Tusculum was about twelve miles southeast of Rome. The Arabs would have called it a 'fat land'—black earth filled with nutrients, sunshine interspersed with moderate showers, ground easily plowable and crops rotated. There were fewer castles than Henry expected but many manner houses. They were all designed similarly: a large, square courtyard in the center, tan plaster-sided buildings circling the courtyard and, more often than not, an eight-foot wall encasing the entire structure. Vineyards were plentiful, bee-boxes ubiquitous and piles of manure lay heaped in readiness for spring spreading. The only aspect of these plantations that didn't seem to fit was the scarcity of workers...but of course it was still winter.

The ancient, cobbled road they were riding north on Henry reasoned was the Appian Way, a road built even before the Caesars. The antiquity thrilled him. Also he discovered that many of the Italians, at least those who appeared to be higher in the social order, spoke Latin. This pleased him because he could ask questions, understand answers and not feel like a foreigner. Thinking they must be nearing Tusculum, Henry asked directions from a young man who was walking in the opposite direction. This fellow had known Benito and directed them to a specific castle only a mile ahead where they would find Caesar Tusculani, Benito's father.

It was mid-afternoon when Henry's troop arrived at the castle. The draw bridge was up and the portcullis down. Since they'd landed in Bari, Henry noted this had been true at every castle they'd passed. It was surely a sign of political instability and perhaps, even aggressive military activity. But of the latter, Henry had yet seen none.

"Hallow," Henry hollered to the unseen castellan who was undoubtedly watching them. "I am Henry of Dol and wish to speak with the father of Benito Tusculani who was my tutor."

A voice called back in Italian which Henry couldn't understand.

"I speak Latin, French, German, Spanish and Arabic. If one of those will do, please speak it. Otherwise please introduce me to Caesar Tusculani."

An Italian word was called back, which Henry hoped meant that the castellan was getting Benito's father. Henry and his group dismounted. They had been alternating walking and riding for several days .

"Who are you?" called out a voice in perfect Latin. The accent was exactly the same as Benito's but the force suggested a speaker of considerable age.

"I am Henry of Dol, one of your son's students. I promised God that if I was ever in Rome, I'd visit you to give my thanks."

"God bless you," responded the voice from just above the drawbridge. "Open the gate. They are friends."

A moment later came a grinding, squeaking noise that was immediately followed by the top of the drawbridge beginning to swing away from the castle and slowly descend toward its lowered position across a dry moat. Eventually the drawbridge ground to a halt and shortly after that the portcullis began to rise, albeit with a baser rattling sound.

Standing just inside the entryway stood four men. The most notable was old, stooped and bald with just a little white hair showing above his ears. It was not this hoary senior's physical appearance though that singled him out but rather his brilliant red coat which shimmered in the sunlight. The other three men who stood beside and slightly behind their patriarch were soldiers each wearing chainmail, hauberk, helmet, and carrying a crossbow. The crossbows were cocked and loaded but pointed at the ground.

"Please come in," squeaked the old man as best he could in his wispy accent. "I am so glad you've come. Benito was my third son and so well educated. We'd thought one day God might make him Pope but sadly that won't happen. Come in, come in."

With little concern for the loaded crossbows, Henry stepped forward. During his last three years, he'd grown accustomed to constant vigilance. He did however hope the three bowyers were calm veterans and not jumpy neophytes.

"Thank you for seeing us," chirped Henry. "My first time through Rome I was on my way to the Holy Land and we didn't take any time to stop." Henry stepped up to the red-shirted elder and stretched forth his hand. "My name is Henry and these are Bart, Ezekial and Rachel."

Bart was holding the horses' reins and simply raised his free hand. Ezekial though, stepped right up to the Italian patriarch and put forth his hand just as he had seen Henry do. Rachel stepped behind Bart and shyly peeked out. "Well met," said the Tusculani leader to Ezekial as he smiled at the boy. Then turning back to Henry, he continued. "My first name is Caesar. Please use it as we are surely friends based on my son's relationship with each of us. Come inside. We have very fine mead or wines, some with great punch if you like." The patriarch turned to lead the way into the castle's keep. As he did, he nodded to one of his soldiers. "Embruglio, I shall be quite safe with this knight. He bears proof of that on his back shoulder. Please take their horses, close the gate and return to your post."

The castle's great-room was quite plush. The chairs and benches had padded leather seats, the dishware was pottery instead of wooden bowls and the goblets were metal but with silver latticed around them in a way that both turned them into artwork and made them heavy.

Caesar directed his guests toward a circle of six chairs that surrounded a low table. He then clapped his hands together loudly. Immediately, a young woman entered the room. In deference to her lord, her head bobbed up and down but the action seemed to go on too long which caused Henry to think of Benito's switch. "Maria, bring us some good wine, mead for the children and some slabs of cheese to munch on." Caesar's head barely nodded and the woman began backing away.

After the mid-afternoon repast had been appreciated, the Count of Tusculum turned to Henry's sergeant. "Bart, would you mind taking the children out and showing them around the castle? One of the castellans will show you the way."

Bart glanced at Henry who nodded his consent. The procurer then waved to Ezekial and Rachel. "Have you two ever been in a castle before?"

Once they were gone, Henry turned to the Count to see what he wished to talk about.

"Thank you for coming to see me," said Caesar. "My son was very dear to me. How did he die?"

"He died bravely," replied Henry. "We had the priest in to administer the last rites and did everything we could to comfort him and relieve his breathing."

"But what did he die of?" interrupted the Count.

"Oh," said Henry, "he developed a fever and both his head and his lungs filled with moisture. This led him to not being able to breathe. We put his head over boiling water hoping the steam would diminish his congestion. It didn't have enough affect."

"You didn't have a surgeon you could call in?" asked the father.

"No," replied Henry. "The nearest surgeon was in Caen. That's fifty miles from Dol. My father sent for him but he arrived two days too late."

"Then you did all you could," mumbled the Count without raising his eyes. "I have one more question though."

The old man lifted his gaze and stared directly at the knight. Henry could see anger smoldering beneath his eyelids.

"Do you know why Abbott Hugh sent Benito to Dol?"

"To tutor my brother William and me," answered Henry.

"But why Benito? And to such a faraway place?" asked the Count with his lower jaw locked so tightly he could hardly enunciate the words.

"I don't know," answered Henry. "Benito never talked to me of Hugh and Hugh never talked to me about Benito."

"You know Hugh!" Caesar said angrily.

"Yes," replied Henry, "but I never heard him speak of Benito."

"How well do you know Hugh?"

"Fairly well," replied the young knight who in his mind had decided not to elaborate on their trip to Spain.

"How would you describe the Abbot?"

"Well," answered Henry as he pondered how to answer the Count's question, "Hugh is a devout Christian and a man of values. He has devoted his life to Cluny and its houses. They have grown in number and are spread from Burgundy to Spain, Germany, Italy and even Jerusalem. In those places, the sick are nurtured, pilgrims fed and communion offered. All in all, I would say that Hugh is a man of God who has devoted most of his life to others."

The Count viscously spat on the floor."You don't know him," he bellowed. Then almost imperceptibly the old man began to sob.

Not thinking that the Count had finished his response, Henry said nothing.

"Have you nothing to say boy?" The old man's voice came shrill and harsh.

Henry looked at his expression. Anger was still etched in his face but it was quickly being washed over by a deep, disconsolate melancholy. Benito's father began to cry.

"You may be surprised," the young knight whispered, "that shortly before he died, Benito asked that I present his eulogy. When I did, I distinguished between his little vices and his two great strengths which were his standards and his knowledge. He held the highest standards, something he probably learned here. When he taught, he always expected the fullest attention. He had a switch with which he reinforced his high standards. He only snapped that stick on my hand once but it got his point across. He used his knowledge to impart wisdom. He did it by reciting stories from Homer and Virgil. His presentations were articulate, profound and always delivered in three parts designed to make the point as strongly as possible. Your son was a man of God and an excellent teacher."

Henry looked at the Count. The man's eyes were wet with tears and his body shuddered uncontrollably. When he finally regained his composure, he raised his eyes to Henry's and whispered. "Thank you. That was very kind of you to share."

For a moment Henry felt tears forming in his own eyes but he smiled and continued. "I respected your son a great deal. But in answer to your question about how and perhaps why he died, I think God simply had another mission for him and called him back."

A period of silence followed during which each man regained his composure. After that, Henry was the first to speak. "Caesar, I see signs here at your castle and at others that suggest concern for security. Am I interpreting this correctly?"

"Sadly, yes," replied the Count in a soft tone. "You have experience beyond what one might expect for your years. Military duty will do that to

a man. In recent years, our situation here in Rome has changed dramatically. Let me think how best to describe it. I shall over simplify but for a
bright, well educated man such as yourself, it is important to start with
how we were when I was your age.

"Rome had fifteen thousand citizens and was a mere specter of its old
self when it had upward of half a million. We had only the Pope, our
churches and our ruins. Our only source of prosperity came from the generosity of pilgrims who came to salve their souls through benediction and
redemption, to visit reliquaries, pursue litigation or petition for some
wrong to be righted. For all Romans, including the vulgar, this flow of
pilgrims provided a means of living whether through the Pope's 'beneficia'
or 'presbyteria,' gifts on feast days or through tolls such as those administered by Cencius Stephani at his tower on the bridge of Saint Peter. The
income was never large but was sufficient to keep us all alive. And most
fortunately because it wasn't large, it didn't draw the great emperors,
kings, dukes and other plunderers to come and rob us.

"That all changed when that blasphemous reformer Hildebrand
became Pope Gregory, may he roast in hell! He immediately proclaimed
himself not God's emissary, but God himself by directing the young Emper-
or, whose fiefs we all live on by his permission, to stop investing his
churchmen with ring and staff and turn that function over to the Papacy.
One might then presume that Gregory would choose the priests and
bishops along the North Sea, which even a fast courier couldn't reach in
less than three or four weeks' time. This effrontery quickly led to excommunication and the schism we have today with two Popes.

"For us here in Rome, this has been devastating! The politics of
Gregory's extremism against the Emperor led to the Papacy pursuing alliances with Matilda, Countess of Tuscany and Robert Guiscard of Apulia
against the Emperor. In 1083 the weasel Guiscard, may he also roast in
hell, offered Rome 30,000 silver solidi if we would keep the city safe from
Henry and therefore protect Gregory. Greed is a powerful motive and the
vulgus of the city accepted the silver; but then, when Henry arrived a year
later with his army at our gates, they let him in.

"After Henry had crowned himself Holy Roman Emperor, he left leaving behind his anti-pope Clement, a devout and reasonable man from
Ravenna. The weasel Guiscard showed up only a few days later and, feeling
betrayed by the Romans, sacked the city most horribly. A third of the

buildings were razed, thousands of men, women and children killed and raped, aqueducts destroyed, even churches smashed and desecrated. Our city, once full of magnificent antiquities, was utterly ruined...all because of that stupid Gregory and his politics.

"Fortunately when he left, Guiscard took Gregory with him. If he'd left him behind, we'd have burned the fool alive for the damage he brought upon us. Clement proved to be a reasonable man with whom we could work.

In the past, when it came to picking Popes and filling key positions in their administrations, the Crescenti and Tusculani families had been great rivals. But with the ascent of Gregory and all the new political entanglements he brought us, we found common ground and began to work together to save Rome from further bloodshed and carnage. You see, the Crescenti hold sway in Sabina and, through the Octaviani, a branch of the Crescenti family, hold even more land in several adjacent areas. The Tusculani hold Tusculum, Velletri and Palestrina with my daughter's family, the Colonna, controlling the strategic Castle Colonna.

"Together we have been able to stabilize the city for eighteen years. But wider politics continue to threaten us. Not only do the German, Tuscan and Sicilian elements plant spies in our midst, they also buy allies and stir up locals in their favor. Fortunately, Theobald Stephani, a Crescenti but also another of my son-in-laws, has been able to hold Castle Saint Angelo, which controls the Tiber bridge and the basilica of Saint Peter. This is key because several families have been paid to wrestle it away from us. Certainly the Pierleoni, Frangipani, Papareschi, Scolari, and Scotti are in that category. They call themselves 'Papal Reformers' or sometimes 'Fideles' but make no mistake, they are in it for themselves and will act accordingly. If they keep contesting our position, they may precipitate another sack of the city. May God protect us from that!

"With the death of Clement last year, we now have Theordoric installed as Emperor Henry's Pope. His counterpart is of course Paschal who, like Gregory, dubs himself a reformer. I have heard he is a Godly man. If he can just refrain from stirring up the Emperor, Kings and Dukes, we Romans may live a little longer without again being sacked, raped and murdered."

THE FACES OF AUTHORITY
February 1101

The next morning, Henry's foursome was again riding north on the Appian Way, this time to Rome. Henry and the Count of Tusculum had talked late into the night. Fortunately Bart and the children had retired early. But Henry was tired. His conversation with Caesar had been long and seemed to have covered every conceivable topic: Roman politics including the Count's family connections, his dislike for Guiscard as well as church reformers like Pope Gregory, the pros and cons of Rome's revenues being entirely drawn from pilgrims and the city's long connection to the Holy Roman Emperor originally Charlemagne and most recently Henry IV. The discourse had eventually shifted to Henry's pilgrimage to Jerusalem: what happened along the way, the leaders, their personalities and squabbles and finally to God's intercessions and the magnificence of their final accomplishment.

Caesar had ended the discussion abruptly by telling Henry that he'd instructed his domestic staff to have breakfast ready at dawn on the morrow.

"Leaving early should get you into the city well before noon. I'll write you a letter of introduction, which should overcome any check, delay, or interference you may run into on your way. You will be impressed with Saint Peter's bascilica. I'm glad you plan to visit it. Sleep well, Henry."

The old man did not appear at breakfast but one of his domestics presented a folded piece of parchment on which was a thick, red wax seal beside the Count's name. The writing was in Latin written in a most florid style yet remarkably succinct—'Grant this man, Henry of Dol, all possible assistance per Count Caesar Tusculani.' In order to protect the seal, Henry folded the parchment very carefully and placed it inside his chess set where he reasoned it would be least likely to incur damage.

After only a mile or two, the rich farm land of Tusculum gave way to a series of mud and wattle shacks that seemed to be scattered aimlessly about. This random squalor reminded the knight of Paris which had been similarly haphazard and disgusting. Immediately after this recollection, Henry saw a shabbily dressed woman step out of her hovel's doorway and toss shit from a bucket onto the path ahead of them. It was, he knew, a 'deja vue'—an exact replication of a similar act performed by a similar woman outside Paris. Henry asked himself if there might be some greater meaning in this seemingly odd event, some message that God was sending him? If there was, he couldn't figure it out. Pegasus simply walked through the excrement.

Once inside the city walls, the riders dismounted and, with Henry going first, led their mounts by the reins. As the foursome walked on, they passed the Baths of Caracalla and then on their right the Coliseum.

"What's that old building?" asked Ezekial. "It looks broken."

"Oh," answered Henry as he waited for Bart and Rachel to catch up, "that's the Coliseum where a thousand years ago the Romans held games. They had gladiators fight there. Do you know what a gladiator is?"

"No," responded Ezekial in a tenor which displayed interest.

So Henry shared his knowledge of gladiators, lions, circuses and Christian martyrs. Each child and Bart as well, stood listening as their immediate surroundings came to life.

Saint Peter's basilica was huge. The structure itself had been placed directly above Saint Peter's tomb and beside it there were numerous mosaics and frescoes depicting scenes from both the Old and New Testament.

"Henry! Is that you?" bellowed a familiar voice from across the basilica's nave.

There was a deeply tanned man dressed in a scarlet robe and wearing a white conical hat springing toward him.

"Bernard!" shouted Henry. "I didn't expect to see you here. How are you?"

The two men clasped each other in a great hug.

"Your mother's bear hug," whispered Bernard as he stepped back with the air squeezed out of his lungs.

"Yes," murmured Henry whose lungs had also been mightily squeezed.

"How are you?" queried the Bishop.

"Very well," answered the knight. "It's been a long time. You've probably seen Abbot Hugh since I have and Brother Bruglio the bursar?"

"Oh yes," answered Bernard, "Hugh is very well and still travelling all over Christendom. Sadly though, Brother Bruglio passed into God's realm only a few months ago. He came down with one of those winter illnesses that take away your breath until you can't breathe at all. He was among the best of Christians though, a man whose soul will surely be saved. And you Henry, did I see a cross sewn on your back?"

"Yes," responded Henry. "I went to Jerusalem with Robert of Flanders and am only just returning."

"Good for you," continued the Bishop. "I'd always thought Abbott Hugh would get you into the Church but I can see he didn't."

"No," replied the knight. "My brother William died and I had to take his place at Dol. I was just finishing my knight's training when Count Robert invited me to go with him on the Pope's great pilgrimage. I even got to meet Urban at Reims. What a speech he gave! Everyone there took their cross right on the spot, the same cross that's now on my back."

"And you were successful!" smiled the Bishop. "But tell me truly Henry, was it as awful as I've heard?"

The knight lowered his eyes for a moment. When he looked back up, he whispered. "God tested us mightily with thirst, hunger, plague and battle. Most of us died. But time after time, He honored us with impossible victories against overwhelming numbers. It was magnificent what He did and what we were able to do with His help."

After Bernard was certain that Henry had finished speaking, he also responded in a very low tone. "Thank you for sharing that...and thank you for going." Then the Bishop elevated his voice to its usual level of buoyancy. "Look how you've grown Henry! How old are you now?"

"Twenty one," answered the knight with just a touch of a blush coloring his face.

"I remember when we were in Santiago de Compostela. You were a bright boy but still just a boy. Now you are a man."

"That was a good time," said Henry, "sitting in that tavern with that woman server tickling my neck...Rosalette! That was her name. She was flirting with me and I didn't even know what flirting was. Do you remember her?"

"I do," Bernard answered quietly as he lowered his eyes. "She was a lovely woman. Too lovely for that place..." The Bishop lifted his gaze back to Henry. "She is now with Brother Bruglio. I was back there a few years ago and asked after her. She died in some sort of accident. Henry, I have an appointment with His Eminence Pope Paschal and I must hurry or be late. I want to see you again before you leave the city. Will you do that for me please?"

"Of course," answered Henry. "Where shall we meet?"

Bernard swung his head around as if appraising the inside of the cathedral. "Right here at prime tomorrow...and just you alone. Your man and the children..." Suddenly the Bishop's face paled. "Are they your children Henry? Are you married?"

"No," answered the knight. "They're two orphans whom I'm looking out for."

"Oh...good," responded Bernard. "They can be near at hand tomorrow with your man but I want to speak confidentially with just you. Is that all right?"

"Of course," replied the knight.

"Good," said the Bishop as he turned away. "Prime tomorrow at Saint Peter's shrine."

The next day, Henry arrived at Saint Peter's a little early. He had left Bart with the children and horses at the Pantheon with a man whom he was reasonably certain knew quite a bit about the various ruins and their history.

To Henry's surprise Bernard, dressed in his scarlet robe and white conical hat, was already kneeling at Saint Peter's shrine. Henry waited until the bishop rose to his feet before going forward.

"Ah," smiled Bernard, "did I keep you waiting?"

"Not at all," replied the knight. "This is a beautiful place to visit."

"It is," said Bernard. "I apologize for asking that your orphans and your page not join us here. You see I have a great favor to ask of you and for personal reasons I wish it to be just between the two of us. Come let's sit down on one of these benches."

Henry's mind raced with anticipation. He couldn't imagine what favor Bernard might want from him but he was certainly eager to find out.

Swinging his arm, Bernard motioned for the young knight to take a place on one of the darkly stained benches. Once Henry had settled, the Bishop sat down too. Each man then turned his head and shoulders to face the other.

Bernard cleared his throat. "I have a ward Henry, a highly intelligent and beautiful young woman named Angeline who is now of marriageable age, fourteen or fifteen I think. Ordinarily her parents would be acting on her behalf to find an appropriate husband. Unfortunately she, like your two children, is an orphan. She is a member of my family but her mother is dead and her father has passed on as well. Accordingly there is no dowry. I have overseen her upbringing for many years and have done my best. What she needs now though is different and not something a Bishop is well suited for. Accordingly, I need to find a landed lord of good character with whom she shares interests. An additional problem is that she is in Spain and I am more and more here in Rome. I simply cannot give her the attention she needs nor, as a Bishop, can I approach people about her without raising issues about a priest's role in such matters."

"So Henry, this is what I'm hoping you will do for me. I want you to consider becoming Angeline's guardian, go to Spain, spend a week with her and then decide if you want her as your ward or not. If not, send me a letter to that effect. If so, take her to Dol with you. If you take her, you'll have sole responsibility for her. You will decide whom she will marry. You can even marry her yourself if you wish.

"I know Spain is out of your way and, if you choose to take her on as your ward, there will be extra responsibility for you particularly since there is no dowry. My only request is that you meet her and devote a week's time to deciding. Will you please grant me this favor?"

"Certainly," replied Henry. "Just tell me where to send word so I can be sure of reaching you and I shall write whether it's yes or no."

"God bless you Henry," whispered the Bishop. "God has sent you here to meet me for this very purpose. Thanks be to you and thanks be to Him."

Henry chuckled. "We must discuss a few more details. Where shall I find her? How shall I go? And what sort of introduction will you give me so she'll know and agree to the scope of my mission?"

"Of course, of course," replied Bernard. "Forgive me for I was thinking of this from my perspective not yours. I shall write you a letter of introduction that you may give to the Archbishop in Barcelona. He has her studying at a seminary there that teaches young women not only the Bible but etiquette, languages and even some medicine. Most of the graduates become nuns and either continue their education in a monastery or work in one of Hugh's Cluniac hostels."

"With such a background, isn't she likely to want to enter a nunnery?" asked Henry.

"No," answered Bernard. "She and I have already talked about that. She wants to have children. You see, while you are from Dol and I am from Sedirac, both north of the Pyrenees where women are sometimes less eager to bear children, her mother was Spanish. Spanish women usually want children.

"Would you like to meet Pope Paschal while you're here Henry? I can introduce you tomorrow. He's 'a Cluniac' too and was a favorite of Gregory. He now resides just a little north of here in the Castle of Saint Angelo. Today he's busy with Bruno of Segni, his prime advisor, but I'm sure I could get you in to meet him tomorrow."

"Oh," said Henry, "ordinarily I would, but Bart and the children are waiting for me at the Pantheon so we can leave for Genoa."

"That's good," responded Bernard. "I mean I'm sorry you can't meet the Pope but, you're going to Genoa ties in nicely with a trip to Barcelona. You see, the merchants in Genoa do a great deal of business in Barcelona, so you'll be able to take ship for there easily. I often come or go by way of Genoa. But..." the Bishop leapt up off the oak bench, "on our way to the Pantheon, we'll go to my office where I can quickly write your letter of introduction regarding Angeline. Then I'll show you the Lateran Palace where Paschal's coronation took place."

GENOA
February 1101

Under the watchful eyes of at least a dozen soldiers, the foursome rode through the city's main gate without being challenged. Nevertheless Henry drew in Pegasus' reins beside the last of the guards.

"Kind sir, can you please direct me to a merchant named Abraham?"

The soldier frowned and gazed back first at Henry, then at Bart and finally at each of the children. When he responded, his tone was cold and adversarial. "Are you Jews?"

Henry stared at the man for several moments before his expression hardened. "No, I am not. Please note the cross on my back." The knight twisted in his saddle to display his cross and then turned back to again face the guardsman. "Abraham?"

The soldier backed up a step and pointed. "The ghetto is to the right. You will see a low wall."

"Thank you," said the knight as he kneed his horse forward.

At the entrance to the ghetto, one soldier was sitting comfortably in a chair. He was an older fellow who looked to be asleep. Not wanting to wake him, Henry walked Pegasus almost through the gate before the sentry spoke. "The gate's locked at dusk, just want you to know since you're not regulars here."

"Thank you," replied Henry as he pulled in Pegasus' reins. "We are looking for Abraham. Can you direct us please?"

"I can," the man answered pleasantly. "First left, second right and a bold red door. He's in the city today but he'll be back before dark for sure."

"Thank you," responded Henry who was pleased not to have been treated as someone worthy of suspicion. "If we're in the ghetto past dusk, do we call over the wall for you to let us out?"

The old guard sat up in his chair. "You're not from around here, are you."

"No," answered Henry even though he hadn't thought the old man's comment was a question. "I'm from Dol in Brittany."

"Well," the guard responded still in a very friendly tone, "here you'll have to be out of the ghetto before dark. That's Council rules and the Jews want it that way too. If they don't know you inside, they may lock you up. In any case if anything happens to you or one of the Jews while you're in there, it may give the Countess an excuse to come with her soldiers and that's a hanging offense as far as the Council's concerned; bring the Countess or the Emperor and they'll hang you for certain!"

Henry kneed Pegasus. "Thank you, sir. We shall be out before dark. Will you be here till then?"

"I lock up," said the old man, "but I can't extend the time. You know these Jews are owned by the Emperor...or Countess Matilda. I can never remember which, so be out before dark and don't be late."

Henry slapped his knees against Pegasus' flanks. The politics here was confusing. He thought he knew a lot about Emperor Henry and Countess Matilda but he wasn't at all certain who this Council was.

Henry knocked twice on the red door. After the second attempt, a glass casement squeaked open above him and a female voice called down. "Abraham's not here." The woman conveyed her message with an accent Henry hadn't heard before.

Henry stepped back and looked up to see who was addressing him. He could see the woman quite clearly as she had her head out through the casement.

"Hello," the knight called up. "I am Henry of Dol and have been directed here to find Abraham of Genoa."

"This is his house," replied the woman whose face was round and flat with eyes that opened narrowly and looked almost slanted. "He is not here now. Perhaps you could come back tomorrow?"

"I shall," responded Henry. "Please tell him that it is Henry of Dol who wishes to speak to him and, if he doesn't remember me, tell him that I'm the boy who returned his notebook in the middle of the forest."

"I will tell him," the woman announced as she shut the window with a clump.

The sun was only a little over the mountains when Henry again knocked on Abraham's red door. Almost immediately the door swung open and Abraham thrust his right hand forward. "Henry, you have grown immensely. I would never have recognized you."

"Thank you, sir. It is good of you to see us."

Abraham ducked his head and peeked about to see if anyone was listening. "Henry," he whispered, "you have forgotten what I told you about calling a Jew sir."

"Oh," said Henry, "you're right. I won't do it again."

"Good," smiled the Jew whom Henry noted looked a lot older than he remembered. "Come in, come in. Are these your children?"

"They are my wards," replied the knight. "Perhaps if you are willing, we could talk together confidentially in a little while?"

"Of course," responded Abraham, "but first we have some cinnamon rolls. I'm quite certain the children will like them and of course you and your man are welcome to some too. Anna," Abraham raised his voice, "please bring the cinnamon rolls." Immediately, the flat faced woman who had leaned out the casement window the previous day stepped through a doorway. To Henry, the room they were in looked like a small great-room. It was furnished with carved wooden chairs and padded benches. There was an ornate table too. Each piece of furniture was elegantly carved and had obviously taken a great deal of time to make.

"Abraham, let me introduce Bart who served my father as his page and now is my sergeant. And these are Ezekial and Rachel who were orphaned in Jerusalem where I became their uncle."

Abraham bowed to the children. "Good morning," he said in Yiddish, "I am Abraham and this is Anna who has some cinnamon rolls for you. Have you had cinnamon rolls before?"

Ezekial, obviously remembering that Henry had told him not to speak Yiddish with anyone, glanced toward the knight. Rachel, however, launched into an immediate response in perfect Yiddish, which Henry had thought she might by now have forgotten. "Oh thank you, Abraham. Yes we have had cinnamon rolls before but not for a long time. Our mother used to make them for us on Sabbath days."

Abraham looked up at Henry and smiled. "These are wonderful children, well behaved, obviously bright and well brought up." He turned back to Ezekial. "Henry will not mind if you speak Yiddish to me. I am a Jew and consider the use of that language an ancestral blessing. And this is Anna who works for me here in Genoa. She is a wonderful cook and home-maker. Her cinnamon rolls are exquisite." Again Abraham looked around. "Let's all of us talk for a while and then Henry and I must discuss some business. After that, we can have lunch."

"Does that mean," asked Rachel, "we can have a cinnamon roll now?"

"It certainly does," answered Abraham who then nodded to Anna.

After about an hour, Henry and Abraham excused themselves and departed to another room. Henry had long been planning what he intended to say, but when they sat down, Abraham spoke first. "Henry, if my wife were still alive, we would gladly take those wonderful children and bring them up as our own. But I am away a great deal of the time. And without my wife, I could never give them the upbringing they deserve. You have done a wonderful thing taking them on. Perhaps when you get to Dol, you could raise them yourself? You know the issue of their religion, while important, is less significant than they're having parents who will raise them to be ethically and morally straight. Is Dol a place where two Jewish children could grow up without being shunned or abused?"

Before he answered, Henry thought for a moment. "If you'd asked me before I left for Jerusalem, I would have said yes. Now I'm not so certain. The prejudice against non-Christians was very strong among many of the members of our army. I was told by a German foot soldier that Count Emich of Leisingen slaughtered as many as five hundred Jews in the Rhineland before even starting out on his pilgrimage. There were similar reports referring to Worms and Mainz where murders took place. Ezekial's and Rachel's parents were most likely killed by Christians during Jerusalem's fall."

"Sadly, I have heard those stories," whispered Abraham.

"But," continued Henry as if he hadn't heard the Jew's lament, "I could probably introduce them as Christians and raise them as such...hide their lineage for their own sake."

"Henry, let me have a day or two to think on this. I might be able to find someone who could help. Our Rabbi here in Genoa is a learned and thoughtful man. May I ask him for his opinion?"

"Yes," answered the knight. "I have to line up a ship to take us to Barcelona anyhow. So I'll go down to the docks and see what I can find out by way of our transport."

"Don't worry about any of that," interrupted the merchant with a fresh smile on his face. "I know all the ship captains and the owners too. I can promise you a safe trip, a fast ship and a fair price. But first give me three days to determine a good solution for the children. I have some ideas. Tonight I want you to leave the children here. They will be safer here than in the city and I shall take excellent care of them, including some more cinnamon rolls."

"Thank you," replied Henry.

"Good," continued Abraham. "Come back here an hour before noon and I'll take you to look for transport to Barcelona."

After Ben nodded them through the gate, Henry noticed for the first time a cemetery on their right. There were numerous grave stones but none with crosses chiseled into them. Instead they bore five-pointed stars.

~**~

"**H**enry, you are here right on time." Abraham and Ezekial had answered the door. "I thought the four of us could visit the wharves today, investigate choices of transportation for Barcelona and teach Ezekial a little about the shipping trade. Rachel is shopping on Cog Street with Anna in order to purchase food for our dinner. We men can have our lunch at the Red Parrot Tavern. It has an entrance in the back to a little room where I do business with many of the merchants in the city. Will that be all right?"

"Certainly," answered Henry.

"Please note my yellow badge," continued Abraham. "The city rules require Jews, when outside the ghetto, to identify themselves in this manner." He looked down at Ezekial and then up again at Henry. "I have informed Ezekial that he must stay close to Henry or Bart and speak only French or Arabic during our sortie to the docks. Isn't that right Ezekial?"

"Yes," responded the boy in French.

"Very good," commented Abraham. "You've even got an accent. If a Frenchman ever asks you where you're from, tell him Flanders, Paris and Marseilles, which is why your accent is hard to discern."

When the troop got to the ghetto's gate, Abraham pulled a penny out of his pocket and flipped it to the gateman.

"Thank you," the man said as he nodded his head in a deferential manner.

"You're welcome," replied the Jew. Then turning to Henry, Abraham continued. "Once a month, we have to pay a toll when we come out of our little ghetto. The gentiles pay taxes on a variety of things, the Jews pay a toll to come and go. I figured it out once and concluded that our fee is only a little more than a Christian's. Don't tell them though or they'll increase it. Henry, you may already know this but Jews are restricted in many ways most of which don't make any sense at all. We can't work in any way that could be deemed agricultural or mechanical. Nor can we work as physicians although many of us are physicians. We just can't be paid by Christians for our services. Legally we are the property of the king, emperor or other overlord who, when he is short of coin, can call on us for a special tax in addition to the usual poll tax. While most of this is quite arbitrary, it nevertheless gives us value. We perform the jobs that Christians dislike: coroner, undertaker, crossbowman, lender of coin. Of course we hope for Christians like Ben back there. We both know that not every Jew can afford the toll. So, some of us pay a little more, some a little less. Ben is smart enough to know that his fee comes out about the same and he makes no issue about our process of payment. If he finds himself getting a little behind, he simply let's one of us know and we make it up to him."

"Now," continued Abraham in an entirely different tone, "if I invest in several companies and am the principal in two…"

"What's a company?" interrupted Bart.

"A company is a commercial venture," responded Abraham, "a cloth manufacturing company, a wine producing company—essentially a group of people who collectively own an entity that produces products like cloth or wine and sells their product at a profit. Let's say that we four put up a hundred denari—Ezekial ten, Bart fifteen, Henry twenty-five and me fifty. If we make a profit, it would be divided among us in proportion to the amounts we put in. So, if the profit was fifty denari, Ezekial would get five, Bart seven and a half, Henry twelve and a half, and I twenty-five. The complexity in a business comes in knowing the costs and the risks. I am an investor in a cloth manufacturing company in Flanders.

"To know all our costs is difficult. The wool comes from England so we must compensate the shepherds and pay for the transportation across the channel. We have to pay the carders, spinners, weavers, fullers, dyers, walkers, slappers, stretchers and knitters. In Ypres, we dye the fabric a magnificent blue which, while very expensive, makes for a very desirable product. We then have to take it to market or perhaps, to a fair to sell. We may be selling in an Italian city, outside Paris or even in Constantinople. Some items travel by cog or carrack, others by wagon or mule train. These last costs must be added to all the others to determine preliminary pricing.

"In addition to knowing those costs, you must anticipate risks. Laborers try to pool together in order to get higher pay. These efforts are called guilds, a means of gouging the eventual purchaser. There are also other risks such as robbers, pirates, ships sinking, a fire in a warehouse, drought, famine, locusts, floods, tolls and fees at fairs. In addition to all these risks, you must even add in an estimated cost for the unknown.

"And once you have thought of all those things, you should still diversify your investments so as to spread your risk. For example, if Ezekial's ten denari were all he had and he'd invested it all in ship 'A' that foundered, he'd be much worse off than his cousin Martin who put half his money into ship 'A' and his other half into ship 'B.' Assuming that only ship 'A' foundered, Martin would get his five denari back from ship 'B' plus a profit of two or three denari. In this case, diversification saved Martin because he was smart enough to spread out his investments. Many people think that doing well in business is just a matter of luck. But in fact, God gave each of us a brain and, if we use it, our business will do better."

"Are you saying that if you are smart enough, you can always succeed in business?" asked Bart.

"No," Abraham answered. "I'm saying that your chance of success is higher if you think carefully before making your investment. God can always make you fail if He thinks you're too arrogant or otherwise undeserving. I knew a merchant once who'd become very wealthy. He was only thirty-two years old when a giant wave washed him off his ship never to be seen again. Nothing guarantees success. You can only hope to improve your chances.

"There is also a great mix of businesses, many of which you might never think of. I do some work in finance abroad, not lending but in bills of exchange. It is always dangerous to carry lots of coin on your person, and it is much more so to do it in distant places where protection from thieves may be minimal. So, when a ship captain sells his cargo...let us say in Barcelona, in theory he would have to bring his payment home in some purse or strongbox. Thus he would be at great risk until he got home safely. But by availing himself of my company's capabilities, he can instead receive a payment voucher in Barcelona from the purchaser of his cargo and submit it to me here in Genoa when he gets home. I then give him his coin and charge him a small fee for the service. He has thus mitigated his risk of being robbed and has only a slight risk to my company failing which I mitigate by supplying him a surety bond guaranteed by one of my competitors."

"But," asked Henry, "how do you get the coin back here any more safely than he could?"

"Ah," chirped Abraham, "you were attending! Good for you. Actually my company doesn't bring his money back here. Instead we hold it for payment to a Barcelona merchant who may have sold his cargo in Genoa. We hold the coin in Barcelona until we can use it there. And before you ask me about an imbalance of trade upsetting that arrangement, I concede that sometimes we must ship coin back and forth lest in a coin-strapped city, we run low and cannot make payment immediately. But even then we can initiate short-term borrowing from other companies similar to our own."

In case his listeners had questions, Abraham paused for a moment. When none sprouted forth, he turned his head toward the boy. "Ezekial, did you follow all that?"

"I think so," murmured the youth, "at least until you referred to an imbalance of trade. I don't know what that is."

"Oh," said Abraham, "you're right. I should have defined my terms."

When they got to the wharves, Henry was struck by the throng. There were baggage handlers pushing two-wheeled carts, mule trains waiting to be loaded, gargantuan work horses pulling four-wheeled wagons under heavy canvas covered loads, sailors skipping into a tavern, scantily clothed women with painted faces and a vast mob of humanity whose role wasn't obvious enough for Henry to immediately identify. Also there were numerous smells and sounds: the crisp scent of freshly spilled tar, the sharp odor of spices, and the ubiquitous stink of offal dropped, spread, thrown, dribbled, leaked or lost. The knight's ears were challenged to identify a carpenter sawing wood with which to fix a damaged mast, the high-pitched squeak of a small cart as opposed to the bass clatter of a wagon, the shriek of circling gulls, the hammering of a workman freeing blocks from under a restrained pallet and, intermingled amongst everything else, the normal talking, yelling, ordering, denying, chatting, and hallooing common to busy wharves.

Henry was trying to keep up with Abraham and at the same time make sure that Ezekial and Bart didn't disconnect and become lost. The boy seemed right at home; but Bart, whose jaw was hanging awkwardly agape, seemed quite likely to get lost if not watched closely. Henry had persevered quite well in this regard until he gaped at a large cog which was tied, nose touching the street, with a mast thrust forward over the street in a manner that forced taller pedestrians like Henry to have to duck under its overhang.

Fortunately for Bart, at exactly the moment when Henry's attention was diverted, Abraham barked forth orders. "Turn here."

The two Jews turned neatly left into an alley and the two yokels from Dol, having been awakened from their period of inattention, followed almost perfectly behind. The alley was narrow, dark, smelly, and filled with obstacles. Henry was disappointed that they were now heading away from the docks. He'd seen this sort of naval crush in Constantinople but only from the city's high walls. Here he was right in it.

"Right here," said Abraham as he pivoted and put out his left hand to point at an open doorway.

Ezekial entered first, Bart and Henry next and Abraham shut the door behind them.

Henry knew they were in the back of one of the wooden commercial buildings that faced the docks. There was a partition between them and the front, which kept him from being able to see what goods were sold there. However, the scent of spices and pepper was apparent.

"Greetings," rumbled forth a vibrant voice in Italian.

The room had only one window so inside it was fairly dark. Nevertheless Henry was able to make out the speaker sitting at a table in the corner of the room.

"And to you," responded Abraham.

The man was short with a tanned face, black mustache and brown, beady eyes that constantly leapt in different directions. On the table in front of him sat a black metal pot from which steam was rising.

"I have been boiling a treat for you," the man said.

"Thank you my kind host," replied Abraham. "But first let me introduce you to Henry of Dol," Abraham pointed, "Bart of Dol, Henry's page and Ezekial of Jerusalem, a ward of Henry's."

The man stood up and bowed. He wore a bright blue shirt that reached down past his knees and brandished a large silver ring on the third finger of his left hand. Despite a deeply tanned and furrowed face, he looked relatively young, perhaps still in his twenties.

"This," continued Abraham, "is Leonardo of Genoa, a man I have done business with for years. He is honest, truthful, shrewd and someone who can take people to Barcelona. He owns several ships that travel to Spain regularly. But enough introductions, if my nose is correct Leonardo has cooked us a drink made from the beans of a plant that grows three hundred miles south of Alexandria."

"That's right," interjected Leonardo, "the coffee plant; although these particular beans came from the east, perhaps half way between Jerusalem and the Indus. Come. There are cups awaiting you, and the brew is ready. If your tongue identifies some residue, do not be dismayed. It won't harm you."

"Tell them of the bean's effect," interjected Abraham.

"It will stimulate your brain, particularly your memory. It is not dangerous, although it may keep you awake if you drink a lot of it."

The group settled back in their chairs and sipped their hot coffee from potter's jars that kept the heat of the drink away from their fingers.

Eventually Abraham revivified the conversation. "Leonardo, I've told Henry that you might be able to get him to Barcelona. When might he go?"

"The next ship to Barcelona will sail the day after tomorrow," answered the Italian, "after that, perhaps a week later."

"And," continued Abraham, "it would be no problem for you?"

"Not at all," replied the Italian.

"And," asked Abraham, "how much would it cost?"

"I've been thinking about that," responded Leonardo. He twisted in his chair to face Henry. "Abraham has told me that you are just returning from Jerusalem and took the cross to go there. Is that true?"

"Yes," answered Henry. "I left with Robert of Flanders in '96 and stayed a year after Jerusalem was taken to help Godfrey defend the city. I am now indirectly on my way back to Dol."

"I see," said the Italian as he leaned forward in his chair. "And in your years as a soldier of Christ, did you know this Baldwin who is now king in Jerusalem?"

"I did," responded the knight.

"And are you close?" asked Leonardo.

Henry tilted his head to one side. "Why do you ask?"

"Because a letter of introduction from someone he esteems would be of great value to my shipping company."

"Ah," mused the knight, "the truth is that Baldwin and I are not friends. We got along but neither of us likes the other. A letter of introduction from me to him might do you more harm than good. But Tancred of Taranto is likely to have become Count of Antioch by now and is a very good friend of mine. Would a letter to him be of interest to you?"

Displaying a missing tooth, Leonardo's face broadened into a wide smile. "Through Saint Simeon, Antioch is a much greater trade route than Jerusalem. If you'll write me a good letter of introduction to your friend Tancred, I'll take you to Barcelona for free and still owe you a favor."

"Done," said Henry as his face also widened into a smile.

On the way back to the ghetto, while Ezekial was walking with Bart, Abraham spoke quietly to Henry. "Our rabbi has found a perfect family to take on the children. I give you my word, the children will be well taken care of.

ANGELINE
March 1101

"**I** am Leone Rassellino the Black Rose's captain." The sailor bowed his head slightly and then, raising his visage, smiled which twisted the scar on his face so that it became obvious that he was blind in that eye. His smile also revealed that his two top, front teeth were missing.

"You did well to choose Genoa," responded the Italian. "On the west coast, Genoa is by far the best of the shipping cities. We do more business in Spain than any other, have more ships in the western Med and carry more goods than any of our competitors."

For a moment the captain's single roving eye caught one of his sailors taking a break. "Step lively there," he bellowed. "Time is coin. Time is coin."

Then turning back to Henry, he continued as if there had been no interruption. "Now when you get to Barcelona, there are a few things you need to be aware of. First, like every city, there are numerous whores, thieves and frauds. Hold onto your purse at all times. Never put it down. If anyone bumps into you, assume they're stealing your purse. Always stay with your sergeant and watch each other's backs. Barcelona's not a charter city like most of the Italian cities. It's not self-governed, hasn't complete control of the constabulary and its laws are different than you might think. Some of the laws come down from Mullahs. So don't be assertive about anything until you know what it is and how your actions might be misinterpreted. Especially, don't approach Muslim women no matter what the reason; even if one is being beaten in the street, stay away. The Koran gives Muslim men the right to beat their wives in public, so be careful. Also the politics in Spain is different than in Outremere. In the east, the Christians, at least those who speak French, German or Italian, can generally trust their fellows. In Spain, the Christians and Muslims hire each other to fight. Muslims often hire Christians to fight Christians. Today's ally can be tomorrow's enemy. It's very fluid as well as very lucrative, at least it is if you know who to help and when."

Leone had described Barcelona perfectly: a Spanish city with three large sections reserved exclusively for the ships of Genoa, Pisa and Venice. The port was alive with arriving and departing ships, couriers, mule trains and all that attached itself to such business ranging from food for the animals to sex for the teamsters. Henry and Bart didn't stay long. The church was easy to find. Archbishop Antonio was a cold, suspicious man who seemed to be in a hurry to do something else. He read Bernard's letter quickly, asked no questions and, pointing to the door away from the sea, spoke sharply. "It is twenty miles that way. The Abbess' name is Maria and there'll be sign posts."

So the next morning Henry, Bart and all their worldly possessions set out for Montserrat. The road was clearly used by wagons, mules and horses. They even came on several mule trains that were returning to Barcelona. And as the Archbishop had said, there were sign posts along the way. What Henry had forgotten was the incessant wind which kept blowing grit into his eyes.

Their objective came into view in only a few hours. The abbey wasn't a particularly large edifice but it did have wide, sprawling gardens on both sides and to the rear. Henry dismounted and approached the large wooden door. It was weather-beaten but still retained most of its dark redish patina. It reminded him of the cross in his family's chapel at Dol. As he reached the entryway, he heard a click and saw the heavy barrier begin to swing back away from him. Into this openning stepped an angel! The most beautiful woman he thought he'd ever seen. Her face was perfectly formed, her eyes brown, her expression serene and her black hair reached down past her waist.

Several moments passed while Henry realized how incredibly struck he was with this woman. He couldn't take his eyes off her...nor could he bring words to his mouth.

"Good day," said the young woman in Spanish. Her voice sounded like a bubbling brook in spring happily dashing downstream. "I am Angeline. Have you come to see the Abbess?"

"Y..es," fumbled Henry. "Abbess Maria please. I am Henry... Henry of Dol."

"Please follow me," said this beautiful seraphim still in her liquid voice, as she pirouetted and started to dance away.

Regaining his own cerebral resources, Henry stepped after her. This was Angeline! His ward for a week or a lifetime. This angelic creature! Should he speak to her? Tell her why he was here? No. First he should give Bernard's letter to the Abbess.

As Angeline reached the second door on their right, she stopped and knocked on the open casement.

"Come in my dear," replied a cheerful voice.

"My lady," continued Angeline, "this is Henry of Dol who has requested an audience with you."

The young man stepped forward.

"Henry," continued Angeline as she smiled at the knight, "this is Abbess Maria."

The Abbess rose from her chair and bowed slightly to her guest. "Thank you Angeline. You may leave us and please shut the door." Once Angeline had exited, the Abbess turned toward her guest. "Do you perchance have a letter of introduction from Bishop Bernard to give me?"

"I do," mumbled the young knight as he fumbled forth his letter. "May I assume that you know why I'm here?"

"Let me read the letter first," she answered coolly.

Henry passed her the letter which was written in Latin.

The Abbess read it quickly and looked up. "Dol is in Brittany isn't it?"

"Yes," replied Henry who was about to explain his role as possible custodian for Angeline when the Abbess interrupted.

"You speak Spanish passably but with a French accent. Do you speak any other languages?"

"I... I," Henry stammered as he began to wonder if he'd just transitioned from the company of one of God's angels to one of the devil's. "I speak several."

"But which ones?" demanded the Abbess in a tone that reminded the boy of Benito.

Henry's sudden irritation actually helped clear his mind. His knight's training had taught him that the more he was being pressed, the more he must focus. "I speak French, Latin, Arabic, Spanish, German and a little Yiddish. Does that answer your question?"

"Speak some Latin," ordered the Abbess.

"Arma virumque cano, Trojae qui primus ab oris Italiam."

"Ah," appraised the Abbess, "your Latin is quite good...although spoken with a Roman accent. Did you have a Roman tutor?"

"I did," answered Henry, "a churchman named Benito Tusculani."

For several moments Abbess Maria stared at the knight. At last she spoke but in a newly pleasant tone. "Well Henry, it seems you speak one more language than I do. Where did you learn Yiddish?"

Henry smiled. "After Jerusalem fell, there were quite a few orphans. I took on two who were Jewish, a boy six and a girl five. They taught me Arabic and Yiddish."

"Did you bring them with you?" asked Maria.

"No. I turned them over to a Jewish man whom I'd grown to trust. After considerable thought, I came to realize that they would be better off in a Jewish family than with me."

"But you were glad to be rid of them?"

"No," answered Henry sharply. "I miss them a great deal. But I know they will do well and be safe where they are now."

"Then it was a hard decision?"

"Yes," murmured the knight, "a hard decision."

"Good for you," complimented Maria. "You acted unselfishly. What are your motives in regard to Angeline?"

"I don't know yet," responded the knight. "I promised Bishop Bernard I'd take a week to get to know her and then decide whether or not to take her as my ward."

"Are you married, Henry?"

"No."

"Then God has blessed you," said the Abbess. "Angeline is an angel."

"Could you please tell me about her?" asked the knight.

The Abbess waved a hand toward one of the two chairs on Henry's side of her desk. She then stepped quickly around the desk to sit in the other.

For the next seven days Henry devoted himself entirely to Angeline. From the beginning, he knew this assessment period had nothing to do with determining whether to take her as his ward. His sole issue was whether or not to marry her. Every sense, feeling and emotion in his body was rushing him forward but he was too rational a person not to take some time to think, to get to know her, to see if they were compatible. He wanted this period of assessment to be a time of serious search for reasons why he shouldn't marry her. He must focus on weaknesses, incompatibilities, values and more. His problem was that his intellect kept being washed away by his feelings, feelings unlike any he'd ever experienced before.

Abbess Maria set some rules: they could ride or walk between breakfast and dinner but not out of view of the monastery. Dinners with the nuns and oblates were obligatory and proved to be quite formal. Otherwise, Bart and Henry were relegated to an out building that was designed as an overflow barn for horses and was regularly inhabited by the abbey's cook who was a fat fellow who smiled when asked a question and farted the rest of the time.

On the couple's first morning together, Henry and Angeline took a walk. The knight had mentally organized a series of topics and duly started with God. Despite the obvious rigidity of his question, Angeline embraced the topic eagerly and wholeheartedly.

"I am not a pantheist," she began, "but I marvel at His creations: the drops of dew on a flower's blossom, the streaks of orange along the bellies of grey clouds at dawn, the singing of the birds as they converse among the trees. His work is everywhere Henry, bright and beautiful. Consider also the spider that sits so motionlessly atop her web. Have you ever wondered how she can spin that thread so perfectly and create a quantity greater than herself? Have you ever felt Him helping you compose a thought? Pop just the right word into your mind? What a wonder God is. Yet so often we take Him for granted. In your travels have you felt him helping you? And known that it was He who helped you?"

"Yes," answered Henry fervently, "I have. Have you noticed that His aid is more likely after a prayer?"

"Oh yes," Angeline answered quickly. "It's as if a prayer invokes Him, calls Him to you. Have you ever examined a coincidence and found His meaning in it?"

"Yes," responded Henry. "I think it's a means God uses regularly, a clear validation of His work. I try hard to always test a coincidence to see if I can figure it out. Of course sometimes we don't have enough information or the message may be for someone else. I believe omens are similar to coincidences. We encountered many on our pilgrimage to Jerusalem. It was amazing how God would signal us what He planned to do. We saw a meteor fall upon a Muslim camp the night before we defeated them in battle."

The next day's topic was children.

"Bernard told me," began Henry, "that you don't want to become a nun because you want to have children. Isn't that a little strange for an oblate in a monastery?"

"Oh, I'm not an oblate," Angeline responded quickly. "I am an orphan and therefore cannot be given to God by my parents. I can enter the monastery as a nun if I wish and I am acceptable to Abbess Maria. The Abbess has told me several times that she would welcome me if I wish to enter. But I don't want to wear the habit. I believe God wants me to bear children and raise them in such a way as will please Him. I cannot explain why I know this other than to say that I am certain. I know it is an answer lacking logic but faith is often called for when logic fails."

On their fifth day, Henry introduced Angeline to his chess set.

"Have you ever played?"

"No," she answered. "I've heard of the game but never played it. Is it hard?"

Henry smiled. "The rules are very simple. Nevertheless it is a game of skill. Would you like to play?"

"I'm willing to try," responded Angeline, "but please don't expect me to be good at it right away."

After Henry set up the chess board and explained what movement each piece could make, they played five games in about an hour's time.

"I lost every game," chuckled the young woman. "Shouldn't you have let me win at least once?"

"Probably," answered the knight. "But you were getting better so quickly, I feared you'd beat me if we played again."

"You know that isn't true," she giggled, "but I did get better at it, didn't I?"

"Yes," said Henry, "you did."

For a moment Angeline stared at her beau. "Henry do you know anything about astrology?"

"Only that some heathens use it to divine various things," he answered. "It's not accepted by the Church and may even be considered heresy. As to details, I know very little about it. Why do you ask?"

"Well," Angeline replied in a slightly guarded tone, "some of the Arab intelligentsia in Cordoba use it to predict the future. Do you think that is possible?"

Henry thought for a moment then smiled broadly. "If you are asking if it's possible they use it, I think it likely. If you are asking whether it can be used to predict the future, I doubt it."

Angeline studied Henry's expression. "You didn't answer with certitude."

Henry looked her squarely in the eye. "No," he answered. "As I've grown older, I've found God's world to be astonishingly complex and very difficult to be certain of. I have come to believe that God Himself is certain and almost everything else is less so. But of you Angeline, I am certain."

The young woman lowered her eyes before responding. "I'm certain of you too Henry."

Three days later the ecstatic couple was riding across the barren plains of northern Spain. Having been overjoyed at the conjugal news, Abbess Maria had found two porters and four horses to help them on their way. At first, Henry and Angeline had passed their time in near giddy glee. But half way through the second day, their thoughts turned to more tangible topics.

"Henry," asked Angeline, "what is your mother like?"

"My mother? She is a kind person, one who sees the good in others. She will like you for your kindness and also for your willingness to listen and consider other's views."

"Is she open to other views?"

"I think so," replied Henry. "What views are you thinking of?"

"Well," Angeline stammered, "we talked of astrology, how the Arab scholars in Cordoba divine future events like the moon's eclipse. They believe astrology is a science, that it does not contradict God's will but rather is a means to reveal His intentions. Yet this same science is used by others to predict all sorts of strange things, some of which seem a lot like witchcraft."

"My mother would be a good person to ask about that science. She will not think ill of you if you ask her opinion. It probably wouldn't be the first thing I'd ask her though."

"Henry!" It was Bart who called out loudly from behind them. "There's a cloud of dust ahead on our right and another following behind us."

"How many can you make out?" rejoined the knight.

"Ahead, perhaps fifty, whose direction will certainly intercept us. Behind it is harder to gauge a number. They're following right behind us, perhaps another fifty."

"Thoughts?" asked Henry.

Bart's response came quickly. "Both groups have seen us. The front group clearly intends to intercept us, the following group probably the same. We can leave our pack horses and ride hard west but I doubt we can shake them."

"I agree," said Henry. "We'll maintain our speed and direction and pray they're not brigands. Helmets on and shields unlimbered."

When Henry turned back to Angeline, he saw her face was ashen. "Don't worry," he said calmly. "We are in God's hands. A prayer though, might be in order."

To make certain they would meet both of these unknown companies simultaneously, Henry slowed the pace of his little group. He reasoned that either of these opposing forces could quickly dispatch his group of five. By meeting both groups at once, he hoped to find their leader and thus diminish the chance of some undisciplined adolescent loosing an arrow. They were definitely Arabs. Their mounts were mares, their weapons bows and their armor limited to small, round shields. This of course didn't lift Henry's spirits. But they hadn't done anything untoward yet.

"We are not an enemy," Henry called out in his best Arabic. "We only seek passage north for my betrothed, my sergeant and our two porters."

As the Arab horsemen closed around him, Henry searched each face looking for the leader. Then one of the lightly armed riders slapped his knees against the flanks of his horse, a fine black, and directed her toward the Christian knight. "Please remove your helmet."

Henry hesitated for a moment. This man reminded him of someone. Then, realizing that he might be offending the Arab, he quickly lifted his helmet off his head.

"Henry! It is you," hooted the Arab gleefully.

"Ali?" responded the knight. "Is that you?"

"It is. It is. Were you expecting someone else?" The Arab leader kneed his black up beside Henry and leaned over to embrace him.

Henry reached forth too and the two men hugged each other awkwardly from atop their mounts.

"How good to see you," gurgled Henry. "I never thought it would be you."

"Nor did I expect to meet you. Allah has blessed us."

"He certainly has," smiled Henry. "He certainly has."

Ali rolled back his head and called out to his men. "This man saved my life at Jerusalem and the lives of many of our men. He is a friend, a good friend."

"Ahhh," the knight breathed out a long sigh. "I feared we were dead but it is you Ali!"

Ali lowered his gaze and spoke in a whisper. "Henry, this force is not as disciplined as were my Nubians in Jerusalem. I think I can set you all free but I shall have to exact some price, something that will avoid these men losing respect for me. Do you understand?"

Henry glanced at the Arab faces near him. Their expressions were sullen and cold. "Yes," he answered. "I shall do as you say."

"Good," said Ali still whispering. "First the woman, is she Arab or Spanish?"

"Spanish," answered Henry also in a whisper.

Ali turned his head toward Angeline and, raising his voice so all could hear, called out. "Are you Muslim or Christian?"

"Christian," Angeline replied.

Ali turned back to Henry and lowered his voice again. "You have chosen well, Henry. She is both beautiful and brave."

"Thank you," said Henry.

"Now," continued Ali, "to the price. I must take the cross from your shoulder. I know it is a symbol of your valor but to an Arab it signifies a great slaughter."

Henry's mind whirled to Reims: Pope Urban's speech, the bishops cutting their robes into crosses, his own feelings of closeness with his cross-bearing brother pilgrims. Then he remembered he still had Reynauld's cross in his kit bag. "All right," he murmured.

"And your horse," Ali continued.

Again Henry's thoughts turned back to their great pilgrimage. Pegasus had been a gift from Count Robert, undoubtedly taken from a dead Arab. He could always get another horse but... Henry suddenly smiled. "Would you play a chess game for him instead?"

For a moment Ali thought. When he finally responded, his voice had a slightly different tenor. "Henry, you have two things of value, the woman and the horse. If my men kill me, they'll take both."

Henry nodded. "You are right, Ali. The horse is yours."

"Thank you," replied the Arab as he smiled. "You may take the saddle and your chess set."

Henry swung his right leg back over Pegasus' rump, dismounted and then uncinched his saddle. Looking up at his friend, he spoke again. "Ali, I shall always remember this kindness. You have saved our lives and I thank you most sincerely. May Allah always watch over you."

"And may Jesus continue to watch over you Henry." For a moment the Arab leader smiled at his friend. Finally he turned to one of his horsemen and pointed to Pegasus. Then turning forward again, he called out to his men. "West!"

SETTLING IN
March 1101

Angeline was cold, so cold she had to clench her jaw shut to keep her teeth from clicking when she shivered. The hours of riding against the wind, drizzle and cold had numbed her body to the bone. That Arab Ali had been right when he'd said to Henry 'may Jesus continue to watch over you.' Even he recognized that meeting was not a coincidence but a miracle!

She again raised her gaze to look at him riding in front of her. As her hood rose, droplets of icy water hit her face. Just beyond Henry, she saw the stone wall of a castle rising up amidst the roiling mists of fog.

"Henry," Angeline called out cheerfully, "you didn't tell me Dol was a castle."

A few feet in front of her, Henry twisted around in his saddle. "I thought you knew," he answered.

Angeline beamed at her knight and giggled. "In the future I shall have to interrogate you more deeply."

Henry's face transitioned into a grin causing Angeline to blush.

Once inside the castle's stable, with Henry's help Angeline dismounted.

"Welcome back," called a voice she didn't recognize.

"Thank you," responded Henry who immediately leapt from Angeline's side to clasp the welcomer's hand. Quickly though Henry turned back.

"Angeline, this is my brother, Edmond."

"Ah," exclaimed Edmond as he grasped the young woman's hands, "you are cold and wet. You two go straight into the great-room where there's a fire and Bart and I will attend to your mounts and bring in your belongings."

"Thank you," said Henry. "That's a very good idea." Then turning to Angeline, he continued. "I'm sure my mother will have some dry clothes and I'll put a chair right in front of the fire for you."

When they entered the great-room, Angeline's first impression was how high the ceiling was...at least three stories. She'd never been in a room so tall before other than a cathedral.

"This is my mother Audrey," she heard Henry say.

In front of her, Angeline saw a tall woman with kind, brown eyes whose head thrust out above a thick, bear-skin coat.

"Oh, my dear," gasped Audrey, "you look absolutely frozen. Here, put on this coat." Immediately Henry's mother drew off her warm winter coat and, brushing off Angeline's half uttered protests, proceeded to run it up one of the Spaniard's arms and then pull it over her back for the other. While sliding the girl's second arm into her coat, Audrey glared at her son. "Now come with me," commanded the hostess, "and we shall get you dry clothes and then put you right next to the fire." Audrey pressed Angeline toward the spiraling stone stairs but before she was out of the great-room, she called out once more. "Henry, send Melinder up to our room with some mulled wine and tell her to be certain it's still hot."

Angeline shivered as Audrey stripped off her wet clothes and then rubbed her dry with a blanket. The room was totally dark except for a hint of light coming through a small loop-hole that had almost been stuffed shut. As Audrey began handing her young protégé clothing to put on, the door to the hallway hesitantly creaked open.

"Lady Audrey, it is Melinder with hot wine for Angeline." The young servant was also carrying a small candle that immediately brightened the room.

"So, your name is Angeline," said Audrey very pleasantly. "What a beautiful name. Was it your mother's name?"

"No," answered the young woman somewhat hesitantly. "I... My parents died when I was quite young so I was named by the Abbess at the Monastery of Montserrat."

"Oh," responded Audrey in a surprised tone, "so you were raised in the Monastery of Montserrat?"

Angeline had been hoping to make a good impression on Henry's mother. She'd planned to ask her what Henry had been like as a baby, what his interests were as a young boy, if she'd read to him, what funny things he'd done. But now, having been with Audrey no more than a few moments, all her well thought out plans for their conversation were falling apart and being replaced by the one topic she knew the least about.

"Yes," answered Angeline as Audrey guided her bear coat back onto the young woman's shoulders.

"Is Sarah of Arras still the Abbess there?" asked Audrey as she beckoned for Melinder to deliver her goblet of hot wine to the now dry and re-clothed Spaniard.

"Oh, no." responded Angeline with great surprise, "Abbess Sarah passed into God's hands eight years ago. Maria of Saragossa is now Abbess. Did you know Abbess Sarah?"

"A long time ago," answered Audrey wistfully, "when I was in the sister Abbey to Bec near Flanders, Sarah was a nun there…a very kind person."

"You were a nun?" questioned Angeline in complete surprise.

"Oh no," replied Henry's mother. "I was neither a nun nor an oblate, rather what I have come to call an intern." As she finished her remark, Audrey noticed Melinder near at hand still holding the steaming cup of wine. "Angeline, take that goblet and drink some of it so you can warm up your inside as well as your outside."

Angeline reached for the simmering drink.

"And," continued Audrey as she turned to the serving girl, "Melinder please tell Matthew the forester to start a fire in Benito's room and then set it up for Angeline to use. We have to remember that our southern brethren aren't used to the cold." Henry's mother then turned back to her young colleague. "Now Angeline, we'll go to the great-room and sit you down right in front of the fire," Audrey glanced about, "right after I find my sheepskin coat."

Angeline nodded her assent and took a tiny sip of the hot wine. It was still too hot to drink but the goblet was warming her fingers wonderfully.

MARRIAGE

September 1101

As he walked toward Abbot Hugh's office, Henry was thinking about his and Angeline's wedding. It was certainly a great honor to have Abbot Hugh and Bishop Bernard personally performing the ceremony and to have it at Cluny! That was practically unheard of. Bernard had sent a letter to Dol making the offer right after he'd heard from Abbess Maria about their betrothal. Henry had immediately convened his family to discuss the possibility.

Walter, Audrey, Edmond, Joan, Angeline and he had all met in the great room. First they established who could not go: Joan was pregnant; Edmond was too busy overseeing the estate's harvesting and Walter simply said 'it was too long a ride for a cripple.' With half his family saying they couldn't go, Henry expected the discussion to turn toward having the wedding at Dol, but it didn't. As was usually the case, everyone looked to the lord of the manor. But Walter immediately lauded Hugh and Bernard as 'two of the greatest Churchmen in all Christendom' and ended his comment with a declarative 'you should not miss such an opportunity.' Audrey then went on to agree 'most strongly' with Walter which, in most of the family's minds, settled the issue.

Nevertheless, everyone still turned to Angeline. Speaking quite softly she proffered that she 'very much looked forward to being married to Henry no matter where the ceremony took place.' Henry knew she really wanted to have Bernard marry them but he also knew she was already capable of reading the family's dynamics. What really struck him though was that his 'north star' had discerned Angeline's inner hopes and put them above his own. And Audrey, who almost always held out for Walter's interests, had gone right along. This outcome caused Henry to see how deeply his parents supported 'others'—a recognition which led him to realize that his third value had come to him from more than just himself.

The other thought that had popped into his mind had been less positive. Bernard's continuing involvement in seemingly everything that Angeline did was beginning to bother him. Constructive outreach to an orphan was a most Christian thing but the Bishop's zeal seemed to go beyond that.

Henry wondered if there was something going on that he didn't know about. His mind wandered into suppositions. Then he consciously dismissed those thoughts. They clouded his mind toward the Bishop and he had nothing specific to base them on.

He'd been hoping he might have time to investigate how far the construction of Cluny's church had come. But a black-robed monk intercepted him bearing a request from Bernard to join him and Abbot Hugh in Hugh's office. It was the same message he'd earlier received, which meant Bernard had either sent two messengers or just sent a second, which of course meant he was in a hurry to start their meeting.

Henry knocked softly on the office door.

"Come in Henry," called out Bernard's ever-cheerful voice.

Henry pressed open the door and was immediately hugged by the Archbishop who wrapped his arms around the young knight and squeezed mightily.

"Henry, thank you for coming." Bernard swung his left arm toward the table behind him. "You remember Abbot Hugh."

"I do," replied the knight as he bowed to his seated friend. "My dear Abbot, I'm so pleased to see you. It is most gracious of you to host Angeline's and my marriage. I thank you...we thank you."

Henry stepped forward and extended his right hand to his mentor.

"Henry," murmured Hugh with a broad smile on his face, "are your values still respect, integrity and others?"

"They are," answered the knight, "and are yours still respect, integrity, and stewardship?"

"They are," said Hugh as his face radiated warmth. "You would have been a wonderful member of the Church. I know though that God has something special planned for you and I trust His judgment. Do you still have your chess set?"

"I do," responded the knight. "Shall we play a game?"

Hugh lowered his eyes. "Perhaps a little later, right now I think Brother Bernard wants to share some political goings on in Rome." The Abbot waved his right hand toward an empty chair beside the table.

Henry and Hugh sat down but Bernard did not. Instead he began pacing.

"Henry, thank you for coming." Bernard paused for another long moment but then seemed to find his words. "Each of you is a 'Fidelis.' You have committed to help reform the Church...to winnow out simony, investiture, the directing of church revenues to others than the church and to keep chaste all those who wear the robes. We know that our reforming efforts go back hundreds of years to 'decretals' written by prior Popes whom God Himself called on to cleanse the world. We do not know exactly when the 'Fideles' started, but we do know that in the last fifty years they have multiplied ubiquitously. Today, friends of the reform movement exist everywhere." Bernard pointed to the Abbot. "It is perhaps to you that we owe so much. Your tireless work on behalf of the reform effort has never ceased. You have I believe, brought us to a new threshold, one which will be more rewarding than in the past but more dangerous as well."

"Our past efforts have been hindered by the election on too many occasions of Popes inimical to our goals or without the...the fortitude to carry them forward."

Bernard stopped for a moment and looked at Hugh. "Let me digress for a moment. I realize that you already know this but I must bring Henry forward as he is younger and has not been placed so centrally as you."

The Bishop turned back to the young knight. "Henry, the process by which we have chosen Popes in the past has been quite haphazard. There are two reasons for this: the greed of the Roman citizens and the avarice of Rome's noble families. The first of these produces the most random results. The citizens have come to see the Pope as a mint spewing forth gold and silver coins: 'beneficia' on his accession, 'Presbyteria' on various feast days and additional remuneration whenever there is some sort of crisis such as in 1083 when Robert Guiscard paid the citizens 30,000 solidi as a means to reconcile them to the Pope. The citizens can be bought and often have been.

"The second obstacle, also driven by greed, has been the intrusion of noble families into choosing or forcing, the choice of their preferred candidate, this done for the sole purpose of ensuring their receipt of political positions of power from which they can squeeze out great sums of coin. For three generations the Crescentii and Tusculani families have controlled the electoral process. More recently with the advent of Gregory and Urban, we have been able to steer the balloting into the hands of only the Cardinal Bishops. Most of them are reformers. But even that approach has limitations. The families control great swaths of the city: Sabina by the Crescentii; Tusculum, Velletri and Palestrina by the Tusculani. They even hold the castles of Colonna and Saint Angelo, which of course gives them control of the Tiber Bridge and the basilica of Saint Peter. A Pope not on good terms with those families would be hard pressed to find a safe place anywhere in the city. And now with the advent of anti-popes, it seems that any noble family, lord, or emperor can have their very own pope.

"But despite this most recent disaster, there is cause for hope. First, there are new Roman families who, while still seeking patronage from the Pope, are quite willing to let the Pope promote a reform agenda and some even support its specifics. These new families are numerous: Malabranca, Papareschi, Parenzi, Scolari, Scotti, Orsini, Pierleoni, and Frangipani. The Pierleoni gave Urban refuge in the church of Saint Nicola in Carcere where he died. And they favor Paschal now. Make no mistake they still act in their own interest, but what's different is that we can now play the two family groups, old and new, against each other and thus have a much freer hand shaping our reforms throughout Christendom.

"The second of our initiatives will help us elect Popes who are really reform-oriented. Urban and now Paschal have appointed more bishops from outside Rome. This means there will be more electors who have no allegiance to local nobles. This not coincidentally, also helps us compete with the anti-popes by establishing direct lines of authority into regions throughout the Christian world. Before Urban there were seven Cardinal Bishops who were the designated electors. Now there are three 'orders' with positions for seven Cardinal Bishops, twenty-eight 'Cardinales' and eighteen Cardinal Deacons.

"Certainly the citizens of Rome will continue to exert influence particularly when they take on the form of an angry mob. The noble families also still have great resources which they can bring to bear. But we believe that reforms and reformers will now begin to take hold more deeply and further afield.

"With this background in mind let me explain your role within it, the role of a 'Fidelis." The Archbishop looked directly at the knight sitting in front of him. "Henry I may at certain times call you to Rome. We may need to protect our Pope or candidate. But more than anything, we shall need men who even if provoked, can restrain themselves, use tact, negotiate, stay calm, yet present a presence sufficiently powerful to cause any sane man to think twice before acting...someone who'd been 'the third knight over the wall in Jerusalem!"

After the wedding was over, Henry cogitated on how the trip to Cluny had gone. The wedding had taken place on a magnificent fall day and the ceremony was highlighted by Hugh's very touching insights into each of the betrothed and how they complemented one another. His comments were sincere, insightful and succinct. Now Henry thought, they could go home to Dol and live their lives quietly together.

LIFE IS WONDERFUL
May 1102

Displaying every shade of green, all the tree leaves were out. A few were still displaying their prepubescent shades of pale orange but very few. Occasionally soft zephyrs lifted the tender fronds exposing their paler undersides. Angeline remembered how the Spanish siroccos used to elevate her skirt when she was young. Of course she had immediately slapped the offending clothing back into its proper place lest one of the nuns correct her. She'd liked it though: the suddenness, the loss of control, that moment of impropriety.

Angeline liked Dol too. It was wetter and colder than Spain but so much greener. She loved Audrey who had so wonderfully accepted her into the family. And of course, she loved Henry who was so caring, thoughtful and handsome. She thanked God every day for this new life He had given her. And now as she touched her fingers to her protruding belly, she had another love, a baby soon to be born. Every day she prayed for her unborn child: that he or she would be born safely and soundly, become a fine human being, a good Christian in God's image, a child that God would be proud of.

Another breeze lifted strands of her long black hair off her back and swirled the dark tresses across her face. She took the twisting eddy as a sign that He had heard her prayer. "Thank you Jesus," she whispered. "Thank you for this wonderful life."

Near the edge of the field, Angeline saw a large, blackened tree stump. Long ago it had been a living part of God's magnificent creation. Now it was decomposing, a sign that life was short. As she sat down on the decaying stump, she promised herself that she would make the very most of every day God gave her.

Then she heard a call and looked up. Audrey was exiting the castle. Angeline waved and Audrey waved back. For the first time in her life, Angeline felt as if she had found a mother. She could talk freely with Audrey and not be nervous about what she said. Audrey was willing to hear anything and not be judgmental. She never shared Angeline's thoughts or questions with anyone else and she only offered her own opinion if Angeline asked for it.

Audrey sat down beside her daughter-in-law and they talked about the beautiful weather, how nice it was that Angeline wasn't experiencing 'morning sickness' and that her child's soul would come from heaven and, when it died, it would return to heaven.

"But," said Audrey, "I've seen a dead person resuscitated! Brought back to life!"

Seeing Angeline's quizzical expression, Audrey elaborated. "When I was at my convent in Flanders, a young nun named Annette and I had been dispatched with wooden buckets to pick apples in a nearby orchard. On the way, we had to cross a small river at a ford. When we got there, to my amazement a young girl of perhaps seven was lying face down in the water. Sister Annette immediately dropped her buckets, ran to the girl, pulled her out of the stream and placed her on her back on the stream's banking. She then touched the girl's throat and after a moment or two, pronounced the child to be dead. This was followed by a series of further actions: Annette rolled the girl onto her stomach, leapt onto her buttocks and began energetically pressing the girl's back with her hands. To my immense surprise, the dead girl began to splutter and then cough, at which point Anna called over to me that she had once seen a man similarly revived who had drowned during 'a trial by water.' In any case, as soon as the dead girl got over her coughing, Sister Annette clasped the child in her arms and called out quite clearly. 'Surely God has brought you back from some horrible place.' The little girl responded immediately and Audrey remembered her exact words: 'Oh no Sister; it was a wonderful place.'

Audrey finished her story by telling Angeline that she was certain the girl was actually dead when Annette found her and that she believed Annette's actions had, with God's help, returned the girl to life from the threshold of heaven. After all, how else could the girl have referred to her briefly held habitat as 'a wonderful place?'

Angeline saw this saving of the child to be a miracle as well as a powerful validation of heaven. For her it was like an epiphany when death took a good Christian to 'a wonderful place' and then returned her to earth. Accordingly Angeline concluded that death was not a bad thing...certainly nothing to fear!

A REGRESSION
Spring 1106

Henry, Bart and Angeline were riding to Vannes, a three day trip for some séance conducted by a woman named Kay Mora. Angeline, with Audrey usually egging her on, had a recurring interest in strange phenomena: abnormal people with unusual capabilities or odd occurrences that seemed to contradict reason. Somehow Angeline always got word about these people or events. Henry thought Mariteth, the midwife, was the principal source of his wife's most unusual information but he really didn't pay much attention. He ignored the most far-fetched topics: intuition, divination, augury, influencing love, weather or illness. A few of Angeline's interests were more staid: potions made from herbs, grasses or flowers which Henry considered 'medicines' if used to provide a cure for something.

When they got to Vannes, a shepherd told them that Kay Mora 'summered' in a hut quite close to the sea. Since it was already fairly dark they made camp, slept over and with Henry pressing, got started early. The designated 'hut' looked like every other serf's' dwelling: a mix of poles, mud and rushes. It showed no signs of life but Henry thought he could smell a hint of wood smoke. Otherwise it seemed that Kay Mora was still asleep. On their left the sun had just risen over the horizon. It shone majes-tically, its beams turning the young tree leaves orange and the sea's rolling swells a translucent green.

Before they could dismount, the deerskin which hung over the hut's en-trance was replaced by an old woman. She had unkempt gray hair hanging hither and yon and a woven blanket pulled over her shoulders which displayed numerous but faded colors. For the longest time she offered no greeting. But finally after the three arrivals had dismounted and walked right up to her, she spoke.

"You are from Dol."

"Yes," answered Angeline in her usual cheerful manner. "Are you Kay Mora?"

"I am," replied the woman. "You and your husband may come in but not the liegeman. It's a small dwelling and too many people will distort the energy."

As Bart took the reins of Angeline's and Henry's horses, Henry wondered what energy the old woman was talking about. But that thought was interrupted as they entered the building. The inside was lit by only one candle; there was a tiny table and several chairs, each holding a knit blanket similar to the one the woman had over her shoulders. To their right was a fire place with a stone chimney rising through the rushes which composed the roof. There were no other openings in the tiny building.

"Kay Mora," said Angeline, "I have heard from a reliable source that you have the gift of telling people where they are going as well as where they have been. These are subjects that interest me. So I am hoping that you might share some of your insights. Would that be all right?"

"Yes," responded the old woman. "I have had some success along those lines particularly in finding people who have become lost...both living and dead." Kay Mora then turned from Angeline and looked directly at Henry.

"And what of you?"

Henry was taken back. He hadn't thought of doing anything at all. He had only come to give Angeline company and provide a second escort. But this old woman was staring right at him expecting an answer.

"I hadn't planned on doing anything...but I suppose I could," stammered the knight. "What are my choices?"

"Not having planned ahead," interjected Kay Mora, "can actually be a good thing. You will not have built up expectations and therefore be more open to the energy."

Henry was about to ask what this energy was but the old woman spoke too quickly.

"Your 'choices,' as you call them can be very specific or quite general. For example, I can tell you things about your next child. No, that's not a good example. I could take you back into a previous life, a life you lived long ago or very recently. Often people learn a great deal about themselves doing that."

"A past life?" Henry murmured. He'd never thought of having had a past life. "I'll choose that...unless," he turned to Angeline, "unless it will diminish Angeline's time with you."

"It will not," responded Kay Mora. "Angeline, you may stay for your husband's regression if you wish but if you do, you must only look and listen. You may not talk nor even sit near him. Do you wish to stay?"

"I think so," Angeline answered hesitantly. "Is that all right with you Henry?"

"Of course," replied the knight who was already wondering what this experience would be like.

"Now," said Kay Mora, "before you sit down Angeline, Henry must choose his chair first."

"Does it make any difference which chair I take?" asked Henry.

"It may," responded the seer evasively. "Each has different fabric, different sorts of pillows and each faces in a different direction."

"I see," said Henry, who didn't think which chair he sat in made the least difference and immediately sat down in the nearest. "Is this all right?"

"Quite all right," answered Kay Mora as she moved a nearby chair closer to Henry's and then sat down beside him.

Angeline quietly eased herself down into the chair that was the furthest away.

"Now," began Kay Mora, "I want you to be comfortable Henry. So please sit back in your chair and, if you wish, elevate your feet onto the hassock and close your eyes."

"I must close my eyes?" asked the knight somewhat uneasily.

"Yes," answered the seer. "It is absolutely necessary. Otherwise your brain will be taking in unimportant information that will hinder your ability to connect with the energy around you. Close your eyes."

Henry did so and immediately began hardening himself to resist anything—energy, vibrations, whatever, if for any reason he felt they might harm him or Angeline.

"Are you feeling relaxed now?" asked Kay Mora.

"Yes," replied the knight.

"Good," murmured the seer. "I'm now going to take you on a trip through some clouds. You don't have to do a thing... Just pass through these big, puffy white clouds...and now some more floating clouds...and some more..."

Henry's fingers clasped the arms of his chair. He was certain he could leap up at any time he wished. "Should I be seeing any of these clouds?"

"Just concentrate on relaxing," the old woman answered in a tone which conveyed a hint of irritation. "Just a few more puffy, white clouds... floating...past you."

Finally she altered her drone. "You are now descending... descending...

You are eight years old...and are now on the ground... What do you see?"

"Nothing," answered Henry.

"Keeping your eyes closed," the woman went on, "look around you...all around you. Do you see anything now?"

"No," answered Henry.

"Look down at your feet."

Henry visualized his feet.

"What do you see?"

"Boots," Henry answered. He wasn't really seeing anything but he felt he should at least be helpful since the old woman seemed to be trying her best.

"What color are they?"

"Brown," Henry replied. He'd made up his answer again.

"Look all around you again," commanded Kay Mora.

With his eyes still closed, Henry elevated his gaze.

"What do you see now?"

"Steep hills and mountains," answered the knight who visualized a steeply inclined meadow with daunting granite outcroppings rising above it, mountains...peaks covered with glistening, white snow.

"Where are you?" asked Kay Mora.

"Tyrolia," answered the boy.

Henry was shocked. 'Tyrolia?' Where had that come from? Certainly not from his conscious mind. He wasn't even sure where 'Tyrolia' was. How could he have said that? Something had radically changed. He was no longer making things up. He was no longer in charge of this... 'this regression.'

"Now," said Kay Mora in a more generous tone, "we shall advance you to forty years old."

"I can't," said Henry whose words now came forth without his consent, without his having formed them as if they were someone else's. "I can only go to twenty-six!"

"All right," responded the seer, "then we'll go to twenty six. What do you see?"

"I'm riding across great grassy plains...plains as far as I can see in every direction." The vastness of the plains filled Henry's consciousness. They went on forever...brown grassy plains...late in the summer and very dry.

"And what are you doing there?"

"We are raiding villages...killing men, women and children...taking their coin, their possessions, their food...burning their homes."

"All right," interrupted Kay Mora, "move on in this life as far as you can... Where are you now?"

"I am looking down at a body... MY BODY! It lies on its back on the grass with a gaping wound in its upper chest and right shoulder. I'm float-ing above it...looking down from behind its head." Henry's voice was clinical, frigid, detached. He felt nothing not even the wound...particularly not the wound.

"All right," said the seer, "it's time for you to come back."

"No. I can't leave my men."

Henry knew he was crying. His body, the one in the chair at Kay Mora's cottage, was crying too. But he couldn't leave his men. He was their leader. They'd followed him, they depended on him, they needed him...

"Henry, you must come back now. Your live body is here. You can't help your men any more. Come back through the white, puffy clouds...the white, puffy clouds... You are in them now...coming back...coming back."

When Henry came to, he was sobbing. Tears streamed down his cheeks. He felt horribly conflicted. He couldn't leave his men but he couldn't help them either...his men...his duty. Guilt gnawed at him...but also relief. He opened his eyes.

~**~

Henry couldn't stop mentally recounting his meeting with Kay Mora. There were three aspects of his regression that he couldn't even begin to understand: 'Tyrolia,' 'twenty-six' and 'I can't leave my men.' Each of those words he'd spurted forth spontaneously. They weren't consciously made up like his 'brown boots' had been. How had that happened? He'd never been to 'Tyrolia.' He wasn't even sure where it was... 'Twenty-six' had also come from out of the blue. He'd just said it...didn't make it up, just said it. And 'not leaving his men.' Where did that come from?

"Henry, you really scared me." It was Angeline riding up beside him. "I was afraid you wouldn't come back."

They were riding back to Dol. Henry hadn't wanted to camp near the seer's cottage. So he, Angeline and Bart had ridden out even though it was mid-afternoon. Now it was getting dark. But he still wasn't ready to talk about his 'out-of-body experience' ... not even with Angeline.

"Yes," he responded, "I was concerned too. How did your time with her go?"

"Oh," replied the young woman, "nothing like yours. We talked about the children mostly. Walter will take up the family's interest in medicine, William will become a man of the Church and Kay Mora said I'd have a third son who'll be a student. Three sons she said...and they'll be favored by God. Isn't that wonderful Henry. Audrey will be so pleased to hear that."

"And what about you?" asked Henry who was hoping Angeline would talk about her experience so he wouldn't have to talk about his.

"We really didn't talk much about me," answered the young woman, "mostly about the children and a little about the family. You don't want to talk about yours yet do you?"

Henry paused. "I do want to talk with you about it but not yet. I have to think it through more."

"Certainly," Angeline responded in her usual cheery manner. "I shall be available whenever you are ready. Now I'm going to drop back a little so you can continue to think. I'm not angry with you or anything like that."

"Thank you," said Henry. "I appreciate your thoughtfulness."

Immediately Henry's mind returned to Kay Mora and his three 'surprises.' After considerable thinking, Henry concluded that one of two things had happened. The most simple and perhaps the most likely, was that his brain had played a trick on him. Somewhere within his head there was some place, some creative center, probably the place where his dreams came from, which had conjured up those three statements... and then delivered perceptible images to go with them, his seeing the plains and his body.

But those images, those created ones, he could still bring them forward in his mind. He could look at them whenever he wanted just the same way he did with normal recollections from yesterday's camp site, his trip to Santiago de Compostela or even his childhood. That brought him to the second possibility, that he'd really had a former life! Was that possible? It didn't fit well into Christian doctrine at least not that he knew of. But...what if it was true? The Greeks and Romans believed humans were returned to a new life after they'd paid for the transgressions they'd committed in their past life. He had only the vaguest grasp of Hinduism; he didn't think he'd ever met a Hindu, but he'd heard Abbot Hugh once mention something about them believing in reincarnation. He'd never given much thought to reincarnation, being repeatedly born into a new life. One's soul moving forward from life to life, taking on a new body each time, perhaps as a caterpillar becomes a butterfly. Death would be a transition to another life, a thought which was similar to that of Christianity, for surely Christians pass into a better place when they die. Reincarnation suggested an eternal soul and many lives, a concept perhaps not all that different.

THE BATTLE FOR ROME
October 1108

The sky was blue, the visibility very clear and the sun deceptively penetrating, similar Henry recalled to Outremere where the humidity could be low but the heat still overwhelming. From the battlements, he stared out over the fields and forests of Dol. It was Tuesday, one of the two days of the week when the freemen and serfs worked on the manor's fields instead of their own. Now that it was September and the weather was good, Edmond was pressing them hard. Henry's brother knew the weather could change at any moment. The hay had to be turned over to dry before it could be put into one of the barns. All but the youngest children were out with a scythe or a rake turning, bundling, carrying and storing. By age four or five they'd been taught specific jobs. Henry knew on a day like this most of these families would have preferred to be working their own plots, but he was certain that the wisest of them knew that if the lord's fields didn't get hayed, there'd be no food for the cows, cattle, oxen and horses, which would lead to shortages for them and their children.

There were really two lords at Dol—Edmond and him. And Henry thought Edmond did more than he did. Edmond even seemed to enjoy overseeing the daily drudgery. Henry did not. The work was boring and incredibly repetitive—plowing, planting, hoeing, watering, thinning, and harvesting every year, after year, after year. Oh, there were occasional surprises but they were usually bad – washouts, droughts, locusts, winds, infestations and rot. At least there had been enough food since he and Angeline had come. That couldn't last. His father had told him several times that bad harvests came at least every fifth year. In the eight seasons since he had come back, they'd only had two weak harvests so a truly bad one was due.

God had blessed him with Angeline. He loved her so much. She was genuinely thoughtful of others, a true Christian in every way and a wonderful mother. She had been right to want to have children. It was a perfect role for her. And she was pregnant again. Their third child should come around Christmas.

Far down the castle's entry path almost where the fields ended, Henry saw a movement. It was a rider who was leading two additional mounts and a pack horse toward the castle. They were cantering. Henry prepared to yell down to the castellan overseeing the portcullis but first he waited to see if there were any more riders. There seemed not to be...so the rider must be a messenger.

"Alert the gatesman," Henry called out. "A messenger is coming."

For a moment he wondered who could be sending them a message. Then he pivoted toward the stone steps which spiraled down into the darkness of the castle. 'Bernard,' he thought, 'it could only be Bishop Bernard.'

The man's name was Luigi, an Italian who spoke French well. Bishop Bernard had sent him with a one word message— 'Hurry.'

They'd heard from Bernard only once since they'd been married, that being two years ago with a two-page written letter that had been very cordial but had ended with a succinct reminder that the bishop might call for Henry at any moment. Apparently this was the moment.

"Are you riding right back?" Henry asked Luigi.

"I was told to bring you directly back," replied the Italian as he looked at the castle and its surroundings. "I don't mean to sound impertinent but do you have extra horses to bring so we can cantor?"

"How long did it take you to get here riding three horses?"

"Ten days," responded the courier. "I rode three and the fourth carried a light load of supplies. I bought fodder, hay, water and food along the way. It will be safer with two of us."

"I'm going to bring my sergeant," interjected Henry. "His name is Bart. We'll be ready to go in less than an hour. Please dismount and rest yourself. This man over here," Henry pointed, "is Jayson. He will get you anything you need." Henry saw Audrey and Angeline exiting the castle. As he trotted back into the castle, he called out to them. "Bernard has called for me. Bart and I shall take five horses in less than an hour."

Half an hour later, Henry and Bart were ready to go.

Henry kissed his mother. "I'm sorry we have to be off so quickly but the mountain passes will be closed by mid-October. I don't know how long we'll be gone, possibly until spring." Then the knight stepped close to his wife and, putting his arm around her back, pulled her so close to him that their noses nearly touched. "Angeline, I love you deeply. It is for you that I thank God every day." Then he kissed her fully on the lips.

"I love you too Henry," offered the beautiful, young Spaniard with tears welling up in her eyes. "God willing, you will have another son when you get back."

"Aye," smiled Henry, "and I shall be most glad to see all of you when I return."

With that said, the three men mounted their horses and rode quickly away.

~**~

Before leaving his two charges, Luigi conveyed a story to them. Should anyone ask, they were a Norman lord and one of his knights in Rome to request a favorable resolution of litigation pertaining to the lord's estates in Brittany.

All this seemed quite odd to Henry since he had been under the impression that Paschal held clear control of Rome and that the Anti-Pope Sylvester, a tool of the German Emperor, was ensconced somewhere in the west. After quite a long wait, Henry finally spotted Luigi returning with someone dressed like a Benedictine monk. The monk of course was wearing a black robe but with a very large hood which obscured his face. Obviously the fellow didn't want anyone to recognize him.

"Henry," whispered the monk, "I'm so glad you've come."

It was Bernard's voice but so quiet Henry could barely make it out.

"Bishop," Henry replied in an equally hushed inflection, "I am glad to see you too. Angeline sends her best."

"We can't talk here," whispered Bernard. "Follow me." Immediately the bishop pivoted back toward the direction he'd just come from. On the back side of the castle, there was a narrow oak door almost obscured by piles of trash and debris which was opened from the inside once the Bishop tapped an odd series of knocks upon it. The horses were barely able to get through the doorway and certainly wouldn't have been able to if they bore riders. When the door clunked closed behind them, Bernard pressed on past the castellans who'd let them in. Eventually, after turning their horses over to an unknown person, they followed the Bishop up three flights of stairs and entered an unlighted room with no loopholes, windows or other openings. After a moment or two of scuffing, Bernard managed to light a candle.

The room was tiny with five chairs, a small table and three 'bunk' beds atop one another. The Bishop set his candle down on the table, pushed his hood back over his head and sat down.

"Now," he said for the first time in his usual ebullient voice, "how is Angeline?"

"She is well," answered Henry. "She's about six months pregnant with our third child and sends you her best."

"I am glad to hear she is well," said Bernard with obvious sincerity. "She is a genuinely open human being with malice toward none as you Henry are also. You and Angeline make a fine couple."

"Thank you," responded Henry.

"No, thank you, Henry, for coming so quickly." The Bishop paused for a moment before continuing. "Our efforts to restore the Church, to put her back onto a more righteous path, we all knew would face challenges from time to time. We face one today. Sit down and I shall explain."

Once every one was seated, Bernard surveyed the three faces that stared back at him through the pale candle light. "Our current situation as best we can tell is as follows: Count Ptolemy of Tusculum, Peter Colonna and Stephen Normannus of the Corsi family have withdrawn their immediate support of Pope Paschal purportably because when the Pope recently left for a tour of some southern cities, he put Petrus Leonis and Leo Frangipane in charge of the city. Paschal has greatly favored these two men for several years, so it is not surprising that some of the other families have finally revolted, this sort of action being in essence a formal complaint."

"Now, we must act quickly and decisively because all the Roman families are watching to see what we will do. Our goal is to maintain the true Pope and his control over the Church: specifically the basilica of Saint Peter, the Castel Saint Angelo and the granting of the city's appointments. Our control of these has never been iron-fisted. But we must acquire sufficient military strength to convince the families that they cannot take control. A hundred years ago they used to pick Popes whose sole purpose was to despoil the Church. Their actions were so venal, so carnal..." Bernard's voice rose an octave, "that they had clowns, wizards and prostitutes performing in the basilica itself. Henry, you and Luigi must go to Duke Richard in Gaeta and ask him to send us five hundred of his soldiers to put down this revolt. If it's a smaller number, the families may fight. But they won't fight against five hundred."

"Almost all of the engagements here have not involved actual fighting.

When the families aren't certain they can win, they won't fight. Their actual numbers are unknown but whatever they are, they can't afford to lose many men lest they become less powerful than another of their ilk. And they don't have many real fighting men, lots of bullies who might fight with their fists on the street but not real knights or soldiers who've actually fought in real combat. When you come back with Richard's force, ride up front with your cross on your back. That alone will be the equivalent of another five hundred men.

"Oh, Henry one more thing before you go," added the Spanish bishop, "when you meet Paschal, as you surely will, please point out to him that he must balance his beneficences broadly among many of the families in order to keep them all pursuing him. They must never think they won't get any more gifts. Once they think that, they'll revolt and our beloved church will fall back into disarray. Our plan of melding our cardinals into a functioning, governing body is making progress especially outside Rome. But like grass, it must have time to put its roots down." Bernard leaned back in his chair and sighed deeply.

Henry wasn't certain whether he and Bart were supposed to depart immediately or await further instructions. But Luigi touched his elbow and when Henry looked to see why, nodded his head as if to say 'follow me.'

~**~

Gaeta was a pretty little town nestled beneath a high-rising block of granite. Richard's castle was perched atop the granite ledge making it nigh-on unassailable.

One of Richard's castellans immediately ushered the three visitors into the stronghold and then escorted them up three consecutive sets of stone stairs to the castle's great-room.

"Guests!" trilled the host who was seated quite near the entryway. "Ah Luigi, it is you. Come in. Come in and introduce your friends." The Duke was short, muscular and flashed two piercing pale, blue eyes at his guests. "Have the cook send up three more meals," he called out and then looking directly at Henry, he continued. "And you, young man, do you prefer wine or mead?"

"Mead thank you sir," replied the knight as he smiled in response to his host's courtesy.

"I am Richard, the lord of this little castle. Come right here and sit beside me." The Duke pointed to an empty chair. "And you two also," he continued while pointing a finger toward Bart and Luigi and then swinging his arm toward a nearby bench.

As Henry took his proffered seat, Richard gasped. "What have we here? Is that a cross on your back?"

"It is," replied Henry. "I am Henry of Dol and this is Bart my sergeant. I believe you already know Luigi. Thank you for receiving us."

Richard sat down. "The pleasure is mine Henry. I don't get real knights here that often but you three undoubtedly have an important reason for coming. So you go first and then the rest of the evening you can tell me what you did on the great pilgrimage."

"Certainly," replied Henry. "We come from Rome where some of the families are presenting a small challenge to Pope Paschal. We hope you will loan us five hundred of your knights and soldiers with which we can cow these troublemakers back into compliance." Henry was about to say something more but Richard was too quick.

"I can have them ready to go the day after tomorrow. Will you lead them or do you want me to?"

"Oh," answered Henry quickly, "I would only lead your men if you could not and that would be a last resort."

"Well said," continued Richard. "I shall lead them then. By chance, is Ptolemy of Tusculum one of the ringleaders of these troublemakers?"

Knowing that Ptolemy's name was among those mentioned by Bishop Bernard but thinking it would be good to get Luigi into the discussion, Henry turned toward his guide.

"He is," said Luigi.

"That's good," smiled Richard. "He's a schemer, not a fighter. We can call in my men tomorrow, march four days to get there, take the strong points on the sixth day, give them a day to figure out they've lost, then on the eighth accept their deserters who will deny ever having been on the other side; the ninth day Paschal can throw us a great feast and four days back makes it all in a fortnight. Of course I'll have to get some men out tonight to line up victuals along the way. What have I left out, Henry?"

"Not a thing, sir," smiled the knight. "Not a thing."

"Good," chortled Richard. He then stood up and walked over to one of his men who was sitting nearer the fireplace. The two men whispered quietly for a moment or two. Then the sitting fellow rose and strode rapidly toward the stairway where he nearly bumped into a young serving girl who was awkwardly carrying in a full pitcher and three cups.

"Ah ha," bellowed the wily Duke as he returned to his chair, "here's our mead. Now if you wouldn't mind Henry, please tell us all about your exploits on the great pilgrimage. We don't get many chances to hear firsthand accounts so I've invited a few more of my men to join us. Don't hold back a thing. I promise we won't fall asleep."

~**~

Richard's schedule held up perfectly with his men entering Rome on the sixth day and quickly taking control of the strong points: the Appia, Tiburtina, Flaminia, and San Paolo gates, the Prefect's office, the Pantheon, the Castel Saint Angelo, the cisterns and the marketplace. The next morning, the opposition sent a young man, a nephew of Ptolemy of Tusculum, to negotiate. The Duke of Gaeta, whose son had been stabbed in the back two years earlier by one of Ptolemy's thugs, had the youth strung up on a makeshift gibbet in the market place and left hanging for all to see. On the next day, various members of the old families began to trickle in to Richard's strong points declaring their undying loyalty to Pope Paschal and their eternal thanks to the Duke of Gaeta for saving them from the evil Ptolemy of Tusculum whom, they said, was rumored to have fled the city.

The next day Pope Paschal who was actually still somewhere to the south touring cities, threw a great feast for the citizens of Rome and most particularly for Duke Richard of Gaeta and his men who had so ably come to the rescue of the city. Of course all the Roman families, 'old' and 'new,' were notably present. The body hanging in the marketplace was left to decompose.

Bernard, now back in his scarlet bishop's robe, sat facing Henry and Bart on a bench beside the entrance to the Pantheon. It was late in the afternoon, which meant for most of the citizenry that eating was over and drinking beginning.

"Henry, it will only take you one day longer. Canossa is less than a half day's ride from the coast, a place you'll be passing right through anyhow. Matilda is the most powerful and loyal 'Fidelis' in all of Italy. It's really important that you get to know her. This sort of uprising could happen again. Please, just one day."

"But what will we do if the pass closes?" responded Henry. "You know it will snow soon. It may have already closed."

"If it closes, you can take a ship or, ride along the coast. It's only one day."

"I can't afford a ship," Henry quipped.

"Oh," said Bernard, "I'm glad you mentioned that." He reached beneath the breast of his scarlet robe and pulled forth a cloth purse. "This is the Pope's thanks for saving Rome. And don't say you won't take it. You've come a long way, risked your life and given a whole month of your time. You'll need this just to get back to Dol, particularly if you have to hire a ship."

Henry stared at the purse then he looked up at the bishop. "Alright, we'll go to Canossa but for only one day...and thank you."

"You're welcome," mumbled the Spaniard. "Would you like me to send Luigi with you? He knows the way, won't bother you and can be very helpful if you run into trouble."

"No," replied the knight, "I like Luigi. He is the kind of man who can be very helpful in a foreign land but we know the way and he deserves a rest."

~**~

Once through Matilda's castle gate, Henry saw at least fifty armed men. To determine whether they were at war, he studied them closely. The head guards paid them very little attention and the men on the walls looked down without apparent concern. Just a lot of soldiers, Henry concluded, which meant while they weren't at war, they were prepared for the possibility.

When Henry entered the Countess's great room, his jaw dropped. "Abbot Hugh!"

In his black robe the aged Abbott of Cluny sat directly in front of him. His head was bare revealing that his hair had dramatically thinned and whitened. His smile though, came quickly and the tone of his voice was unchanged if slightly fainter. "Henry, is that you?"

"It is," called out Hugh's once youthful student as he rushed forward to greet his mentor.

Hugh squinted at the knight. "Ah," he murmured, "it is you. My eyes aren't as good as they used to be." The Abbot then turned his gaze toward an old woman who sat next to him.

The woman's hair was grey and shorter than was the current style. She was not a particularly big person but her hands were large and her face looked weathered as if she'd spent a lot of her life outdoors. It was, Henry noted, a characteristic that made her look like a serf. But he could tell by her arrow-straight posture that she wasn't. She must be 'la Gran Contessa.'

Henry was just starting to bow to her when Hugh continued speaking. "Respect, integrity and others," the Abbot declared definitively. "Isn't that right Henry?"

Very awkwardly Henry completed his bow to the Countess as he simultaneously twisted his head toward Hugh and said, "Yes."

Matilda chuckled and then, to cover her social indiscretion, put her right hand over her mouth. In only a moment she regained her composure and became again the Countess. "Greetings knight. You are obviously an acquaintance of Abbot Hugh and one he holds in high esteem. Am I correct that your values are 'respect, integrity and others?'"

"Yes, my lady," answered Henry.

"It is unusual that I know a man's values before I know his name."

Henry was about to put forth his name but Matilda continued. "Perhaps though, this putting values ahead of names should become a new social custom. I rather like it."

"Henry of Dol," said the knight. "I was Hugh's student long ago on a trip to Spain. He is a good friend."

"Yes," interjected the Countess, "he is." Matilda glanced toward an arrow loop which had been letting a little of the remaining sunlight into the great room. "It seems the sun is setting," she whispered as if to herself, "but," her voice rose, "we can keep warm in here, have our dinner and if you are willing, share a few stories."

Both men nodded and the Countess pointed to chairs for Henry and Bart.

The knight sat down and soon discovered that his hostess and mentor had a practiced routine. Hot mead was delivered and as the evening wore on: wine, venison and bread. During this leisurely dinner, the hostess and Abbot alternated telling stories. But after the break for venison, Hugh twisted toward the knight and spoke.

"Henry, did I ever tell you the story about Emperor Henry coming here to Canossa to meet with Pope Gregory? Let's see, I think it was December of seventy seven. Yes, seventy seven. It was a brutal winter: cold, icy and lots of snow. Matilda had invited Gregory to stay here for a while. He was a German through and through: hard-headed, combative, stubborn, determined, and unyielding if he thought he was right and he almost always thought he was right. At times he'd even burst into tirades not listening to anyone's advice. I learned a lot from his stubbornness. You couldn't disagree with him right out. You had to appear to agree with him but ask questions. Questions made him stop and think. Despite his humble birth and lack of any sort of classical education, he was a good thinker. And once you got him thinking, there was a chance of him opening his mind. Even then it would only be open for a moment or two. So you had to strike at just the right moment. You couldn't make it obvious or he'd jump right back to his original thesis. But if you were oblique and didn't articulate your case too clearly, he'd clarify your position, your thesis, make it crisp and narrow. And then once he'd done that, it would be his. He really had a good mind. He just couldn't stand the Aristotelian method of debate.

"He was totally in support of the reform movement—celibacy for priests, the peace of God and the problems created by letting secular lords appoint priests and bishops. He'd seen how all that corrupted the parish priests and the bishops even more. But once he got behind something, it was all or nothing. He couldn't compromise even if he got almost all of what he wanted.

"He and I used to travel together as young church delegates. We rode far and wide and became good friends. In many respects he and I complimented each other. I of noble family educated in Greek and Latin and a political compromiser, and he a rough hewn peasant, educated in 'the world of hard knocks' and totally committed to complete, wrenching change. His favorite quotation was from Jeremiah: 'Cursed is he who keeps back his sword from blood.' And of me, he used to say, 'you are an urbane tyrant.' By 'urbane' he referred to my skill in handling people and encouraging them to see my point-of-view. By calling me a tyrant, he meant that I was just as committed as he in believing my way was best.

"Anyhow, the essence of Gregory's belief was that the Pope, by his God-given appointment, was the highest ruler in Christendom; secular kings, emperors, lords or other humans so appointed, held lesser positions. He saw the Emperor as the 'protector' of the Church not its 'ruler.

"Now as you both know, Henry was my godson. I knew him when he was a child. I gave him counsel and on occasion he took it. But he was a German too: head-strong, self-centered, obstinate and used to getting his way. Additionally, he was raised by a mother who taught him to mistrust his father; and when taken from her, he was dipped into all sorts of sinful activities and, worst of all, he was taught by everyone that there were no rules which applied to him, none at all. So he ended up with only one value—'himself.

"And so these two male bears wrestled each other most violently here in Matilda's castle to determine which was the prime ruler of Christendom; who could make appointments and who could not; who could invest a priest and who could not.

"Gregory started the battle by excommunicating five of Henry's advisors who had recommended that Henry appoint certain churchmen to high positions in the far north of the Emperor's provinces. Henry angrily responded by ousting the Bishop of Milan, a strong supporter of the reform movement. And when Gregory asked to meet with Henry to attempt resolution of the issue, Henry simply told the Pope that he was 'deposed.' Enraged, Gregory excommunicated the Emperor.

"But it turned out that these thrusts and parries were of unequal affect. Henry's control over his barons in Saxony and other northern realms was weak. With priests no longer able to relieve their parishioners from sin through absolution, they used the Emperor's excommunication as an excuse to rebel. Without being able to assuage people of their sins, Henry quickly began to lose his kingdom. And so Henry came, a beggar, here to Canossa castle during Christmas week. Right in that courtyard that you just walked through Henry, the Emperor stood three days and nights barefoot in the snow. Gregory was nothing if not a stubborn man. I talked to him every day, entreated him, cajoled him, begged him. Three whole days went by, and I almost gave up. Finally though I went to Gregory and simply said, 'Christ thought forgiveness was sublime. Do you put yourself above our Savior?

"I then left his room and let him think. Several hours later he went out into the snow and forgave my godson. That evening in this very room, we all dined together. I sat across from Henry and watched him drum his fingers loudly on the table and not take a single bite of his food. I knew then that it was only a matter of time until he'd do it all again. Such willful men!"

"Countess, what story would you like to tell?"

"Oh," said Matilda, "I haven't anything as important to tell as that. Let's see. How about I share a little of what we've been doing here to support the reform movement? Henry, do you know who 'the Fideles' are?"

"Yes," answered the knight modestly.

"Arhum," gurgled Hugh. "Henry, aren't you a 'Fidelis' yourself?"

"Yes," responded the knight. "I am on call to come to Rome when the need arises."

"And," continued the Abbot, "haven't you just been to Rome as a 'Fidelis?"

"Yes," replied the youth, "but let me share that story after our hostess has recited hers."

Hugh looked back at the Countess.

"Well," Matilda said in a quiet tone, "I am a 'Fidelis' too, probably for the same reason that you are Henry. I believe the reforms we work for – eliminating simony, clerical celibacy, retention of Church lands from seculars, consanguineous marriages, the peace of God and the election of Popes by an unfettered cardinalate—are all reforms that will lead to more souls being saved. In essence we intend to cleanse the Church in ways that will free her to do even better for her flock.

"My way of helping is perhaps somewhat like yours Henry, serving as an intermediary to protect the rightful Popes and their supporters. God has granted me some worldly power with which to achieve this goal and He has placed me in a position between Rome and the Emperors. My inheritance came to me in seventy six when my parents left me Lombardy, Mantua, Modena, Cremona, Verona, Lucca, Canossa, Upper Lorraine, and the 'Quattro Castelli'—Montezane, Montelucio, Montevatro and Bianell – as well as clouded rights to Florence and the western passages through the Apennines. I am also uniquely related to several of the principals involved in the disputes. Emperor Henry III was my first cousin once-removed and Henry IV my second cousin. These relationships, although frayed at times, are based on primary blood lines that favor my connections and give me legitimacy when I have to stand up to my cousins. In this way I have been able to fight delaying actions to hold or delay an Emperor from reaching

Rome, unseating a Pope or replacing a false one on the throne of Saint Peter. Also I have been able to provide succor to various reformers or, in other cases, disaffected parties. These have included Anslem of Canterbury, Bonizo of Sutri, Pope Gregory and the fleeing wife and son of Henry IV.

"One other thing may be worthy of mention. In eighty I came upon information that Emperor Henry was plotting with Robert Guiscard to have their children marry. 'The weasel' needed legitimacy, which such a marriage would have given him and Henry wanted a free hand in Rome. I passed that information on to Robert's relatives in Sicily and the marriage plans were dropped. All in all, my position in the middle has served the reform movement well over the years."

For a moment Matilda paused. "Henry, now it's your turn. Please share some of your exploits on the great pilgrimage as well as your involvement in the bubblings of Rome."

Henry had completed telling his 'hurrying to Rome' story and was arriving at Antioch in the great pilgrimage rendition when the evening's stillness was interrupted by a shout from the main gate. Someone was calling to be let in. Getting a castle to open its gate in the middle of the night was a commonly used ruse in which an armed force bursts in as soon as the gate is opened. Henry had seen Matilda's sentries and knew they would not be making any mistakes regarding who entered. Accordingly, he finished covering Antioch and was just starting for Jerusalem when one of Matilda's knights entered the great-room and called out an introduction.

"My lady, a messenger from Rome—Luigi Delasandro."

Assuming that this Luigi was the same Luigi with whom he'd just travelled to Rome, Henry began to rise. At the same moment, it occurred to him that whatever news the courier was bringing, must have arrived in Rome just after he and Bart left. Henry stared toward the dark entryway. The great room was very dark: its loop-holes black, its candles guttering and, where the fire had once blazed, there were only red embers remaining. When Luigi entered his face was the only part of his body visible and it, like the coals in the fire place, was a pale reddish shade which seemed to float all by itself in the darkness.

"What news do you bring?" asked the Countess coldly.

Luigi took another step forward and, as if by magic, his shoulders and torso took on form. His face though still held its reddish hue. "I have a letter for Henry. It came from Dol right after he left."

"Well, bring it to him," commanded Matilda still employing a strained tone suggesting she was miffed by the interruption.

As he walked toward Henry, Luigi's boots clicked on the wooden floor.

For some reason Henry stood stock still, waiting.

"It is from your mother," said the messenger as he pulled a parchment from his sleeve and held it out.

"Thank you," whispered Henry nervously as he clasped the letter and held it up to the paltry candle light.

"Do you need another candle?" asked Matilda.

"No," Henry answered. "I can make it out." His eyes passed over the words. 'Dear Henry, Your beloved Angeline has died in child birth. Her last words expressed her love for you and thanked God for fulfilling her desire to become a mother. Your new son Bernard is well. We pray for Angeline's soul and shall have a service for her when you return. May God be with you. Audrey.'

SECTION II

ME

BETRAYED
November 1108 – April 1109

Henry had never been so powerfully affected by death: not for William, not for Walter, not for Benito, not for Reynauld, not at Dorylaeum, not at Antioch, not at Jerusalem. But his tears lasted only a short while. To make them stop, he clenched his jaw tight-shut and forced his mind into sword's point focus. With that done, he slew his feelings and put his rational mind back in charge.

Aware that everyone was watching him, he stood up. "Countess Matilda, thank you for having us here; Abbot Hugh, you have always been kind to me. Thank you for sharing your wisdom... Luigi, thank you for riding so quickly to bring me this news." The knight turned to his sergeant. "Bart, we'll ride before dawn and hope to be through the Mount Cenis Pass the day after tomorrow. Good night everyone."

Despite his apparent control, Henry did not sleep well. His mind leapt through memories of Angeline: his first sight of her in Montserrat opening the abbey's door, her courage on the Spanish plain when surrounded by Ali's men, her look of concern when first asking about his mother, her beaming expression as she first held up their son Walter and her forced smile when he rode away to answer Bernard's call. Intermittently these recollections stabbed Henry throughout the night but he only let them do so until morning.

Henry had been riding for about an hour when he concluded that he had been betrayed...betrayed by God! After all, he'd just been answering Bernard's call, the Church's call to help the Pope. He'd been called to do God's work...and then God had taken Angeline from him. Was there any justice in that? Some reason for such a heinous act? Was Angeline's death punishment for him killing that woman in Antioch? That had been an awful sin but it was a visceral reaction, a reflex. Every day since, he'd prayed for forgiveness. Of course he'd committed lesser sins as well: that girl in Flanders in the barn, Brinette in Jerusalem...but after he'd met Angeline he had never philandered, never sullied their relationship. Did any of those actions justify taking Angeline's life? He didn't think so. Anger squeezed his lungs, pressed bile up his throat, pummelled his head. How could God have done this to me? I've served His mission on the Great Pilgrimage, stood by for Bernard's call, left Angeline and my family to serve Him. If You are so angry with me Lord, why didn't You just take me? It wasn't right. Your act was irrational. Your hand's erratic! Angeline was an innocent. You betrayed her...and me!

On the second day riding toward the pass, Henry's mind was focusing on a lesser abuse, the purse Bernard had given him. He hadn't looked to see how much the Bishop had given him, how many coins, whether gold or silver. But whatever it was, it wasn't enough. He'd spent years being ready to leave on a moment's notice, letting people know where he could be reached, keeping his saddle bags filled and ready, having the kitchen staff always prepared with emergency victuals. How many years had he been doing that? Seven...eight? In the future if Bernard wanted him ready on a moment's notice, he'd have to pay for it. Actually with Angeline gone, perhaps he ought to just go to Rome and hire on. There was nothing in Dol to really hold him. Well his children, of course, but they were still too young to need his instruction. Walter was six, Henry two, and Bernard just born. Audrey and Joan would be watching over them for years to come. With regular pay in Rome, Henry thought he could compensate Edmond and the women too. And when the boys were old enough to need him, he could bring them to Rome.

The funeral was held in the castle's chapel. Father Andrew, the priest from Dol who had been a friend of Henry's father, presided over the service. He'd become a stooped, old man whose steps were short. But his voice was still strong and, as he stood beneath the rood beam and completed God's blessing, he called upon the congregation to share their recollections of Angeline. Henry's cousin, Carla, spoke kindly of the times she and Angeline had walked their children. Joan shared the kindness and comfort that Angeline always exuded when they marshaled their children within or without the castle. And Audrey, whom Henry knew was as deeply bereaved by Angeline's passing as he was, spoke about the young woman's keen interest in all God's doings and also of her appreciation of reading, how the two women had written poetry together and read it later to the children. Henry had planned to speak, but as it got near his turn, the import of the others' words caused his lower lip to quiver and he knew he couldn't do it. He just lowered his head and shook it negatively when Andrew looked to him.

Later in the winter, Henry began to read his *Aeneid* to his oldest son, Walter. They spent time every morning except Sunday with the father reading and the boy answering occasional questions about the story. Eventually Henry asked his mother to join them. Audrey attended several sessions before asking the question.

"It's very nice of you to have invited me to these readings but what exactly are you hoping I'll contribute?"

"Do you think Walter needs a tutor?" asked Henry.

"Can we afford a tutor?"

"Not as things currently are," replied the knight, "but that doesn't answer my question."

Audrey's countenance held a quizzical expression. "Well then," she continued, "yes, he does. He is just as bright as his parents and would benefit greatly from a well rounded education. There, now that I have answered your question, please share with me how you might go about getting a tutor for your son."

"Well," answered Henry, "I've been thinking of going to Rome. I think Bishop Bernard would hire me as a Papal guard. It might pay enough to hire a tutor."

"It would take a princely sum to get a qualified tutor to trek all the way to Dol and stay. Do you really think..."

Henry interrupted. "I'm thinking of taking Walter to Rome with me and putting him in a lyceum there."

Audrey's back straightened. "You don't really like being here anymore, do you?"

Henry took his turn staring back at his mother. "No," he finally answered. "I love you, my children and my relatives but I don't feel as if I fit in. The work here doesn't interest me. Most of it is repetitious, mundane and boring. I don't know if it's my education, my time in other places, my military experiences or what. I always have the feeling of having to move on to something else."

"Did you have that feeling before Angeline died?" asked Audrey.

"Yes," replied Henry. "It's just worse now. Angeline kept me here. I loved her very much. She diminished my craving, my itch to keep moving. I thought she was helping me find God but I now see that there really wasn't one to find."

"Oh Henry, don't say that. You're bereaved. God is still there for us. It's just difficult for us to understand why He does some things the way He does."

"Fine," replied Henry. "I won't say it...but it's true."

Again Audrey stared at her son. "When will you go to Rome?" she finally asked.

"The passes usually melt in April. Does this mean you think I should go?"

"Yes," quipped Audrey, "but not because I want to lose you and Walter." The grandmother's voice mellowed slightly. "But because you need to find your calling...and a fine education will be good for Walter. But Henry, promise me one thing."

"Of course," responded Audrey's son.

"Promise me that you'll come back to Dol occasionally with Walter so your doting mother can be happy."

"I promise," breathed the knight. "Anyhow I shall want to see the younger boys too."

ROME'S LYCEUM

June 1109

As Henry trudged up the twisting, stone stairway of Castel Saint Angelo's keep, he was thinking about their trip. He, Walter and Bart had departed in late April leaving Audrey, Edmond, Joan, Henry and little Bernard at Dol. Henry was certain that in his absence the remaining adults would raise his two youngest sons as if they were their own. He would be responsible for Walter and would keep his promise to his mother to return to Dol at least every two years.

His oldest son Walter was climbing the castle stairs right behind him. The boy had done remarkably well on their trip. He'd ridden quite well with only a sore butt in the first week and keeping up thereafter.

They made one unplanned stop in Genoa. Henry decided, since their progress was going so well, that they had time to visit Abraham, Ezekial and Rachel. The knight wasn't sure the children would remember him. But he still wanted to see them if only to relieve his own concern about his decision to leave them in Abraham's hands.

They spent their first day at Abraham's home discussing all sorts of things: Leonardo had secured 'prefered' trading rights in Antioch; Acre had been taken by the Christians; Alexius was still Emperor in Constantiople; Venetian pirates were accosting Pisan and Genoese merchants but how much was unclear; the wool market was strong and the price of food stuffs had soared due to droughts in the Crimea.

On their second day, Abraham had taken them to a different part of the ghetto where they were met by Rachel, a beautiful young woman, who'd rushed up to Henry and clasped her arms around him with sincere joy. Ezekial was equally sincere but with a handshake. He'd grown into a serious young man and, judging by his dress and dignity, was already a member of the Jewish business community. Henry inquired about the two's progress in life since he'd last seen them and they sought out his doings as well. These summaries were fairly brief but Henry got Ezekial to share the name of his shipping company and some information about where they went and what they carried. The young man was not particularly effusive, causing Henry to recall that even as a young boy, he hadn't been loquacious. They had lunch together and then Abraham took Henry, Walter and Bart back to his house. There the Jew sat Henry down and told him there were some things about Rome he wanted to share before they left.

The core point which Abraham put forth was that Rome had become a politicized city and therefore there would be no one there whom Henry should completely trust. Henry thought he already knew that. But Abraham continued by telling the knight that there was one man in Rome whom he knew, a haberdasher named Martin, who could be trusted. 'He will be your friend if you need one.' Abraham went on to explain that this Martin was not officially a Jew, so Henry should be very careful not to say anything that might compromise him. Furthermore, Abraham cautioned the knight not to meet Martin more than once because as someone new in the city, Henry would be being watched and all his contacts would be noted. Henry thought Abraham, as a Jew in sometimes unfriendly surroundings, might be overly suspicious but just in case he thought he'd still heed his friend's advice. With that subject covered, Abraham took Henry, Walter and Bart to the Ghetto's gate where they watched him toss a coin to a young guard they didn't know.

At the third level of the stairway, Henry turned to his right and began to look for the mustering room that he'd been directed to by one of the guards. The room was lit by sunlight coming through several arrow-loops and offered six bunks, a table and, hanging neatly inside the doorway, several crossbows with boxes of quarrels on the floor below them. Henry, Walter and Bart slung down their saddle bags and sat around the table. Bishop Bernard had been sent for but they had no idea how soon he'd arrive. Accordingly, after a short while Henry got up and took his chess set out of his smaller travel bag and set it on the table.

"Walter, do you want to play a game?"

The boy who'd been closely watching his father from a few feet away, leapt up and moved to a chair nearer the chess set.

"White or black?"

"White," answered the boy.

Sitting opposite each other, 'the two would-be players' set out their pieces while Bart lay down on one of the bunks.

"Your turn to start," offered Henry after all the pieces had been placed.

"Will you show me the beginning of the double-entendre move this time please?" asked Walter.

"I will when I see it myself. Sometimes it doesn't come to me until enough pieces have been moved around. But I'll tell you when I do."

The game progressed perhaps fifteen turns before a noise in the hallway interrupted the players' concentration.

"Henry!" bellowed Bernard as he rushed into the room. The Bishop was wearing a workman's clothing: a linen shirt, dirty leather leggings and boots. Henry hadn't seen him dressed that way since they'd ridden together to Santiago de Compostela years ago.

"Bishop Bernard," responded the knight somewhat formally as he stood up and stepped forward to hug his long-time friend.

"Henry, I'm so sorry about Angeline. Such a tragedy. You have my condolences."

"Thank you," whispered the knight.

"Ahh," continued the Bishop as he withdrew his arms from Henry's shoulders, "this must be Walter. Even in this light I can see that he is Angeline's son, the same beautiful brown eyes. Henry, even as God has pained us so deeply, He has blessed us with this child." The bishop reached forth his hand to Walter and continued. "My son, I knew your mother very well. She was a wonderful person: kind, unselfish and always thinking of others." Bernard completed his handshake and then wrapped his arms around the boy and hugged him tightly.

When Bernard finally withdrew his grip, he raised his right hand to his eyes and wiped away some tears. "Forgive me," he continued. "You remind me so much of your mother." Then the bishop advanced to the chair that Walter had previously been sitting in and sat down. Then, seeing Henry's sergeant lying on a bunk, he spoke again. "Hello, Bart. I didn't see you when I first came in. Please don't be offended by my poor manners. You are well I trust?"

"I am, sir."

Perhaps to see if there was anyone else he hadn't seen, Bernard scanned the small room. Finding no one else, he turned back to Henry.

"I got your letter only a couple of days ago. You must have made a fast trip. Is Walter that good a rider?"

Henry smiled. "He is now."

"Good for you," said Bernard as he looked at the boy. "Do you know that Normans are considered the finest horsemen in the western world?"

"Really?" responded Walter.

"Yes really," said Bernard whose attitude had returned to its usual effervescent state. "Now Henry, I have assigned you to be the Captain of the Papal Guard. It is an honored position that also carries with it great responsibility. Ordinarily a convoluted vetting process would have been necessary but in your case, I simply explained that you were the third man over the wall in Jerusalem and there was no contention. But that doesn't mean there won't be push and pull. Let me explain what the role entails. Counting you, there are six guards whose function is solely to protect Pope Paschal."

"The other five will report to you, and you to me. The five are all on personally good terms with Paschal. That means nothing in regard to their trustworthiness. You must determine that for yourself. You can relieve any or all of them at any time on a moment's notice...but I recommend that you not do so in a dark alley. My best guess is that there are three who've been bought by the Emperor, the Normans in Sicily or one or more of the families here in Rome. In the past I have found when one has sold himself, he is likely to have sold out to several masters. Quite simply, the pay is better. Almost always the Pope will be in a place overseen by a lord whose men will out-number you. This is not necessarily a bad thing. Here for instance, we are in Castel Saint Angelo. Its master is Petrus Leonis of the Pierleoni family. He is greatly favored by Paschal and accordingly is loyal. Currently, Leo Frangipane, Petrus Leonis and their families dominate the city politically. That of course can change.

"You will need to establish a close relationship with each of these guards, with many others and with Paschal himself. This is important because to guard His Eminence, you'll need to know not just where he currently is but also where he is going to be. Paschal is often the least likely to know the answer to that question. You should talk to me daily. I will tell you all that I know, all of the rumors of the day and answer your questions or concerns. Do not assume that my opinions, or any of my sources, are necessarily correct. You'll get the hang of it but whatever you do, never trust anyone. Here people sell out for coin more readily than any other place in the world. Oh, I forgot to mention that there are also factions within the band of Cardinals. Some favor aligning with the Emperor, some with the southern Normans. These leanings usually intertwine with strong support for the 'Reform Movement' or the newer belief that reform has become a divisive issue."

Bernard smiled broadly. "Don't worry Henry, you'll get good at this but it will take some time. Oh, also you'll have to set up some escape routes. There's always the chance that the Emperor, the south Normans, or a powerful grouping of families might take the city and try to capture Paschal. We'll need at least two escape routes, each with a code name and secret processes in place to sneak the Pope safely out of the city. Only you and I will know them, no exceptions! We can also establish some canards through people less likely to be loyal, which will lead our enemies in the wrong direction. We'll talk more about that later. You may want to make Bart one of your guards. He's certainly qualified and you can trust him. You know about Maginulf the anti-pope. You'll have to keep up on him too: where he is, what he's doing, who's supporting him."

Racing forward, Bernard switched subjects. "Now we need to get Walter into the Lyceum. We've still got time this afternoon." The Bishop looked around the room. "You can leave your luggage here for now and tomorrow we can find a permanent place for you to stay. Right now, follow me and I'll tell you about the Lyceum while we're walking over there."

Henry immediately began to pick up his chess pieces and place them in their box.

"Don't worry about the game," said Bernard who was already standing in the doorway. "You can get it when we return."

"I'll take my book and my father's chess set with me," replied the knight. "After hearing what you've said about all the people who can't be trusted, I don't want to leave these behind."

"Will Walter have a tutor similar to Benito Tusculani?" asked Henry.

"The Lyceum is the best school in the city," answered Bernard. "One or two of the families still retain a single tutor for their children but most send them to the Lyceum. It offers near certain passage into the Church, the civil ministry, business or finance. The latter seems to be the thing nowadays but sticking to the Trivium and Quadrivium, at least in the early grades, makes the best sense. That's what you did isn't it Henry?"

"Yes," answered the knight. "But the changes are so rapid now, particularly as you said, with business and finance. On our way here we visited a friend in Genoa. He's in shipping and finance and was explaining some of the complexities inherent in those trades. It was incredibly complicated:

shares of ownership, diversifying risk, insurance through off-setting guarantors. It's much more complicated than I would have expected."

"It sounds as though you know it better than I do," replied the Bishop. "I have trouble keeping up on the politics here in Rome. Adding business and finance would sink me like a ship foundering in a horrific storm. But you're younger than I am Henry, smarter too. You can absorb all these new things. For us old folks, the pace is leaving us behind. But of course that's why you want a good school for Walter. Ah ha! It's this building coming up on our right." Bernard pointed toward an old stone edifice that had several shabby-looking, wooden additions appended behind it.

The Lyceum didn't match Henry's expectations. He wasn't entirely sure why, but it conveyed a sense of being cobbled together, of being in some sort of transition and barely keeping up.

"How many students does it have?" asked the knight whose need for credentials was suddenly sprouting.

"I don't know," responded Bernard, "but we can ask Brother Mendichio, the Master. He's expecting us."

"Welcome to our Lyceum," called out a huge fellow in a black robe. "I am Brother Mendichio, the Master here and this is Roberta one of our teachers."

THE BEST LAID PLANS
June 1109 – February 1110

After his meeting with Bernard, Henry had a clear idea of what he had to do: replace Paschal's existing five guards, set up two escape routes in case of emergency and establish sources who would keep him up to date on everything going on in the Church, the city and beyond. He would need a network of friends and informers through whom he could get up to speed on what everyone of importence was doing, thinking and planning. Some informers he would have to pay, some threaten but most he would have to give information to get information. So he needed learn what information he could give up and what he should not. As a new arrival in Rome, he didn't have many contacts. But because of his new role as the Pope's principal guard, he expected he would meet a lot of people who could help him and most likely there would be a lot of people seeking him out as a source of information for themselves.

He remembered his first meeting with Tancred in which the young lord of Taranto had pressed him for information as if Henry was one of Tancred's own liege knights. Henry had politely rebuked the Norman but offered to share his knowledge if Tancred would do the same. The two had quickly become fast friends. Bernard gave him names of potential sources who Henry began to find ways to meet. Simultaneously, Henry discovered that he was on other people's list. Many men, and some women, seemed to run into him. Some were quite direct, others played their roles, but all departed with an ongoing relationship established. There were so many with such varying interests and information that Henry created a notebook in which he recorded name, time, date, topic of conversation and any odd or unusual references that might prove significant. He reviewed the book regularly to determine what sort of information the person seemed to be interested in and how they went about working their way into the subject.

After a few months, Henry could review a person's conversations and usually identify their topic of interest and, even more interesting, their methodology for getting it. The former usually allowed him to identify who they were getting information for and the latter allowed him to learn new questioning techniques that he hadn't previously thought of. The best of his questioners initiated their conversations with general topics, often interesting ones, but nothing that suggested any greater meaning. Given time though, they would edge their conversation into something more specific, then ask what he thought about it and what pros and cons he may have heard that might shine a brighter light on the subject. When Henry started his notebook, he usually had no idea which conversations to track. Accordingly, there were many that were entirely benign. One however, was someone he never would have suspected who after several months turned out to look very suspicious. This was a priest who worked in the Vatican as a secretary for the Pope!

Of course most of his sources were quite clear as to their opinions and perfectly willing to share them. When it came to the Papacy's ongoing dispute with Emperor Henry over investiture of bishops and priests, Henry had only to ask the softest questions on the subject and he quickly learned that there were two camps among the cardinals. Leo of Ostia, Cuno of Palistrina and Bruno of Segni were opposed to any compromise whatsoever. On the other side were several of Paschal's closest advisors: John of Gaeta, Peter of Porto and Peter Pierleone who saw benefit in compromise. Henry quickly determined that those who proffered their opinions quickly and clearly were sincere. He became suspicious though of the cardinals who avoided sharing their thoughts. Some were simply too old or too slow witted to advocate. But there were others, just a few, who simply wouldn't share.

Outside this inner circle, there were a great number of people coming and going every day. Some were regulars with defined functions and some were more shadowy figures whose roles were almost impossible to determine. These took up a lot of Henry's time since any one of them might be an assassin planning to poison Paschal's wine or stab the Pontiff should an opportunity present itself. However while this was a concern, Henry delegated the moment-to-moment protection of the Pope to his five guards. The knight reasoned that killing any pope would only lead to a quick replacement. Therefore, unless the killer knew the likely replacement and wanted him to become Pope, there was little gain to warrant an assassination. Most of the associated parties simply sought to wring out greater 'beneficia' from the existing Pope. This caused Henry to pay close attention to Leo Frangipane together with the Pierleoni clan, since they were the most favored by Paschal.

The political issue of the day was 'investiture'—the appointment of high ranking churchmen in various kingdoms. In the past kings had picked the lords in their lands because those lords were seen first and foremost as 'the king's liegemen' who served militarily when called to do so. More recently, the Pope was claiming that any lord whose title was a Church one, like 'Bishop', should be picked if his first duty would be churchly functions. This issue of who should appoint the most powerful 'churchmen' in various kingdoms, the Emperor or the Pope, had been going on for years. Henry IV had been excommunicated for it. Pope Gregory had been undone by it. Since then, negotiations between the Pope and various kings had been progressing unevenly. Essentially the Church's position was that bishops and priests were God's personnel to be appointed by God's representative on earth, the Pope. The kings, particularly the German Emperor, believed a lord overseeing lands in his territories, be they churchmen or lay, owed homage, both fealty and service, to the Emperor for their use of his land. Accordingly the Emperor, being already the overlord of the proposed 'churchman', would be the proper person to make appointments.

Henry thought both positions made sense...except when actually applied. Take for example a bishop in Utrecht who oversaw churchmen and church functions in far northern Germany while simultaneously performing civil court duties and giving knight's service to the Emperor. In small, distant places like that there just weren't enough qualified men to fill multiple positions. Negotiations had been going on for years but they usually came back to the issue of local control. The Saxons in northern Germany had used the Emperor's excommunication—no one in all Germany being able to receive relief for his or her sins—to weaken the Emperor and thus promote their own ambitions.

Meanwhile, Henry released three of Pope Paschal's guards and replaced them with Bart and two veterans of the great pilgrimage whom he knew, Archard of Auxerre and Rotrou of Issaudun. Each of the latter Henry promised to keep on for at least a year with a significant payment at year-end so they could embark, if they wished, knowing that they'd have enough coin to get home and purchase a fief from some local lord.

When Henry met with Bishop Bernard to establish escape routes, he found that Bernard already had two that had been in place for three years. Based on how long they had been 'up' and how many people were involved in them, Henry thought they should be changed immediately. But Bernard put him off 'at least for a while.'

What Henry did have, which was unknown to anyone in Rome, was a name—'Martin the haberdasher.' So on his day off, Henry set out for the clothier district. He left Walter with Roberta whose rental was close to his and set out. Because he didn't want to ask for Martin by name, his search took him through a great deal of the commercial part of the city. Eventually he came upon three successive haberdashery shops. In the first, when he asked the owner his name, the answer was 'Luigi.' Accordingly, after the fellow had shown him some trousers, Henry deemed them 'not quite what he was looking for' and moved on to the second shop.

There the proprietor was short, with graying hair and a bulbous nose. "My name is Martin," answered the man as he bowed to his potential customer.

Seeing no one else in the shop and not knowing how long that would last, Henry rose quickly to his task. "Martin, my name is Henry of Dol. I am a friend of Abraham of Genoa who suggested that I call on you. One day I may need a place to hide and then escape the city, south preferably. I would likely have my son, a woman and two or three others. Can you perhaps help me with a place to hide and a process by which to escape?"

For what seemed like a very long time Martin stared at the knight. At last he spoke. "Did this Abraham fellow of whom you speak say anything or give you anything which might help me know him?"

It was Henry's turn to pause. "He told me a little about you but I'm loathe to reveal it since I'm now not certain that you're the Martin I seek."

"Ah," responded the haberdasher, "tight lips are almost always a good thing among new acquaintances. Did this fellow you talk of perhaps have a housekeeper?"

Henry smiled. "He did. Her name is Anna, a flat-faced woman from the Ukraine who served delicious cinnamon rolls."

Martin's expression changed into a broad smile. "Let us talk quickly for, God willing, a real customer may enter at any moment. Six I can handle but their quarters will be tight. No notice will be necessary but you must get here without anyone following you. That is the most important thing. Would you be coming all together or separately?"

"Probably all together but I'm not certain of that," answered Henry.

"I sleep in the back," said Martin. "Knock twice and then a third time after a pause; and when you say south, do you mean to Tusculum or Gaeta?"

Henry hesitated.

Martin hurried on. "I do not need, nor want to know your reasons for leaving secretly. But if you need to go further south than Tusculum, it will be by boat. That's the reason I ask and I'm assuming a quick departure will be desired?"

"Yes," answered Henry, "and by boat."

Martin nodded affirmatively. "Then this conversation is completed. Please give my best to Abraham when you see him. Now may I show you some trousers?"

~**~

As his knowledge of all the families and factions increased, Henry settled into the rush and crush of Rome. Guard duty became more routine. He developed a process by which the guards did their daily work and he concentrated primarily on the shifting alliances of the Roman families, the politics of the Emperor and the south Normans, the anti-pope Maginulf and the push-pull of factions within the college of cardinals itself. Despite the feeling of relief that came with routine, Henry made a point not to let his mental focus slip. On pilgrimage he'd learned that routine could become a nap from which one wouldn't wake up.

Naturally as one year passed into another, Henry got to know Pope Paschal. At first he'd seemed a quiet leader, unlike most that Henry had gotten to know on his treck to Jerusalem. At synods the Pope was deferential toward his cardinals and even to priests and monks who were in attendance. Only once in a great while did the man burst forth against someone or some subject usually the Emperor relating to investiture. Eventually he came to see that Paschal's bombastic self was really only for show. It was his way of giving direction, inspiring his men and pointing out the principal enemy.

One late afternoon in Paschal's office behind the basilica, Henry found himself alone with the pontiff. Each of them was watching the orange glow of the remaining sun light rise on the wall across from the window. Conversation had ebbed.

Eventually though Henry broke the silence. "Your eminence, may I ask you a question?"

Paschal turned his head toward his mastiff and smiled. "Certainly."

"I've noticed that you use forcefulness in your language only on rare occasions, to show direction I think, somewhat like a leader on the field of battle pointing to just the spot he wants his men to take." The knight paused to gain a sense of whether or not he was getting himself into trouble.

Paschal nodded his head in affirmation, so Henry continued.

"I notice that most of your...your outbursts are lodged against the Emperor over investiture. Why do you choose that issue to attack?"

The Pope stared at his guard for quite a while before responding. "That's a very good question Henry and you are a very observant fellow. During the winter when you were a boy in Dol, did you ever have to go out and chop a block of ice out of a frozen pond, bring it back into your great-room and put it into a bucket near the fire to melt?"

"Yes," murmured the knight, "but our well hardly ever froze."

"Ignore the well for a moment," smiled Paschal. "Considering your entire job from cutting, to carrying, to placing the block in the bucket, to waiting for it to melt, to drinking the water, what was the hardest part?"

Henry answered quickly. "Cutting it out and carrying it in."

"Exactly," agreed Paschal. "Bishop Anslem fought tooth and nail for seven years with King Henry in England over investiture. He even refused giving him homage. For Anslem it was a very hard job. But King Henry finally backed off and agreed not to invest Churchmen in England. And we agreed to accept bishops who hadn't been invested but had nevertheless done homage to the king. A similar agreement was worked out with Philip of France. We had to chop a lot of ice, but once compromise was reached, the block of ice put into the bucket, the issue melted away. These kings returned to overseeing their lords and the Church returned to saving souls. In the Emperor's case however, we've not yet gotten him to give a little. So we're still chopping the ice. Someday though he'll have a change of heart and investiture will be put into the bucket to melt."

Henry was in bed with Roberta when loud banging on her front door woke him. It was late in February and still quite dark. Half dressed but with sword in hand, Henry opened the door and found Bart whom he'd left the previous evening with Walter at their rental only a few buildings away.

"My lord," Bart began as he tried to catch his breath. "Bishop Bernard wants you to come at once to Castel Saint Angelo."

"Bart, get Walter with necessary belongings and bring him here. Then you and I shall go to the castle to see what's afoot."

Once inside the Castel Saint Angelo, Henry dispatched Bart to alert the other Papal guards and began looking for Bishop Bernard. It turned out he was in the same third level mustering room they'd met in before.

"Henry," Bernard breathed a deep sigh of relief, "His Eminence received a message from Countess Matilda last night, one of great importance. Sit down and I'll summarize it for you, then I'll want your assessment."

Quickly Henry sat down.

The bishop was out of breath but immediately began. "Sometime in January, Matilda's cousin, the Emperor, announced his intention to move into Italy, subdue the northern provinces and obtain the imperial blessing from the Pope. Matilda believes that he has consolidated his position sufficiently throughout his realm so he can raise an army of as many as thirty thousand soldiers. And if he does, she says she cannot prevail even in delaying him and will therefore seek peace without stipulations."

Henry responded instantly. "Is there any chance that this message could be a ruse or a trick of some sort?"

"None," sighed Bernard. "Her message bore her seal, contained certain notations to authenticate it and the messenger is one of her most trusted men whom we know well. What shall we do?"

"The passes won't be open until April and even in the best of circumstances thirty thousand men is an unwieldy force. The Emperor will still have to negotiate with the cities—Venice, Mantua, Genoa, Lucca, Milan, Bologna, Pisa, Ravenna and Florence. To intimidate them, he'll have to have his army at least near enough to get their attention. But if he's willing to grant concessions, he shouldn't have much trouble. Thirty thousand men will be very intimidating. But all that will take time. The soonest he could get to Rome would probably be late in the year. Of course that presumes he'll consolidate his position by befriending all the various political entities along the way. If he wants them to become his vassals, he'll have to make time for them. If he just wants the crown from Paschal, he could just rush to Rome in which case he can be here by May. But he won't do that. He's a man who wants the whole cake not just a big piece of it. Meanwhile, our task will be to determine what sort of compromise we can work out. With thirty thousand men standing behind him, he won't give up much."

Bernard sighed deeply. "That makes sense, Henry. Thank you. I shall take your assessment to our meeting this afternoon. And," Bernard looked up and smiled wanly, "we shall see what we shall see."

~**~

In March, His Eminence Pope Paschal convened a synod in which he stated: "Henceforward a layman performing 'investiture' on any bishop or priest must be deposed and likewise he who consecrates the candidate."

Henry himself was on duty at this synod and heard Paschal's very words. He concluded that the Pope was still chopping his block of ice out of the German king's pond.

CONCERNS
May 1110 – February 1111

In the late spring, rumors began trickling into Rome relaying the German king's activities in northern Italy. By midsummer it was clear that King Henry's army was very large and was handily imposing its will across the countryside. Cities were bowing, counties genuflecting and local lords kneeling. But distinguishing reports from rumors was difficult. As the king's army came closer, the cacophony of clamor grew ever more boisterous and in many cases, more ridiculous. Rumors that should have been dismissed due to their obvious silliness, spread like a wildfire during a drought. 'The entire population of Florence had been put to the sword for not surrendering quickly enough. Genoa had been burned to the ground.' Perhaps the most silly of all warned that 'a Muslim army had landed near Naples.' As foolish as these were, there were daily departures of citizens leaving Rome with their children and worldly possessions heaped high on wagons.

Pope Paschal's head guard remained calm. He was though, irritated. Almost a year ago he'd given Bishop Bernard a pretty fair summary of what King Henry would do and when. Bernard had taken those insights and recommendations to Paschal but that was the last Henry had heard of them. He'd gotten neither feedback about the Pope's plans in regard to the German King nor even any direction as to what to do differently, if anything, to protect the Pope. He hadn't even been able to get Bernard to update the two antiquated escape plans. Most recently he'd prodded Bernard quite forcefully asking to be told what was going on. But the more he pushed, the more it seemed the Bishop didn't know either.

This startled Henry. Was Paschal in the grip of some stifling paralysis? With the German king's armed sortie into Italy, the investiture dispute between Paschal and King Henry had changed dramatically. It was no longer a contest of exchanging erudite letters from afar. Now one of the combatants was actually closing on the other. Shortly it would be a face-to-face confrontation. And if it came to that, Henry thought Paschal would lose. Accordingly, on a chilly morning in January, Henry trudged through the Lateran complex to the Pope's little office and knocked on the door. He didn't wait for the Pontiff to ask him in. He simply pushed the door open and entered. Paschal was sitting across a small table from Cardinal Deacon Peter Pierleone. Peter was the son of Petrus Leonis Pierleone, who among the Roman families was Paschal's most powerful supporter. Henry considered Bishop Peter to be one of the most astute and reasonable men within the College of Cardinals.

Each of the churchmen seemed taken aback by the rude entry the Captain of the Guard had just made.

"Your Eminence," Henry's voice was clear, bold and decisive, "I must talk with you now."

Peter glanced toward the Pope but before either of them could respond, Henry continued.

"Cardinal Peter, you may stay." Looking back at Paschal, the knight continued. "Your Eminence, when King Henry arrives here with his army, I will no longer be able to protect you. If you have a plan, I must hear it now. If you don't have a plan, I have one to offer. Whatever the case, we must determine our next steps immediately." Still staring at the Pope, the knight pulled the nearest empty chair out from the table and sat down.

Paschal, who was sitting forward in his chair with both his arms resting on the table, cleared his throat to speak but Peter reached over and placed his hand atop one of Paschal's.

"Your Eminence," Peter pronounced decisively, "may I suggest we hear the knight's plan."

Perhaps sensing a reprieve, Paschal responded quietly. "Oh yes. Henry, please share your plan."

As if looking for further permission, Henry glanced at Peter. The Cardinal nodded affirmatively and smiled. So Henry began. "If we wait for the king to get here, we shall be completely at his mercy. I recommend that you come up with your best compromise proposal on investiture and dispatch a delegation to some agreed place outside of Rome and propose it to him. This approach allows us to present something we are willing to live with as opposed to having to just accept his terms, which will surely be worse than any we would propose. Additionally the setting will appear neutral and that may cause him to be less demanding. In any case, we have a weak position. If we press too hard, he can put you in a dunjon or do something to further anoint the anti-pope Maginulf." Henry paused and hardened his tone. "What is our best compromise proposal?"

"Well," answered the Pope whose tone indicated eagerness to share his dilemma, "we've been thinking of returning all the marches, counties, markets and duchies that the Emperor has given us over the years—'the regalia'—in exchange for the king not performing any more investiture of churchmen in his realm. We would lose a number of estates and their income but the bishops and priests would be freed from their administrative roles and could actually look after their flocks. By eliminating the putting on of hands by the king, no simony can occur. It would be a good compromise in that we and the king each will have given up something. We don't think he and his advisors will go along with it though."

Henry glanced at Peter.

The Cardinal Deacon nodded his head approvingly.

"Good," said Henry. "Let Cardinal Peter and me ride forth to find the king and see if we can establish a process to reach agreement. If there are refinements called for, will you let Peter negotiate them?"

The Pope glanced at Peter. "Yes."

~**~

Henry was elated. It took him and Peter only a day's ride to locate the king and his army. Henry hadn't seen so many soldiers since Dorylaeum. He noted though that there were no sentries, nor any scrutinizing of their incoming group. It was obvious that this army hadn't faced any real opposition.

When he and Cardinal Peter were taken to the German King, Henry was surprised to find that the monarch was five to ten years younger than himself. He had a ready smile and a troop of advisors who followed him around. Henry introduced Peter and himself.

"Henry of Dol?" pondered the King. "I think I've heard that name. Did you serve with Robert of Flanders in the east?"

"Yes," answered Henry.

"Ahha," continued the sovereign as he thrust forth his hand, "you were the third Christian over the wall at Jerusalem! I've talked with Ludolf and Bartholomew of Tournai. Come, have a drink with me and tell me your story. I want to hear every detail." The young monarch turned to one of his assembly of advisors.

"Gerard, hold forth with this fellow." He pointed to Peter. "What was your name again?"

"Cardinal Deacon Peter," replied the bishop.

"Of course," continued the King to Peter. "Find Gerard over there among that riff-raff," the King pointed almost aimlessly toward a group of his men, "and get started on this...this investiture issue. Henry and I will be discussing heroic deeds in heroic times."

Peter and Henry met with Gerard again on the 4th of February in the church of Saint Maria in Rome and then confirmed their agreement five days later at Sutri just outside the city. Henry had been nervous about the negotiations for two reasons. First, it seemed odd to him that an issue that had been broiling for thirty-five years should be seemingly so simple to settle. Peter had reported little resistance to Paschal's proposal and even less scrutiny of the details. Second, it nagged at the knight that King Henry seemed so willing to pay so little attention to the whole thing. He delegated the negotiations entirely to Gerard and, as far as Henry could tell, didn't review the agreement at all. Meanwhile the king's coronation—to be annointed 'Holy Roman Emperor'—was scheduled for noon on the 12th. But on the 11th Gerard communicated to Peter that the King wanted the agreement read at nine bells the next morning so that all his lords and churchmen could hear it.

As the bell tolled nine, Henry assessed the crowd. It was large. Pope Paschal stood just in front of him together with most of the College of Cardinals, a number of priests and a few monks. Opposite them stood King Henry with many of his lords and churchmen as well as a great throng of knights and soldiers. It was apparent to Henry, if their agreement wasn't accepted, that there would be little he could do to hold back the King. In his mind he beseeched the Almighty: 'God, please be with us.'

After the ninth gong had echoed away, Bishop Peter twisted toward one of the monks behind him and nodded. It was Brother John whom Henry knew to have once been a Cluniac monk. The little man stepped smartly forward, stopped, glanced back to Cardinal Peter and, having received a second nod, pulled a parchment from his robe, cleared his throat and began.

"Pope Paschal, servant of God to his beloved son Henry and his successors forever: It is decreed by divine law that priests should busy themselves with secular cases, or should go to the public court only to rescue the condemned or for the sake of others who suffer injury. In portions of your kingdom, bishops and abbots are so occupied by secular cares that they are compelled assiduously to frequent the court and to perform military service. Which things are scarcely, if at all, carried on without plunder, sacrilege, and arson. Ministers of the alter are made ministers of the king's court in that they receive cities, duchies, margravates, monies and other things which belong to the service of the king. Whence comes also the custom, intolerable to the Church, that elected bishops should not receive consecration unless they had first been invested through the hand of the king."

At this point in John's reading, a murmur began to rise among the lords and churchmen on the king's side of the basilica. Its resonance grew very quickly. Despairing at the interruption, Brother John stopped his reading.

"No! No! No!" the King yelled out as he leapt forward. His face was bright red and contorted by rage, his hands gesticulated wildly in the air, his voice strident and shrill. "You can't do this. Don't you understand that these lords...their fathers the original inheritors received their lands from my line in perpetuity and swore their loyalty to give knight's service, to adjudicate in the courts, to protect their people! You cannot separate these functions. How will I defend the realm if you take away my soldiers? No! The 'regalia' as you call it cannot be split up into pieces. You cannot have those you like and not the others. Do you think I'm a fool!"

With his eyes glowering rage, the German King advanced toward Paschal.

Henry stepped forward so he stood shoulder to shoulder beside the Pope.

Seeming not to have noticed, the King kept coming. But his knights and soldiers had noticed. Intending to protect their lord, they too rushed forward. The King stopped directly in front of Paschal. "You old fool..."

But Henry interrupted the monarch's tirade by insinuating his shoulder slightly between the two.

King Henry seemed surprised by this physical intercession but he didn't cease his harangue against the Pope. "I've spent a year coming here for my crown old man and I'll not let you spoil my day. We'll do the coronation right now! Do you hear me?"

"I cannot," issued Paschal in the voice of a church mouse.

"You what?" screamed the King.

"I cannot until you cease laying your hands upon God's disciples," answered the Pope in a slightly firmer tone.

The King turned away. "Round them all up," he yelled. "Take them to our camp to...to learn some reason."

The King turned back not to Paschal but to Henry. "I apologize to you sir." The monarch's voice had dropped three octaves and he was smiling. "You have been a brave man on pilgrimage and again today when you interceded here. I must of course take you too but I promise you all good treatment and will consider any requests you may have for yourself or any of this group."

"Thank you," Henry nodded as he wondered at the monarch's ability to quell his anger so quickly.

~**~

For a large army, camp life in Italy was exactly the same as camp life in Outremere. Each man had to devote most of his time to foraging for food. There was rarely any shelter which, in February and March, meant being cold and often wet. Disease was rampant. Nearby food supplies—cattle, chickens, eggs, vegetables, grain, feed, and hay—were consumed in two days or less, which meant the army had to relocate constantly. Henry wondered how the peasants from whom this food was taken survived, but after thinking about it, he concluded that many of them probably didn't.

True to his word, the King treated Henry's charges—Pope Paschal, sixteen bishops and thirty-some others—better than his soldiers in that they weren't required to forage. The problem was that most of them were old and totally unused to living out in the open. Their dislike for outdoor life was also indelibly compounded by the fact that soldiers shit and pissed wherever the urge hit them. Many of Henry's wards complained bitterly about their proximity to such defecations but nothing was done to stop it.

To help keep up Paschal's spirits Henry played chess with him. For a few weeks the game and the comradery that accompanied it seemed to have a positive effect. But as time passed, it became clear to Henry that the Pope was failing. The man anguished constantly over his administrative flock: those held captive, those in Rome and those in greater Christendom.

Also he mentioned that his contest with the King over investiture was only aiding Maginulf the anti-pope.

When a monk named David died horribly after eating a mushroom, Paschal cried and, with tears running down his cheeks, told Henry that the monk's death was a sign from God. Paschal then called forth the King and announced his capitulation.

HUMAN WEAKNESS
March 1112

Alone Paschal sat in his tiny office. One tiny candle flickered...and it was nearly out.

"Today I conceded to the majority of the College—the 'Reformers.' I swore my belief in God and His course as laid out in recent years by Gregory and Urban, that we must strive for celibacy in our priesthood, eliminate simony from tainting church appointments and allow investiture to be only put forth on behalf of a churchman by a churchman. And I revoked my evil privilege by which I'd granted Emperor Henry the right to invest churchmen, a deed that again puts that divisive issue front and center.

"When I became Pope, I was just like them, pushing for power: power over kings, power over other churches, power over dissenters. Urban stirred up trouble for the Emperor in Saxony. I did the same thing when I encouraged his son to revolt against his father. I even gave the son forgiveness for breaking his oath of allegiance. Just recently I rebuked Emperor Alexius of the Greek Church who extended a feeler to see if we might be willing to investigate possible ways to bring our churches closer. I repeated our usual 'clap-trap' about our church's 'primacy.' How arrogant! Has God put us here on earth to amass power...or save souls?

"I'm weak to let them bully me back into chasing power instead of saving souls. I tell myself I've compromised. After all, with compromise we can get half of what we want instead of none. On the other hand, perhaps I've just made my life easier. I won't excommunicate the German King though! That's what they'll want me to do next. He'd just make another anti-pope and split the Church further apart.

"The Pope's supposed to be God's representative on earth, not God Himself. Each of us is human, capable of making mistakes. I've made bad appointments, worse than some of Henry's. What makes us believe that we're so perfect? We play politics in Henry's lands to force him to accept our terms. But while we're pursuing that improbable goal, how many souls have we saved? So much time wasted! Our list of reforms has turned into 'dogma'—a theoretical logic carrying us toward a theoretical end...but with hardly a soul saved along the way!"

LIFE IS A PRISM
THROUGH WHICH WE PASS IN ORDER TO DIE
April 1112 – July 1112

Henry sat at the table within the tiny patch of light his candle cast. Beyond the pale glow, the room was entirely black. When he had realized no one ever used this mustering room, he had taken it for his office. There he mostly wrote letters, took naps and thought. His notebooks, chess game and *Aeneid* resided in a large, locked wooden box beneath the table that had his name branded onto its top. At the moment he was crafting a letter to his mother, a task he performed devotedly every third month. This month, he was updating her on Walter's progress at the Lyceum and asking questions about Henry and Bernard.

The knock on the door startled him. He jumped up bumping the table and wobbling the candle. The taper's glow seemed to roll for a moment as if it were in a ship at sea. With quill still in hand, Henry steadied the candle holder. "Who is it?"

"It's me," wheezed Bart's voice, "with two letters my lord."

"Come in," rasped the knight.

The door creaked and a second taper's light entered the room. Immediately Henry's candle fluttered again, caused perhaps by air the opening door pressed across the tiny table.

"It is you," growled Henry. "For a moment I wasn't sure. How long have you had that wheeze?"

"Oh," replied Bart, "I get that when I hurry up stairs."

Henry exhaled. "The letters?"

Bart raised his right hand and reached forth two envelopes.

The top letter bore the seal of Flanders. Henry immediately felt guilty for not yet having gone to visit his friend and mentor, Count Robert. He'd promised he would but hadn't yet gotten around to it. He clasped the envelope, broke Robert's seal and pulled forth the enclosed parchment. At the bottom it was signed by Clem.

'Dear Henry, Count Robert died in combat fighting the Conqueror's son Henry, who reneged on a debt he owed Robert. My husband held you in high esteem Henry. I wanted you to know. Clemantine.'

Henry crumpled the paper in his hand. He'd intended to call on Robert to thank him for his knight's school, his leadership training and the trust he'd shown when he appointed such a young knight to be his coordinator. Robert had never been self-promoting like so many of the others. He was a serious pilgrim bent on keeping open the path to Jerusalem for others. Similar Henry thought, to the line of crosses Taticius' engineers set into the ground every mile along their way to show future pilgrims the route to salvation.

The second envelope was sealed with the sign of Dol, once Henry's father's but now his brother Edmond's. A chip of the wax seal had broken off but not a big enough peice to cast any doubt on who the letter was from. Henry passed his finger beneath the seal and broke it.

'Dear Henry, Our mother has passed into God's hands...'

Henry sank back into his chair. Audrey dead? That couldn't be. He was in the midst of writing to her, planning his trip with Walter back to Dol. Then with tears filling his eyes, he slumped forward onto the wooden table. He remembered his last conversation with his mother, her promise to look after Henry and Bernard if he'd bring Walter back to Dol every two years. He'd promised he would. That was just after Angeline died, almost four years ago. "Damn!" He pounded his fist on the table making the candle light flicker again. "Damn, damn, damn!"

"My lord?" queried Bart.

Henry's shoulders jerked up. His sergeant's words had startled him. "Bart, I'm sorry. My mother has died."

"Lady Audrey?" Bart effused. "I'm so sorry, my lord."

"So am I," Henry murmured. "So am I."

The next evening Henry made his usual stop at the Castel Saint Angelo's kitchen where he returned yesterday's wicker basket and picked up today's, which was filled with potatoes, a cooked chicken, and two loaves of paynedemain bread. For only three it was a large meal but Walter was growing fast and had a ravenous appetite. At Roberta's rental after hands were washed and grace spoken, there wasn't much conversation until the food was eaten. Henry then asked Walter if he had anything to report from the Lyceum, to which the boy answered that he did not. Usually Henry pressed this question a second time, but on this occasion he simply sent the boy home to practice his recitals of the multiplication tables. After the door had closed behind his son, Henry twisted in his chair so he could see his consort. Before he spoke he cleared his throat.

"Roberta, we must talk."

Catching her paramour's tone, the 'Magistra' settled back into her chair. "What must we talk about?" she asked.

"I received a letter yesterday from Edmond. My mother has passed into heaven."

"I'm sorry Henry. I know she was a fine person. Is there anything I can do?"

"Perhaps," replied the knight, "but first let's discuss our relationship. We respect one another, we sleep together and we oversee Walter's up-bringing. Yet we have not spoken of marriage and we avoid having children. Is this what you want?"

"If it weren't, I wouldn't do it," replied Roberta in an edged tone.

For a moment Henry waited to see if she intended to add any more. Finally he continued. "You have nothing more to add or ask?"

"Look," she rejoined in a tone which clearly did not leave room for disa-greement, "I've seen how a marriage can wear out, how one person can abuse another as age, injury or sickness comes; how the death of one can put the other into an unmanageable situation; how children can die and, in doing so, ruin both their parents' lives. Our relationship is a good one but it can sour at any moment. And if it does, I can send you to your rental and go on with my life without undue pain or bother. That's why I don't want any children. I'm happy to teach Walter but I want to be able to walk away at any time it pleases me."

Henry stared at his partner. He'd never realized how rational their relationship was, each using the other without commitment, sel-fishly...equally selfishly!

"I shall be going to Dol for Audrey's service. It will probably make sense for me to bring Henry, they call him 'Bishop' now, back to Rome and, if Joan won't continue to oversee Bernard, I'll have to bring him back too. Does that work for you?"

"I'll be happy to oversee Bishop but Bernard is too young. Bishop is ready to be taught. Bernard is still a child."

Henry sighed. "Would it work if I hired a woman to watch over him?"

"No," answered Roberta, "It becomes too complicated, the two older children or none."

~**~

In late June Henry, Bart and Walter returned from Dol with Henry's second son Bishop. He wasn't quite six yet but Henry was certain that Roberta had agreed to oversee him and also accept him into the Lyceum as a new student. This was important as he'd be leaving for Jerusalem almost immediately. Paschal had delayed the departure of a Legate's trip by a month so Henry could attend Audrey's funeral. Henry knew it was a kindness not bestowed on anyone. But he and the Pope had a good relationship, one which Walter had recently enhanced when he'd talked with the Pope on the subject of values. After the discourse, Paschal announced that he was very impressed with the boy's 'gravitas.' Many of the Papal Curia thought Paschal to be a vacillating and inconsistent pope. But Henry thought him to be a deep thinker who, more often than not, preferred compromise as an approach that would avoid conflict.

King Baldwin had written to Pope Paschal requesting legates be sent to Jerusalem to determine whether the Knights of Saint John were worthy of receiving the protection of Saint Peter, a designation that would elevate them to the level of monks and canons. Henry disliked Baldwin but more importantly, he disliked his title. Godfrey, and to a lesser extent Raymond, had turned down the title 'king' not wanting to offend Christ whom they saw as Jerusalem's real King. Godfrey had taken the title 'Advocate of the Holy Sepulchre.' Baldwin however, had himself crowned 'King.' Cardinal Bishop Peter Pierleone would be the official Legate whose recommendation back to the Pope would most likely become the official answer to the request.

On the first day of July, the legation departed Rome for Bari where a Pisan ship was to meet them. There were six men riding out: Cardinal Bishop Peter, his batman, a Benedictine monk named Osbert who would act as scribe, Henry and two recently hired guards. The latter, George and Randulf of Chalon, had ridden with Abbot Hugh of Cluny for many years. Henry had been with them on one of Hugh's sojourns and trusted them. The honored Abbot who had reached his nineties, had died three years before which had put the two younger brothers from Chalon out of work. When they came to Rome and found out that Henry was 'Captain' of

Paschal's guard, they quickly looked him up. Thinking of the upcoming mission to Outremere, Henry hired them. Each was a pious Christian, quiet and loyal.

The ride to Bari, the sail to Jaffa and the short hop to Jerusalem went perfectly. There wasn't a single stormy day, the winds were favorable and no unknown ships came into view. Cardinal Peter, Osbert and Henry met Baldwin in the Tower of David. As Henry entered the immense castle, he recalled his negotiations with Iftikhar, his trips to Ascalon with Ali and later with Iftikhar's son Nur.

Baldwin looked much the same: black hair, dark eyes, a set jaw and no smile. He did however have a short-cropped beard sprinkled with gray hair that was new. Nevertheless Henry suspected the subject of the day would quickly turn to what the Pope could do for Baldwin.

As their meeting was an official one, Cardinal Peter wore his crimson robe and white conical hat. Henry thought his friend probably wanted to make the point that Baldwin was meeting with God's appointed represent-tative.

Standing just behind the King was a pudgy older man who was dressed even more splendidly than the Cardinal. He wore a white robe adorned with gold filigree all along its front and a white conical hat exactly like Peter's but with gold sequins on its sides. The fellow looked familiar but Henry couldn't quite place him.

As Peter's threesome stopped directly in front of the King, the white-robed man with all the filigree stepped forward. "Welcome, your Honor, I am the Patriarch of this most holy city. My Christian name is Arnulf of Chocques. Am I correct that you are Cardinal Deacon Peter Pierleone of Cosma e Damiano whom our blessed Pope Paschal has sent to hear our request for official recognition of our devoted Knights of Saint John as monks of the Benedictine order?"

"Cardinal Bishop," Peter corrected. "Pope Paschal has..."

"My lord," interrupted Arnulf, "let me introduce you to our King." The Patriarch swung an arm toward Baldwin. "This is King Baldwin, King of all the Christian east, conqueror of all the Muslim hordes and most just ruler of this land."

Baldwin took a step forward and dipped his head slightly to Peter. "Cardinal Bishop Peter, welcome. Let us be seated." The King pointed to a nearby table upon which was laid out a large map. There were four chairs, two on each side of the table.

Immediately Henry knew that Baldwin intended to expel him from the meeting.

Arnulf pointed Peter and Osbert toward the chairs nearest them.

In a more commanding voice, Baldwin then conveyed more specific directions. "You won't need your guard here in the Tower of David."

Peter turned to face the King. "My lord, I'm certain that you have this tower well protected and that I shall be safe within it. But I have grown accustomed to Henry's presence," Peter glanced at his guard, "and I wish him to remain within this room during our discussion. I'm certain that will suit you, will it not?"

Baldwin's expression never changed. "Certainly," he answered.

Henry took up a spot nearby and stood there for several hours.

Using the map, Baldwin gave a detailed presentation of his kingdom's four regions: Edessa, Antioch, Tripoli and Jerusalem; identified the fractious Muslim elements that had been 'harrying him'; explained his defensive weaknesses and finally summed up everything quite succinctly. "If Christianity is to exist for long here in Outremere, we shall need a great many more knights and soldiers sent to us from the west."

Peter nodded his head. "Thank you, your majesty." The Bishop then turned to the Patriarch. "Arnulf, do you have time to take us around the city this afternoon? I have not been here before and want to visit the holy places before we leave."

"My time is entirely yours," responded the Patriarch, "but we have a lunch prepared. May we eat first?"

~**~

Hoping to meet some old friends, Henry spent some time wandering through the hospital. Almost immediately he met a man coming the other way who looked familiar. "Hugh!"

It was Hugh de Payens, the knight he'd met long ago in Antioch when he'd gone to ask Bishop Adhemar to hear his confession.

"Henry!" called out his erstwhile compatriot, "how good to see you. Are you living here now?"

"No," answered Henry. "I'm with a legation that will be here only a week or two at most. How about you?"

"Oh," answered Hugh, "I've been here for several years. But I'm thinking of going home to visit my family in Troyes."

"I've found going home sometimes doesn't meet my expectations," commented Henry as he swung an arm in the direction of the low stone wall.

Hugh sat down. "I don't think I'll stay there long. It seems I can't put down real roots anywhere."

Henry sat down beside his friend. He and Hugh had connected well years before when they didn't even know each other. He expected they would connect again.

"What have you been doing here?" Henry asked.

"Well," replied Hugh, "I'd been feeling as if I needed to do something constructive, something for others. So I've gotten a few knights together to watch over the pilgrims who come here from Jaffa. There's a great deal of brigandage here, pilgrims being robbed and murdered all the time. We try to protect the road, sounds like a small enough task, but it isn't."

"Really!" said Henry with real spirit in his voice. "What a good idea! But how do you feed yourselves and your horses?"

"You probably know this already Henry but it is very different here than back home. Here there are marauders all the time, sometimes one or two, sometimes hundreds. A lot are locals but some come all the way from Egypt or Damascus just to plunder Christian pilgrims. And here there are so few knights that brigands are safe practically everywhere."

"But," interjected Henry, "you've got a band of knights?"

"Only a handful," responded Hugh. "It would take several hundred to provide real protection here and they'd have to be really dedicated, dedicated like a monk, willing to give up home and family."

"A lot of us did that on our way to Jerusalem".

"A lot of our men were prideful, greedy and blood-thirsty too," Hugh reproached.

"You're right," answered Henry. "I wonder if it's possible to be a monk and a knight?"

"Are you acquainted with the word 'malicide?" asked Hugh.

"A bad death?" asked Henry who'd tried to untie the meaning of the word through its Latin roots.

"No," said Hugh. "It refers to killing a 'bad person'. The Church forgave us for killing Muslims because they fought against Christ and therefore were bad people."

"So," jumped in Henry, "a knight could be a monk if he were only killing bad people...but would he have to avoid other sins too? Always tell the truth? Not steal? Be chaste?"

"I don't know," answered Hugh.

"Greed would be hard for some knights too," Henry added, "but stealing, lying and swearing, those would be fairly easy. The oath for a Benedictine monk obligates a man to obedience, poverty and chastity."

"Well," said Hugh, "I'm certainly poor and I've learned to obey. I wouldn't have survived all the way to Jerusalem if I hadn't followed orders. That just leaves chastity."

"You know," Henry said cheerfully, "we couldn't get every knight with chastity in our oath but I think we could get quite a few."

"That gets us back to your earlier question," said Hugh, "the one about how we would feed ourselves and our mounts."

"Yes," responded Henry, "but if we were doing God's work protecting pilgrims, great lords might donate to our cause and thus improve their chance to get into heaven."

The two ebullient knights talked on till dusk when Henry realized Bishop Peter might be looking for him.

"I must go Hugh," said the Papal guard, "but please tell me how to reach you should we want to talk again."

Hugh answered quickly. "At Troyes, twenty-some miles southeast of Paris or here through the hospital."

That night at dinner, Henry's mind was still alight with the concept of a monk-knight, so alight that he brought up the discussion he and Hugh had had with Cardinal Peter.

"That's interesting," said the Legate. "It's almost the same discussion that Osbert and I had with Baldwin although Baldwin's was from the perspective of his need for soldiers to defend his realm while yours seems to have been more focused on the meshing of potentially conflicting attributes within a man, whether he could be a monk and still a knight. That's the same central question in our review of these Knights of Saint John. Did you and Hugh reach a conclusion?"

"Not exactly," answered Henry. "We remembered that many of our knights going to Jerusalem were bloodthirsty, greedy and unchaste."

"That is true with any large group," interrupted Peter, "but were there not still many who were true to God's dictates?"

"Yes," Henry answered, "but it is very difficult not to sin when you are constantly under the pressure of combat; deciding who to kill and who not to, often without sleep or food, making instant decisions without a moment to think."

"I'm sure that's true," whispered Peter, "but I think you're the kind of man who would hold to his values, stick to God's directives if he possibly could."

"I killed a woman in Antioch," interrupted Henry. "I didn't mean to but she came at me from behind."

"Then you didn't do it on purpose. If you were twenty feet above the ground building a cathedral wall and putting a wet rock into place when it slipped through your fingers and fell on some person below, I'm sure you'd blame yourself but I don't believe God would blame you. Monks after all are sinners too. They fight temptation but on occasion can be overcome by arrogance, greed, lust and many other things. A Godly man is he who tries his best...not one who never sins. No human being never sins. I'm inclined to think some knights could be monks. The trick would be in figuring out which ones."

Peter changed his tone. "Now I have something else to ask you. But first I must put forth a disclaimer. I didn't ask for your opinion of Baldwin before I met him because, as a Legate, I wanted not to prejudice my meeting with him. But now that I have met him, I'd like to hear what you have to say about him and the Patriarch too."

Henry smiled. "First, let me thank you for not dismissing me from the room, which was clearly what Baldwin wanted and second, I wish to compliment you on not letting him treat you like a lackey."

This time Peter smiled. "Thank you."

"As to Baldwin," Henry continued, "everything he does is to benefit himself. I'll share one story that was told to me first by Tancred, God rest his soul, a man with weaknesses but one whom I never knew to lie. Before we got to Antioch, Baldwin split off from the main group and went east looking for a principality he could take for himself. Along the way he acquired an Armenian guide, a man named Bagrat, who eventually led him to Edessa. Bagrat made the mistake of bringing his lovely young wife with him. Not too much later, Baldwin accused Bagrat of treason and had him beheaded. The wife was saved... in Baldwin's tent. I've heard two other men tell that same story and, if you wish, I can tell you a dozen more just like it."

"No," said Peter, "one's enough. But what do you know of this Arnulf fellow, the Patriarch?"

"Oh," replied Henry, "Arnulf is an interesting fellow. He came on the great pilgrimage as Robert of Normandy's chaplain. He'd been a teacher at the Cathedral school in Caen and tutored the Conqueror's daughter, Cecilia. The Normans used to sing ditties about his activities with women. According to those songs, he was an aggressive 'wencher.' He is bright, politically astute and he speaks well. Before I left He was the Patriarch but still subject to the Pope's confirmation. Just before I left, a fellow named Daimbert, an Archbishop from Pisa, came as the Pope's designated replacement and Arnulf was out. Obviously though, he's back."

"Apparently," added Peter. "He's actually been Patriarch three different times which certainly speaks to his political acumen. Do you think you could introduce me to your friend Hugh de Payens?"

HENRY'S NOTEBOOKS
March 1117 – March 1118

Henry was sitting on an elegant bed in one of Robert of Capua's castles near Naples. He, the Pope and His Emminence's entire retinue had again been driven out of Rome. The German Emperor was pressing for repudiation of the synods of 1112 and 1116 in which Paschal had formally reneged on his promise to grant the Emperor the right of investiture. The Emperor's Saxon vassals were again calling for him to reach a settlement with the Pontiff. Frustrated, the German king had finally decided to descend on Rome again. Accordingly the Papal entourage had left the city in the middle of the night with Henry only having enough time to get his things from his mustering room and say goodbye to his sons at Roberta's.

So the chief Papal Guard was now reading his notebooks looking for answers. The castle was just a little east of Naples, so their ride south had been about hundred miles. Along the way, Henry's mind kept nagging him about what was changing. There was the obvious: Countess Matilda had died in 1115 and her lands were sequestered by her cousin, Emperor Henry. That eliminated the buffer between Rome and the Emperor. Consequently, whenever the Emperor was south of the Alps, he could descend on Rome with only a moment's notice. This meant Henry had to have the entire Curia ready to ride on very short notice and simultaneously be able to avoid Ptolemy of Tusculum on their way south. But there was more. The Fideles, who like himself were committed to help the Pope when called upon, seemed to be slipping away. A lot, like Matilda and Abbot Hugh, had died. But it wasn't that they were dying as much as they weren't being kept close, cultivated and communicated with. And there was less clarity too. Investiture was a prime example. It had changed from being a sin only six years ago, to being a granted privilege and, most recently, to being both permissible and sinful at the same time. Henry had even heard Paschal utter words of ambivalence on the subject.

While these three things—the rising threat from the Emperor, the diminution of the Fideles and an increasing lack of clarity – were taking the Church into rough waters, Henry was trying to figure out why these changes were occurring. He hoped he could find the answer in his notebooks. When studied in detail, these books helped him see where things were headed and why. After considerable study, he'd found five mainline subjects.

The first was the staple list of Gregorian reforms: simony, celibacy, loss of church property to laymen, consanguineous marriages, the truce of God, indulgences and lay investiture. Many of these were being accomplished on a fairly broad front. Investiture though was still being contested with the German Emperor. As Henry reviewed his list of the Church's most fundamental priorities and the comments members of the Curia were making, to his surprise he discovered an outlier: 'saving souls.' It was a simple term fundamental to the Church's purpose. He couldn't remember ever hearing the phrase spoken in his first few years in Rome. But now it was ubiquitous. He heard it most from the newer members and often pronounced in an almost wistful manner as if speaking of a wonderful person who'd recently died. It was defined by both the new and old members in exactly the same way: each priest's and cardinal's duty was to help save people's souls. What was different, though, was that the older churchmen seemed to take for granted that it was still going on while the newer members thought of it as something lost. This discovery caused Henry to recall remarks that Paschal and Bernard had uttered shortly after Paschal had divided Bernard's Spanish 'see' into two parts by which the province of Braga became a new apostolic subdivision under a newly appointed Cardinal, Maurice of Braga. Paschal's comment was that the division of the see would allow the bishopric 'to stay close to its flock and thus save more souls.' Bernard's remark directed at the new Archbishop, had been less complimentary. 'He dresses well and talks of saving souls.'

The second of Henry's baseline topics was the Roman families. There were at least fifteen noble families in the city who lived mostly off papal patronage: receipt of city offices, roles within the city's churches, dealing with litigants and petitioners, overseeing courts, policing the streets, collecting tolls, and distributing the Pope's 'beneficia' and 'presbiteria.' There were old families, the Crescenti and Tusculani, and newer families like the Pierleoni, Frangipane, Colonna, and Corsi.

For years Petrus Pierleone had dominated Paschal's patronage. And he was currently rumored to be in line to become the city's next head prefect. This had caused dissention on the part of the Frangipane family who apparently felt they deserved a more equal share of the spoils. Many of the families had outside ties to either the Normans in the south or the Emperor in the north. This last factor sometimes moderated discord but could also exacerbate it. Henry wondered whether the Frangipane family might be realigning itself toward the Emperor. If so, that would place them against Petrus Pierleone who was closely tied to Roger of Sicily. This would upset the balance of power in the city and also account for the Emperor's recent interest in entering the city too...as well as why the factional fighting had recently grown so strong.

The third baseline was the growing factionalization within the Cardinalate. By Henry's count, the college contained five cardinal bishops, nineteen cardinal priests and twelve cardinal deacons. The number grew and shrank as popes made additions and death made subtractions. The older were, almost without exception, in the 'reform' camp. These included John of Tusculum, Leo of Ostia, Bruno of Segni, Guido of Vienne, Josceran of Lyons, Adalbert of Mainz, and Cuno of Palistrina. These men were outspoken in their beliefs and hardly ever shrank back when called on to share their opinions. The newer and younger, tended to be quieter, were more likely to be from north of Rome and were often difficult to get definitive opinions from. A great number of these inscrutable members had been personally picked out for promotion by Paschal himself. The Pope's opinion was increasingly the key determiner for an appointee. Just in the short time Henry had been the Captain of the Guard, it was apparent that voting within the Cardinalate had become almost perfunctory. The members seemed more and more to see their role not as debaters but as facilitators. Accordingly the only vote that really revealed a member's position on anything was when a new Pope was elected. The Aristotelian form of proactive debate, which Henry had been taught by Benito, was less and less practiced. Henry thought at least part of the reason for this silencing of personal beliefs was due to there being anti-popes. Being too open with opinions could narrow one's opportunities.

Henry's fourth baseline issue stemmed from the location of Rome and therefore the Church, being between two powerful, political and military personalities—the German monarch in the north and the Norman suzerain in the south. Emperor Henry and Count Roger each maintained some degree of hegemony over Rome and the Church. The Emperor laid claim by means of his predecessors having been crowned Holy Roman Emperors, Roger by means of his willingness to protect the Pope, a point not long on credibility but fertilized nevertheless by occasional calls from the Papacy. Whatever the theory, each man was a loadstone whose iron magnetically pulled or pushed Rome and the Church. Conversely, factions in both the city and the Church often reached out to one or the other of these powerful men calling on them for help. Trying to twist the Emperor's arm regarding investiture, Pope Urban had stirred up the Emperor's Saxon vassals. Similarly members of the Cardinalate had sought a tighter relationship with Roger hoping it might diminish the Emperor's incursions into Rome.

The last of Henry's baselines was the most difficult to discern. Over time his notebooks had shown which of the Cardinalate to be suspicious of, even which of the clerks, scribes and lesser workers to watch, but the inscrutable category was growing and he wasn't sure why. Perhaps it was simply that he wasn't as perceptive as he had been in his youth. Perhaps it was because he was seen as a reformer, a Fidelis, and therefore people didn't want to offend him by sharing contrary beliefs.

However, there was an oddity that he'd noted in his conversations with several new members of the college. They tended not to respond when he brought up the topic of medicine. In his youth when riding with Abbot Hugh, every topic relating to new ideas, topics, or subjects was received like green grass by a horse. With Hugh, Henry had long discussions about illnesses, injuries, rashes, symptoms and cures. Similarly other new subjects were eagerly picked up as well: geometry, astronomy, horoscopes, castle building, engineering of catapults and even interpreting the meaning of natural events. But with these inscrutable Cardinals, it was as if they weren't interested, didn't care or hadn't any intellectual curiosity. In one case, Henry had referenced insights Abraham had shared about insuring business ventures by means of shared ownership with others and thus diversifying risk. To his surprise the Cardinal Priest with whom he was speaking responded quite dismissively. 'Christ will shun them.'

~**~

January 21st was a clear, chilly day in Rome. Henry was doing his best to keep Paschal's death a secret. Without dissent the Cardinals had set the 24th for their election of a successor. Henry hoped the secret could be kept and an undisputed election would pass the purple robe on without chaos. Waiting had been intolerable but when the meeting was finally convened in the church of Saint Maria in Pallara, the Captain of the Guard was pleased to see the hands of nearly the entire assembly rise in approval of Cardinal Deacon John of Gaeta. John had been the Chancellor and primary advisor to Paschal writing the Treaty of Ponte Mammolo and taking the Pope's confession before he died. The two men were very similar: each cautious, each a believer in compromise and each aware of his own human frailties. As the votes were counted, Henry wondered if 'Gelasius,' John's chosen new name as Pope, would stand up to the Emperor over investiture. In normal situations Henry thought the new Pope would stand tall, under real pressure though, he was less certain.

But just as that thought passed through Henry's mind, the front door of Saint Maria's church smashed open and, sword in hand, Censius Frangipane burst in. Henry immediately drew his sword and stepped forward to place himself between the Pope elect and his antagonist. For several moments Henry and the oldest Frangipane brother faced each other with perhaps five feet of open space between them. During that time the church filled with Frangipane 'soldiers.' Simultaneously, Cencius' two brothers, Leo and Robert, stepped up on each side of their brother. All had swords drawn.

Henry assessed his opponents. Cencius was the oldest, the biggest and the leader. His face was flushed almost red and it showed signs of dampness, probably sweat. His reputation was that of a bully, not a coward, but like most bullies usually an aggressor against a smaller or less able opponent. Henry judged the man might attempt to browbeat but only attack if he had first riled himself into a fit of irrationality. Leo stood on Cencius' right and slightly behind him. His eyes were furtive, never directly meeting Henry's gaze. He was a schemer not a leader, a man who preferred to instigate, to inveigle but not to personally act. His first step would be back. The youngest son, Robert, stood on Cencius' left with his left hand just touching his sword at the tip of its blade. His eyes were calculating and fixed coldly on Henry. This one was a threat. Henry knew behind him were five veterans—Bart, Archard, Rotran, George and Randolf—who would die if need be in order to defend each other and the Pope. There were too many Frangipane soldiers for them to fight successfully but they could certainly cut a broad swarth before they fell.

Henry cleared his throat and looking squarely at Cencius Frangipane, spoke in as gravel a tone as he possibly could. "Have you come to kiss

Gelasius' ring?"

In a tone that betrayed relief, Cencius responded. "Put down your weapons and we will let you live."

Still employing his gravel tone, Henry responded. "Cencius, if you or any of your men move toward us, I promise that you and your two brothers will be the first to die."

"But you will die too," responded the bully.

"Probably," replied the knight, "but each of us who is a Papal guard has already received God's promise of eternal glory in heaven for our participation in the great pilgrimage. Do you expect similar forgiveness for accosting God's Pope in this holy place?"

Cencius dropped his gaze.

"Henry," it was Gelasius' voice, "sheath your sword. There are too many of them."

Henry's heart sank. The Frangipane leader had been in the process of losing his nerve. "Your Eminence," Henry answered without taking his eyes off the three brothers he faced, "are you certain?"

"Yes." John's voice was frail and weak.

"My lord," responded Henry, "we shall do so but only after that one," he pointed his left hand toward the youngest Frangipane brother, "has sheathed his sword first." Henry then turned his gaze back upon the oldest Frangipane.

Seeing an opportunity suddenly bloom amidst horrible risks, Cencius turned upon his youngest brother. "Robert, sheath your sword."

As a moment or two passed, it became clear to everyone that Robert really wanted to kill Henry.

"Robert," growled Cencius again.

The youngest Frangipane then looked around at all the men gathered in the church: Henry's guards, his own two brothers, the Frangipane soldiers, the Cardinals and then at Henry. Finally his lips separated, his teeth showed and with his smile complete, he sheathed his sword with a sweeping flourish.

~**~

It had been dark outside for quite a while but for some reason, Henry had not been able to fall asleep. Gelasius was back, rescued from the

Frangipane family by Petrus Pierleone. It always amazed Henry how many people there were in Rome who knew so much more about what was going on than he did. And he spent all his time at it. Then he heard a horse's hooves coming fast down his little street. He was at the door before the rider knocked.

"The Emperor has again entered the city," gushed Bart. "The other guards are bringing Gelasius here."

"Good," responded Henry. "To this house or Roberta's?"

"This house," answered Henry's sergeant.

"Good," repeated Henry. "We won't tell Roberta and the children. It will take too much time. Let your horse go. We'll be walking from here."

"Walking?" queried Bart in obvious disbelief.

"Yes," answered Henry as he turned for his clothes. He quickly put on his mail shirt, boots, belt and sword; grabbed his kit bag, dropped in a loaf of bread, his chess game and some quarrels for his cross bow and finally placed his helmet on his head and his shield on his left shoulder. He'd just started for the door when he remembered something important and trotted to the rental's back door and ran his fingers along its casement. Years before, he'd chiseled into that very piece of wood the knocking code for Martin's shop, a good thing since he'd long since forgotten it. On his way back to the front door, he picked up his crossbow, a weapon he had wanted ever since watching Godfrey use his so effectively in Jerusalem.

At Martin's shop Henry tapped the correct sequence on the door and quickly prayed for God's help. It had been years since he had set up this escape route. He should have checked with Martin every once in a while to be certain that nothing had changed. Behind Henry with the five guards stood Pope Gelasius, a small man wrapped in a black robe. The only aspect of him Henry could see was his face. In the darkness, even that was heavily shadowed. A moment or two passed and Henry began to fear that Martin wasn't in his shop. But suddenly on the other side of the door, a dead bolt clunked and the door's hinges squeaked.

"Speak my name," bid a voice from within the tiny haberdasher's shop.

"Martin," Henry whispered as loudly as he dared.

The door opened slowly.

"Be very quiet," continued the voice, "no lights and no unnecessary talking. Is one of you Henry?"

"I am," whispered the knight who was standing directly in front of the speaker.

"Oh, I couldn't make you out in the dark. I'm Martin. Now form a single line and each of you take hold of the person in front of you... Good...now follow me. Remember...absolute quiet."

The line wove through the shop, out a back door and through alleys and yards for what seemed like a very long time. During their march, it stopped raining but there was still a heavy mist which caused Henry to shiver. Eventually their line entered some sort of stable. Henry couldn't see much of it but he could smell hay and hear the animals occasionally move in their stalls.

Martin stopped. "Gabriel, are you here?"

"Yes," responded a new voice from somewhere in the dark.

"Can you have two carts ready for seven to Gaeta first thing in the morning?"

"Yes," replied Gabriel's voice from a different location than before, "it will be tight but seven should just fit."

"Each of you," whispered Martin in a slightly louder tenor, "will be put into a barrel. They are wide enough to be reasonably comfortable. In them are some blankets to cushion butts and elbows. There are two carts with four barrels each. On the back of the second cart, one of the barrels is filled with merchandise. Don't try to get in that one. It will be used to fool anyone who might wish to verify our load. Your ride tomorrow will be long and uncomfortable. You must not make any kind of noise. Don't talk, whisper, sigh or fart. We shall be going right through public places. As long as you don't give yourselves away, it is the best possible means of escape. There will be two breaks, each in a barn where no one can see you. We shall give you water there. You won't like this ride but it will get you out of Rome safely."

A SECRET LEGATE
1119 - 1122

After completing their barrel ride out of Rome, they took ship to Gaeta. The new Pope had been Cardinal Deacon at Saint Maria's and was still held in high regard there. Of course Gelasius' hope was to return to Rome as soon as possible in order to take up his duties at the Church's principal administrative seat. In March, the Emperor ordained a second anti-Pope, Maurice Archbishop of Braga in Spain. Henry couldn't help recalling Bernard's comment about Maurice: 'He dresses well and talks of saving souls.'

Once the Emperor had created his second schism, he left Rome and crossed back over the Alps undoubtedly planning to tell his factious vassals that he had the support and blessing of the Pope. Henry doubted that such duplicity would get him very far. His leaving however freed up Rome for Gelasius to reinhabit. Sadly though, that didn't happen. Cencius Frangipane and his brothers who'd become henchmen of the Emperor, had enough power in the city to make it dangerous for Gelasius. Accordingly, Henry led the vagabond Pope and his Curia on to Cluny where the knight knew a sincere welcome and safe stay would be offered.

But by the time they arrived at Cluny, it was clear to everyone that Gelasius was mortally ill. His symptoms were loss of weight, lack of energy, bleeding from several ugly, greenish-black sores and considerable pain. Henry administered some white powder from a small packet Abraham had given him. The merchant had said it was from the east and would dull pain if administered in small doses. It did help but was used up several days before the Pope died. Nevertheless while the powder held out, Gelasius was able to make some decisions. Since he knew he was dying, he sent for Bishop Cuno of Palistrina, hoping to talk his friend into accepting the Church's highest office. But Cuno declined and instead recommended Guido of Vienne 'due to his prudent mind and his secular virtues.' On February 2nd at Cluny with the agreement of the Curia, Guido of Vienne was selected to succeed Gelasius with the pseudonym 'Calixtus.' The new pope was of noble birth, had always been a staunch Gregorian reformer and was unlikely to be a Pope whom the Emperor could intimidate. Since Cluny had no ties to noble Roman families, no Emperors, no southern Normans and no apparent rifts in the Curia, the election went smoothly. Henry believed Calixtus was a good choice.

With the successor Pope elected and on safe ground far from Rome, four of Henry's guards—Archard, Rotran, George and Randulf—approached their supervisor.

Archard took the lead. "Henry, we have enjoyed our service with you. You rescued us when we were penniless and offered us an honorable way to earn silver enough to purchase fiefs when we get home. Long ago you told us we could leave but we stayed on because of the risk to the Pope and to you. Now things appear to be in hand, so we would like to take our leave and go home. We thank you."

"It is I who should be thanking you," replied the Captain of the Guard. "Each of you has been loyal and keen. I have never served with better knights."

So these four men parted with good cheer in their hearts and coin in their purses.

The next day, Henry met with Calixtus to report the guard situation. After Calixtus had heard Henry's introduction, he interrupted. "Henry, this is very good timing. I have other plans for you and Bart. I've received information that suggests the Emperor wishes to resume negotiations in regard to 'investiture'. Our past negations have failed. I believe the Emperor has not sufficiently involved himself in regard to details. You've been there Henry, do you think that's the problem?"

"Absolutely," replied the knight. "The Emperor delegates the entire process. If we could get him directly involved, we'd have a much better chance of success."

"I think so to," murmured the Pontif. "He respects you Henry... If I send you there, just you and Bart, do you think you could come up with a process which would involve the Emperor in the details enough to give our effort a chance to succeed?"

~**~

On November 19th, Henry set out with Bart to meet the Emperor. The sky was stuffed with scudding grey clouds, the wind was whipping icy granules of snow against his face and the cold numbed his fingers and toes. Whenever Henry came upon a barn, castle or peasant shack, he would call a halt and the two knights with their mounts would press their way into the dwelling to avail themselves of whatever heat there might be. Will-power was the primary thing which got them to the Emperor's castle.

~**~

"Henry," called out the German monarch, "how good to see you. What's this? Your face is blue. Come over here by the fire. You too, Bart. Take off your coats and wrappings. Sit right up close," he pointed to the fire. "God-win, bring more logs. We need to warm our visitors. Constance, bring mulled mead and be quick. It won't do to have my friends freezing in my castle!"

And so the unofficial visit with the Emperor started very pleasantly: mulled mead, fresh venison and blessed heat. By evening everyone was mellow and warm again.

"So, Henry, have you come in this awful weather to see me or are you passing through for some other reason?"

Henry cleared his throat. "Your Highness, Pope Calixtus has asked me to visit you...unofficially, to talk of possible settlement of the issues that currently plague both his Church and your monarchy."

The Emperor raised his hand interrupting Henry's explanation. "Con-stance, please take Bart on a tour of the castle. Show him whatever he wants to see." The King then turned to the remaining men in the great-room. "Perhaps you could turn in a little early tonight. Henry and I have to talk."

The room quickly emptied leaving only Henry and the Emperor remaining within the circle of dancing firelight.

"Now Henry, please continue."

"My lord," began the third man over the wall of Jerusalem, "Pope Calixtus believes an accord between his Church and your monarchy would serve both by allowing each of us to stop hobbling the other. It would allow us to address and hopefully settle, the myriad of other pressing issues we face. He is hoping that you and I might talk, just the two of us, and perhaps make some progress toward an agreement."

"Well," replied the Emperor, "that is a noble goal but I thought that's what we tried to do last time. I had pleasant talks with William of Cham-peaux and thought we'd reached an agreement. Then I got that written gobbledlygook all in Latin which, when my scribes translated it, wasn't what William and I had agreed to. I think at times the Pope in Rome thinks we don't have anyone here who can read Latin. Can you read Latin?"

Since the Emperor's voice had risen revealing his irritation, Henry wondered how to answer without further angering him. At last he gave up and just answered. "I can but that's why Calixtus sent me, so I could be certain that what you agreed to is what the parchment says."

For a moment, the Emperor just stared at Henry. "You are sincere?"

"I am," replied the knight as he nodded affirmatively.

"All right, I shall trust you, but don't say one thing and mean another and be completely candid with me as I will be with you. Are we agreed?"

"We are," responded Henry. "How would you like to proceed?"

"Let's start by sharing our objectives, our challenges and our points of view on this issue of the laying on of hands, 'investiture' as you call it."

"All right," said Henry, "which of us would you like to go first?"

"You," answered the Emperor with a thin smile on his face.

Henry twisted slightly in his chair. The fire light caught the Emperor's head so that the right side of his face was almost orange and the left heavily shaded. For a moment Henry wondered what that might portend. "The primary goal of the Church is to save men's souls. We attempt to encourage good behavior and discourage bad. To do this, we must have priests, bishops and monks who devote themselves to following Christ's teachings, a very heavy burden. Accordingly we expect them, our men and women, to give themselves over to God by swearing vows of chastity, poverty and obedience. They must do their best to avoid the lures of sexual intercourse, self-will, wealth and power. Each churchman must do his best to save every member of his congregation just as a sheepherder watches over his flock. To do this we must have priests and bishops who are chosen for their sincerity and ability, not for simonical greed. Investiture conveyed by a layman disconnects God's hand from this process."

"That is all very interesting," responded the Emperor, "but those men are my liegemen whose fiefs they hold from my hand. They owe me fielty and I expect them to perform their courtly duties and serve their annual military obligation or pay the difference. If I stop putting my hands upon their shoulders when they receive their appointment, how long will it be before they have forgotten whose land they administer and what their obligations are to me?"

"You have a point," responded Henry, "but we've not yet listed our challenges."

"Ah," nodded the Emperor, "please continue with the Church's challenges."

"Well," said Henry, "since the Church's purpose is to save men's souls, the Pope is disconcerted when an anti-pope is created. That act lessens his time for useful effort and diverts him to having to make a case to Churchmen everywhere just to validate himself as Pope. It also bestirs various noble Roman families to take sides in order to benefit themselves."

"You know, Henry, I didn't tell this to William of Champeaux but I've already promised the priests and lords in my kingdom that I shall renounce the anti-pope and recognize Calixtus. So your Pope could have ended this period of being disconnected long ago if he'd only kept to the agreement that William promised."

Henry stared at the monarch. "You mean all those things were agreed to and we still couldn't get it done?"

"Yes," answered the Emperor in an exasperated tone. "Now let me share my objectives and challenges. I think I've already explained my position on investiture."

Henry nodded.

"As king, my purpose is to keep my kingdom intact, to defend it and expand it some when possible. I owe my liegemen my support just as they owe me theirs. My challenges come largely from the disrespect some of them show me. Many of the Saxon lords wish to create a kingdom of their own, a separate entity. Oh, they talk of unity but in their hearts they long for a justified rebellion. Also the Magyars are a constant threat. They nibble at my eastern border and seek to attack me when I'm busy elsewhere. And of course there's the Church. In Metz, Munster, Merseburg, Wildesheim, Osnabruck, Liege and Magdeburg they've demanded a series of canonical elections and rejected my investing of them. This is what I mean about disloyalty. They've forgotten who granted them the privilege of using the land, whose land it really is. Mine, Henry...my land!"

For quite a while neither man spoke.

Finally Henry broke the silence. "It seems clear to me that both Church and kingdom have today made a strong case for compromise."

"Perhaps," responded the Emperor, "but I'm now again negotiating with the Saxons. When that falls through which it assuredly will, I'll send a messenger to bring you back. Perhaps then we can get this done. But you must stay for Christmas Henry. The weather's awful for traveling. By the way, you play chess don't you?"

Henry didn't return to Cluny until January and then he found that the Pope and Curia had left for Rome. This concerned him because he doubted that the Pope had hired enough guards to protect him from the Frangipane family. When he finally got to Rome in April, he was even more startled to discover that the Pope's new guards were none other than Cencius Frangipane's men. When he asked Calixtus how this could have happened, the Pope explained that the Emperor had diminished his support of the anti-pope so much that the Frangipanes had reached out to the Church, promising that if Calixtus would accept their guards, they would drop their support of the anti-pope and open Rome to 'the true' Pope. Henry understood the politics but doubted the long-term merits of the decision.

Thus having checked in with the Pope, Henry went directly to Roberta's place hoping to find all three of his sons. Both Bishop and Bernard joyfully ran up to him and bowed. Henry threw out his arms and the two boys rushed forward again but this time into a giant hug. Each of the young men had grown tremendously. Bishop's face showed signs of whiskers. When the three person hug ended, Roberta took her turn. Then missing his oldest son Henry asked, "Is Walter not here?"

In a slightly querulous tenor, the mistress of the family responded. "Walter has gone to Barcelona. He completed his courses in medicine at the Lyceum last fall and graduated. But he still wanted to learn more, so together we discussed several places he could go for more advanced study— Paris, Constantinople, Alexandria and Barcelona. He told me that he'd heard you say that Bishop Bernard thought Barcelona was the most advanced city in the civilized world, not only in medicine but also in many other disciplines. We have not yet received a letter from him so we don't know if he's settled in there yet with new Masters."

Henry remembered Roberta's positive statements about the expansive medical knowledge held by a number of Masters in Barcelona. He also recalled the glowing comments Bishop Bernard had proffered long ago, the ones Roberta had just referred to, about the magnificence and modernity of the city and how the Arabs, Jews and Christians get along together there, making the city a wonderful place in which to learn.

"Well," the knight finally responded, "I wish I'd been here to share in the discussion but Barcelona is certainly a seat of learning. We shall look forward to receiving a letter from Walter in order to learn how he is doing." Then looking directly at Roberta, he continued. "Thank you for helping him make his choice and for teaching him so well. How are these two doing at the Lyceum?"

"Oh very well," replied Roberta now with a smile on her face. "Bishop has advanced into the upper level and is concentrating on law and Bernard is about to choose his subject of priority in the upper school which he should enter next year. He is extremely precocious."

Not long after he arrived in Rome, Henry received a letter from Hugh de Payens in Jerusalem. The news was bad. In one fell swoop, three hundred Christian pilgrims had been slaughtered on the banks of the Jordan River. The murderers were apparently a band of Muslim raiders from either Egypt or Damascus. Hugh bemoaned at length the insufficiency of his tiny group of knights who were attempting to protect the very road these pilgrims had been traversing. He did have some good news. His band of knights had picked their self-defining values—chastity, poverty and obedience. And they were now reciting these values at least weekly to the new Patriarch in Jerusalem, Garmond of Picquigny. Hugh ended his letter with a rousing comment. 'For the first time since the great pilgrimage, I feel that I am truly serving others.'

In January, Bishop completed his advanced studies in law at Rome's Lyceum. Father and son, together with Roberta, discussed various next steps. They finally settled on Henry's recommendation, which was to seek an internship in Genoa with Abraham and Ezekial as a legal acolyte. Given that Henry had already been discussing the possibility with Abraham, the arrangement came together very quickly and Bishop was off to Genoa.

~**~

In September a terrible epidemic swept through Rome. Young Bernard, Roberta and Henry all fell ill. Before he physically succumbed, Henry set out cups and a bucket of water but the illness came on him so quickly, he could do no more. He tried to identify his symptoms but all he could recall was disgorging all his stomach's contents and then having a horrible fever. He thought he shivered and sweated profusely, but he wasn't really certain since his brain was racked by delusionary fits interspersed with wild dreams. He lost all sense of time leaving him with no idea whether his illness had lasted for a day or a week. All he was sure of was that he was sicker than he had ever been in his entire life...deathly sick.

When his fever finally broke, he became vaguely aware of Bart giving him sips of water. Eventually he mustered up enough energy to ask the question. "The others?"

Bart nodded positively. "You must rest. We'll talk tomorrow."

Immediately Henry's eyes closed and he fell into a deep, nurturing sleep.

The next morning when he woke, he realized he was still lying on the floor. Weakly he sat up. Then Bart, whom he hadn't noticed, clasped his arm and moved him to a chair.

"The others?"

"Both Bernard and Roberta have died!"

~**~

Only a few days later, Calixtus received a letter from a priest named Beno in Saxony that stated there had been a conclave in Wurzburg from late September through mid-October in which the rebellious Saxon nobles had presented their Emperor an ultimatum: 'The Emperor shall obey the Pope in the complaint which the Church has against him. A settlement shall be made!' With the letter still in his hand, Calixtus called Henry into his office and announced that he would immediately dispatch his Head Guard to meet with the Emperor together with Bishops Lambert of Ostia, Gregory of Saint Angelo and Cardinal Priest Saxo of Saint Stefano. Just before the legates departed, Calixtus convened the group and, to the Churchmens' surprise, told them that he wanted the issue settled. He then went on to share that Henry had been working with the Emperor and would therefore have the final say in the negotiations.

Lambert and Saxo accepted the Pope's direction without comment. Gregory however was far less tactful.

"If Henry is going to make the important decisions," the bishop huffed, "why send us?"

Calixtus was equally blunt. "Gregory, if you won't support Henry's decisions, I don't want you to go. Do I make myself clear?"

There was a long pause before Gregory finally responded. "I

understand our charge and I shall bend to Henry's will."

"Good," said Calixtus. "May God be with you."

The actual negotiations took place for more than a week. Henry established a process by which each morning the Emperor would hear the topic of the day and put forth his comments and opinions. The legates and imperial advisors would then retreat and prepare a draft that would be taken back to the Emperor for review. Henry was careful not to appear to be telling the monarch what should, or should not, be modified until they were alone together. He also made a point to always ask the three legates for their opinions before he set a course. Give and take took place in steady steps. The Emperor renounced investiture with ring and staff and conceded canonical elections. After considerable discussion with his three bishops, Henry agreed that the election of bishops and abbots could take place in the presence of the Emperor at the imperial court as long as no simony or violence occurred. Also the monarch could confer the regalia with a touch and receive the homage of the elected prelate at the same time.

At the end of this process, all the identified details had been addressed and agreed upon. Henry knew that he'd given up some points that the legates would not have but most of those points had to do with the moment when the priest and Emperor were together, a place bound to be three to six weeks distant from Rome. Accordingly Henry thought he'd given up what the Church couldn't really control.

On the 23rd of September, the Papal Legates and the Emperor signed the agreement. The monarch seemed nervous that he might have given away more than he should have, but he was clearly pleased with the process and understood exactly what he'd agreed to. Two of the three official Papal Legates signed willingly. Gregory glared at Henry before touching quill to parchment. Nevertheless, Henry felt he'd done what Calixtus wanted...as well as performed a significant role for others.

THE SELFISH AND THE SELFLESS
September 1122 – January 1125

"**H**enry," beamed Calixtus, "in this effort you have been the hand of God. A wonderful outcome! Thank you, thank you, thank you."

The knight was very appreciative of the Pope's effusive praise. He did wish though that Calixtus had delivered it privately instead of in front of Lambert, Gregory and Saxo. Nevertheless, the issue of investiture had now been settled in England, France and Germany, which meant the Church could go back to saving souls.

In his euphoria, Calixtus increased Henry's stipend and promoted him to 'legatus natus', a rather vague title but one which Calixtus obviously intended to be a great honor. Thereafter since he was no longer overseeing the Pope's personal guard, Henry's actual duties diminished to escorting papal legates, various specific missions and performing occasional courier duty. Calixtus made it clear though that he wanted Henry available for negotiations with lay lords who, like the Emperor, might relate better to a peer than a bishop. Accordingly Henry spent most of his time 'standing by.'

To fill his time, he continued to record his meetings with various bishops, church officials and visitors, which turned his notebooks into a sort of personal diary...and he continued to reread his notes out of habit. One day while doing this, he noticed that almost all of Calixtus' appointments of new bishops followed immediately after one of his meetings with Cardinal Haimeric! Haimeric was an officious fellow from Saint Maria Nuova whom Calixtus had recently appointed to the College of Cardinals and only two years later promoted to Chancellor of the Curia. At first Henry had thought him to be a very earnest church mouse whose opinions almost always adhered to Henry's own beliefs. But with this discovery, Henry changed his mind.

The epidemic that had taken Henry's lover and youngest son had also swept through the ranks of the Curia, taking in a very short time fully sixteen cardinals and, according to Bishop Bernard, almost all the most able. With this in mind, Henry searched further to see whether these newly appointed cardinals had any consistencies worthy of note. He found they did. Without exception they all tended to be young, often from one of the new orders, Cistercian or Augustinian, favored compromise in regard to the old Gregorian reform platform, were from northern Italy or France and preferred the German Emperor over Roger of Sicily.

During Calixtus' tenure, the political positions of the Bishops had become increasingly hidden. Votes were hardly ever taken. Instead the issuance of 'fiats' was employed. When the Pope expressed in a meeting that agreement had been reached, a bishop would call out 'fiat' and all the others present would then call out 'fiat' as well. This method of reaching agreement built harmony but obfuscated dissent. Over time it made it practically impossible to determine individual bishop's positions. Were it not for Henry's notebooks and his laborious review of them over a long period of time, he would not have noticed these consistencies among the newer Curia appointees. But of course the notebooks had been created for the very purpose of exposing otherwise obscure opinions, activities or plots.

Henry's obvious conclusion was that Haimeric was steering Calixtus toward men who held certain beliefs. Henry already knew there were two factions existent in the Curia: 'The Pierleone,' which supported Gregorian reforms, tended to be older, were usually from south of Rome, had matriculated through Cluny and favored the Sicilian Normans as opposed to the German Emperor; and the 'Frangipane,' which included many of the replacement bishops, tended not to hold the Gregorian reforms very high and prioritized 'saving souls.' Henry wasn't certain exactly how Haimeric's spoon would stir the pot. But of the two existing factions, Haimeric's choices appeared to align more closely with the Frangipane faction. But, due to the prevalence of 'fiats', Henry could only identify with certainty the positions of about two thirds of the Curia. Henry's notebooks also raised the possibility that a third faction might exist, which might presage a greater likelihood of trouble electing a Pope!

~**~

Calixtus died on December 13th. For the knight from Dol, this was a sad occasion. Calixtus had valued him highly and always treated him with great respect. The Pope's passing had another impact as well. Because Henry's role as 'legatus natus' was uniquely attached to Calixtus, it was no longer clear to many in the College of Cardinals whether Henry still held an official

role within the Curia or not. This doubt immediately diminished his relationship with a number of his long-standing associates. They were still
polite but not forthcoming. Only Bernard treated him in exactly the same
way he always had. But this didn't help much because Bernard had never
truly shared information in its deepest sense. Instead the Bishop tended to
talk with Henry in a very focused manner, often asking a question but not
explaining why he asked. Henry had grown used to this, but he found it
frustrating when on the day after Calixtus died, Bernard showed up in his
office and asked him to 'keep an eye on' Cardinal Theobald of Saint
Anastasia.

"Should I become his fulltime bodyguard?"

"No, no," responded Bernard. "I don't want anyone to know you're
watching him. Just make a point of being where you can see him, so you
can help him if he needs it. But be subtle!"

"Just during the day?" responded the knight, "and what if he goes next
door to the Monastery of Saint Pancratius? Should I follow him?"

"Henry," rejoined the Bishop, "just do your best to keep him near without anyone noticing. Just do the best you can."

"It might make it easier," replied the knight, "if you told me why I'm to
do this."

"I can't tell you," answered Bernard, "but it's very important."

So on the 15th, the knight trailed Bishop Theobald around as surreptitiously as he knew how. During this distant escort service, Henry considered what was probably occurring. The process of choosing a new pope
must have begun, at least informally, and Bernard knew that Theobald was
a candidate, probably of the Pierleone faction. And if Bernard wanted
Theobald protected, he must fear contention from the Frangipanes. Henry
concluded he should also keep his eyes open for any signs of them.

When the day passed uneventfully and Theobald finally retired into the
Lateran complex where most of the cardinals ate and slept, Henry and Bart
took up their shields and headed for Henry's rental. Dusk had fallen and
dark shadows permeated the narrow streets and alleys.

"They'll wait for three days," Henry said, "then convene..."

Thwack...THUMP!

"I'm hit," croaked Bart as he stumbled.

Henry knew the sound of a crossbow releasing its bolt and instantly
elevated his shield.

Thwack...THUMP, THUMP.

He felt his shield take two bolts. Three shooters! Drawing his sword, the knight instinctively charged the dark alley ahead from which he'd heard the crossbows release their quarrels. As he rushed into the shadows, he focused on the shadowed objects forming ahead of him. There were several but it didn't matter. He had to attack or be killed from afar and he had to protect Bart. The nearest figure was bent over his crossbow re-cocking it. Henry thrust his sword viciously into the man's side and instantly withdrew his blade. A second shadow was raising his bow but he was too late. While knocking the crossbow askew with his shield, Henry buried his sword almost to the hilt in the man's chest. As he did, he felt his shield take a sword's blow from his left. It was an untrained blow that Henry knew had left the wielder exposed. He lifted his shield and paid forth another thrust which immediately yielded a piercing screech. Henry knew the villain would be dead before the scream ended. As he continued his pivot, Henry saw two more adversaries each with his shield up prepared for close combat. For only an instant Henry allowed his eyes to glance toward Bart. His sergeant, back to a wall, was combating a single foe.

With powerful self control, Henry moved his eyes back onto the two men in front of him. His adversaries were clearly trained. Each was stepping away from the other intending to expose Henry's back to one or the other of them. Knowing it would leave him with a delayed thrust from the second man, Henry charged the man on his right. The soldier parried Henry's sword with his shield but in so doing, couldn't keep Henry's full weight from crushing him back against the wall of the building behind him. For a moment the two men were so pressed together that neither could bring his blade into action. But Henry had planned for this and wickedly brought up his sword's pommel into the man's face in the meanest way possible. Blood gushed from the enemy's left eye.

As Henry saw this, he felt a blade penetrate his mail shirt on his left side. He winced with pain but, still in control, pivoted to his left bringing his shield around against this foe. As Henry's screen made contact, he felt the backstabber's blade exit his side with a searing slice. He knew his shield would quickly pass across his enemy's front and then expose the man to his blade, which was already sweeping forward with deadly intent. As his shield cleared, Henry saw his adversary's sword rising to intercept his blow.

Quickly Henry adjusted his thrust in order to target the man's shield arm. Henry felt his blade penetrate just below the shoulder. A high-pitched screech reverberated off the alley's walls. Henry pulled his sword free and immediately aligned it for a final thrust, but just at that moment he felt a wincing pain in his side. He gasped for air; he knew this spasm wasn't from a fresh attack but rather from the way he'd turned. He lowered his arm and the pain lessened slightly. In the moment he'd stayed his thrust, his opponent twisted away. Henry took a deep breath and gritted his teeth to blot out the agony. In this moment the two remaining assailants began to run away. Knowing he couldn't catch them, the knight hobbled toward his sergeant. As he went, he thanked God and then with considerable anguish, reached his left hand over his right shoulder and touched Reynauld's cross. "Thank you my friend."

Bart was slumped back against a building. His helmet was pointing up so Henry knew he was still alive. With help from several of his neighbors, Henry got his sergeant to Castel Saint Angelo. There they laid him down on a table. Henry immediately dispatched his helpers for bandages, boiling water and additional torches. Even without more light, Henry could see that his life-long friend was dying. The crossbow bolt had entered his left upper chest and was causing Bart to bleed from his mouth. Henry quickly dispatched a castellan to seek out Bishop Bernard, or any other churchman to come immediately to hear Bart's confession and give him absolution.

Lowering his lips to his friend's left ear, Henry whispered. "We've certainly gotten into a mess this time. I've got bandages coming for you and a priest just in case."

Bart couldn't speak but he moved his head slightly to acknowledge Henry's words. His eyes and Henry's locked together.

"When the bandages get here," continued Henry, "I'll take the quarrel out and see if we can stop the bleeding in your throat."

Almost imperceptibly Bart shook his head sideways.

Henry felt tears welling up in his eyes and moved his head so they wouldn't drip onto Bart's face.

With a gurgle Bart murmured. "Y...ou?"

Henry barely heard his friend but nevertheless grasped the meaning. "I have a sword wound in my side but, God willing, I shall live. Can I do anything for you?"

Again Bart moved his head sideways.

Wiping the tears from his eyes Henry spoke again. "Bart, you have been a loyal and able sergeant to me just as my father said you would be. Thank you."

Bart's face twisted into a semblance of a smile...and he died.

When Henry's helpers returned with cloth and hot water, the knight set to work cleaning and bandaging his own wound. He couldn't see it but he was quite sure that no organs or arteries had been cut. He then implored God to accept Bart into Heaven and immediately fell asleep.

~**~

"Henry, I just heard. What happened?"

Henry was deep in sleep and only vaguely recognized Bishop Bernard's voice. When he opened his eyes, the first thing he saw was Bart's body across the room still on the table. It took him a moment to get his bearings—Bart dead, himself wounded, the middle of the night and Bernard waking him up. Unwittingly the knight twisted to rise but his wound emitted a poignant, piercing pain and he lay back.

"Are you all right?" stammered the bishop who, despite his earlier gush of questions, seemed to have just noticed Henry's condition.

"I am recuperating," murmured the knight.

"I'm so sorry," continued Bernard. "I didn't know you'd been wounded."

Henry delayed his response until his pain lessened.

"Bart and I were attacked by six men who clearly meant to kill us. They had three crossbows and hit Bart from close range before we even saw them... I'm not certain who they were but if I were to guess, I'd say Robert Frangipane... Of the two who survived, I wounded one in his left arm just below the shoulder... As to why, you may know better than I."

"What... what do you mean?" asked the Bishop in a quavering voice.

"I mean," replied Henry quite sternly, "that Calixtus is dead and the papal succession is underway... The Frangipanes have previously shown a willingness to kill for it and you only yesterday appointed me to watch over Bishop Theobald... I don't believe in coincidences."

"Oh," whispered Bernard as if to himself, "I never dreamed it would come to this. I'm so sorry Henry. I should have realized there might be danger for you."

"Thank you," replied Henry, "but it is Bart you should apologize to."

Bernard glanced at Bart's body on the adjacent table. For a moment the bishop's face wrinkled up and then he wiped a tear from his right eye. "Oh Henry, I'm so sorry. I should have thought more clearly. I don't know what to say."

"You need say nothing more," replied the knight. "It is not you who killed Bart... But please keep me apprised of upcoming papal events and, if you see the man with the left shoulder wound, please give me his name."

"I will," responded Bernard. "The events as you call them, will begin this morning. We hope to get Theobald voted in but of course nothing is certain...and I will do my very best to find out who murdered Bart, the man with the wounded left arm. I'll have every member of the Church looking for him Henry. I promise."

Henry slept the rest of the night and most of the day... In the afternoon a clerk named Stephan, whom Henry'd befriended years before, brought him mead and some roasted chicken legs.

Bernard returned well after dark. "Henry, it was Robert Frangipane. But let me tell you of this wicked family's sins today. Unconscionable, Henry, unconscionable!" Bernard's face flushed red with anger. "The Curia gathered this morning in the monastery of Saint Pancratius to consider possible choices to replace Calixtus. After thoughtful discussion, Jonathan of Cosma e Damiano nominated Theobald whom we all voted for. It was unanimous, 'unanimitas,' the sign of God's will. Theobald had taken up the purple mantle as 'Celestine,' and we were actually singing the 'Te Deum' when Robert Frangipane burst in with his soldiers. He with his left shoulder bandaged, harangued, bullied and threatened us with sword in hand until Theobald finally resigned his papacy. But that wasn't the end of it. Next Robert forced us to elect Lambert of Ostia, which after many tears and great wailing, we finally did. So now Lambert is 'Honorius' and the Frangipanes control the Papacy. I can't begin to tell you how horrible it was. Some of us plan to meet tomorrow but I fear we have already conceded the Papacy to those ungodly devils. Henry, I apologize for not staying longer but I must run in order to plan for tomorrow."

By the morning of the 17th, one day before his birthday, Henry was feeling so much better that he asked Stephan for bacon and eggs.

"Henry," it was Bishop Bernard looking even older and more tired, "Bishop Peter of Porto and I have tried to do over the election. Robert

Frangipane and his soldiers weren't there so we thought we had a chance but we didn't. Lambert wouldn't renege. I made the mistake of telling the whole Curia that Robert Frangipane had killed Bart and wounded you but that didn't seem to matter to Lambert. He claimed no knowledge of the deed and simply said that he was now Pope and wouldn't resign after God had placed him in the seat. And the impact of my telling them that it was Robert who was the killer had the opposite effect of what I expected. Instead of raising their indignation, I think it simply intimidated them more."

The following morning, Henry thought his wound had passed the point of risk to septicemia. He thanked God and, since it was his forty-fourth birthday, promised to rededicate his life to 'others.'

Moments later, Bernard appeared with yet more news. "Henry, you won't believe this, but last night Leo Frangipane and Bishop Haimeric bribed Peter Leonis by giving him the city of Terracina and the castle of Formello! Can you believe it! Now, Honorius' papacy is without doubt."

"You said Leo and Haimeric?" asked Henry.

"I did," replied Bernard. "Can you believe it?"

"Yes," replyed Henry. "I believe I can."

Several days later when Henry had begun to get around some, he made a point of visiting the new Pope. Of course he'd known him as 'Lambert of Ostia.' They had been on several legations together, the most notable to Worms to consummate the investiture agreement with the Emperor. Henry was certain that Honorius hadn't known anything about Robert Frangipane's plans to kill Bart and himself. Lambert had always been a good Christian, a man without an evil bone in his body. Henry simply wanted to wish the new Pope well and take his leave. During the knight's recuperation, he'd spent a lot of time thinking, particularly after he'd heard that Bishop Haimeric had helped Leo Frangipane negotiate Petrus Pierleone's bribe that sealed Honorius' position as Pope. The 'me-firsters' as Henry called them, the Frangipanes and now Haimeric, had finally taken over. He doubted that Haimeric had prior knowledge of Robert Frangipane's intentions to kill him and Bart, but the Chancellor had certainly known about the Frangipane's actions before he joined Leo's bribery initiative.

Henry also used his days of recuperation recalling his regression with Kay Mora when he and Angeline had gone to Vannes: how he had spent his prior life enmeshed in ungodly activities, killing and plundering innocent people. He wasn't going to repeat that selfish life again. He was going to commit himself to 'others' and join Hugh de Payens in Jerusalem – chastity, poverty and obedience with the single goal of protecting pilgrims!

~**~

"Henry, have you heard about Bernard?" It was James, one of the young clerks who worked with the bishop.

"No," answered the knight. "What about him?"

"He has a great pain in his chest!" gushed the neophyte. "He's in Saint Pancratius' chapel."

"Take me to him," commanded the knight.

"Ah Henry," croaked Bernard, "I'd hoped Jammie would find you in time." The bishop was sitting in a wooden pew. His once black hair had grayed and thinned, the sparkle in his eyes had waned and the zest in his voice was now merely a throaty rumble.

"What are your symptoms?" queried the erstwhile medic as he knelt before his long time friend.

Before he answered, Bernard carefully breathed in some air. "It's passed right now…" he whispered. "It's a great contraction in my chest… It will take me next time Henry but I want to give you my confession."

"But I'm not a priest."

Bernard weakly raised his left hand signaling Henry to cease his interruption. "I am Angeline's father…and your sons' grandfather… I wish I'd told her. May God forgive me. I wish I'd told her." Suddenly the bishop gasped for air…then his forehead furrowed and his eye lids fluttered.

Henry caught Bernard's body as it tipped forward. "She knew," he whispered. "I'm sure she knew."

SECTION III

OTHERS

A FRESH START
January 1125 – April 1125

Henry made a list of the things he needed to do before he left for Jerusalem. Item one was to write a letter to each of his sons. He had not yet received a letter from Walter in Spain. But the School of Medicine in Cordoba was renowned and surely would pass along a letter to one of its students. Coincidentally, Honorius would soon be sending a courier to Toledo to notify the 'see' of Bishop Bernard's death and ask for suggestions regarding his replacement. Henry had heard that Honorius already had someone in mind, but the politics of such important choices always created an opportunity to recognize a number of people before finally resolving the 'difficult' choice.

In any case, Henry thought the courier could get his letter to Toledo and from there the Church would have reliable connections with Cordoba. Henry made a point of giving Walter the hospice of Saint John in Jerusalem as his address. He also invited Walter to visit him and stoked that fire by mentioning at some length the Nestorian medical schools of Nisbus near Edessa and Jundishapur in Persia.

In his letter to his second son, he asked for an update on Bishop's business activities: where his ships sailed, what products they carried and whether internecine piracy among the Italian cities was still going on. He also mentioned his intent to join Hugh de Payens protecting the Jaffa road. As with his first letter, he proffered his new address and encouraged a visit should his son sail abroad. At the end he asked Bishop to give his best to Abraham, Ezekial and Rachel. This letter, being to Genoa, could easily be added to the packet of any Church courier bound for France, Flanders, Normandy, Brittany or England.

Henry's second item was to write to his brother Edmond. Thinking it possible that he might never see his family in Dol again, he thanked his brother for taking on their fief and thanked Joan profusely for her help raising his children. At the end he asked one favor, that each Christmas they stand beneath the cross in the family chapel and pray for the souls of Angeline, Audrey, Walter, William and young Bernard.

The final item on Henry's list was to personally part with those in

Rome whom he'd worked with for so many years. Of course quite a few had died: Calixtus, Gelasius, Paschal, Hugh, Brother Bruglio, Bernard, Matilda and even Martin the 'haberdasher.' But there were still many whom he felt he should personally thank for their friendship and help, certainly Bishops Peter Pierleone, Saxo of Saint Stefano, Theobald of Saint Anastasia, Renaud of Reims, Master Aubrey also from Reims, Master Mendichio at the Lyseum, the courier Luigi and of course the clerks, accountants and secretaries with whom Henry had always gotten along very well. The knight offered 'Dominus Vobiscum' many times before he left.

When Henry had completed his farewells, he went to Marco, the bursa's clerk, to collect the retention fee that Bernard had promised each of the guards long ago. Marco was prepared as Henry knew he would be. The young man was bright, helpful and a friend. But when Henry asked for Bart's fee as well as his own, the youth blushed and, after saying that he would need permission, turned and walked toward Honorius' office. Henry thought that odd since Marco reported to Clive, the Curia's bursar who was a mercurial fellow and had never scored highly in Henry's notebooks. Shortly though, Marco returned smiling with a second purse in hand. Henry had been debating whether to give Bart's coins to the hospice in Jerusalem or to a man in Rome he knew who might be willing to exact justice for Bart. However he'd decided that killing Robert Frangipane, no matter how appropriate, wouldn't really serve others. So he left Robert in God's hands.

Unlike his previous trip to Jerusalem, Henry's ship encountered contrary winds, relentless rollers, deep swells and cold rain. Fortunately, they stopped at Limasol, which gave some relief. By the end of March, Jaffa was finally reached. But Henry's luck didn't get much better. Standing in the very same stable where he and Peter Pierleone had hired horses in the past, Henry found neither a horse nor a camel. In the entire building there was just a single, old Arab whose only solace was quintessentially succinct. "You're out of season."

So wearing his chainmail, helmet and belt with sword and carrying his two shields and crossbow, the knight set out upon the road on which the three hundred Christian pilgrims had been slaughtered only a few years before. Henry was quite tired when he finally saw a lone horseman ahead on a tiny hillock. At first he couldn't make out whether the man was Christian or Arab, soldier or traveler. But as he walked on, the fellow kneed his horse toward Henry which allowed him to discern by the man's helmet, crooked nose guard and muscular horse, that he was a Christian soldier... perhaps, Henry thought, even one of Hugh de Payen's knights guarding the road to Jerusalem.

"Good day," said Henry hoping the French he was speaking marked the horseman correctly.

"Good day to you," replied the rider in perfect French. "You're out of season."

"Yes," chuckled Henry. "I was told that in Jaffa."

"You've walked quite a way," continued the horseman. "Put down your equipment and rest for a while then we can figure out how to get all that gear onto this horse with the two of us as well. But don't worry, Balmung has carried similar loads before."

"Wasn't it Sigmund who pulled Balmung from the Branstock tree and slew Fafnir?" asked Henry somewhat tentatively.

"Aye," responded Balmung's rider with a broad smile on his face. "You must be Norman."

"It's been a long time since I've heard Balmung's name. My mother's midwife used to tell me stories about the old Norse gods. She knew them all and I believed her too. But of course I was only four or five then." Henry reached forth his hand. "I'm Henry of Dol."

Leaning forward in his saddle, the erstwhile Norseman clasped Henry's hand. "I'm Goeffrey Bison of Champagne. I ride this road to protect merchants and pilgrims. This time of year though, there's not many of either. Let's get your gear up on Balmung and on our way to the Temple; you can tell me why you're here."

"Most gladly," smiled Henry. "Most gladly."

GOD'S GRACE
April 1125

When their dinner had been consumed, Hugh de Payens cleared his throat. "Henry of Dol is here with us tonight."

Looking at Hugh at the head of the table, Henry noted he had the same modest voice, the same dark hair and the same hooked nose—essentially the same physiognomy that he'd had twenty five years ago when they'd first met...except perhaps for the depth of the lines in his forehead.

"I first met Henry just after we took Antioch when he and I were waiting for Bishop Adhemar to hear our confessions. Henry served throughout the campaign with honor and valor as did all the knights seated here this evening. Today Geoffrey met him walking here from Jaffa with all his worldly possessions on his back. Then they rode here, two knights atop one horse, just as our emblem depicts two poor knights sharing one mount. Henry, would you care to speak?"

"Thank you, Hugh," responded the knight from Dol as he rose to his feet. "I know only a little about your efforts here. Hugh and I have shared some correspondence and met once a few years ago when we talked about values and the oath of obedience, poverty and chastity that you have taken. With so little knowledge, I hope not to offend you when I say that I have come here in hope of helping your troop protect others."

For a moment Henry paused to give way for his rejection should these soldiers not want him. A period of silence followed.

"Thank you for your willingness to hear me. I shall take a moment to fill in what else you may wish to know. Prior to joining our great pilgrimage, I was a second son and had been started toward a place in the Church. I was tutored, sent to the Abbey of Bec, and taught to write and speak Latin. Sadly, my older brother died causing my father to switch me into knight's training at Count Robert of Flanders' school headed by its Master of Warcraft, Reynauld of Flanders. He was one of the bravest knights I ever knew. He died unhorsed outside Antioch. As I'd had the good fortune to learn several languages, Count Robert chose me to be his coordinator. After Ascalon I stayed on with Godfrey but when his brother took the Advocate's position and anointed himself 'king', I decided to go home. Most of my time since then has been spent as a papal guard for Popes Paschal, Gelasius, Calixtus and Honorius. However the rapacious greed of the Roman families and their willingness to do anything to achieve power has caused me to reassess my life's activities. I wish to commit the rest of my life to others. My wife died years ago in childbirth. I have two grown sons and my sergeant was recently killed in Rome. My values are respect, integrity and others. What more would you care to know?"

A few moments passed before Hugh spoke again. "Henry, it seems our troop has heard enough. But please let me share some of our history lest you join us and find we are not what you expected. Most of these knights are related by blood or marriage and come from Champagne. I'd like to formally introduce you to our knights and sergeants."

Hugh stood up and began to point along the table. "This is Godfrey of Saint Omer, this Payen of Montdidier, Archambaud of Saint Agnon, Andre de Montbard, Hugh de Rigauld, Raymond Berenger, Hugh d'Ambroise, Geoffrey Bison with whom you've ridden and our sergeants Rossal and Gondamer. We joined the great pilgrimage under the banner of Count Hugh of Champagne and served variously first with Hugh of Vermandois and after Antioch with Godfrey of Bouillon. Five years ago when we decided to come back here for good, we intended to become Augustinian monks. Their creed, as I'm sure you know, revolves around others, especially the poor and down-trodden. When we got here we took ourselves to King Baldwin...the second, not the first. He dissuaded us from becoming monks and instead implored us to become protectors of the Jaffa road. He believed as knights, God had already molded us into soldiers capable of protecting others. He said we should use our existing skills to protect wayfarers: pilgrims, merchants, rich or poor. But in order to avoid the avarice, whoring and bloodshed often propagated by ordinary knights, he agreed that we should, like monks, commit ourselves to a vow of obedience, poverty and chastity. This said, the King would allow us not only to pray for travelers but to watch over them as well. And if we'd so swear he said, he'd let us use this stable and pay us a monthly stipend that would allow us to do our job but not make us rich. We swore our oath and now years later, we're still here.

"But we still have two problems, nothing to do with our oaths or functions, we need more men and just as important, the coin to train, feed, shelter and oversee them. We don't know how to make those two things happen and neither does King Baldwin."

After Hugh stopped talking, there was a long silence.

"May I offer some thoughts?" asked Henry.

"Of course," responded Hugh.

"You have been here much longer than I, so my ideas you may have already considered and found wanting. If so, please stop me."

The knight cleared his throat. "What I have heard you say is that patrolling the Jaffa road is not the strategic goal. The strategic goal is to protect the Holy Land and thus make it safe for all pilgrims today and forever into the future. If this is so, then our tactical goals must be to raise a quantity of men capable of defending the kingdom and a quantity of coin capable of maintaining them. Several years ago, I think it was at the synod in Benevento, Pope Paschal officially recognized the Hospitallers for their work in their hospice here in Jerusalem. The Pope's sanctification of their order allowed them to request donations from kings, dukes, counts and lesser lords with the assurance that God will smile on the giver of such donations. Thus, sinners can receive a degree of amelioration for their sins. Papal sanctification of our order would allow us to approach the wealthy with similar requests and we would be doing the donor a favor to ask him for some of his coin. Simultaneously we could solicit knights from those same lords: second sons, un-landed knights, even excommunicated knights who seek redemption. But," said Henry quite vociferously, "this all depends on getting sanctification from Honorius. I know him well enough to ask, but we really need our request to bubble up within the Church. That's how most successful sanctifications work. Do any of us have powerful connections within the Church?"

For several moments Henry's question hovered in the candle light above their table.

"I might," declared Andre de Montbard. "Bernard of Clairvaux, one of the leaders in the new Cistercian Order, is my nephew. He's also Hugh's first cousin. I don't know if he'd promote our troop or not, but I'm certain he'd listen to us."

"Thank you Lord!" bellowed Henry at the top of his lungs as he raised his hands in supplication and dropped to his knees. "Thank you Lord!"

Everyone in the room crossed themselves.

Instantly Henry stood back up. "Brothers, this is no coincidence but a true sign of God's grace! How else could we have a bloodline directly to the most vibrant and articulate Churchman of our day. Bernard of Clairvaux is the perfect man to speak for us. Never have I seen God's hand so clearly. We must start right away: a letter to Bernard, a meeting with King Baldwin, a trip to Rome but only after Bernard's sagacious wisdom has had time to percolate. Oh, thank you Lord!"

NEXT STEPS
April 1125

Having sat through the Sunday service at the Holy Sepulchre, Hugh, Andre and Henry were trying, amidst the exiting throng, to catch up with King Baldwin and his entourage.

"My lord," called out Hugh, "may we please have a word with you?"

Obviously intending to see who was calling him, King Baldwin turned. He was dressed in shimmering green satin trousers, a billowing peach-colored shirt and a plump iridescent turban which changed color as he moved.

"Good day Hugh... Henry, is that you!" called out the king as he stepped forward and clasped the Breton's hand. "I haven't seen you since... I can't remember."

"Before Antioch, my lord," the knight responded, "and that was a long time ago. It's good to see you."

"The pleasure is mine," replied King Baldwin as he inclined his head to Hugh and Andre also. Then, as if catching himself, the monarch turned to the woman with whom he'd been walking.

"Rebecca, this is Henry of Dol, a brave knight who rode with us on our pilgrimage to Jerusalem and served as coordinator for Count Robert of Flanders."

The woman was of eastern descent, probably still in her thirties, slim and had long black hair dropping almost to her waist. Her eyes were brown, full of life and penetrating.

"Henry, this is Rebecca," continued the King. "She is my sister-in-law and very insightful in all things, particularly politics."

"My lord is too kind," murmured Rebecca as she swung her gaze back to Henry and bowed slightly.

Henry lowered his head in response. He sensed her obeisance was more for courtesy than anything else but he wasn't sure. There was some-thing about her...

"Do you speak many languages?" she asked.

"I speak several," Henry answered. "Among all our pilgrims, we spoke nineteen different languages."

"What ones do you speak?" asked the King's sister-in-law.

Henry was taken aback. This woman wasn't just reciting pleasantries. She actually wanted to hear the answer to her question. For a moment he looked at her...trying to measure her.

"I speak French and Latin well," he answered, "and am passable in Spanish, English, German, Arabic and Yiddish."

Rebecca smiled. Her teeth were perfectly aligned. "Where did you learn Yiddish?"

"After Jerusalem fell, I took on two Jewish orphans. They taught me Yiddish and I taught them French."

"They were children?" asked Rebecca.

"Yes," answered the knight, "Ezekial was six and Rachel five."

"And what did you do with them?" questioned the woman somewhat forcefully.

"I searched out a Jewish friend of mine in Genoa and he helped me place them in a good Jewish family."

For a long while, Rebecca contemplated Henry's response. "For that act Henry, God will surely reward you." She then looked back at Baldwin.

The King turned to Hugh. "My friend, what may I do for you?"

"Your Highness, Henry's arrival has caused our little group to focus more sharply on our strategic goals. We would like to meet with you at a time convenient to discuss how we can raise more men and coin to support us."

"By all means," replied Baldwin. "No other subject could suit me more. Would tomorrow at the palace be soon enough? Perhaps Terce?"

"We shall be there," responded Hugh, "and thank you."

The King and the sister-in-law continued their trek toward the palace.

"How well do you know this Henry of Dol?" asked Rebecca.

"Not very well," Baldwin answered. Suddenly the King's head snapped around allowing him to lock his eyes on his sister-in-law. "Are you interested in him?"

Changing neither her tone nor looking directly back at the King, Rebecca responded offhandedly. "Perhaps."

"Really?" choked the King, "after just asking him what languages he speaks?"

"We also discussed the two Jewish children." Rebecca still didn't make eye contact with Baldwin. "Do you think he really turned them over to a Jewish family in Genoa?"

"I don't know," replied the King, "but Henry has a reputation as an honest man. Why would you care about that?"

Rebecca finally turned her eyes on King Baldwin. Her glare was unmistakable. "I'm wondering if this man, a Christian knight, might actually be capable of judging people one by one instead of by the group—Arabs, Christians and Jews."

"You're serious?" asked the King.

"Of course. I said perhaps, didn't I!"

"Well," said Baldwin, "I don't want to do all this again if you're not going to go through with it. Do you want me to talk with him?"

"Yes," answered Rebecca as she turned her eyes back to the road.

~**~

The next day right after breakfast, Henry, Hugh and Andre went to the formal entrance of what had been the al-Aqsa Mosque and entered King Baldwin's palace. They were quickly ushered through the large, high-ceilinged 'prayer room' and taken down a hall to a relatively small chamber. In it there was a magnificent, multi-colored Persian rug with numerous pillows scattered across it. Baldwin sat in the middle of the rug and looked quite at ease atop a plump orange pillow with his legs crossed in front of him. Beside the monarch sat a little, officious-looking fellow who was clearly a clerk. The poor man obviously hadn't any experience sitting on pillows.

"Come in, come in," called Baldwin as he signaled the guide who'd brought the trio in, to go. "This is Clarence. He's an able clerk who may take notes or otherwise help us should we need his skills. He's Italian and just arrived from Venice; so new, he can't yet sit on the floor with his legs crossed. Please sit, please sit."

The three knights settled onto cushions near the King with only Henry finding the position uncomfortable.

"Thank you for coming," said Baldwin. "More men and coin! What can I do to help accomplish these lofty goals?" The sovereign's voice rippled with anticipation as he looked at Hugh.

"My lord," responded Hugh, "please let me defer to Henry. He's the one with the good ideas."

Baldwin swung his head toward the knight from Dol.

"My lord," Henry began, "we believe that if we can gain Pope Honorius' sanctification of our poor knights of Christ in a manner similar to Paschal's blessing of the Hospitallers, we can more effectively ask for knights and coin from kings, dukes, counts and lesser lords throughout the west. When we were discussing how to get sanctification I, having been with Paschal, said that the way these things get approved is to have many respected voices 'bubble up' to the Pope and Curia in a manner that shows broad support throughout Christendom. I then asked if, among our committed members, we had any connections within the Church. The answer was so profound that I'm certain God's hand brought it forth. Hugh and Andre are Bernard of Clairvaux's cousin and uncle, Bernard the most revered churchman of our day, a speaker who moves any person he speaks to and a writer who motivates every member of the Church. This bloodline connection is no coincidence. It's a certain sign of God's will in action. Therefore with the certainty of God's support, we wish to do three things: I shall write letters from Hugh to Pope Honorius and Abbott Bernard to explain our mission and ask for their support to achieve sanctification; you my lord, we trust will also write to the Pope and the Abbot expressing our purpose and calling for support; and third we intend to go to Rome next year after the bubbles from our letters and yours have risen and warmed the Curia with zealous support for our sanctification. Honorius will then call for a Synod to formalize our sanctification.

"And after our order has been so blessed, we shall devote the next few years to soliciting every monarch, lord and vassal in the west; asking for knights who are second sons, knights who need to cleanse their souls and knights who simply want to serve our Lord and Savior...and of course for donations of manors, fiefs, markets and coin."

Baldwin's smile was so wide that Henry thought he could see every tooth in the King's mouth. "Aye," roared the Monarch, "I'll send the letters and take them myself if I must. This is a wonderful idea. Henry, coordinate your letters' content with Clarence. We'll get this done right away. God favors us. I knew He would. I knew it."

Before the knights could rise to leave, Baldwin spoke on a different issue. "Henry, I was embarrassed yesterday. I didn't remember where you were from. I'm sorry. But so it won't happen again, please spend a few moments and tell me about yourself: where you learned Latin, how you got from the Abbey of Bec to being a knight, why you left Jerusalem after Godfrey died, whether you have a wife and children, how you got to be a papal guard and why you came back here. I don't mean to delay you but you have so many skills and so much experience, I want to be certain that you will get all you hope for here...and that Outremere will get all it can from you."

With that said, Baldwin politely dismissed Hugh and Andre and then directed Henry through a detailed accounting of his life. The process was very friendly but caused Henry to wonder what was behind it. At the end of his interrogation, Baldwin paused.

"Henry, based on this conversation, I want you to not take your oath with Hugh for a month. Will you promise me that please?"

"I suppose I can," replied the knight, "but may I ask why?"

"I cannot answer that question yet," said Baldwin, "but I promise you my intentions are honorable and that I shall not contradict your final decision." Baldwin quickly clapped his hands together to summon a servant.

"Have you ever had coffee Henry? It stirs my brain," chortled the monarch. "It stirs my brain."

~**~

Early the following Saturday morning, a messenger called for Henry at the hospice. If able, Henry was asked to report immediately to the King.

"Thank you for coming," said Baldwin as he led Henry across the magnificent, multi-colored rug and pointed to the cushion nearest his own. "I've been working on some ideas for you Henry. Sit here and I'll share my thoughts."

The two men sat down and for a moment just stared at each other. During this hiatus Henry watched the King's expression shift from genial to serious.

"If I understand the plan you and Hugh envision, it's first to get the Pope to sanctify the order and second in the next few years, to visit all the kings, dukes, counts and lesser nobles in the west in order to ask them for knights and donations—coin, fiefs, manors, markets and whatnot. Is that correct?"

"It is, my lord."

"Well, I've talked with Hugh and he thinks you could do all that and only be a 'confrere' member in his order. Do you know what a 'confrere' member of an order is?"

"I think so," replied the knight. "It's someone who is a member but whose commitment is somehow qualified: a lord who is dying and joins a convent hoping to be closer to God and pays a sum for the privilege or a lord who participates but limits his role in some way. Is that what you mean?"

"Yes," said Baldwin. "That's exactly what I mean. I've talked with Hugh and he agrees that you could join his order and do all those things we've talked about without giving an oath or even living with his troop. Do you think that's possible Henry?"

"If Hugh agrees," answered the knight, "but why wouldn't I want to swear the oath?"

"Ah," responded Baldwin, "that brings me to my second thought. My sister-in-law, Rebecca, is a widow. Her estates are large, their revenue significant, her advice sage...and she's my ward. As you know Henry that means I can commit her to any man I think appropriate."

Baldwin paused. "She'd be a fine wife for you and you could still go all over the west helping Hugh's order make safe the pilgrim routes to Jerusalem. What do you think of that?"

Henry's expression changed to pensive but he responded immediately. "I shall need to talk with Hugh, then to Rebecca and, before I commit one way or the other, think on it. Is that all right?"

"Of course," said the King. "I can talk to Rebecca this afternoon so you could meet with her as early as tomorrow morning."

"One more question," said Henry with a wide smile spread across his face, "have you not talked with her about this already?"

~**~

"**T**hank you for meeting with me," said Henry as softly as he could. He and Rebecca were seated on pillows in the center of Baldwin's meeting room. It was their first meeting alone together and each was nervous.

Henry cleared his throat. "I'm hoping that today each of us will share our deepest thoughts regarding our proposed marriage and be completely candid as to our priorities and desires. Neither of us is yet committed, so we should be open and honest in everything we say. This will improve our chances of making the right decision. Does that sound all right?"

Rebecca bowed her head slightly. "Yes."

"Would you like to go first?" asked Henry, "or would you like me to?"

For a moment Rebecca stared fixedly at Henry. Her gaze searched for validation, corroboration, certainty that he actually might let her speak first.

"Since you offer," she finally said, "I will choose to go first. My husband has been dead for many years." She rushed her words as if they'd been locked away for a long time. "When we married his lands, fiefs, manors and coin came from my dowry, my father's wealth meant for me and my issue. I do not think it proper for you to take it and pass it on to your children. I know Franj law works that way but I'd rather die a widow than permit the theft of my son's inheritance." She put forth these last few words almost angrily.

Feeling this rushing torrent, Henry sat back on his cushion. He hadn't expected such an outburst but he was certainly glad she'd spoken first. If he'd spoken first, he knew she never would have heard a word he said.

Rebecca halted her outburst apparently expecting a counter stroke.

Smiling inwardly but not daring to display his feelings outwardly, Henry spoke even more softly than before. "Rebecca, I have no interest in your lands or your coin. If we marry, I will not consider them mine. My sons live well without need of an inheritance. Your concern for your son is admirable but unnecessary."

Rebecca scrutinized Henry's every twitch, breath and heart beat. "Many Franj have stolen estates just that way," she proffered.

Henry wasn't sure whether she'd heard his comment declining interest in her son's inheritance. In any case, he was certain that he shouldn't respond too quickly. "I shall write a codicil into our marriage agreement if you wish, which will explicitly exempt your estates and coin from being left to either of my sons. Would that allow us to move on in our discussion?"

Rebecca stared at Henry. "You would?"

"Yes," replied the knight.

"All right," she responded in a tone that said the subject was now closed.

"Good," said Henry. "I have a related question for you. If we have a child, would you divide your estate between your son and this new progeny?"

The question obviously took Rebecca by surprise. "I suppose we could, each of us."

"Fine," whispered Henry. "What else do you have for issues?"

Rebecca's posture straightened. "I'm a Christian...but a Greek Christian. And I prefer not to change." Her tone was no longer combative.

Henry guessed she could be pressed to compromise but he didn't care. He'd never thought the differences between the Roman and Greek Churches were fundamental. "That's fine," he said. "What other issues do you think might be important to bring up?"

"You really don't mind if I stay on in the Greek Church? Many Franj consider the Greek church...heretical."

"Do the Greek Christians believe that God sent Jesus here to save our souls?"

For a moment Rebecca tested the question in her mind. Finally she answered. "Yes, they do."

"The Roman Church believes that too."

"Those two things were what I wanted to bring up." Suddenly she smiled. "It must be your turn."

Henry smiled back and then took a deep breath. "I believe my values guide my life. I certainly hope they do. They are respect, integrity and others. I may not always achieve them but I try to every day. I'm sure you know the meaning of the first two." The knight paused to allow his potential consort to ask about them if she wished. When she didn't, he continued. "My third value, 'others', I'm now trying to focus on. I'm planning to give over a great deal of my time to helping the poor knights of Christ in their endeavors to defend the Holy Land and, more particularly, protect the pilgrims who attempt to get here and return safely. In the next decade, I could be gone for two or three years in the west urging kings and lesser lords to give us knights and treasure in order to better insure safety here." Again Henry paused to give Rebecca time to respond.

"I would think," she whispered, "when you are absent, that my pain would be no more than it is now...and probably less because I'd have hope of your return."

Henry liked her answer.

"When my first wife, Angeline, and I met, she was my ward. We were both young and knew very little about marriage. We agreed to spend a week together to measure our compatibility. I made a list of topics to cover...values, education, the way God's hand controls events and she made a similar list which, to my surprise, asked where the line between heresy and Christian doctrine lies and what I thought of astrology. Was it a science or a sin? We spent seven of the happiest days of our lives sharing our thoughts on these and other subjects. By the second day, I knew I would be hers if she proved willing. She never told me when she decided but at the end of the week, she agreed. I loved her very much, so much that I've feared remarrying, perhaps thinking that it could never be so good again." Henry's comments waned.

"Henry," whispered Rebecca, "my first love was similar to that: a rush of warmth, a sense of partnership, shared beliefs, a complete surrender. We are older now, more mature, more set in our ways but perhaps still willing to take a chance. If we spend a week together, God will show us His favor or not. I'm willing to investigate our prospects if you are."

Henry stared into Rebecca's deep brown eyes. She looked a lot like Angeline and seemed to think the same way too.

By the fourth day as they walked the streets of Jerusalem, Henry knew he would take the chance and that Rebecca would too. He had found her to be keen, direct, fair and thoughtful. At times she responded assertively but always respectfully. What he found most interesting though was that, despite her religiosity, Rebecca like Angeline was very interested in topics tangential to doctrine; so much so that the knight was considering telling her about his past-life regression.

"Henry, is that you?"

Henry looked up. He and Rebecca had just turned at the city's Josaphat Gate and were walking back toward the Holy Sepulchre. Coming toward them was an Arab boy leading a long string of camels. The boy was clearly the person who'd called out his name but was not someone he knew. Assuming the boy was calling to another 'Henry', the knight turned his head in several directions to see who might be the target of the boy's hello. There was no one else nearby!

"Henry," called out the boy again, "it's me...Peter Maillesais."

Henry's head jerked back to face the boy. Still holding the first camel's leash, the youth stood just ten feet away…looking right at him.

"What did you say?" queried the knight in a tone of suspicious disbelief.

"Henry," trumpeted the youth, "it is you!" Immediately the boy dropped the camel's rein, ran forward and clasped his arms around the tall Christian's midriff.

For a moment Henry stood stock still. Then he put his hands on the boy's shoulders and pressed him slightly back. "What did you call yourself?"

"Peter Maillesais," responded the youth as he looked up at Henry with ebullient, glowing happiness filling his face. "Bec," he squealed, "your mentor at Bec."

"But," gurgled Henry, "that can't be. Peter died. He'd be my age." Henry frowned. "Did someone put you up to this?"

"No, no," pronounced the boy. "It's really me Henry. You remember…when we were going to the infirmary, we stopped in the church and I showed you Herluin's sarcophagus."

"Let go of my boy!" growled a burly man who'd just trotted up.

Henry raised his eyes to the new arrival. The man stood quite close, was obviously angry and was touching the handle of his sword which was still in its scabbard.

"I mean no harm," Henry said in Arabic as he lifted his arms from the boy's shoulders.

"Father," said the boy, "this is Henry of Dol. We were friends in my last life…"

Still glaring at Henry, the Arab man yelled at the boy. "Shut up. We're leaving."

"But father…"

"Shut up," commanded the man again as he grabbed the child's arm and started to pull him away.

For just a moment the boy turned his head back toward Henry. His joyous physiognomy had descended into the most crestfallen expression Henry had ever seen. Then just for a moment, Henry saw the boy's lip quiver!

"Peter," called out Henry, "I recognize you…I recognize you!"

Henry watched Peter, his father and the camel train until they had all passed through the Josaphat Gate. He was so startled by their meeting that he had forgotten he was with Rebecca until she spoke.

"What was that all about?"

The knight's head turned. "I don't know," he mumbled. "It was very odd. That boy was someone I knew...thirty some years ago. I know that can't be... but I'm certain it was him."

"What makes you sure it was him?" asked Rebecca in a tone which was not disputive.

"His comment about us going to Herluin's sarcophagus, no one else could have known that...and his lip quivering! I'm certain it was him." Again Henry shook his head. "My mind must be playing tricks on me. Perhaps I need to sit down in the shade."

"I have heard stories," Rebecca whispered softly, "of little children who talk like that about their former lives: having different parents, a different home, different brothers and sisters, what they did, who they knew. It is rare but not unheard of."

"Really?" responded Henry.

"There is much," continued Rebecca, "which we don't yet know...or understand."

Henry glanced around as if to see whether someone might be listening. At that moment he and Rebecca were the only humans standing on the street.

"I once had occasion," Henry began, "to be taken back into a former life... It was very jarring, an experience I rarely share."

Rebecca stared at him. It was a deep, penetrating stare. Eventually she spoke. "God favors you, Henry, to be picked out like that...and like this. He shows you great favor. If you don't want to share, I will understand. But if you'd like a confidant, I'd very much like to hear your story."

On their seventh day, Rebecca took Henry to her estates. They were large and run differently than western manors. There were of course wheat, barley, beans, squash and other food crops grown to feed the estate's workers and owner. The vast majority though were 'coin crops' which the estate sold. These were sugar, cotton, olive oil and some spices. What surprised Henry was how effectively the tenants—Arabs, Jews, Roman Christians, Greek Orthodox, Maronites, Jacobites, and Nestorians—handled their tracts. They gave Rebecca's overseer half their food stuffs, paid him half their income from cash crop sales and additionally paid a poll tax of one dinar annually. These takings Henry noted left the farmer with a strong incentive to produce and sell as much as possible. Furthermore, Rebecca needed fewer overseers since their task was so simple. They kept track of all sales, collected coin and performed court duty when called for. From discussions with several farmers, mostly Muslim, Henry also learned that they found the Franj fairer in their legal decisions than prior Muslims had been. Apparently this was due to the animosity between Shi'a and Sunni, which took itself down even to the level of the local courts. Henry was also surprised to find that slaves preferred Christian rule because the Franj were willing to offer a slave his freedom if he met pre-agreed quotas of production over some period of time. Henry was also struck by the irrigation systems that included piped water, cisterns and even Archimedes' screws in order to pump and spread water to adjacent fields.

So Henry married for a second time. He and Rebecca each felt they had found a special person. In Henry, Rebecca found a man comfortable enough within himself to be able to see the good in others. He didn't need to have everything his way. He listened before he decided. Most of all, he respected her. In Rebecca, Henry found a good Christian woman who could diagnose extremely complex issues and, after reducing them into a few parts, make the subject simple to understand and thus bring a solution into view if one was needed. Her assertiveness and directness could be very blunt. But the ability to deal with haughty, yet insecure, men was a skill Henry had learned long ago. Best of all, he could still help the poor knights of Christ and yet be married. All in all, their marriage seemed to each of them to be a fresh start with a good person.

BIRTH
1127

They had originally planned to start their 'communications' to Kings, Dukes and Counts of Europe after their sanctification had officially taken place. But Abbot Bernard had written them stating that the 'bubbling up' process had not yet set in sufficiently among the southern bishops who would make up a significant part of the sanctification voters. Accordingly the Abbot suggested they delay their official sanctification one year. Since Abbot Bernard was their principal promoter, they took his advice but only in regard to scheduling the Church's vote for sanctification. Otherwise Henry thought, with Hugh de Payen's agreement, it made sense to begin visiting the Christian Kings, Dukes and Counts during the year's delay to share what they had been doing and were planning to do after their official sanctification. But they'd first go to Rome to make sure the Pope was in full agreement.

So Hugh, Henry, Godfrey, Payen and Andre visited Pope Honorius in Rome. The Pope was effusive about sanctifying the 'Templars.' Bernard was apparently working on a 'Rule' which would list activities, roles and restrictions appropriate for an order of monk-soldiers. Balancing the purpose of a knight, whose most basic function at least in war was to kill, with the functions of a Christian monk who was fervently expected to commit no sins and particularly draw no blood, was apparently not a problem. Based on Bernard's clearly written enumerations, Honorius defined the killing of an enemy of Christ as 'malicide'. This meant that a warrior-monk could kill without sinning as long as he was defending Christians or Christendom. Henry found the entire discussion to be an identical replication of the conversation he and Bishop Peter Pierleone had had in Jerusalem several years before.

Completing his audience with the knights, Honorius referenced an already scheduled synod at Troyes in January of '29, which was to discuss the progress of the 'Truce of God'. The Pope thought because Troyes was quite near Champagne where Hugh de Payen's family resided and because it was also very near Bernard's Abbey of Clairvaux, that putting the sanctification of the 'Templar Order' on that synod's agenda would be 'perfect.'

He went on in considerable detail, to explain just what Hugh should discuss at the Synod and how he should comport himself, the latter being the most important since many of the convened bishops would envision future 'Templars' to be like Hugh. Henry thought this was both an insightful and propitious remark since Hugh was one of the two most devout knights he'd ever known, Godfrey of Bouillon being the other.

While Hugh and his small enterage left Rome for Clairvaux to meet Abbot Bernard, Henry split off toward Genoa hoping to find his second son Bishop. He'd already written to his son extolling the possibilities that might blossom after Hugh's knights were sanctified. In Genoa's getto Anna cooked him cinnoman rolls, told him Abraham had died peacefully and that his son Bishop, had sent Henry a letter just before he'd taken ship.

~**~

The Abbey of Clairvaux was so new that its dormitory's wooden sides still displayed the pale cuts of the adz. Henry estimated the dormitory wasn't more than ten years old. Nevertheless, the abbey was a busy and prosperous place. Like Cluny, it was surrounded by fields, gardens and outbuildings. Soft zephyrs were rippling the green grass and vegetables were sprouting ubiquitously, promising a bountiful harvest. The only significant difference between Clairvaux and Cluny that Henry could see was that the monks here wore white Cistercian robes instead of the Benedictine black.

Henry was immediately intercepted by two boys whom he assumed were oblates. One took his horse and the other led him into the dormitory. A right turn took them to a door at which the oblate knocked.

"Come in, come in," crowed a cheery voice from the other side of the door. "It's not locked."

The boy bowed to Henry and pointed indicating that the knight should enter.

"Ah ha," called out a little man in a white robe' "you must be Henry of Dol."

This fellow looked to be not much older than the two oblates. He had an unusually thin face and a voice which seemed perfect for singing hymns. His 'tenor' suggested pre-puberty but his white robe testified that he was older than that.

"I am," replied Henry. "Have I the pleasure of meeting the Abbot of this most magnificent abbey?"

"The pleasure is mine," replied Abbot Bernard. "Hugh has been telling me about how you have helped his small troop focus on becoming sanctified in order to raise men and coin more quickly." Putting out his hand, the Abbot stepped forward. "I am Bernard...and you Henry, are now our guest. If you need anything, anything at all, please call on me. I want you to feel right at home."

The Abbot paused but not long enough for Henry to speak. "In the future, I see this little group of Christ's soldiers swelling into a vast army, an army dedicated to overcoming the Church's enemies, defending pilgrims, protecting the poor and helping the sick. And we can do it with your help Henry. Sit down right here," Bernard pointed to one of three chairs beside his broad desk.

"Thank you," responded the knight as he sat down.

"You know Henry, God gives us so little time to do big things. But for those who believe in Him, fervently believe in Him, there is no challenge too large. Henry, you were on the great pilgrimage. You must have felt God's hand carrying you forward, read His signs, heard His voice and known that victory was certain. All God's will Henry...God's will! Surely though you are about to embark on another such journey, the creation of another army, men so close to God that they'll be His monks and men so close to God that they'll be His soldiers too. Henry, you are blessed by God for He has surely chosen you to participate not just once in His glorious efforts but twice. He has called you Henry! He has surely called you."

Henry liked this man. He was someone who saw God's hands in action, knew what they could do and understood the power of faith in making it all happen.

"You know," Bernard continued in a softer tone, "I had an earlier mission...also from Him. It was much smaller than yours, much less signifycant. It was building this abbey. God directed me, showed me the way, helped me. It was Him Henry. I could feel Him. We, He and I, set at it and...and the pieces came together. Twelve monks to begin with, then the gift of land and coin from Hugh of Champagne, then learning all the things we had to do...and doing them. We, He and I, and many others built this monastery in only twelve years. Only possible with God's help Henry...the only way great things ever get done...with God's help!

"Now," continued the Abbot, "Hugh and I have been talking about a

'Rule' for your order, a set of directions that will place inductees on a righteous path. It's clear that Hugh de Payens has given this a lot of thought. His vow of obedience, poverty and chastity goes right to the heart of a monk's calling. Do you know what 'contemptus mundi' means?"

"I believe," responded Henry, "it means having contempt for material things: food, pleasure, sex, hunting and dice."

"Very good." smiled the Abbot. "I'm still working on Hugh's Rule," continued Bernard. "Do you know that Honorius has set the date and place for the sanctification as January 1129 at Troyes? This gives us some time but not much since I'll need to soften up a number of cardinals particularly south of Rome. My core ideas for this Rule are: Hugh's vow of obedience, poverty and chastity, the concept of 'contemptus mundi' particularly in regard to sex, greed and power and the absolute avoidance of women. Let's spend some time Henry, on what you think we should include. No doubt you have given it some thought."

"Actually I have. I agree with those you and Hugh have settled around. I do have an 'outlier' though that I could use some help with. When trying to think what sort of knights we may receive when soliciting, it occurred to me that some of the very worst might be sent to us if only to get rid of them: murderers, rapists and robbers who wish to gain some hope of redemption. Some of these would surely be fine picks and others would ruin our reputation. How should we address that?"

"I've thought of them too Henry. It's a very tricky proposition as well as an opportunity."

~**~

The next evening at dinner, the Abbot tapped his spoon against his bowl and rose to speak. "Your brother Hugh de Payens has asked me to make an announcement." Conversation ceased and Bernard continued. "Count Hugh of Champagne, who sits among you, has given you, the poor soldiers of Christ, a magnificent piece of land and a castle with accompanying buildings, castellan, twelve attendants, fifty-two serfs and fourteen freemen. Count Hugh, please stand up and receive our thanks." Applause filled the room.

Henry had not expected many entire manors to be donated. He'd thought knights, horses, weapons, equipment, coin and even some tolls from bridges and fords were likely but entire manors with tenants, fields, forests, fish ponds and even bee hives! This was different. They'd need to be overseen the way Edmond did at Dol. They'd need men with different skills: administrators, accountants, scribes, overseers and all of them would have to be trustworthy or the revenue would never get to Outremere. He'd have to identify 'outliers' just as brother Bruglio had done to track the peer performance of each of Cluny's brother and sister abbies. There would have to be regional oversight… a bursar!

~**~

At Anjou, Hugh de Payens introduced Count Fulk as a close friend. The Count had toured Outremere in 1120, getting his palm, staying for several nights at the Temple and even donating enough coin to support two knights for an entire year.

After dinner on the second night of their stay, Hugh de Payens somewhat peremptorily sat Henry down next to Fulk. The great room of Anjou's castle was a very comfortable setting. Servants plied all sorts of wines and a summer breeze came in to keep the day's heat at bay. Being both polite and seemingly interested, Fulk plied Henry with all the usual questions about his background and his experiences on the great pilgrimage. When those had been covered, Henry responded by asking Fulk about the goings on in his vast estates.

"Oh," answered Fulk, "that's a very timely question. Together with my half brother, Louis 'the fat' and several other nobles, I've been fighting King Henry of England, 'Beauclerc' we call him because he's such a learned fellow. Not that it's done him much good. Henry has a temper. He once got so mad at a merchant that he threw the man off the roof of a castle. But times change; his daughter and heir, Matilda, will marry my son Geoffrey in the fall. So now 'Beauclerc' and I are allies against Louis, a reversal well worth the effort. My son will rule Anjou, Normandy and England and, when we defeat Louis, Paris and most of central France as well. He'll be more powerful than the Emperor in Germany. What's the new one's name?"

"Lothar," answered Henry.

"Yes, yes. That's the one," continued Fulk. "Do you play at dice, Henry?"

"Not really," answered the knight. "I play chess."

"No, that won't do," replied Fulk. "I only play games of chance."

~**~

"Ah," said Louis, "Henry of Dol. Suger has told me about you, a man of values whose word is as good as gold. I like you Henry. If we had more like you, we'd live in a better world. Come sit with me and share how France can be of help to the knights of the Temple." The King turned toward a long wooden table. "Do you mind if I have my sons sit with us? When I was their age, my father let me listen in on his conversations with important people. I found it very educational."

"Of course," responded Henry, "please have them join us."

Louis waved an arm in the direction of two boys who looked to be about six and eight. Their eyes already being on their father, they leapt up and almost ran to the table.

"This is Phillip," pronounced the father, "and this is Louis."

Henry bowed slightly and received back similar obeisance from the boys.

"This," uttered the monarch to his sons in a very serious tone, "is Henry of Dol. Please note that he and his fellow knights each have red crosses stitched on their back shoulders. These are the brave men who rescued Jerusalem from the wicked Muslims and have returned to ask us for help to continue holding the center of our Christian world. This man has earned our attention and our assistance."

"As you know," began Henry, "the Holy Land is full of murderers, cut-throats and heathen armies. Christian pilgrims are robbed and slaughtered regularly. These men here with you today represent about one third of our entire troop. We are committed to protect pilgrims on the road from Jaffa to Jerusalem, a route of about twenty-five Roman miles. Our most committed have sworn an oath of obedience, poverty and chastity. They intend to live like monks. What we hope you will do for us is direct some knights into our ranks and, if you are able, also send us some war-horses, equipment and coin."

"How have you been responded to so far on your trip?" asked the king.

"I should have mentioned that," replied Henry. "At Champagne, Count Hugh committed a very large manor—its castle, castellans, serfs and free-men. At Anjou, we had a warm reception from Fulk who received his palm in Jerusalem several years ago. His commitment is not yet specified. In Maine and Poitou, the same."

"I'm going to be very candid with you Henry. Although I'm a King, I'm one with many disloyal vassals. I've given them no cause to shirk their duty, no diffidatio, but they still renege on their obligations simply because they have the power to get away with it. Both Fulk of Anjou and Henry of Normandy owe me fielty. Neither gives it." Looking at his sons, Louis continued. "They seek to bring us to our knees but, God willing, that won't happen. They're not our only problem either. We're plagued with robber barons. Engerrand of Coucy has constantly been assailing his neighbors—stealing sheep and cattle, robbing merchants, plundering fiefs and even towns. I actually had to take an army to Amiens just to protect the bishop and inhabitants there. Engerrand just retreats into his castle and waits me out. It would take a year to starve him out and my men require pay after their forty days are up. I can't afford to lay a siege on him long enough to bring him to heel."

~**~

"**H**enry of Dol," mulled Henry 'Beauclerc' who was both the King of England and Duke of Normandy. "My father spoke several times of a Henry of Dol, said he was saved at Hastings Field by a charge that man lead. Are you perchance his son or, more likely, his grandson?"

"I am," answered Henry. "My grandfather lead that charge. He and my uncle died there and my father had to use crutches the rest of his life to get around. But your father never forgot our family's deeds. He even became my brother's godfather. Your family is held very high by mine."

"Ah," sighed the King, "loyalty, real loyalty! But I see a cross on your back. Obviously, like your progenitors, you have also been a brave warrior. Sit down Henry and tell me about yourself."

The King was neither tall nor heavy set. His hair was black and his eyes blue. He had as far as Henry could discern no particularly distinguishing characteristics. He did direct their conversation to topics he wanted to hear. But of course he'd been king for twenty-some years.

"Well," began Henry, "as you know I'm from Dol and was the second son in my family. I spent my early years with a tutor learning to read and speak Latin..."

"Arma virumque cano," interrupted the King.

"My lord, I've never known a king to quote Latin."

"Ha ha," smiled the monarch, "and I've hardly ever heard a knight speak Latin...a bishop or a priest of course, but not a knight. You know Henry, a king without an education is really no more than a crowned donkey. I couldn't do my duties if I hadn't learned to read, write and do sums. It's no wonder our world is coming to an end. The kings are as ignorant as the serfs.

"Let me give you an example of what I mean. Most kings, particularly if they're born into the crown, haven't any idea what to do other than some vague sense of perpetuation. I was fortunate. My brother William, we called him Rufus, took the crown when our father died because he was closest to the treasury. I don't think he had any clear idea of what to do but he was smart enough to grab the coin.

"That got him thirteen years as king...and he'd still be king if it weren't for a stray arrow shot by someone who wasn't paying proper attention. Well, having seen how Rufus got the kingdom, I did the same thing, immediately took control of the treasury. But the key, Henry, this is where the education comes in, is that you not only have to have a brain, you have to focus it on what you need to do for others in order to stay in power. People who haven't been taught to think don't ask the right questions. And if you don't ask the right questions, you'll never know what to do.

"A king is one man, no more, no less. All the nobles, knights, sheriffs, burgers, bishops and freemen don't have to obey him if they choose not to. Knowing that is the most important thing a king can learn! Once he learns it, it's fairly easy to figure out what he should be doing. The nobles want certainty of their positions; the bishops want harmony between the king and the Church; and the burgers want safety and fair taxation without abuse; the sheriffs want consistent enforcement of the law, no favoritism; freemen the same. Most of all, a king needs to be fair and not arbitrary.

"I immediately initiated financial and judicial reform. We now have itinerant officials who mete out taxes and justice to every class just the same way. There are no longer some burgers who pay and others who don't. The courts are overseen in order to be certain that justice is given equally to all. I even reinforced the old Saxon legal tradition. It was always sound and we needed one system, not two. I wrote a charter that defined the privileges of lords and bishops. Arbitrary enforcement has gone away.

"When I first married, I picked Edith, daughter of Malcolm of Scotland, niece of Edgar Aetheling and great-granddaughter of Edmond Ironside, half brother of Edward the Confessor. You see, I tied my line to both Normans and Saxons equally, fair to both. I speak English as well as French. My charter of guarantees protects both Church and nobles from arbitrary diminution of their standing. I simply don't have the power to take them down without just cause. I had to go even further with the Church. Bishop Anslem confronted me over investiture and after a long battle, we compromised much as I'm told you did with the German Emperor for Calixtus. I've even used my illegitimate childrens' marriages to build bridges with powerful families so they'll feel safe.

"Of course sometimes I've reached out and failed. My oldest son, William, to whom I taught all these things, I married to Fulk of Anjou's daughter to induce Fulk to become an ally instead of an enemy. Sadly William and his wife drowned in the White ship...on November 25th, 1120. The monks at the Abbey still pray daily for them. God has blessed us though in that our original intent will soon be consummated with the marriage of my daughter Matilda, the widow of Emperor Henry, to Fulk's son Geoffrey. May God watch over them and their issue. I've had other failures too. My oldest brother Robert..." the King paused, "did you meet him on your pilgrimage?"

Henry nodded.

"I gave him Normandy but, as you probably know, he eventually contested for the throne. He's a kind man, not at all evil, but he's not a thinker, not focused on much of anything. Well, he got himself surrounded by a grasping group of want-to-be's, so we finally went to war and had a battle at Tinchebray. It was an odd contest. Neither one of us knew the other was coming, so it was more of a running skirmish than a real brawl. Anyhow, we captured Robert retreating. I had to put him away where he wouldn't get used again. Eventually I moved him to Cardiff where he could ride and hunt and be relatively free. Unfortunately he broke our agreement and tried to escape. But, he rode his horse into a bog and we recaptured him. After that we had to eliminate his riding and hunting privileges."

The King turned his head toward Henry. "I got you off your subject Henry but I'll twist Fulk's arm at the wedding and get him to give your knights of the Temple a big donation. He's not well practiced in the art of giving but, if I give you a big gift, he'll feel obliged to give one just as big or bigger. Now, I want your group to go to Scotland. But you have to be back to cross the channel no later than October. You have enough time but you won't be able to go on any hunting trips. They like those in Scotland...not much else to do I think."

SANCTIFICATION
January 1129

Even though benches had been drawn together in the center of the church at Troyes and a fire had been burning on its stone floor for hours, the high vaulted ceiling together with the open doorways made any hope of warmth a fantasy. The bishops, archbishops and cardinal deacons were all dressed in their best regalia, conical white hats and scarlet robes, but most of their spectacle and color was muted by their overlayment of wool blankets, leather gloves and, in one case, fur earmuffs. Henry knew most of these churchmen. He had worked closely with several of them: the lead legate Bishop Matthew of Albano, Peter of Porto, William of Palestrina, Gregory of Saint Angelo, John of Crema, Conrad of Sabina and John of Ostia. Among the newer he recognized Chancellor Haimeric, Victor of Paris, Rusticius of Saint Ciriaco, Diego of Compostela, Hubert of Lucca, Norbert of Magdeburg, and Peter of Saint Susanna. All the older members of the Cardinalate had greeted him very pleasantly. The younger had been polite but less effusive. He assumed his presence caused most of them to recall Bart's brutal murder which, for those supported by the Frangipane family, must have been extremely embarrassing.

The Synod had commenced with a brief service led by Bishop Matthew and then it launched into a review of 'The Peace of God' which for years had been attempting to limit combat among nobles to only a few specified days of the week. Several of the cardinals gave detailed reports of violations in their dioceses and concluded by offering up names of the most egregious perpetrators for anathema and excommunication. These reports droned on for most of the morning and touched entirely on feuds, actions and people whom Henry didn't know. He fell asleep about mid-morning but was elbowed back into consciousness by his friend Geoffrey of Bison.

After that, Henry's mind fell into a review of his trip. He was immensely glad that it was almost over. They had rushed from place to place throughout the Christian west: Rome, Champagne, Anjou, Maine, Poitou, Paris, Normandy, England, Scotland, Flanders, Upper and Lower Lorraine, Burgundy and Provance. He himself had additionally visited Genoa, Barcelona, Toledo and Cordoba. All this had left him very tired. He'd hoped to pass through Dol to see Edmond, Joan and their children but the rush to cross the channel before it closed kept him from visiting Dol because they had to take a ship bound for Boulogne. Of course he'd sent a letter but he now thought it likely he'd never see that part of his family again.

Landing at Boulogne allowed them to pass through Flanders on their way south. Even though Henry knew Count Robert had been killed long before, he stopped at Robert's castle hoping to see Clem. He was told that she had married Godfrey of Louvain whose estates were only a short distance to the south east. So their group stopped there, which was propitious since Godfrey gave the knights of the Temple a large manor that Henry thought could become their preceptory for the entire region where the French and the German languages overlapped.

From there, he had gone to Tournai hoping to convice his knight's school chum Bartholomew, with whom he had trained under Reynauld, to join the knights of the Temple as their trainer in Jerusalem. They had already acquired seventeen knights who were traveling with them to Jerusalem. God willing, there would be many more. They would need training in unit tactics and team coordination. Henry was certain that those two skills, after God's favor, had contributed most to their victories in Outremere. He intended to have them become standard practice for the knights of the Temple. When he rejoined the other Templars, Hugh de Payens told him that due to distance and time constraints, he had decided not to go to Spain. Henry suggested that he could go to Barcelona and Toledo and still be back at Troyes in time for their sanctification. Hugh agreed. So with an extra pack mule and an extra horse, he and Bartholomew set out along the Rhone River to Marseilles. From there they took ship to Barcelona.

In Spain, pushing back the Muslim Moors was called 'the Reconquista' and had been going on for hundreds of years. Conflict was a norm and finding volunteers relatively easy. The real challenge was calling for Spanish knights to go to Jerusalem when they could just as well fight Christ's war at home. Furthermore the last major battle fought against the Almoravid Muslims had been a decisive Christian victory at Valencia. So the Spanish were keen to fight but loathed to give up men and coin to fight in foreign places. After consideration Henry concluded that, if Hugh agreed, it might be possible to create an arm of the Templars in Spain which could provide organizational skills without taking men and material away to foreign places.

When searching for Walter, they came upon a teacher who explained that a school in Cordoba was not like the Abbey of Bec or the Lyceum in Rome where students sat at a desk listening to their teachers. In Cordoba the setting was open and extremely informal. Because of the warmth, classes were usually held outdoors in courtyards and were open to anyone who cared to listen. The fellow quickly explained that teachers had specific times reserved for them at various places in the city and that attendance identified the most popular topics and teachers. Narrower topics drew fewer students and usually met at a street corner, tavern or even a bridge. Following this man's direction, Henry and Bartholomew finally found Walter and two students in a small tavern engaged in an animated conversation about infection.

Walter's thesis was that prior to treating a wound, a physician should put some cloth into boiling water and then use it to scrub all around the patient's wound with the objective of thoroughly cleaning the area. It mattered not he said, how big or small the wound was. The two students could not see why such an approach should make any difference but Walter simply responded that an old Jewish doctor, whom he had studied under, had found the approach significantly reduced infections. The debate went on for quite a while before Henry interjected that since the scrubbing was unlikely to do harm and that there might be a benefit from it, then employing it would be riskless and wise. This the two students couldn't rebuff, so they departed leaving Henry, Bartholomew and Walter to have lunch together.

That evening at Walter's adobe hut on the outskirts of the city, he introduced Anita, who was apparently his Spanish concubine and mother of Edmond, his two-year-old son. The boy was enchanting and quite taken with his grandfather. When asked, Walter declined going to Outremere or the two Nestorian schools of medicine further east. Nevertheless, pleasant conversation continued well into the evening mostly with Walter and Henry discussing various medical theories and experiences. The next morning Henry and Bartholomew set out for Troyes.

~**~

"**W**e shall now hear Brother Hugh de Payens, the requestor of sanctification for 'the Knights of the Temple," called out Cardinal Matthew of Albano, a call that jolted Henry's mind back to the present.

"Your honors," murmured Hugh almost inaudibly, "in answer to Pope Urban's call, our tiny group of knights went to Jerusalem many years ago. When we last went back, it was with the intention of becoming Augustinian monks to serve others. King Baldwin however asked us to serve others in a different way—to guard the road from Jaffa to Jerusalem where Christian pilgrims are regularly slaughtered by Muslim infidels. While we have saved some lives, our ranks are too few and too poorly equipped to save all who take that road. To help us meet our task, we ask that you sanctify our troop as you have the Hospitallers who serve an equally Christian purpose of nurturing the sick. Sanctification, as you know, will encourage our countrymen to donate men, arms, equipment and coin to our cause. With your blessing, we can save more pilgrims and better protect Jerusalem." Hugh sat down.

Henry looked at the churchmen around him. Not one was asleep.

"Thank you," responded Cardinal Matthew in a barely audible voice. "Now to speak in favor, Abbot Bernard of Clairvaux."

Several moments passed before Bernard rose to his feet. He cleared his throat and then, when there wasn't the slightest whisper from anywhere in the entire church, he spoke. "Brother Christians, we have a momentous opportunity before us today. With just one word of support, we can create a new kind of Christian soldier, a soldier of God! From men so chaste, so humble, so devoted and so dedicated, we can anoint, bless, create and sanctify these men, these men who have already of their own accord, just like a monk, vowed before the Patriarch of Jerusalem their pledge of poverty, obedience and chastity. These men, as much as any group of monks, have given themselves over to God, denied their flesh, their will, their greed, their every natural desire in order to give themselves to Him. They epitomize 'contemptus mundi.'

For what seemed like a very long time, the Abbot stood stock still. Finally he completed his remarks. "Members of the Curia, these knights seated among you deserve your anointment and your sanctification." Abbot Bernard sat down.

A few moments of silence followed before Cardinal Matthew spoke again. "Is there anyone who wishes to speak against sanctification?"

Several more moments of silence followed.

"Then," continued the Pope's Legate, "with the power that Pope Honorius has placed in me, in God's name we sanctify these 'Knights of the Temple."

Henry glanced toward Hugh who, with a broard smile on his face, was staring right back at him.

GROWTH

May 1129 – August 1131

"As I see it," began Henry, "our mission has been expanded from protecting pilgrims on the Jaffa road to protecting the entire Holy Land." He paused to see if Hugh and Andre had come as far as he had in defining the Templars' role. Hugh nodded his agreement and then Andre bowed his head as well. The three men sat facing each other, Hugh with his back against the main mast and Andre and Henry each leaning slightly to their left so as to offset the carrack's starboard tilt. They had taken the ship out of Venice for Jaffa. So far the winds had been light out of the northwest which promised, the Captain said, fair weather and only a two or three week trip.

"Our role in the west," continued Henry, "will be to acquire knights, equipment and sufficient coin to keep them in the field. To do this, we must establish six to eight regional preceptories from London to Louvain to Toledo. Each must fund itself and be able to put forth at least one able solicitor in its region contacting nobles, abbots and priests to gain their assistance. Donations must be sought continuously. The solicitor can also ask the courts in his region to offer pardons to errant knights if they'll agree to become Templars. Of course these knights must gain our approval first. And our solicitors must seek out accountants, smiths, cooks, sergeants, archers and other support personnel. Similarly, we shall need warhorses, palfreys, swords, lances, hauberks, trebuchets, mangonals, timber and iron bars. And coin can be procured through manors, mills, fairs, docks, bridges and fords. We shall have to put very able solicitors abroad to establish networks of helpers in each community as we did when we asked Abbott Bernard to write letters of solicitation for us.

"As we increase our preceptories, we must manage them to produce significant amounts of coin. To do this well, we will need regular reports. I'm thinking three four month-end reports a year in October, February and June, with a list of every building, field, forest, fish pond, crop, animal, man, woman, child, and an accounting of everything and everyone sent to Outremere during that period of time: knights, sergeants, horses, equipment, arrows, coin and whatever else. Do you know that a castle needs 30,000 arrows to defend itself against a siege? These reports should come from every property we possess and roll up into the regional preceptory's report, which will then be rolled up by us here in Jerusalem into one summary report. We can then initiate 'outlier' reports that will identify properties suspected of weak performance to which we shall send someone to investigate opportunities for improvement."

Gaining momentum, Henry continued. "We can also offer some services to our pilgrims that will benefit both them and us. Often when a lord leaves his fief to go to Santiago de Compostela, Rome or Jerusalem, he doesn't have someone he can trust to put in charge of his demesne. He fears that whoever he designates will be incapable and ruin the property or so grasping as not to give it back when he returns. Our local preceptory could offer to look after a lord's fief while he's away. This would give him piece of mind and we could take the income from his lands while he's away as our payment."

"How much would that be?" Andre quickly asked.

"It would depend on the size and efficiency of the fief," replied Henry, "but probably several silver pennies a year."

Astonished, Andre's eyes grew wide. "Enough to pay a knight for a year!"

"Another possibility," Henry continued, "would be for us to secure a large part of a pilgrim's coin that he otherwise would risk carrying on his person. For example, in Paris before our pilgrim departs for Jerusalem, he could deposit half his coin with us and then retrieve it in the holy city. His risk of loss would be cut in half and he'd have our guarantee that he could collect his money in Outremere whenever he got there. Again we could charge him a fee for the service."

"But Henry," interjected Andre, "how can we be sure we can get his coin to Jerusalem before he gets there and asks for it?"

"We won't give him his coins," smiled Henry. "We'll give him our coins at the same value that he gave us in Paris, less our fee of course."

"But," said Hugh, "how will you know that he's really our pilgrim and not some charlatan attempting to steal the pilgrim's money?"

"A very good question," responded the knight from Dol. "Let me explain step by step how this might work. Let's say one of Louis the Fat's counts wants to go on pilgrimage to Jerusalem and wishes to protect half his coin by placing it in our hands and not in his purse all the way to the holy land.

He would come to our nearest preceptory and hand over half his coins. The preceptor would give him a cheque, a piece of parchment, with our name, his name, the date and his deposit amount. It would also have space for a series of numbers and letters...a code. The code would identify the man by name, rank, home location, chosen password, amount of his deposit and the name and number of our preceptory. The code would be written in Latin and facilitated by the use of Virgil's first page in the *Aeneid*, something we'd need to have in every preceptory. This would allow us to identify the Paris depositor as the Jerusalem withdrawer and it would further allow us to verify the value of the deposit. Our preceptor in Jerusalem would then be able to turn over the pilgrim's coin in any currency he wanted and even continue to hold some for a longer time if the pilgrim desired." Looking at Andre, Henry added. "Our fee still needs to be worked out but it might be enough for us to pay the upkeep of two to four knights a year.

"We could also recommend where a pilgrim could find a ship at a reasonable price, tell them the ship's schedule and have arrangements with the shipper by which we'd get a commission for each pilgrim we placed on one of their ships, again a service to the pilgrim and a stipend for us."

For a moment no one spoke. Finally Hugh cleared his throat. "Henry, we're simple knights, not knowledgeable in Latin, codes or cheques. But God has sent us you who is honest, educated, intelligent and one of us. Go forward with your plan and let me know if you need help on anything."

~**~

Henry reined in his horse. In front of him was Rebecca's Castle. The outer wall's gate was closed so he waived to the small turret above it and called out. "Henry of Dol."

"Welcome back, sir," responded a pleasant voice which Henry recognized as that of Mortamor, one of the Armenian soldiers who'd come south with Rebecca years before. "Open the gate. It's the Master."

Having left his mount with the stableman, Henry walked quickly toward the stone ediface. Its oak door was already open.

All at once, Rebecca burst forth. "Henry, you're home!"

Henry leapt forward and wrapped his arms around his wife. "I'm so glad to see you."

"Henry, I've missed you," Rebecca squealed. Then quite suddenly she pushed him back breaking their embrace. "But there's a little boy here who wants to meet you."

Henry looked up and saw a smiling servant trotting toward him with a big baby in her arms.

"He's your son!" exclaimed Rebecca, "a fine baby boy...big and strong like his father."

Henry reached for the boy and with some effort lifted his son high into the air. "What's his name?"

For a moment Rebecca paused. "We haven't chosen his name yet. It is for you to choose."

"But," responded the knight, as he bobbed his son up and down drawing forth giggles and smiles, "you must have been calling him something." Pulling the boy to his chest, Henry pivoted back toward Rebecca.

"We've been calling him Gabriel after my father," she responded quite softly, "but it's for you to choose his name."

"Then Gabriel it is," shouted Henry as he again tossed the child into the air drawing yet further giggles from Gabriel.

"Oh thank you, Henry!" stammered Rebecca. "You're sure?"

"Yes," answered Henry as he caught sight of a young man who was just exiting the castle.

Seeing this, Rebecca's voice rose another octave. "And Henry, you have another son here to see you too, Bishop of Genoa."

Later in the castle's great room, Henry leaned back in his pillowed chair. Across from him sat Rebecca holding Gabriel and next to her sat his son Bishop fresh off a Genoese ship that had birthed two days earlier.

"So," commented Henry as he looked at his middle son, "you must have gotten my letter."

"Yes," answered the merchant. "Do you still carry my grandfather's chess set?"

"I do," smiled Henry. "That chess set and Benito's *Aeneid* are my two most cherished possessions coming only behind my wife and children." Henry smiled at Rebecca then turned back toward Bishop. "I'm so glad you got my letter and have come to visit. Are you here for a while or is your ship heading right back?"

"Well," responded Bishop, "that depends. Before I left Genoa, I asked Ezekial to oversee my investments so I could look into some of the things you referred to in your letter: the possibility of helping your Knights of the Temple with shipping, preceptories and reports. Your letter was enticing but not plump enough with detail for me to really know if I could do the things you suggested or would want to."

"Ah ha," chuckled Henry quite shrilly as he sat forward in his chair, "God is still with us. Our tiny group of knights, the Templars, have just received formal sanctification from Pope Honorius. We have established three regional command centers in the west: Champagne, London and Louvain. We'll have three more within a year. We've experienced a waterfall of donations these past two years. Our mission is to defend the holy land against the infidels. We solicit donations of manors, mills, bridges, fords, ferries...anything that can produce coin. Also we seek knights to come east and join our brethren...second sons, poor knights, those seeking redemption from their sins, soldiers dedicated to God who will do His bidding. Our network of preceptories will extend throughout the west: Scotland to Spain, Brittany to the Holy Roman Empire. We need a dedicated administrator, someone who can put good men in place, clearly define their tasks and hold them accountable. I'm in that role at the moment but it's too big a job for me. And I'm too old. We need someone with better business skills, someone who is used to reports, ships, making a profit, all those sorts of things."

"Does that mean I'd have to become a monk?" asked Henry's son.

"No, not at all," answered Henry. "We have 'confrere' members whose commitment is given in lengths of time. You must have values though, iron values such as integrity and respect and honesty is a must! You will be dealing with a lot of coin that isn't yours. But you'll have the satisfaction of helping others and knowing that God Himself is watching over you. You'll have to travel, create reports, hire so the pilgrims won't have to carry so much coin and be at such risk to robbers."

~**~

Two days later, Bishop agreed to take on the job that Henry had described. The two men then had a brief interview with Hugh. The Master said nothing about the Templar job. Instead he asked a lot of questions regarding what Bishop had been doing in Genoa. The young man responded succinctly explaining his involvement in shipping, the places he'd been, the groups of investors he'd worked with, the manner in which they identified risk and tried to diminish it. At the end, Hugh shook Bishop's hand and nodded his assent to Henry. The very next day Bishop sailed off with lists of names, places and things to do. Henry was greatly pleased. He knew Bishop had the values, energy and knowledge to do the job.

~**~

During the next year, Henry kept in close contact with Bishop through letters he would send and receive. The young administrator was making rapid progress. He had created 'tertiary' and 'outlier' reports, established additional preceptories in Supplinburg, Paris and Barcelona and sworn in Templars to oversee them. Notable among his successes were Brother Hugh de Rigauld in Barcelona, Raymond Berenger, Count of both Barcelona and Provence and King Alphonso of Navarre and Arragon. Meanwhile, Henry sent letters to various nobles throughout the west to update them on Templar activities and ask for their help.

'AS A DREAM DIES AT THE BREAK OF DAY'
September 1132

Henry was riding when he felt a sharp pain in his chest. He couldn't catch his breath and slumping forward, he almost fell off his horse.

"Dear Lord," he whispered, "first let me kiss Rebecca and Gabriel...then I'll be ready." Immediately the squeezing in his chest diminished. He reined in his mount and repeatedly gulped in deep breaths of air. "Thank You Lord."

Henry knew his heart would not survive another such attack. God had granted him a reprieve but likely just for a brief time. He slapped his knees against his horse's flanks and began to cantor. As he rode, his mind took him back to the past-life regression he'd shared with Angeline and Kay Mora: his startling responses of Tyrolia, twenty-six and not leaving his men; and then to Peter Maillesais, their meeting in Jerusalem, his friend somehow coming back. But how did it work? And most important, why had he been put into his current life? Was it a random process or a crafted thing? These thoughts rippled through his brain all the way to Rebecca's manor. When he reined in, he knew there was only one thing he really was certain of: God watched over and guided him...but of the logic and the process, he still knew too little.

That night in the dark, having kissed his wife and son and telling each that he loved them, Henry pulled his blanket up over his torso and recalled his friend Hugh de Payens who had recently died in his sleep. Hugh had been a good man, a man of God and a brave soldier in the service of Christ. For some reason, perhaps the setting, Henry then thought of his brother, William, a fine young man whom God had recalled before he could make his mark. Thinking of his brother always made him sad. He remembered when he had returned to Dol how, even though he knew William was gone, he had reached under the blankets hoping to feel the heat of his brother's body...where William had always been but was not anymore. And he thought of his parents, Audrey and Walter, who had slept in the bed just beyond William. His father straight and strong in his judgments and never giving in to his crippling wound, the North Star of the family...and his mother whose love was as warm as the sun, always there for others whatever the need. He hoped he would see them again.

He wasn't aware of falling asleep...but he was aware of having a dream. He was hurtling through a black void. There seemed to be a strong wind blowing. He was traveling very fast. He wasn't quite sure how he knew...but he was certain. After a while, his sense of sluicing forward diminished and the darkness of the void began to brighten...at first slowly and then much more rapidly. As the light increased, he experienced a powerful feeling, more poignant than any he had ever felt before...a sense of warmth, acceptance, affection...love! As this happened, he realized his travel had slowed...to a stop. His surroundings though, were very strange. There was an overwhelming brightness, so powerful that he was nearly blinded. Then all at once, he did see something...someone walking toward him through the light.

"Father!" he heard himself say. "Father, you're walking...without your crutches!"

CAST
OF
CHARACTERS

Abbot Odilo – Hugh's predecessor at Cluny.

Abraham Trebyianni – a Jewish merchant in Genoa.

Adhemar of Le Puy – bishop assigned by Pope Urban as the Church leader of the great pilgrimage.

Al-Afdal and Duqaq – Muslim Sultans in Egypt and Damascus.

Alexander – priest to Steven of Blois, a student of signs.

Alexius – Emperor of Constantinople.

Alfonso VI – King of Castile, Leon, Galicia and Toledo at various times; murderer of his brother Sancho.

Alfonso VII – King of Castile and ruler (1126 – 1157)

Alfred and Glendon – sons of Walter's knight Manion (deceased). Glendon goes with Henry on the great pilgrimage.

Ali Abduli Kafa – Egyptian commander of the Sudanese cavalry unit in Jerusalem; later in Spain.

Almoravids and Hammidites – Muslim tribes in Spain and North Africa.

Andrew – a priest and friend of Walter who went to Hastings field under Henry the Healer; later the priest to Henry's family.

Angeline – an 'angel' who became Henry's first wife and bore him three sons.

Angelos Choniates – a Proedros skilled in languages and diplomacy.

Anna – a young woman currying horses who becomes Henry's first bedding partner.

Anna – Abraham's housekeeper.

Anslem – the Abbot at Bec.

Archard of Auxerre and Rotrou of Issaudun – knights hired to be Papal guards.

Arnulf of Chocques – chaplain to Duke Robert of Normandy and later Patriarch of Jerusalem.

Audrey – mother of William, Henry and Edmond by Walter of Dol.

Bagrat – an Armenian guide hired by Baldwin of Boulogne.

Baldwin II – King of Jerusalem (14 April 1118 – 21 August 1131), cousin of Baldwin I King of Jerusalem; came in the great pilgrimage as Baldwin of le Bourcq, then governed Edessa; four daughters including Melisende and Alice.

Baldwin of Boulogne – youngest brother of Godfrey of Bouillon; his first wife was Godvere; later the first king of Jerusalem (25 December 1100 – 2 April 1118).

balmung – a hammer in Norse mythology.

Bart – a page to Walter; later a sergeant to Henry.

Beniglio – a ship captain.

Benito Tusculani – Henry's tutor, born of a powerful family south of Rome.

Bernard – Abbot at Sahagun, bishop in Spain and becomes Henry's confidant.

Bernard – Henry's son by Angeline.

Bernard of Clairveaux – Cistercian Abbott of a monastery in Clairveaux and the most notable churchman of the day.

Bohemond – leader of a large Norman force from southern Italy going to Jerusalem; oldest son of Robert Guiscard, uncle of Tancred.

Brinette – a Tarfur in Jerusalem, formerly a consort of Odo of Caen.

Brother Bruglio – Cluny's bursar.

Brother George – the giver of values to Hugh.

Brother Minolo – a Spanish monk at Bec who studied medicines.

Bulgars – a vicious tribe from the plains of Rus.

Caesar – Count of Tusculani

Canka – a Turkish pirate.

Cardinals – Leo of Ostia, Cuno of Palistrina, Bruno of Segni, John of Gaeta, Peter of Porto, Peter Pierleone, John of Tusculum, Guido of Vienne, Joscernan of Lyons, Adalbert of Mainz, William of Champeaux, Lambert of Ostia, Gregory of Saint Angelo, Saxo of Saint Stefano, Theobald of Saint Anastasia, Jonathan of Cosma e Damiano, Renaud of Reims, Rusticius of Saint Ciriaco, Diego of Compostella and Hubert of Lucca.

Censius Stephani – a powerful Roman.

Clementia – 'Clem,' Robert of Flanders' wife.

Cumans – a wild tribe from the great plains of Rus.

Daimbert of Pisa – Pope Paschal's appointed Patriarch of Jerusalem.

Danishmends – a Turkish sub group.

diffidatio – an abrogation of a feudal relationship by either lord or vassal.

Drogo of Nestle, Everard of Le Puiset, Thomas of Marle and Raimbold of Crotton – four bloodthirsty knights.

Duke of Norfolk – a member of Duke Robert's retinue.

Edmond – Henry's younger brother; wife is Joan.

Eldebrand of Arras – liege man to Robert Duke of Normandy.

Embriaco brothers – two Genoese brothers with knowledge and equipment for building siege engines and towers.

Emich Count of Leisingen – a slaughterer of Jews.

Ermenberga – Abbot Anslem's mother.

Eustice – older brother of Godfrey of Bouillon.

Ezekial –a Jewish boy whom Henry adopts; the boy's younger sister is Rachel.

Fagan – a poor freeman.

Fatimids – Egyptian soldiers.

Fideles (Fidelis = singular) – members of a group of western Christians supportive of the Church's reform movement.

Firuz – Arab traitor within Antioch.

Frangipane Brothers – Cencius, Leo and Robert.

Frigg – Norse goddess to midwives.

Fulcher fitz-Gerard of Chartres – the first man up the rope ladder at Antioch.

Fulcher of Chartres – a member of the great pilgrimage and an historian of it.

Gaston of Bearn – French knight with experience in Spain building siege engines.

George and Randulf of Chalon – Abbot Hugh's two armed retainers; later papal guards.

Gerard – a kind overseer of the hospital in Jerusalem.

Godfrey Duke of Bouillon – 'Advocatus Sancti Sepulchri' (1099 – 1100); one of the principal Christian leaders on the great pilgrimage with a large force from Lorraine, later 'Advocate' of the city.

Henry I of Dol – Henry's great grandfather, 'the Medic.'

Henry I of England (1100 – 1135) and **Duke of Normandy** (1106 – 1135) – third son of William the Conqueror after Robert and William; called 'Beauclerc' for his scholarly interests.

Henry II of Dol – Henry's grandfather, 'the Healer.'

Henry III – Walter's older brother, killed on Hastings field.

Henry IV of Dol – son of Walter and Audrey; key character.

Henry V of Dol – Henry's son by Angeline.

Herluin – the founding knight of the Abbey of Bec.

Hildebrand – Pope Gregory's pre-papal name.

horses – a knight's horse played a pivotal role. Henry of Dol's horses: Robin, Meredith, Pegasus.

Hugh – Abbot of Cluny and distinguished Churchman.

Hugh of Vermandois – brother of the king of France; leader of a small force on the great pilgrimage.

Hugh, Othocar, and Thorvald – young men present at Henry's knighting.

Humphrey of Monte Scabioso – a casualty south of Nicaea.

Iftikhar – Egyptian political officer in charge of Jerusalem.

Joan – wife of Edmond; Henry's sister-in-law.

John Comnenus – Greek governor of Dyrrhachium, relative of Alexius.

Johnnie – a young orphan taken in by Robert of Flanders.

Kay Mora – a seer with unusual abilities who helped Henry with a 'past life regression'.

Kerbogha – Muslim Sultan of Mozul.

Kilij Arslan – a Seljuk Turk leader encountered near Nicaea.

King Ferdinand – a past king in Hispania.

Lambert Count of Claremont – a deserter at Antioch.

Leone Rassellino – captain of the Black Rose.

Leonardo of Genoa – a shipper.

Louis VI, King of France – (1108 – 1137); 'the fat'.

Ludolf and Bartholomew of Tournai – two brothers at Robert's Knights School; participants in the great pilgrimage; Bart eventually becomes the trainer of the Knights Templar.

Luigi Delasandro – a papal courier.

Maginulf – 'Anti-Pope' Sylvester (e. 18 November 1105 – deposed 12 April 1111).

Magwolf – a trusted knight of Walter's.

Malregard – a small manufactured fort outside Antioch.

Manuel Butumedes – a Greek engineer.

Marco – the pope's bursar's clerk.

Mariteth – the midwife at Henry's birth.

Martin – a Saxon working for a Roman family.

Martin 'the haberdasher' – a recommended tailor in Rome.

Matilda – 'la Gran Contessa' and a Fidelis.

Melvin Borrin – a Jewish merchant.

Mendichio – a Master at the Lyceum.

Mildrid – a hand maiden to Audrey.

Milicent – Audrey's aunt.

Niketas – Alexius' prime advisor.

Nur – Iftikhar's son.

Odin – Norse god of war.

Odo de Lagery – Pope Urban II (c. 12 March 1088, d. 29 July 1099) and a past student of Hugh's.

Odo of Bayeux – William the Conqueror's half brother and bishop of Caen.

Oikoumene – the Greek civilized world defined by the Greeks as 'that of Christ.'

Old Ben – the ghetto's gateman in Genoa.

Osama – a sage Arab.

Outremere – the Holy Land.

Paulitians – a minority group in the Greek empire.

Pechenegs – a tribe from the great plains of Rus; used by the Greeks as military police.

Peter Bartholomew – a visionary.

Peter Desiderius – a respected priest who rallied financial support for the Tarfurs.

Peter Maillesais – an oblate at Bec assigned to be Henry's mentor.

Peter of Castillon – liegeman of Raymond.

Peter Pierleone – cardinal priest of Saint Maria in Trastevere, 'anti-pope' Anacletus II (c. 23 February 1130 - d. 25 January 1138).

Peter the Hermit – an unwashed preacher who inspired approximately 20,000 poor people to follow him to Jerusalem.

Petrus Leonis – leader of the Pierleone family.

Phillip I, King of France – (1060 – 1108), 'one to avoid'; brother of Hugh, Count of Vermandois.

Pope Calixtus II (c. 9 February 1119 – d. 13 December 1124) – the former Guido archbishop of Vienne.

Pope Gelasius (c. 10 March 1118 – d. 29 January 1119) – John of Gaeta, cardinal deacon of Saint Maria in Cosmadin prior.

Pope Gregory VII (c. 29 June 1073 – d. 25 May 1085) – a reformer Pope who died in exile.

Pope Honorius II (c. 16 December 1124 - d. 14 February 1130) – Lambert, cardinal bishop of Ostia prior.

Pope Pascal (c. 13 August, 1099 – d. 21 January, 1118) – Rainer, cardinal priest of Bleda prior.

Pope Victor III (c. 9 May 1086 - d. 16 September 1087) – Abbot of Monte Cassino, cardinal priest of Saint Cecilia.

Proedros – a highly trained Greek bureaucrat specializing in any of a wide variety of skills such as: ambassador, linguist, accountant, etc.

Poulains – those in Outremer of mixed blood – Franj and local.

Provencals – Raymond's southeastern Franks who spoke Occitan.

Ptolemy of Tusculum – a powerful conniver south of Rome.

Rainald Count of Toul – one of Godfrey's liegemen.

Randolf Vulphy – one of Godfrey's knights.

Raymond Count of Toulouse and Saint Gilles – leader of the southern Franks who spoke mostly 'Occitan'; wife Elvira and younger son Alfonso.

Raymond of Auguilers – carried the Holy Lance at Antioch.

Raymond Pilet, William Sabran, Peter Narbonne and Isoard the Count of Die - all Raymond of Toulouse's liegemen.

Rebecca – Henry's second wife, an Armenian princess.

Reynauld – a knight under Robert of Flanders who trained young men to become knights; 'the Master of Warfare.'

Richard Duke of Gaeta – a Fidelis with a small army south of Rome.

Robert Duke of Normandy – the oldest son of William the Conqueror, nicknamed 'Curt-hose.'

Robert I – Count of Flanders – had gone as a pilgrim to both Jerusalem and Constantinople.

Robert II – Count of Flanders – one of the leaders of the First Crusade and Audrey's cousin.

Robert of Capua – a powerful south Norman.

Roberta – a master and teacher at the Lyceum in Rome; watched Henry's sons when he went away.

Roger Borsa, Count of Apulia – his wife, Adela, was sister of Clem.

Roman families with political clout: Crescenti, Tusculani, Octaviani, Velletri, Palestrina, Collona, Pierleone, Frangipani, Papareschi, Scolari, Scotti, Malabranca, Parenzi, and Orsini.

Rosalette – more than a bar maid.

Roussel of Bailleul – a Norman knight who, prior to the first Crusade, tried to carve out a kingdom of his own in northwest Turkey.

Rudolf – Count Robert's seneschal.

Saul Rabinowitz and Omar Sayyid – 'doctors' at Jerusalem's hospital.

Shams – son of Yaghi-Siyan.

Siegfried – Godfrey's page.

Sister Anna – a friend of Audrey's when growing up.

Stephen of Neublans – a knight who went on the great pilgrimage and knew why.

Steven – a visionary priest.

Steven Count of Blois – 'the poet' and 'leader' of Blois' contingent on the great pilgrimage; married to Adelade daughter of William the Conqueror.

Sunni and Shi'a – the two primary religious divisions within the Muslim faith.

Tancred – Bohemond's nephew and friend of Henry's.

Tarfurs – the poorest of those on the great pilgrimage.

Tatikios – a Greek soldier who commanded the engineer regiment which Alexius sent as guides for the Christians.

Templars – the very first group of warrior monks organized by Hugh de Payens: Hugh de Payens (Master) of Martigny in Burgundy, Godfrey of Saint Omer, Payen of Montdidier, Archambaud of Saint Agnon, Andre de Montbard, Geoffrey Bison of Champagne and two sergeants – Rossal and Gondamer. Later joiners included: Hugh de Rigauld, Raymond Berenger and Hugh d'Amboise.

Thoros – lord of Edessa, an Armenian Christian.

Thumble – a friend of Walter's and compatriot at Hastings field.

Verangian Guard – body guards to Emperor Alexius; many were Saxons who'd left England after the battle at Hastings.

Walter – Henry's father, Walter 'the Fair.'

Walter – Henry's son by Angeline; nicknamed 'Bishop'.

William – Henry's older brother.

William and Aubrey of Grant-Mesnil – deserters at Antioch.

William, Bishop of Orange – Churchman in Raymond's contingent, 'coordinator' for Raymond.

William I, 'the Conqueror' – Duke of Normandy, King of England, 'The Bastard' and good friend of Henry's grandfather.

William II, 'Rufus' – King of England (1087 – 1100)

Yaghi-Siyan – the Turkish commander at Antioch.

BIBLIOGRAPHY

Addison, Charles. The History of the Knights Templar. Charleston, South Carolina: Biblio Bazaar, 2008.

Asbridge, Thomas. The First Crusade - A New History. Enland: Oxford University Press, 2004.

Bartlett, Robert. England Under the Norman and Angevin Kings. Oxford, England: Clarendon Press, 2000.

Bradford, Ernle. The Sword and the Scimitar. Barnsley, England: Pen and Sword Books LTD, 1974.

Fagan, Brian. The Great Warming. New York: Bloomsbury Press, 2008.

Farrington, Karen. Historical Atlas of the Holy Lands. New York: Checkmark Books, 2003.

Frale, Barbara. The Templars. Mulino, Italy: Societa editrici Il, 2009.

Gravett and Hook. Medieval Siege Warfare. Oxford, England: Osprey Publishing Ltd, 2002.

Harl, Kenneth. The Era of the Crusades. Chantilly, VA: The Teaching Company, 2003.

Harris, Jonathan. Byzantium and the Crusades. London, England: Hambledon Continuum 2003.

Houben, Hubert. Roger II of Sicily. England: Cambridge University Press, 2002.

Kostick, Conor. The Siege of Jerusalem. London, England: Continuum International Publishing Group, 2009.

MacKay, Angus. Atlas of Medieval Europe. England: Routledge, 1997.

McCall, Andrew. The Medieval Underworld. Gloucestershire, England: Sutton Publishing, 1979.

Moody, Raymond. Life After Life. New York: Harper Collins Publishers, 1975.

Mullins, Edwin. Cluny. Oxford, England: Signal Books Ltd., 2006.

Nicolle, David. Knights of Jerusalem. Oxford, England: Osprey Publishing, 2008.

Nicholson and Nicolle. God's Warriors. Oxford, England: Osprey Publishing, 2005.

Phillips, Jonathan. Holy Warriors. New York: Random House, 2009.

Phillips and Taylor. Crusades and the Crusader Knights. Lorenz Books, Anness Publishing Ltd.

Robinson, I.S. Henry IV of Germany 1056-1106. England: Cambridge University Press, 1999.

Robinson, I.S. The Papacy 1073-1198. England: Cambridge University Press, 1990.

Robinson, John J. Dungeon, Fire and Sword. New York: M. Evans and Company, 1991.

Runciman, Steven. The First Crusade. England: Cambridge University Press, 1951.

Shepard, William R. Historical Atlas. New York: Barnes and Noble, 1956.

Seward, Desmond. The Monks of War. London, England: The Folio Society, 2000.

Sire, HJA. The Knights of Malta. New Haven, CT: Yale University Press, 1996.

Spufford, Peter. Power and Profit - The Merchant in Medieval Europe. New York: Thames and Hudson, 2002.

Stark, Rodney. God's Battalions. New York: Harper Collins Publishers, 2009.

Stevenson, Ian. Twenty Cases Suggestive of Reincarnation. Virginia: University of Virginia Press, 1974.

Toy, Sydney. Castles. New York: Dover Publications Inc., 1984.